SURVIVING DEATH ... ?

Though he had killed countless times in his career as a Mech Warrior, Galen Cox had never before felt like a murderer. Looking through the observation bay window, he saw the dead body of Joshua Marik and knew a healthier double had already taken Joshua's place.

Galen shook his head. "Games and deceptions. I wish life was simpler."

Curaitis watched Galen carefully. "Dying is about as simple as it gets."

"But dying doesn't make things more simple."

The security man's eyes narrowed. "It does for him. We flick the switch and he dies easily. The hard part, the complex part, is what we have to do."

"Right." Galen's mouth tasted sour. "We have to make sure the Inner Sphere can survive his death."

BATTLETECH.

BRED FOR WAR

Michael A. Stackpole

A ROC BOOK

ROC
Published by the Penguin Group
Penguin Books USA Inc., 375 Hudson Street,
New York, New York 10014, U.S.A.
Penguin Books Ltd, 27 Wrights Lane,
London W8 5TZ, England
Penguin Books Australia Ltd, Ringwood,
Victoria, Australia
Penguin Books Canada Ltd, 10 Alcorn Avenue,
Toronto, Canada M4V 3B2
Penguin Books (N.Z.) Ltd, 182–190 Wairau Road
Auckland 10, New Zealand

Penguin Books Ltd. Registered Offices:
Harmondsworth, Middlesex, England

First published by Roc, an imprint of Dutton Signet,
a division of Penguin Books USA Inc.

First Printing, January, 1995
10 9 8 7 6 5 4 3 2 1

Series Editor: Donna Ippolito
Cover: Boris Vallejo
Mechanical Drawings: Duane Loose
Copyright © FASA Corporation, 1995
All rights reserved

 REGISTERED TRADEMARK—MARCA REGISTRADA

To Brian Fargo,
the only man I have met with
the vision to see the future
and the skills necessary to realize it.

The author would like to thank the following people for their contributions to this work:

Patrick Stackpole for his demolitions expertise, J. Ward Stackpole for his medical advice, Kerin Stackpole (of Barrymore & Loots) for legal expertise, Sam Lewis for editorial and story advice, Donna Ippolito for rendering me readable, Liz Danforth for tolerating me while I put this book together, John-Allen Price for the continued loan of a Cox, Larry Acuff for again contributing generously to charity in return for his appearance here, Ron Wolfley and Dave Galloway for perspectives on being professional athletes, and the GEnie Computer Network over which this novel and its revisions passed from the author's computer straight to FASA.

The following books and articles were invaluable in the preparation of this book:

Ranger Handbook, United States Army Infantry School
A History of Warfare, by John Keegan
The Dictionary of War Quotations, edited by Justin Wintle
Simpson's Contemporary Quotations, compiled by James B. Simpson
The Oxford Dictionary of Quotations, Oxford University Press
"The Shadow of a Gunman from World War II," by Robert Wernick, *Smithsonian Magazine*

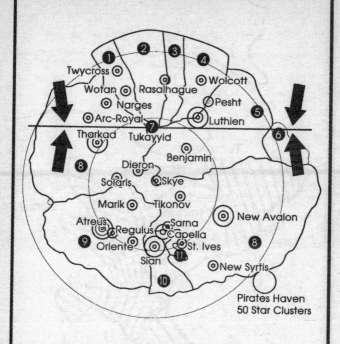

MAP OF THE SUCCESSOR STATES

CLAN TRUCE LINE

1 • Jade Falcon/Steel Viper, 2 • Wolf Clan, 3 • Ghost Bear,
4 • Smoke Jaguars - Nova Cats, 5 • Draconis Combine,
6 • Outworlds Alliance, 7 • Free Rasalhague Republic,
8 • Federated Commonwealth, 9 • Free Worlds League,
10 • Capellan Confederation, 11 • St. Ives Compact

Map Compiled by COMSTAR.
From information provided by the COMSTAR EXPLORER SERVICE
and the STAR LEAGUE ARCHIVES on Terra.

© 3056 COMSTAR CARTOGRAPHIC CORPS.

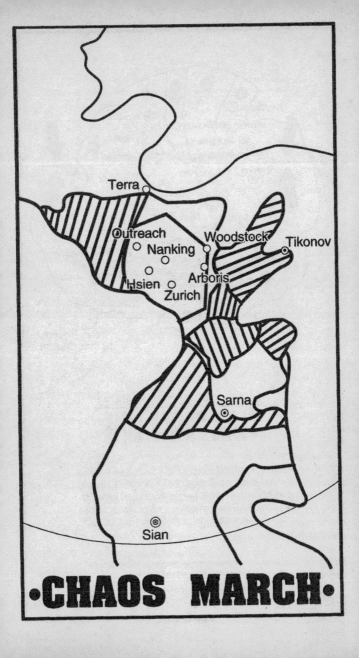

Terra

Outreach
Nanking
Woodstock
Tikonov

Hsien
Arboris
Zurich

Sarna

Sian

·CHAOS MARCH·

1

A single death is a tragedy. A million deaths are a statistic.
—JOSEPH STALIN

Avalon City
New Avalon, Federated Commonwealth
20 May 3057

Though Galen Cox had killed many an enemy in his career as a MechWarrior, this was the first time he had ever felt like a murderer. Standing there with Agent Curaitis and Dr. Joseph Harper in the observation deck of the Passive Life Maintenance Unit, he knew part of his uneasiness stemmed from the fact that he really was no longer Galen Cox. That person had died in an explosion on a planet more than four hundred light years away, a faked death from which Galen had been resurrected as Jerrard Cranston, national security advisor to Victor Davion, Prince of the mighty Federated Commonwealth.

If I weren't here under an alias, I probably wouldn't feel like a criminal participating in a crime. He looked around at the others. "Anyone else feel like we're killing this boy?"

Curaitis, the ice-eyed giant standing between him and Harper, showed not the slightest flicker of emotion. "We can't prevent his death, but we can keep it from causing the deaths of many others."

Dr. Harper nodded. "We've tried everything. The boy's hung on far longer than anyone expected. It's time to let him die with a little dignity, Mr. Cranston."

Galen looked down at the emaciated body of Joshua Marik through the observation window. Son of Thomas Marik, heir to the Captain-Generalcy of the Free Worlds

League, Joshua had been diagnosed with acute leukemia six years before and later sent to New Avalon for treatment. The New Avalon Institute of Science, the finest research and medical center in the Inner Sphere, had been his best hope, but five years of treatment had left him sallow, bruised and, finally, all but dead. If not for the respirator pumping away beside his bed and the dialysis machine cleansing his blood, the boy would have given out weeks ago.

No one looking at this disease-ravaged child would have wished him one more instant of suffering. But he was so much more than a hapless child that machines had extended his life well beyond any rational period. While Joshua still lived, it gave Thomas Marik a wedge against Sun-Tzu Liao. Sun-Tzu was betrothed to Isis, the other Marik child, but Thomas had been stalling on the marriage for several years. Though Thomas had recognized Isis as legitimate, Joshua, the only child of his marriage, had been named as his heir. Because Sun-Tzu dreamed of nothing short of the destruction of the Federated Commonwealth, anything that kept him from assuming the power of Thomas' throne meant more peace and security for the whole Inner Sphere.

Galen touched the glass separating them from Joshua's room. "I just wish we could have done something more. I feel so impotent knowing that this child is dying from the same disease that has killed people since long before our ancestors left Terra and spread throughout the Inner Sphere."

Harper shook his head sadly. "I share your frustration," he said. "We've done everything possible to save Joshua's life, but even that wasn't enough. It saddens me even more because I've come to like this boy in the five years he's been here. You're afraid his death will lead to war with the Free Worlds League, but my regret is that Joshua will never grow up to take his father's place."

"Having a Captain-General who'd spent some of his formative years here and owed his life to the Federated Commonwealth certainly wouldn't have hurt us."

"It's more than that, Mr. Cranston. Joshua was a bright boy. Charming, yet inquisitive and intelligent. He could be a normal little child with the other young patients when he was well enough, yet he knew how to play the role of a noble for important visitors." Harper pressed his lips together into a thin line. "His death is a loss for the future as well as his family."

Galen focused beyond his own reflection in the glass onto Joshua's face. "That's our job now, Doctor, to make sure the loss isn't catastrophic in scope."

The doctor nodded understanding. "Things have been arranged as Curaitis ordered. Once we let the boy die, his body will be cryogenically preserved so that he can be sent back to the Free Worlds League later. The double was inserted in Joshua's place six months ago and has been fully accepted. Staff members who've worked with the real Joshua Marik have been transferred to other facilities both here and on other worlds—though that's another loss. Those transfers have virtually gutted our oncology research projects."

From his greater height, the stiff-backed Curaitis looked down at the physician. "Those people are continuing their work at their new posts."

"You don't understand. For this kind of difficult research, there's not a single other facility like the New Avalon Institute of Science in known space. You're setting cancer research back by centuries."

Galen tried to calm the doctor. "Orders have already gone out for all your people to have priority access to any medical research and procedures recovered from old Star League records. They'll also get priority routing anytime they want to exchange data with their colleagues."

Harper wearily rubbed one hand down from his receding hairline and across his face. "Look, there's a difference between this research and the other advances that the discovery of Star League records have made possible. The recovery of library cores and old Star League equipment have helped us bring our war toys back up to the specs our ancestors considered normal, but they've done nothing for cancer research.

"The Star League scientists didn't know much more than we do today. In the same three centuries that saw BattleMechs develop from crude machines to powerful engines of war, genetic research foundered. The little that was done was directed toward finding cures for the various and sundry new diseases human settlers were encountering as they colonized planets across space. Much of it was also directed at preserving life and extending our life spans. It's true that we know how to control many of the diseases that kill us as we age, but juvenile diseases and genetic ailments that happen later in life both have been neglected."

Harper stopped suddenly and held both his hands up. "Forgive me, gentlemen. I know this rant is well outside your reasons for being here. It's just that I've seen too much research money going to projects aimed at recovering military technology from old Star League records instead of being directed into new research. Granted that a lot of genetic research has led to nothing but a dead end, but what about the Clans? If what I hear about their breeding programs and genetic manipulation is even half true, they've made incredible breakthroughs. Some of that could have helped here."

Curaitis smiled slightly. "Could you clone Joshua?"

"I doubt it. Clones created beyond the embryonic stage don't seem to be viable. But I can't rule it out as a possibility. If the Clans—with their military focus—did it, we could too. But that would require funding we just don't have right now."

Galen scratched at the beard he'd grown since becoming Jerrard Cranston. "I'll speak to Prince Victor about it, Dr. Harper. You won't get your team back—at least not for the few more years we need to maintain the illusion that Joshua is still alive—but after that we might be able to reunite you."

From the look on Curaitis' face, Galen knew the intelligence man would fight that idea as a breach of security, but Galen didn't care. "What's important right now is making certain no one in this hospital except us knows that Joshua has died."

"Don't worry, Mr. Cranston, all my people are professionals and patriots. The transition has gone smoothly. Your double's been fully accepted up in the hospital. The real Joshua will die down here, but up there he'll continue to live." Harper turned and pointed to a pair of switches mounted on the wall between the observation window and the door beyond it. "All the life support equipment has been routed through this red switch. Most folks think it's rather ghoulish to watch while a patient in the Passive Life Maintenance unit dies, so the green switch closes the drapes on the other side."

While Harper seemed unable to take the final step up to the switches, Galen was not. He was willing to accept the responsibility for shutting off Joshua's life support, yet his reach faltered an instant in the enormous gulf between willingness and desire. In that moment of hesitation, Curaitis moved forward and reached for the switches.

"Wait, please," Harper said softly. "I know that Joshua really died weeks ago and that he can no longer hear or see anything, but I'd like to be in there with him when he goes."

"And I'd like to join you," Galen said.

Curaitis looked from one man to the other for a moment, and Galen shivered beneath the tall man's icy gaze. "I'll wait until you give me a sign, then I'll shut off his machinery."

Dr. Harper passed through the door, but Galen stopped and looked back at Curaitis. "I get the feeling you think Harper and I are two sentimental fools."

"Not at all."

"But you'll stay in here."

"My job, Mr. Cranston, is to see to it that the universe that permits you to harbor such delicate sentiments continues to exist. Part of that job is turning off Joshua Marik's life support."

Galen frowned. "That's it?"

"I'm sorry the boy's dying, but I didn't make him sick and all my best wishes won't keep him alive any longer." Curaitis stared off unseeing for a moment, then looked back with electric intensity into Galen's eyes. "I didn't know him and, had he grown up, he'd have been as dangerous to the Federated Commonwealth as were his father or grandfather."

"What if he'd turned out to be a man who could reunite the warring nations of the Inner Sphere?"

"A thin line between that and someone who *thinks* he can reunite the Successor States and starts a war to prove it." Curaitis' gaze did not waver. "The death of a mere boy is sad, but to project anything beyond that is hypothetical and I don't deal in hypotheticals. Can't cover all the possibilities when you do."

"Do you think Victor is right in replacing Joshua with an impostor?"

"Not up to me to second-guess the Prince."

"Especially when you're the one who suggested this course of action."

"I made him aware of the operation his own father had initiated. He chose to employ Project Gemini."

Galen frowned. "Deceiving Thomas Marik this way is bound to cause big trouble."

"Thomas Marik is a pacifist and idealist. His Knights of the Inner Sphere are successful because of the skilled personnel he's recruited, not because of his grand philosophy. Besides, Thomas has other things to worry about."

Galen nodded. "I read the confirmation of the report on the condition of Marik's wife." He narrowed his eyes. "Her injuries weren't caused by one of *our* operations, were they?"

Curaitis was unruffled. "No. We prefer more subtle means."

"Like killing a child?"

"At least here he isn't going to die from the violence that's plagued so many Mariks right in their own realm and even among their own family."

"I doubt that's much consolation to a little boy who'll never grow up," Galen said, his eyes on the failing little boy. "Sometimes I wish life were simpler."

"Living and dying are as simple as it gets, Cranston. All else is just a question of volume and statistics."

"It doesn't seem to me that dying makes anything simpler."

"The boy will get it right." Curaitis nodded toward the door. "Go on, go see him off. He could do worse than have someone like you with him when he goes."

"You could join us."

The intelligence man shook his head.

"Got something better to do, Curaitis?"

"Yes, I do. While you're in there dealing with his death," Curaitis said quietly, "I'll start making sure we can survive his legacy."

2

Nothing is ever done in this world until men are prepared to kill one another if it is not done.

—GEORGE BERNARD SHAW, MAJOR BARBARA

Tharkad City, Tharkad
District of Donegal, Federated Commonwealth
21 May 3057

Caitlin Kell's mouth gaped open as she stared at Katrina Steiner-Davion. "Katrina, are you sure you should be telling me this? That Ryan Steiner was the man behind the assassin who killed our mothers?"

Caitlin slowly lowered herself into a dark leather chair. She had once thought of the furnishings in this room as warm and inviting, but now the leather felt cold as her body sank into it. "Oh, God, and to think I was so sorry for what happened to him."

Katrina knelt down on the thick carpeting in front of Caitlin and took her cousin's hands in her own. "Cait, if there was any other way to let you know this, I would have. The way Ryan died *was* horrible, but no more horrible than what he did to *my* mother and *your* mother and father. When I think of Morgan and the pain on his face when he buried your mother, I . . ." Katrina's voice faltered and her lower lip trembled.

Caitlin squeezed her cousin's hands and bit back tears of her own. The same bomb blast that murdered their mothers had also destroyed Morgan Kell's right arm. The loss of his wife Salome had injured Caitlin's father more than anything he'd ever suffered, including the death of his brother so long ago. Melissa's death had also hit Morgan hard, as it had the whole of the Federated Commonwealth, and Caitlin thought that her father's fierce desire to avenge himself on whoever was behind the assassination was the only thing that had driven him to recover from his wounds.

"My father is strong." Caitlin forced the words past the lump in her throat, as much to convince herself as to comfort Katrina. "And it's probably lucky that a sniper got Ryan on Solaris first because even with one arm gone, my father would have torn him apart."

Katrina swiped at her eyes, the tears smearing some mascara across her cheeks. "You're right. Morgan would have gotten him even though he was an aerospace pilot."

Caitlin smiled grimly. "I'd forgotten Ryan was a pilot. He would have been mine."

Her golden-haired cousin sniffed. "At least you could have done something. All I could have done was snub him at a party. Maybe even seated him next to the Baroness de Gambier!"

"Even I'd not have been that cruel." Caitlin shook her head, the ends of her dark hair swinging slightly. "Don't sell yourself so short, Katrina. You might not be a warrior or pilot, but you'd have had Ryan all tied up."

Katrina frowned. "What do you mean?"

"I may spend most of my time on Arc-Royal training with the Kell Hounds, but it's not that much of a backwater. I've seen how effectively you dealt with Ryan, mediating between him and Victor. You stopped the two of them from doing things that would have split the Federated Commonwealth in two. Victor's decision to return to New Avalon lets you calm things down here."

"Perhaps, but I'm nowhere near the mediator my mother was." Katrina covered her face with her hands. "I miss her so much, Cait."

Caitlin worked herself forward in the chair and leaned over to put her arms around Katrina's neck. "I know, I know." *Poor Katrina. First her mother is killed by a bomb, and then her sweetheart Galen Cox is killed the same way. With Victor gone and Peter vanishing, she must feel abandoned.* "We all miss your mother, Katrina, but in you she has a worthy successor."

Again, Katrina brushed tears away. "My mother was an institution. With one cold glance or—more like her—a warm smile and firm handshake, she always seemed able to persuade people to do what she thought was best for the Federated Commonwealth. Everyone loved and respected her and looked to her for leadership. She was so beautiful and vibrant. She was a strong foundation to hold up the Federated Commonwealth and, at the same time, the glue that bound it together."

A smile came easily to Caitlin as she thought of Archon Melissa Steiner Davion. "I don't think anyone, meeting her face to face, could have refused anything she might ask. That's why the assassin had to use a bomb. If he'd tried to shoot your mother, he couldn't have pulled the trigger."

"I suppose that's why she had to die." Katrina swallowed hard. "This might sound morbid, but ever since I learned that it was Ryan who ordered my mother's death, I've tried to get inside his mind to understand why he did it."

"That's not morbid. It's understandable." Caitlin stroked Katrina's fair hair. "I've also wondered about what sort of person would plant a bomb, knowing it would kill so many people. Killing your mother was bad enough. Maybe he was just a stupid bastard who was afraid the plot wouldn't work otherwise. Ryan probably told him to do it that way."

Katrina stood and shook her head. "No, Ryan wasn't stupid. Anything *but* stupid."

"Killing your mother was stupid, Kat."

Katrina stood up and began to pace back and forth with her long-legged strides. "Ryan saw my mother as a stabilizing influence. With her as Archon Princess, my father's policies—as modified and humanized by her—would have continued. We'd have spent the remaining years of the Clan truce coming together as a nation. We'd have been preparing for the Clan onslaught and even building alliances with other nations to make certain the Clans would never succeed in conquering the Inner Sphere.

"Ryan couldn't abide that. Stability for our nation meant stagnation for him."

Caitlin snarled in disgust. "He should have found himself another line of work."

"He couldn't. He was ambitious and hungry for power, with goals tied to both things. As sainted as my mother was, not everyone agreed with her policies. People like Ryan had legitimate doubts about my mother's plans for the future."

"True, Katrina, but most people felt free to bring their concerns to your mother so she could incorporate them into her plans. Ryan brought her a bomb."

"Yes, but I think he had a fundamental disagreement with the nature of the Federated Commonwealth. You know as well as I do that the Clans carved twenty-five percent of their conquests from the Lyran half of the Federated Commonwealth. To Ryan, that was a mortal wound. He wanted to push back against the Clans, but my mother wanted us to rebuild and train and be ready for when the war resumed." Katrina stopped and leaned against the back of another of the room's plush chairs. "Ryan thought my mother was destroying the Lyran Commonwealth."

"And to save it he wanted to make the Isle of Skye independent?"

"Fomenting the rebellion was a way to wake my mother up to how serious the problem was. He still remembered how the Lyran Commonwealth saved the Federated Suns' economy after my father seized the Sarna and Tikonov Commonalties from the Capellan Confederation twenty-five years ago. Then he saw frightened people fleeing the Clan invasion, abandoning the Lyran half of the Commonwealth for haven in the Davion part of the nation. My mother did nothing to prevent them, confident they'd return once they saw the Clans had been stopped."

"And they were coming back, Katrina. We all know that."

"Yes, but not quickly enough. The rate of return didn't match the rate at which people ran. And those returning were often the ones who didn't have sufficient money to make it in the Davion sector. Government programs financed their relocation. Worse than that, I think, for Ryan was the fact that no one else viewed the situation as he did. He thought my mother was lulling the nation to sleep with her kindness. Until my mother was eliminated, there could be no change, no progression."

Caitlin's green eyes blazed for a second. "Thank God his was a minority opinion."

"Minority, yes." Katrina shuddered. "Unique, no."

"What are you saying?"

"Don't ask me that, Caitlin."

Caitlin stood up quickly at the sight of Katrina trembling. "What's wrong, Kat? You can tell me."

"No, no, I can't. It's too horrible."

"More horrible than our mothers being vaporized by a terrorist bomb?" Caitlin grabbed Katrina by the shoulders. "Look at me. What could be more horrible than that?"

Katrina's mouth opened in a silent cry, then she sagged forward against Caitlin's chest. "I don't think Ryan was acting alone."

The sound of Katrina's tears faded to the background as the full implication of the words hit Caitlin. Ever since Melissa Steiner's death, the Federated Commonwealth had been rife with rumors of conspiracies connected with her assassination. Most had tried to pin the murder on Victor Davion, but Caitlin had known Victor for years. They had all played together as children. She'd dismissed those rumors out of hand.

Katrina's outburst suddenly brought them all back. It was true, after all, that Victor and Galen Cox had been the ones to discover Hanse Davion dead of a heart attack. It was also a fact that Victor had missed his mother's funeral on Tharkad, though her other children, who'd had to travel all the way from New Avalon, managed to make it. The death of Melissa gave Victor his seat on the throne that made him the sole ruler over an empire spanning the furthest borders of the Inner Sphere and containing trillions upon trillions of people.

And the latest rumors about a growing rift between Galen and Victor had taken on a sinister note after Galen died in a bomb blast similar to the one that had killed Melissa. People were whispering that Victor had killed his own father in Galen's presence, promising Katrina's hand in exchange for his silence, then Victor reneged and had Galen killed because Cox was on the verge of revealing the truth about the deaths of Hanse Davion and Melissa Steiner Davion.

"Katrina, how can you say that? What makes you think that?"

"I don't know, Caitlin. It's just a feeling, but it all begins to add up. After Ryan's death, Victor told me that the mystery around our mother's assassination was solved. He said that Ryan had done it and had paid for the crime with his life. Then he said that Ryan had worked alone, all alone. He said it was done. It was time to move on. It was time to do things for the Federated Commonwealth that our parents could never have conceived of."

"But you don't think Victor had anything to do with their deaths, do you? You can't."

Katrina shook her head, her tears pasting golden strands

of hair to her face. "No, of course not. Victor couldn't have . . . no, I'd bet my life on it, but . . ."

"But?" Caitlin felt her stomach tightening. "But what?"

"But all those reasons why Ryan would have killed my mother, they work for Victor, too. And me. And Peter and Arthur and Yvonne. Each one of us gains from the deaths of our parents."

"But Victor? He couldn't have killed your mother or your father."

"Of course I don't believe that, Caitlin. Of course I know he didn't do it, but I have to remember who I am and what my responsibilities are. It's *that* which makes me take a long look at Victor and start to wonder."

Caitlin frowned and seized her cousin by the hand. "Katrina, what are you talking about?"

"Well, his return to New Avalon, for one thing." Katrina freed herself from Caitlin's grasp and began to pace again. Occasional sniffs and sobs punctuated her words, but she spoke firmly. "Yes, the seat of government used to alternate back and forth between Tharkad and New Avalon, even during the years of the Clan invasion. And, yes, the people of the old Federated Sun felt short-changed when the throne remained on Tharkad after our mother's death, but the throne *should* be here. I begged Victor to stay, but he was determined to go back to New Avalon."

Caitlin looked down, thinking, one hand plucking unconsciously at the silk sleeve of her blouse. "But with the Isle of Skye arrayed against Victor, don't you think his leaving will let things calm down?"

"I could have calmed things with him here. By running away he made his enemies in Skye think they can frighten him off. Meanwhile, those who love him believe he's left them high and dry. I mean, he gave Grayson Carlyle a title and demanded an oath of personal fealty in return, then did nothing to help Carlyle's Gray Death Legion in the fighting on Glengarry. In fact Victor left for New Avalon months before the situation was settled. He abandoned Carlyle the same way he's abandoned others."

"I think, with all that's happened, you're the one who's feeling abandoned, Kat."

Katrina stopped and smiled at her cousin. "But not by you, Cait. You came as soon as you could."

"And I'm happy to be here, despite the circumstances."

"You're my strength, Caitlin. You've always been stronger than I am."

"Remember what I said before? Don't sell yourself short, Katrina."

"Maybe once I did, but no more." Katrina took a deep breath and brushed her hair back from her face. "I'm a Steiner and it's my responsibility to see to it that my people are protected. This government has been on autopilot during the transition. Now that Victor's people are all on New Avalon with him, I'll use what Victor's left me to do what must be done. And the first order of business is healing. Healing the political rifts, healing the pain of the Skye rebellion."

Caitlin smiled. "Laudable goals."

"Oh, I'll do more. And healing will be the key. I'm going to focus on medical research, building hospitals, repairing the damage done by the uprising, and healing the hatreds threatening to split the Commonwealth apart. If I can do that, we'll have nothing to fear from the Clans when the truce expires."

Caitlin nodded. "And Victor?"

Katrina hesitated, then looked down at the floor. "My first responsibility is to my people, the people his actions have harmed. I don't want to believe Victor is a monster who could resort to murder, but if I learn that he is, then I will have to deal with him. No matter what happens, though, I remember who comes first, and I will never let Victor harm them again."

Daosha, Zurich
Sarna March, Federated Commonwealth

Noble Thayer smiled as Ken Fox slapped him on the back. "I appreciate the fact that you're willing to rent me this apartment so quickly, Mr. Fox, but I can't let you believe I'm a veteran like yourself." Noble ran his left hand back over his brush-cut black hair. "Just because I have the same cut you do doesn't mean I served in the Armed Forces of the Federated Commonwealth."

Fox frowned, resting his hands on his ample belly. "A fellow your age would have served against the Clans, am I right?"

Noble smiled and set his two duffel bags inside the door of the furnished apartment. "Should have, yes. When I heard about the invasion I was living on Garrison and went to sign up with some friends. We had a car accident on the way there, and I ended up with my right leg snapped in two places." Thayer bent and worked one trouser leg up to show the scar from the surgery performed to set the bone. "My friends got action and I got traction."

Fox winced and chewed on the end of an unlit cigar stub. "I always hated surgeons cutting me open to pull things out. It's worse than the enemy."

The older man looked Noble up and down. "So if you aren't a vet, how come the haircut and the duffel bags? I mean, I look at you and I says to myself, 'there's a guy with self-discipline and a military bearing.' "

Noble's smile carried right up into his dark eyes. "The military wouldn't take me because of my leg. I volunteered for Civil Defense and discovered I was good at explaining things to youngsters. One of my supervisors had a brother who ran a small military academy on Hyde—Stevenson Military Preparatory Academy. Maybe you've heard of it?"

Fox gave a noncommittal grunt.

"Well, I got a job offer there and spent the last three years teaching chemistry and general sciences."

"But why have you come to Zurich? We got no schools like that here."

Noble Thayer nodded. "That's what attracted me to this place."

"I don't follow."

"My grandfather died about six months ago and left me some money. I'd told him, once upon a time, that I wanted to be a writer, but I never had the nerve to sit down and do it. This world is so far away from Hyde that I can't return to the security of teaching or my family. It's sink or swim."

"An inheritance is one hell of a life vest, Noble."

"Well, there is *that,* yes."

"So why Zurich?"

Noble shook his head. "I want to write thrillers and, well, about a year ago I saw a holovid bit on a woman doctor who faced down and disarmed a member of the Zhanzheng de guang and I decided I wanted—no *needed*—that sort of atmosphere to write."

Fox started laughing, his fat rippling up and down under

his plaid flannel shirt. "Well, you got atmosphere in spades here, Noble. This was that doctor's apartment."

"No!"

"Oh, yes. Hell, you're picking up the last month of her lease." Fox nodded proudly. "Dr. Deirdre Lear and her son David lived here. She paid me to keep the apartment open in case she decided to return to the hospital where she'd worked. My daughter used to mind her son.

"We got a message from Dr. Lear about two months back saying she was going to stay on St. Ives for a while. Then some of her friends from the Rencide Medical Center came by to pack up her stuff and put it in the storage locker in the basement. They put a lock on it, so you'll have to wait till they come to get her stuff out. The key to the other lock on the storage area is here on your key ring. Her friends are waiting for a ship heading out for St. Ives—ought to be one within the month. Hope that won't be a problem."

"No, not at all. All I've got is in those bags." Noble shrugged. "You're very trusting to give me a key to that storage area before it's cleared out."

Fox shrugged. "I can judge folks. You ain't the thieving type. You *are* going to need some stuff to fill this place, though."

"Beds, desks, and chairs ought to be easy to get," Noble said. "I figured I could buy some computer gear for writing and all, but I wonder how available such equipment will be around here."

"Just a bit pricey, that's all. My son-in-law, Fabian, can fix you up with something."

"Excellent." Noble dug into the inside pocket of his jacket and pulled out a bank check for a thousand Federated Commonwealth Kroner. "This should cover rent and deposits. Anything left over you can credit for future rent. We can figure it out when you draw up the lease."

"Works for me. Good to have you here, Noble." Fox went out the door, then paused on the landing and smiled back at his new tenant. "I live in the duplex just down the street. If you ever want to hear about some of the things I did with the Twenty-second Avalon Hussars in the War of Thirty-Nine against the Snakes, I'll show you some *real* scars."

"I'll bring the beer."

"Deal."

Noble Thayer closed the door and looked around the modest apartment. The living room led into the kitchen, and a corridor off to the right led back to two small bedrooms and a full bathroom. The walls had been painted a light blue and the floor carpeted in a deep navy. The furnishings were serviceable enough, but cheaply manufactured and never intended to last long.

That was all right with him. He'd come to Zurich to escape his past and to move toward his future. Ending up in the apartment Dr. Lear had rented . . . now that was a stroke of luck he couldn't have foreseen. No one would believe it.

He laughed aloud and hoped Fox couldn't hear him. "This is the first day of the rest of your life, Noble Thayer. Here's hoping such good fortune marks the rest of it."

3

> Neutrals never dominate events. They always sink. Blood alone
> moves the wheels of history.
>
> —BENITO MUSSOLINI

Marik Palace, Atreus
Marik Commonwealth, Free Worlds League
23 May 3057

Sun-Tzu Liao inhaled the peace of Thomas Marik's candle-lit study and resolved to make his case without disturbing the serenity of the chamber. Thomas would expect him to be angry, but he had more to gain by keeping Thomas off guard. *If an enemy cannot define you, he cannot begin to destroy you.*

"I thank you for agreeing to see me this evening, Captain-General." Sun-Tzu held up a holodisk. "I received your message and I wished to speak with you personally about it."

Thomas Marik turned from the hearth and its blazing fire to look at Sun-Tzu. The glow of the firelight fully illuminated the left side of the Captain General's face, leaving the scarred half cloaked in shadow. "Please, Sun-Tzu, make yourself comfortable."

The younger man stopped and deliberately snapped to attention before assuming a more casual stance with hands clasped behind his back. The military precision of the movement made Thomas stiffen, as though bracing for a confrontation, which was exactly as Sun-Tzu intended. No emotion showed on his face, but he let the soft tone of his voice bespeak compassion. "I am aggrieved to learn of your wife's worsening condition. As much as I have desired an end to the delay and that a date be set for my wedding to your daughter, it would be inhuman of me to intrude on your grief. If there is anything I or my nation can do . . ."

Thomas shook his head and the light of the flames flashed white over the scars crisscrossing the right side of his face. "She is receiving the finest of care here. Even sending her to New Avalon would only prolong her life another few years at most. Here at home she might have as much as three, though the damage to her lungs is irreparable. Given the debilitating nature of her condition, she has chosen the time of her own passing."

Sun-Tzu's jade green eyes narrowed. "I have misinterpreted your message then. I did not realize she had chosen to end her own life."

"Sophina was the Duchess of Oceana before I married her nine years ago. Perhaps because Oceana has never been a rich world, its people have developed a tradition in which the terminally ill do not attempt to prolong their lives. They believe the money and resources are better directed to the good of the community." Thomas stopped as pain furrowed his brow. "I would hold on to her for every possible moment more, but I love her too much to see her go on longer than she desires."

Sun-Tzu marked Thomas' pain and filed it away for future use. *If I loved someone that much, I would* force *her to undergo treatment. You're a weak, passive fool, Thomas Marik.* Aloud he said, "You prove yourself a brave man in abiding by her decision. Were I wed to your daughter Isis, I am not so certain I could let her go so easily."

Thomas' shadowed eye glinted at Sun-Tzu. "Though any father wishes a love match for his daughter, I know love is not part of your desire to mate with mine. You love only the power of what she will bring with her to the marriage bed—the chance to rule the Free Worlds League."

"No, Thomas, it is a closer tie between my Capellan Confederation and your realm that Isis brings me."

Thomas chuckled coldly. "Is that so, Sun-Tzu? And you believe that a good thing?"

Sun-Tzu hesitated, unable to read Thomas' sudden shift in mood. "I do, and so do you."

"I might at that." Thomas tapped his chin with a finger. "Perhaps I shall propose marriage to your aunt Candace, binding the St. Ives Compact to the Free Worlds League, and then perhaps I shall marry Isis to your cousin Kai. We depose you and merge all three realms together."

The younger man felt icy tentacles of dread slithering through his guts. "If the scandal vids from the Federated Commonwealth are to be believed, my cousin Kai has taken up with a woman they claim is the mother of his son. He has brought her to St. Ives and presented her to his mother. Kai will marry her, despite the fact she is a commoner from the Federated Commonwealth. Of this I am certain. I expect the announcement to be made soon."

"And you wish a date set for your marriage to my daughter before Kai's announcement can be made?"

Sun-Tzu shook his head and carefully chose his words, gently escalating the volume as he went on. "You, as have many others, interpret all my actions as reactions to what my cousin does. It may be true that my mother decided to conceive me after hearing that her sister was with child, but that familial rivalry does not extend to my generation."

Thomas held a hand up, then slowly patted the air as if to bring down the volume of Sun-Tzu's words. "Then why protest so vehemently?"

"Ah, you are suggesting that I fear the future. From that charge there is no defense. Yet I might consider that you may the one who avoids facing the reality of the future of the Free Worlds League."

"Impertinent as always, Sun Tzu," Thomas said mildly. "But my curiosity begs you continue."

"You don't deny you were raised as a ComStar adept . . ."

Thomas' brown eyes sparked angrily. "I was raised as a Marik."

"Forgive me, my lord, but as Janos Marik's seventh child you had little hope of inheriting his power. You became a member of ComStar at age sixteen, I believe, and you were thirty-one when your father decided to designate you his heir. It was not until you were forty-one years old that you began to rule in your father's name. Then, everyone thought you had died in the bomb explosion that killed your father and your eldest brother. When you miraculously reappeared alive and well a year and a half later, it was only because ComStar had cared for you in secret. You will forgive me if I do not underestimate ComStar's influence in your life."

Thomas' head came up. "And this *influence,* you believe, is what leads you to say I am unrealistic about the future?"

Sun-Tzu shook his head ruefully, trying to buy time to pick his way through the minefield of Thomas' question. "ComStar's concerns, and indeed your preferred areas of research, have focused on the recovery of technology lost after the collapse of the Star League three centuries ago. You are at your most animated, my lord, when discussing technical matters with technicians." He opened his arms. "Though you surround yourself with candles and books and other antiques, perhaps it is because they offer you refuge from the complexities of life in the Inner Sphere today.

"You will be sixty-six years old this year, sir, and though many of us can hope to live at least another three decades beyond that, the life expectancy of Inner Sphere rulers is not nearly so long. In four years you will be Hanse Davion's age at the time of his death—and he died of natural causes. Takashi Kurita, Melissa Steiner, my mother, and even Ryan Steiner all died prematurely at the hands of an assassin."

Thomas arced an eyebrow. "That could be read as a threat, Sun-Tzu."

"It is reality, my lord. You realize, of course, that I would have no reason to assassinate you until after your daughter and I are wed."

"An excellent reason why I should never permit the union."

"An understandable line of reasoning, but it is flawed. Right now, an alliance between the Free Worlds League and the Capellan Confederation means that Victor Davion must think hard before trying to complete what his father started thirty years ago. With you as Captain-General, Victor will never try to finish off the Capellan Confederation. Should you be slain after I have wed Isis and the throne go to her, Victor could play the various factions within the Free Worlds League off against each other by pointing to me as an enemy in their midst. They would not support her, and my realm would die."

"You would do well, then, to keep me alive."

"Indeed, that is my wish. Should you die before I wed your daughter, things become even worse for your nation. You bind the Free Worlds League together. By forming the Knights of the Inner Sphere, you have provided its people a high ideal to which they can aspire." *Foolish and antiquated as it is,* Sun-Tzu might have added, but didn't. He made sure the smile in his heart never reached his lips. "Without you, this confederation of worlds will balkanize and Victor will gobble it up piecemeal."

The Captain-General nodded patronizingly. "You paint a bleak picture of the future, Sun-Tzu. It sounds like you see no way to avoid a war with Victor Davion."

"None."

"And your solution to this dilemma?"

"I have one, but I don't think you want to hear it now." Sun-Tzu frowned, the dim light accentuating the lines on his forehead and around his almond-shaped eyes. "As you know, I have placed agents and subversives throughout the occupied Sarna March. They go by various names and under various guises. I have continuously used them to probe and test."

"Testing your Uncle Tormano's Free Capella Movement?"

"It does seem that way, does it not? In reality, I am testing Victor and his responses to my actions. He worries about the threat of the Clans and, for the time being, lets others deal with problems in his realm. He has given his sister the task of settling the fallout from the Skye Rebellion. He used to have my Uncle Tormano to neutralize my operations in the occupied territory, but now Kai has assumed control of the Free Capella Movement. Before the Clan invasion, Hanse Davion and Melissa had attempted to integrate the Sarna and Tikonov Commonalties into the Federated Commonwealth. Now Victor treats them like colonial provinces while he prepares to fight the Clans."

"If he is so preoccupied with preparing for war with the Clans, why should he fight us?"

"He is a Davion. Duplicity and opportunism are in his blood."

Thomas smiled. "You see him as his father reborn."

"And you see him as his mother incarnate."

"No, Sun-Tzu, I view him as a mixture of both. He has his father's martial and leadership skills and his mother's vision for the future. He has not honed them to the edge his parents had, but he is young yet. As are you."

"Maybe so, Thomas, but mark me well because I have studied history and I foresee what is to come. Someday— and I fear it will be sooner rather than later—Victor Davion will realize that only by unifying the Inner Sphere can he hope to defeat the Clans. On that day, he will come for us."

Thomas nodded slowly, thoughtfully. "And you have a plan to counter him?"

"I do, one that undergoes constant revision and refinement. Whenever you are ready to see to deal with Victor Davion, I will make the plan available to you." Sun-Tzu bowed and started to turn toward the door, then stopped. "Of one thing I am certain, my lord, and it is this: when war is inevitable, it is better to fight on your enemy's soil than on your own."

"A preemptive strike?"

"If survival is the goal, my lord, would you not prefer to kill the cobra *before* he strikes?"

Sun-Tzu bowed, then turned and slipped from the room, the door closing soundlessly behind him. *And if you cannot see the wisdom of that yet, Thomas, I will have to find a way to make it even clearer.*

4

Avalon City, New Avalon
Crucis March, Federated Commonwealth
26 May 3057

Victor Ian Davion, First Prince of the Federated Commonwealth, groaned. "If this is the kind of luck that's going to mark my reign, I might as well abdicate now. Do you want the job, Jerrard?"

Galen Cox shook his head. "No, sir, I do not." He smiled despite the adamance of his tone. "This was a bit of bad luck, but I think we can turn it to our advantage, pending a full report from Curaitis."

The Prince brushed the sandy blond hair back from his forehead and sighed. "What kind of odds do you think we could have gotten on Solaris on the chances of an exact double for Joshua Marik showing up at the Davion Peace Park Zoo and getting spotted by a scandal-vid reporter?"

"Long odds, and longer still if they knew the real Joshua had died and been replaced with a double." Galen gave a slight shrug. "It looks like pure coincidence, though. Once the child took off her cap and you could see the shock of red hair spilling down her shoulders, well, it was pretty obvious that *she* wasn't Joshua. The oversized clothes she was wearing and the amateur application of cosmetics gave her that sunken-eyed look."

Victor stepped out from behind the massive oaken desk that had served his father so well for almost forty years.

"Thank you for getting a quick jump on the story and killing it. *And* the follow-up story."

"You've got to hand it to those gossip hounds. They have great imaginations. Instead of killing the story when they found out that Joshua can't be Joshua because he's a *she*, they get ready to run 'Victor to wed sex-change Marik heir.' " Galen laughed aloud. "Would have been the wedding of the century."

Victor gave Galen a withering stare. "I fail to see the humor there. Drawing attention to Joshua is not a good idea at this time."

"I know that, sir, and that's why I think this whole affair could work to our advantage. We'll arrange for a video of a meeting between Missy Cooper and Joshua. It will make her famous and show everyone that Joshua is doing fine. Frankly, folks know better than to believe the scandal vids. If strange stories about Joshua start showing up there, it will cast doubt on anything else said about him."

"I wish that held true for stories about me and the conspiracy to kill my mother." Victor rubbed his eyes, then dropped onto the sofa near his desk. "You know, of course, that I had Galen Cox killed because I was covering up the murder of my father right here in this office."

Galen nodded as he came to sit in a wing-backed chair to Victor's left. "So I've heard and, just so you know, I don't think there's more than an ounce of truth in that story."

Victor laughed in spite of himself. "Thank you, my friend, for putting all this into perspective. In a world where perception can become reality, I have to remember that reality is what I must deal with. So, in that vein, what have you been doing about this scandal vid?"

"Suppressing it would only make it become more valuable, so I've sent instructions out to all Intelligence Secretariats explaining what happened and including some background information on this Miss Cooper. I've promised them follow-up material. The *Tattler* is going to run the Cooper/Joshua material as a human interest piece in about a week. All our people will have that material two days before it hits and will be encouraging local media outlets to run their own look-alike contests."

Victor nodded. "Very good. How did you get the *Tattler* to agree to shifting the focus of the story?"

Galen swallowed hard. "I told them you'd give them an

exclusive statement on the announcement of Kai Allard-Liao's engagement. I played up the angle about your knowing them both during the Clan war, back on Alyina and Twycross. Five minutes, no more."

"That's five minutes too much, dammit." Victor's hands knotted into fists, then he forced them open and released his anger. "No, wait, I have to do it. You were right in setting it up. Katherine would be so polite to the *Tattler* that it would pain them to say anything bad about her. More people end up seeing their material than anything official we send out, so I might as well get myself humanized by them."

"I hoped you'd see it that way."

"I'm certain of that, Jerrard." Victor looked around the wood-paneled office and noted that ever since he'd become First Prince, the chamber no longer looked as grand or felt as warm as during his father's domain. During that time, in the years Victor was growing up, it had been a place of power, a place where decisions were made affecting the lives of billions of people.

Creating a double for Joshua had been one of those decisions—the Gemini Project, a final legacy of Hanse Davion's reign. Alive and well, Joshua was Thomas Marik's heir and the greatest obstacle to any secret hopes Sun-Tzu Liao might have of ruling the Free Worlds League. But everyone knew Joshua was incurable. The boy would soon die, opening the way for Sun-Tzu.

Thomas had been stalling on Sun-Tzu's marriage to Isis for years, but he couldn't put it off forever. Once Liao married Isis, he would be poised to control both his own fanatical Capellan Confederation and the industrially powerful Free Worlds League.

No one could doubt what Sun-Tzu would do with that power if Thomas Marik, died by natural or unnatural causes, and Isis inherited his throne. Sun-Tzu wouldn't waste an instant mobilizing to take back the Liao worlds lost to the Federated Commonwealth in the Fourth Succession War. Hanse Davion's armies had seized half of the Capellan Confederation in the war, more than a hundred planets that became the basis for what was now named the Sarna March. Those worlds, which had previously thrust like an angry finger between the Lyran Commonwealth and the Federated Suns, now belonged to Federated Commonwealth. Nothing stood between the alliance of their two great star empires.

Victor had thought long and hard about whether to continue the Gemini Project once his advisors brought it to his attention. The idea of replacing Joshua with a double and deceiving Thomas Marik about his son's death went totally against his grain. But in the end he'd been persuaded that it was the only way the Federated Commonwealth could buy enough time to prepare to meet the potential threat of Sun-Tzu Liao. Two years were what his close advisors estimated would be needed to do that while simultaneously trying to prepare for the next stage of the war against the Clans. The Federated Commonwealth was rich and strong, but its borders were vast and there were only so many troops to defend them.

They would allow Joshua to die when the boy no longer had any hope, but would keep the double in his place for at least two years. At the end of that time they would send Thomas Marik the sad news of his son's demise and return the body of the real Joshua Marik to his final resting place in the Free Worlds League.

Given the more pressing problems he had in his realm, Victor agreed to defer dealing with the Sun-Tzu threat by using the double. After all, two years was not much time, but it was time Victor needed for preparation and for handling the other serious threat to the Federated Commonwealth.

"My sister had nothing to do with Missy Cooper?"

Galen shook his head. "Preliminary reports contraindicate that possibility, but Curaitis is doing some final checks before he signs off on that idea. In any event, there is no way she could have known about Gemini because the whole operation took place here on New Avalon and it was top secret. Even your mother didn't know about it."

"What?"

"I think that was Alex Mallory's doing. Alex probably thought she'd kill the project if he told her about it, so he never did. Only if Joshua had died would he have proposed activating Gemini." Galen frowned. "I don't know that I'd have made the same decision, which is why I might not be the best replacement for him."

"No, you're the perfect replacement for Alex. Aside from being bright, you know me well. And Katherine too. You two were actually discussing marriage, I hear."

"Yes, well, I don't think I'd feel too comfortable doing that now." Galen shuddered. "If I was looking for a wife, I think I'd rather have one who would answer yes to the question, 'You know someone is going to kill your husband. Do you warn him or not?' "

"Remind me to put that one on *my* list, too. My point is, though, that you've been closer to her than I have. You know her mind."

"I *thought* I did."

"So did I, but that was before she let you die and before we uncovered evidence linking her and Ryan to my mother's assassination." Victor turned to face Galen and was surprised to see his friend looking slightly pale. "Anything new on that front?"

Galen shook his head. "Unless we can decrypt some of the records we seized from Ryan's office after his death, I think we have as complete a picture of the plot as we're going to get. The assassin was paid with the proceeds of a land deal in which worthless property was bought at an inflated price. The land was then donated to the state for rehabilitation as a wetlands habitat for birds. The corporation got a big tax write-off and the CEO of the company, at your sister's behest, was given a title and a land grant."

Victor slammed a fist into the arm of couch. "*My* government paid for the assassin who killed my mother."

"A point I'm certain your sister would make much of if we tried to accuse her of complicity."

"Which is exactly why we won't do that. No, we've got to let her hang herself, and we've got to give her time enough to manufacture the rope to do it. She's going to have to come after me somehow."

Galen nodded. "True, but right now she has to calm the Isle of Skye worlds and that's going to take a lot of her attention. The victory of the Gray Death Legion over the rebels on Glengarry has taken the steam out of the uprising. Some people in the Skye March are still scrambling to pick up the pieces of Ryan's organization, which leaves the door open for trouble in the future. In the meantime we've pulled most of our troops, which means Katherine will have to reinforce any hot spots with her own people. The latest reports from Tharkad indicate she's concentrating on sponsoring repair and recovery programs, which should help."

"Good. She's got my mother's gift for bringing out the charity in others. A clever strategy." Victor frowned with concentration. "Has she had any visitors of interest?"

"No one incriminating. Just the usual functionaries. Caitlin Kell is staying with her. Do you think Katherine's trying to get the Kell Hounds to align with her instead of you?"

Victor waved that idea away. "No, that's not a worry."

"But they did refuse to accept a contract with the Federated Commonwealth about a year ago. They still have no contract."

"I know how that looks, Jerrard, but I'm not worried. Morgan Kell knows me. Dan Allard knows me. They'll never turn against me. Like all right-thinking folk, in fact, they're staying focused on the Clans, and we should be doing the same. Unfortunately, I have concerns that range beyond the Clans and my sister's treachery. Reports from the Sarna March?"

"Sun-Tzu Liao is stepping up his trouble-making in the Sarna March, just as we anticipated when Kai took over the Free Capella movement from good old Uncle Tormano. Kai seems determined to use Free Capella as a means of social reform and advancement, while Sun-Tzu's people are making it difficult to access the services offered. The Zhanzheng de guang guerrillas have increased their activities on Styk, Gan Singh, Zurich, and Liao, with new cells operating openly on Acamar, Fletcher, and Nanking. Their activities range from graffiti and vandalism to bank robberies and shootouts on Zurich and bombings on Styk and Fletcher."

"Those are all old Tikonov Commonalty worlds. Trouble is to be expected there. As we pull troops out of Skye and send them into the Sarna March, Sun-Tzu will have to back down. Kai doesn't want to have to arm the people, so if we supply the troops to keep Sun-Tzu quiet, Kai can lay a good foundation that will stabilize the area. My mother had been doing that before the Clans came, but the Sarna March has been neglected since their invasion."

"Kai's efforts and our reinforcement of that area *could* prompt Thomas Marik to strike against us if he fears an attack."

"Never happen—we have his son." The Prince pressed his hands together, fingertip to fingertip. "Sun-Tzu has to be pressuring Thomas to act, and Thomas has fended him off. We have to assume Thomas is walking a tightrope there and he doesn't want anything to upset his balance. Any more word about his wife?"

"It now seems that she wasn't on the train when the chemical cars at the Semidam Station caught fire. She was in Semidam itself, but was downwind of the fire at a school. Sophina helped get the children into a civil defense shelter, but then she collapsed. She's had allergic asthma all her life and the gases must have seriously damaged her lungs. She's recovered, but can barely breathe. She's not a good candidate for a transplant and apparently was raised in a tradition that wouldn't accept that option anyway."

"How long does she have?"

"A consultant over at the NAIS told me two years without extensive treatment, maybe four if she came and had work done here."

The Prince nodded. "Set up an audience with the Marik ambassador here on New Avalon. We'll offer to do anything we can to help her." Victor looked up and saw Galen watching him oddly. "Yes, I know it's hypocritical to hide the fact of Joshua's death from his parents, on one hand, then offer to do what we can to save the boy's mother on the other, but both acts move us further from a potential war with Sun-Tzu and the Free Worlds League. If I have to play both ends against the middle to hold off the war forever, I will."

Galen smiled. "I wasn't thinking you were being deceitful. I was thinking that anyone else—Sun-Tzu, your sister, perhaps even Thomas—wouldn't have hesitated to use Sophina as a new hostage to replace Joshua. But you really want to help her."

"No one will benefit from a war. If preventing the death of one person can forestall the deaths of many, I'll do anything in my power to save that single life."

5

> As peace is of all goodness, so war is an emblem, a
> hieroglyphic, of all misery.
>
> —JOHN DONNE, *DEVOTIONS*

DropShip WST Starbride, Inbound Woodstock
Sarna March, Federated Commonwealth
30 May 3057

Peering out through the porthole of the DropShip *Starbride*,
Larry Acuff felt a shiver run through him. Woodstock, the
world he'd left seven years ago after volunteering to fight
the Clans, slowly spun beneath its thin canopy of clouds.
Equal parts land mass and oceans, Woodstock was a bounti-
ful world of rich and varied fertility. In fact, the planet's fecundity had created a surplus trade balance that raised the
per capita income higher than most worlds in the Federated
Commonwealth and considerably better than almost any
other world in the Sarna March.

The day he'd left Woodstock it had been dark and stormy.
Crowded into a military DropShip with other men destined
for the front lines deep in the Lyran half of the Commonwealth, he'd caught only glimpses of his home planet as
they'd headed away from it. The lightning flashes searing
through the dark clouds had seemed like the world protest-
ing against the human harvest being reaped by the ship.

Larry smiled. It was just the sort of fanciful thought that
had often come to him while still young and romantic. Back
then he'd believed that his journey from Woodstock was the
start of a grand adventure. But that was before he'd been assigned to the Tenth Lyran Guards—the same unit of which
young Price Victor Davion was a member. He'd spent many
hours imagining fighting shoulder to shoulder with the

Prince, forcing the Clans off planets they'd taken and sending them back out into the void from whence they had come.

After the Clans had been vanquished, he would return to Woodstock a hero. There he would find himself a wife and, as his father had done after a stint in the Fourth Succession War, he would settle down and raise a family. He would raise strong children and, should some future war demand that one of them fight for the Federated Commonwealth, he would send that child forth with brave words and a fierce embrace—as his father had done when Larry left Woodstock.

Touching the innermost glass layer of the porthole, Larry felt the cold of the void and recognized in it the chill of war. Fighting the Clans on Alyina had burned out of him all fantasies about the romance of war and any dreams of a normal life. War was a machine, an engine, that gobbled up human beings, only to belch them out as corpses and cripples; men and women and broken forms of each; cowards and demagogues and heroes, grand heroes. War left no one unchanged and when it was done with you, it was waiting to hammer on you and pound you again until you either escaped or broke entirely.

Larry didn't think war had broken him, but it had come close. After being blown out of his BattleMech on Alyina, he'd wandered for days until the Clans captured him and took him to a ComStar reeducation and labor camp. Though his wounds were only superficial, healing had been slow on the sparse and at times nonexistent diet provided by ComStar. Many captives died from injuries that would have healed easily with proper medical attention and sufficient food.

From the first day he'd arrived at the Firebase Tango Zephyr camp, Larry had vowed to survive—and on his own terms. The camp's ComStar operators were more than willing to grant privileges to those who wanted to study their quasi-mystical doctrine and accept their ways. Until then, Larry had always believed ComStar to be the benevolent organization that made possible hyperpulse communications between the stars. But at Tango Zephyr they were the ones who guarded the wretched prisoners of war, freeing up Clan troops to hunt down even more Federated Commonwealth troops on the planet. Meanwhile the camp's operators offered their starving prisoners re-education, preaching the superiority of Inner Sphere humanity over the Clans and promising that the Clans would one day be subject to ComStar.

That did not strike Larry as a bright future because nowhere did that message speak of freeing Inner Sphere humans who did not submit to ComStar. He'd resolved never to bend to their will and even made plans to escape, but the paucity of food and the prevalence of informers among the prisoners made any escape attempt difficult. Punishment for attempting to flee was confinement in a small cage left open to the elements.

Throughout the three days of his stay in a cage, it rained cold and hard. Larry got sick, very sick, and his ComStar captors did nothing to help him recover.

He should have died, but he didn't. What did die were all the romance and optimism of his youth. Larry decided that a descent into the bitter self-pity he saw in many of the other prisoners would be a victory for ComStar, so he promised himself that someday he'd have his freedom, and his freedom would come in a universe very different from the one his captors described.

Then Kai Allard-Liao and a Clan Elemental, Taman Malthus, came and liberated Tango Zephyr. They helped the survivors bury their dead and arranged for their transfer off Alyina and back to the worlds of the Federated Commonwealth, back to their life before the Clans.

But Larry knew the Clan invasion had changed him and he could never go back.

"We'll be landing in a half an hour, Mr. Acuff." The flight attendant in the Woodstock SpaceTran uniform smiled at him. "I trust you enjoyed your trip with us?"

"Very much, thank you." Larry smiled at her. The *Starbride* had come to meet the JumpShip *Luxingzhe* at the nadir jump point of the system's star, from there to shuttle the passengers to the fourth planet in the system. Larry was actually on his way to St. Ives for Kai Allard-Liao's wedding, but he had decided to stop at Woodstock for a reunion with his kin.

"If you don't mind me asking, are you coming to Woodstock for fights?"

He shook his head. "No, ma'am, just for family. I've got a cousin who's marrying one of the other recruits I knew here on Woodstock. I hear there's a new municipal arena in Charleston, but I won't be doing any fighting."

She nodded, then blushed a bit. "I'm sorry to have pried, but another flight attendant and I have season tickets for the 'Mech duels there. The local talent isn't bad, but it's not quite the same thing, you know, as on Solaris."

"Have you been to the fights on Solaris?"

"No, but I've seen a lot of the holovids. I saw your fight with Jason Block. I thought you were going to win that one."

"So did I"—he glanced quickly at her name tag—"Ms. Hoglind, so did I. Jason, he had other ideas."

"Call me Meta, Mr. Acuff. I think you'll get him next time."

"Then call me Larry. I hope so. We've got a re-match scheduled for September." Larry reached into the pocket of his jacket and pulled out a holograph card. "If you can make it to the fight, let me know. I'd be honored to have you as my guest in the Cenotaph Stable box. We'll be fighting in Boreal Reach, in a blizzard, so I think it should be interesting."

"Thank you very much." Meta Hoglind slipped the card into her uniform smock pocket. "I've got some free time coming, so maybe I'll be there."

"Good."

Larry watched for a moment as the young woman moved forward in the cabin to check on the next set of passengers, then smiled and turned back to the view of the planet Woodstock filling the porthole. The Larry Acuff that had left Woodstock eight years ago would never have spoken with someone as beautiful as Meta Hoglind, not even someone half as beautiful. It was less a question of nerve than of not being the sort of man who would attract such a woman's attention. Though Larry had once dreamed of being the hero of a romantic epic, he'd never been more than just an ordinary man. Maybe there was nothing wrong with that, but nothing special about it either.

When the truce came, he'd avoided coming back to Woodstock, realizing he'd always wanted to return as a hero. He knew, deep down inside, that what he'd done was as heroic as many of the acts that earned medals during the Clan War, but his experiences had none of the obvious glamour of conspicuous gallantry in combat. Survival—the primary goal of every soldier in any war—was not as valued by noncombatants as committing a foolishly self-destructive act and dying because of it. The fact that he'd been taken prisoner seemed less than glorious, and he resisted returning home where his family would feel constrained to make excuses for his performance on Alyina.

And so Larry had headed for Solaris, the Game World, where MechWarriors fought each other in BattleMech duels that some called sporting events and others viewed as pandering to a people addicted to sanitized violence. For Larry it was the logical place to prove his mettle. Although he was a member of the Reserve Armed Forces of the Federated Commonwealth, he was sure the RAFFC wouldn't reactivate him. On Solaris, he could turn the skills that had let him survive on Alyina into a way of restoring his reputation and self-esteem.

When he reached Solaris, he discovered that Kai Allard-Liao had also made Solaris his haven. Kai gave Larry a warm welcome and offered him a spot in Cenotaph Stables—the newly renamed corporation that had been on Solaris since Kai's father had been champion in 3027. Working his way up through the Solaris arena system, Larry soon become a headliner in Solaris City contests, and his fame had spread throughout the Inner Sphere.

Though Larry was quiet and often shy by nature, his new celebrity status meant that people he'd never have dared approach now came up to approach *him*! He knew of course that most of them only wanted a piece of his public persona: Larry Acuff, 'Mech combat fighter, but he also realized that many mistook the public person for the private one.

His return to Woodstock left Larry sorting out the paradox of who he had become. There was no doubt that he was decidedly changed from the naive young man who'd gone off to war from Woodstock. By the same token, he was not the person most people perceived him to be. He dwelt somewhere in the middle, but on Woodstock he was bound to encounter people who would expect him to be one extreme or the other, not the person he was.

As the aerodynamic DropShip lowered its landing gear and swooped down to the darkened runway on the outskirts of a nightclad Charleston, Larry nodded to himself. *Here begins the last battle of the Clan War. I left Woodstock to guar-*

*antee its people the freedom to live the life they've come to
cherish. In defending them, did I lose them?*

Meta came back to where Larry stood in the gangway to
the spaceport terminal. "All clear, Larry. Not a scandal-vid
reporter or holovid cameraman in sight."

"Thanks, Meta. And remember, let me know when you're
on Solaris."

"I will."

Hiking his transit satchel over his shoulder, Larry headed
toward the reception lounge. Because Solaris' gravity was
slightly heavier than Woodstock's, he felt surprisingly energized even after weeks of space travel. Coming around the
corner he saw the four people waiting for him and broke into
a grin. His mother waved and his father threw him a casual
salute. Beside them, Hauptmann Phoebe Derden—a comrade
from the Tenth Lyran Guards—and his cousin, George
Pinkney, stood linked arm in arm.

He hugged his mother first, then his father.

"Good to have you home, son."

"Thanks, Dad. It's good to be here." Larry hesitated a moment, trying to figure out if he'd said that because it was
true or because he wanted to put his parents at ease. He decided the answer was yes to both. "And it's good to see you
both looking so well too."

"Your father has a touch of arthritis now in his back." His
mother gave Larry a critical look. "But look at you—you're
too skinny."

"Anne, for heaven's sake." Larry's father tugged with irritation at the bill of his Nebula Foods cap. "He's got to
maintain a fighting weight. Right, son?"

"Right, Dad. Cockpits are cramped enough as it is." Larry
turned to his cousin and friend. "George, you're a very
lucky man getting Phoebe to agree to marry you." He offered his hand to George Pinkney, whose grip was a bit
stronger than Larry remembered. The cousins were both of
average height and slender build, and resembled each other
enough that in the old days they were often mistaken for
twins. George had grown a bit taller since then, and his
brown hair had begun to thin. But what impressed Larry
more were the confidence in George's smile and the firmness of his grip.

"Lucky I am, Larry." George winked at Phoebe. "I got my

doctorate earlier this year and Phoebe has agreed to marry me, so I'm a happy man."

Larry shook the hand of the trim blond woman standing beside his cousin. "Went for a man of letters did you, Phoebe?"

"A man of science, Larry." She shook his hand, then leaned in to kiss him on the cheek. "How have you been?"

"Good, really. You and the rest of the Tenth did a great job rescuing Hohiro Kurita from the Clans on Teniente."

"Thanks. We did it to avenge troopers like you on Alyina." Phoebe's gray eyes grew distant for a moment, then she smiled. "We should have known the Clans could never beat soldiers like you and Kai."

Larry's father stepped up and held out the chronometer on his wrist. "We should get Larry's luggage, then head out. If we're quick, we won't have to pay the spaceport authority for your reminiscing."

Larry looked at his mother. "Arthritis or no, he's not changed, has he?"

The elder Acuff brought his head up. "And I won't, not ever. Why vary perfection?"

George laughed. "What can you say to that?"

"Nothing, Dr. George." Larry's father patted his son on the back of the head. "It is good to have you home again."

"And definitely good to be here." Larry smiled and meant it all the way.

6

It is but seldom that any one overt act produces hostilities between two nations; there exists, more commonly, a previous jealousy and ill will, a predisposition to take offense.
— WASHINGTON IRVING, *THE SKETCH BOOK OF GEOFFREY CRAYON*

Tharkad City, Tharkad
District of Donegal, Federated Commonwealth
10 June 3057

Katrina Steiner-Davion smiled graciously as she shook the hands of her visitors. "Thank you both, Dr. Price and Dr. Wu, for spending so much time explaining all this to me. Your input has been invaluable in shaping my plans for research grants."

Both men took their leave of her reluctantly, but Katrina was used to that. From an early age she'd learned to use her charm to manipulate others as easily as a fish swims or a bird flies. A smile, a wink, the press of her hand against someone's arm, a conspiratorial whisper in an ear or a glance sharing a silent joke bound people tightly to her.

Katrina saw her charm as a tool, but others seemed to seek it like a drug. Growing up, she'd learned from her mother, a master of charm, how potent it could be in winning others over to her point of view. Melissa Steiner had combined it so effectively with her innocent idealism that few could stand against her. Her cousin Ryan Steiner had seen that early on, and since he couldn't neutralize Melissa by marrying her, he'd sought another solution to the problem.

Katrina had determined that she would not make the same mistake as her mother, a decision made long before the deaths of either of her parents. Melissa, in being so loved, felt safe in her role as a benevolent figure. After all, she had

Hanse Davion, her husband, as the force to destroy those she could not charm.

Unfortunately, as it happened, the stick died, leaving the carrot unprotected.

Katrina had anticipated that turn of events and resolved never to leave herself so vulnerable. Her natural abilities combined with diligent work had built up her own network of loyal agents who provided her with all manner of information about her enemies. David Hanau had been her spy in Ryan Steiner's camp, though his warning about Ryan's plan to kill Galen Cox had come too late for her to do anything about it.

She shrugged. Chances were that any attempt to change Ryan's mind about Galen would have failed. Ryan had built up an immunity to her charm. He'd seen as much value in using her as she did in manipulating him. In his efforts to destabilize Victor's hold on the government, Ryan realized that Katrina could become a rival whom it would be difficult to vanquish.

What he did not grasp was that she had already strengthened her position in the Federated Commonwealth and was benefiting from the results of Ryan's treasonous activities. This was especially so in the Lyran half of the nation. In adopting the name of Katrina—that of her beloved grandmother—Katherine had won over many Lyrans who might have criticized her because she'd been raised on New Avalon. With the name change and the way she berated both Victor and Ryan for squabbling over the Skye March, in the people's eyes she became the person who would accept responsibility for the fate of a nation savaged by the Clans and almost voiceless since the death of Melissa Steiner.

She had charmed them into believing that. She had charmed Galen Cox. She had charmed the doctors and she would charm everyone else. No one should be able to resist her, but if they somehow did, she would find another way to deal with them.

As she had to find a way to deal with Victor.

Victor had never been prey to her charm. Like any older brother, he usually found her antics annoying. Though only two and a half years her senior, he had dismissed her as frivolous until lately. Even then, he only paid attention to her because she was a weapon for use against Ryan, sword to plunge into the heart of the rebellious Isle of Skye.

He who lives by the sword, so shall he die by it.

Katrina wondered if Victor knew what he was doing. In questioning the two doctors about leukemia, she'd learned that though the disease could easily make the brain swell and that the anemia resulted in much bleeding and bruising because it reduced the blood's ability to clot, it would not cause strokes. What the doctors didn't know was that she'd received a security briefing nearly a year before indicating that Joshua Marik had suffered a stroke resulting in some memory loss and affecting his speech, but that he was recovering quickly. The doctors had noted that, short of the miracle of spontaneous remission, no one recovered from anything concerning leukemia quickly.

As the doctors left the room and the doors clicked shut behind them, Katrina sat down on the white leather couch, her blue eyes narrowing as she thought about Joshua Marik. The stroke was a nice cover, *if* Victor was doing what she suspected. It wouldn't have been his plan, of course, but probably something begun by their father. Victor wouldn't have had the stomach to do what was necessary to create a double for Joshua Marik.

That sent her thoughts back a dozen years to a stormy October day in the palace on Tharkad. Her mother had been curiously quiet that morning and Katrina had instinctively sensed Melissa's need to talk to someone. She'd trailed after her around the palace and, when Melissa had started to bundle up for a trip outdoors, Katrina had silently joined her. Melissa smiled her approval, and they had ventured out into the icy city without notice or fanfare.

The driver took them to a small cemetery where the Twenty-fourth Lyran Guard buried its dead. There Melissa led her daughter to a grave site. After they'd cleared away the snow and laid flowers on the grave of Jeana Clay, Melissa knelt down to say a silent prayer. Seeing her mother cry, Katrina hugged her tight, then they returned to the car and rode silently back to the palace.

The next day Melissa told her daughter about Jeana Clay, who acted as her double in the time before Melissa Steiner married Hanse Davion. After the marriage, Jeana had taken Melissa's place on Tharkad while Melissa stayed with her husband on New Avalon. When the Fourth Succession War began, Skye separatists—every bit as troublesome then as they were now—had tried to assassinate Archon Katrina

Steiner and Melissa. Jeana had discovered the plot and killed the assassins, but died defending the Archon.

If not for hearing that story and her own close brush with death in the blast that had killed Galen, the idea of creating a double for herself would never have occurred to her, nor would she have spotted the problem with Joshua's stroke. And she could not be certain that the use of the term "stroke" had been only carelessness on the part of the Intelligence Secretariat. Katrina knew that if she had Joshua and a double, *and* Joshua was dying, she wouldn't hesitate to make the switch to keep Sun-Tzu at bay.

Everyone knew he was just waiting for the chance to strike back at the Federated Commonwealth to regain the dozens of worlds lost in the Fourth Succession War. The Capellan Confederation was no match for the Federated Commonwealth, but those fanatics would become plenty dangerous if Sun-Tzu could draw on the industrial might of the Free Worlds League.

And once Joshua was dead, what would stop Sun-Tzu? Sooner or later Thomas Marik was going to have to let him marry Isis—and then Thomas better watch his own back. As long as everyone believed Joshua still lived, the status quo would continue. Once the boy died, everything would be up for grabs. Katrina knew it. Thomas knew it. Sun-Tzu knew it. And Victor also knew it.

She smiled to herself as her secretary buzzed to let her know that her next visitor had arrived. *I'll have to watch how you handle this, Victor. This may be exactly what I need to learn just how dangerous you truly are.*

Tamar
Wolf Clan Occupation Zone

Phelan Kell Ward smiled as he looked over to where Natasha Kerensky lounged casually in a camp chair in the office of ilKhan Ulric Kerensky. "You are very confident that your Alpha Galaxy will beat my Beta Galaxy in these exercises, *quiaff?*"

Self-assurance sparkling in her eyes, the flameheaded Khan nodded at him. "Aff, Khan Phelan. I cracked the defenses of Tamar City when that lunatic, Selvin Kelswa, was defending it six years ago." She leaned back, letting her chair balance on two legs. "The city's defenses are not enough to stop the Dire Wolves."

Brushing a few stray black hairs from his eyes, Phelan forced a yawn, then glanced at the white-haired man seated at the desk across from both him and Natasha. "It seems, ilKhan, that Khan Natasha is getting rather cocky in her dotage."

"Dotage!" Natasha rocked her chair forward, bringing her booted feet down with a heavy thump. "I may have been fighting and winning wars before your father was admitted to the Nagelring, but I've not lost any of my edge. And if you try to argue, as the Crusaders have, that my age has made me use my influence to reduce our fighting, I'll turn you over my knee."

Phelan laughed, his green eyes flashing. "I would never suggest that you have become a pacifist because of your age. The Crusaders are foolish to imply that is the reason you support the truce the ilKhan struck with ComStar after the battle for Tukayyid. The fact that I support it and that Ulric negotiated it, and that we're both very much your junior undercuts their argument."

Ulric nodded. "You would prefer, Natasha, the Crusaders fighting a battle they cannot win to having them turn their efforts to something more useful, *quiaff*?"

"Aff, but having to answer challenges from Crusaders within Clan Wolf is becoming annoying."

The Khan of Khans smiled. "You are doing wonders thinning out the Crusader ranks when you defend yourself."

"I can see that, but the only ones I'm getting are those who have earned Bloodnames, with plenty of young Crusaders waiting to step into their places." Natasha curled her lip in disgust. "I would resign, but with Dalk Carns as Loremaster, I would be surrendering my position to a Crusader, and surrender is something I will never do."

The Wardens and the Crusaders were the two main political divisions within the Clans. The Crusaders believed it was the Clans' destiny to conquer the Inner Sphere in order to restore the glorious Star League. The Wardens disagreed, believing it was the Clans' mission to wait in readiness to protect the Inner Sphere against dangers from without.

Phelan frowned. "We could get someone to challenge Carns, oust him and replace him with a Warden."

Ulric arched a white eyebrow at the younger Khan. "Could we?"

"Carns is Loremaster, but that is because he is a better politician than he is a MechWarrior. Athen Kederk or Alita Winson from my Beta Galaxy could unseat him."

"I agree, but that does not answer my question." Ulric leaned forward at his desk. "Could we get a Warden elected to the position of Loremaster, *quineg*?"

The addition of *quineg* to Ulric's question surprised Phelan. It meant the ilKhan clearly expected a negative response. "I am the first person to admit I am not a politician of any skill, but I was unaware that sentiment within the Wolf Clan had shifted so sharply toward the Crusader point of view."

Natasha rested her elbows on her knees. "The shift has been gradual, Phelan, and comes from the youngest ranks of MechWarriors. They were hearing the great tales of our victories as we invaded the Inner Sphere. Knowing they would be finished with their training and in the field by the time the final assault on Terra began, they dreamed of great glory. Because we Wolves were the Clan that had pushed most deeply into the Inner Sphere, the honor of the assault would go to us, and they eagerly imagined the day they would participate in that great victory.

"When Tukayyid resulted in a truce, our young warriors were frustrated. Clan Wolf did not suffer great losses on Tukayyid, so the younger warriors have been left with few chances to compete for Bloodnames. The severe losses suffered by the other Clans opened up whole ranks, and new warriors in the Jade Falcons or Nova Cats have been able to move into positions of higher responsibility. Because the glory dreams of our young warriors have not died, many of them want us to break the truce and finish what we started."

Phelan shook his head. "So they view the right to attack Terra as something positive for Clan Wolf?"

"Aff. Our young have become Wolf supremists." Ulric narrowed his blue eyes. "They are misguided. It's true that they repudiate the beliefs and aims of Crusaders like Clan Jade Falcon, but they are willing to follow Wolves who accept the line of the Crusaders."

Natasha nodded. "Chief among their ringleaders is Vlad."

Phelan's nostrils flared. Vlad, of the House of Ward, was the MechWarrior who had captured him eight years before and brought him into the Wolf Clan. Vlad was a Crusader, fully embracing the idea that the Clans were destined to conquer the worlds of the Inner Sphere and rule over humanity in a newly resurrected Star League. In a strange twist of fate, Phelan and Vlad had ended up battling in a Trial of Bloodright for the coveted surname of Ward. Suffering defeat at Phelan's hands had only intensified Vlad's hatred.

Phelan, who had been born in the Inner Sphere of Morgan Kell and his wife Salome, was what the Clans reviled as a *freeborn,* an individual conceived and born by natural means. That Phelan had managed to defeat the fruit of generations of selective Clan breeding to produce superior warriors infuriated other Clansmen—Crusaders in particular—because his skill challenged their notions of superiority over the freeborns of the Inner Sphere. For a man like Vlad—full of ambition and dedicated to the Crusader mission—losing to Phelan opened a wound that would never close.

"So Vlad is using the young warriors' inexperience and lack of sophistication to push against the Wardens and the truce?"

Ulric nodded in reply. "The idea he is preaching is very attractive to those warriors who have little or no chance of nomination for a Bloodname without warfare to prove their worthiness. He is using your elevation to prove that I have embraced the Inner Sphere, and he uses Natasha's age to suggest that no upward movement in the Wolves will take place because we are not cycling our personnel as other Clans do."

Phelan punched one fist into the palm of the other. "Vlad persuades the youngsters that they have no future, then offers them a solution that means more war and destruction."

Natasha plucked nervously at a thread on her gray jumpsuit. "The problem with the Warden position has always been that it advocates caution and hesitation in a people who are warriors. That never goes over well. Because Nicholas Kerensky was the founder of the Clans, and because Kerenskys have always led the Wolves, we have been able to promote the Warden point of view with impunity. Restlessness among the other Clans finally resulted in the invasion, but only by leading, as a Kerensky must, has Ulric been able to prevent a complete slaughter of the Inner Sphere."

Phelan nodded grimly. "But as long as Ulric remains ilKhan, the Crusaders are stymied."

"True, but sooner or later they will try something to rekindle the war."

"Like the Red Corsair."

The other two Wolves fell silent at Phelan's mention of the renegade Jade Falcon warrior who had almost broken the Truce of Tukayyid with a unit made up of volunteers. Phelan, working in unison with the Kell Hounds, had defeated the Red Corsair and the Crusader plot to reignite the warrior against the Inner Sphere. He had been able to isolate knowledge of the plot—even Ulric and Natasha had not learned *all* the details—and control the damage. Even so, the nature of the plot suggested that the Crusaders and those Clans they dominated, like the Jade Falcons, would use any opportunity to destroy the truce and conquer the Inner Sphere.

"Let us hope they never again become that ambitious, *quiaff*?"

Natasha nodded at the ilKhan. "Aff."

A light knocking at the door of the ilKhan's spartan office brought Ulric's head up. "Come."

Phelan turned to look, then stood as Dalk Carns marched stiffly through the doorway. Unlike the two Khans, the Loremaster wore gray ceremonial Wolf Clan leathers and carried an enameled wolf's-head mask in the crook of his left arm. In his right hand he held a tightly rolled piece of parchment, sealed in red wax. Two small black ribbons trailed out from it.

Carns stared directly at Ulric. "Are you Ulric Kerensky, ilKhan of the Clans?"

"I am Ulric Kerensky."

Dalk extended the scrolled sheet toward Ulric. "This is an indictment generated by an internal Wolf Clan investigation."

Phelan reached out for it, to relay it to Ulric's hand, but Dalk pulled away. "Khan Phelan, do not interfere with a Loremaster in his capacity as High Bailiff."

Phelan opened his hands and raised them in mock surrender. "Forgive me. I was not aware of the protocol."

Natasha slowly rose, smoothing her jumpsuit. "And I, Loremaster, was unaware such an investigation could be undertaken without a Khan's approval."

"As you may know, Khan Natasha, a Loremaster does not require a Khan's approval to conduct an investigation when there is suspicion that one or more of the Khans of the Clan might be implicated in the charges."

The woman shook her head. "That I know. Who did the investigating?"

Carns frowned. "A competent individual who knows the facts of the case."

Phelan looked at Natasha. "Vlad?"

She nodded. "Who else?"

"You will learn in good time, my Khans." Carns held the scroll out to Ulric again. "Receive the indictment."

Ulric slowly came around from behind his desk. He held out one hand to accept the document, but Natasha stayed the hand.

"Yes, Natasha?"

"This indictment comes through an unsanctioned Loremaster's investigation. If you do not accept it, he cannot press the charges. The Loremaster has no jurisdiction over the ilKhan."

Ulric smiled indulgently. "That is true. The charges would founder for a while, but if I do not accept the indictment, Dalk will convince someone in the Clan Council to pass a resolution of no confidence. That leaves me open to unseating by the Grand Council."

"We will demand a Trial of Refusal and kill them if they vote against you."

"Natasha, I will not be a party to pitting Wolves against Wolves."

"*He's* not concerned about that." She glared at Carns. "Don't accept it. Force him to go through the proper steps."

"And suggest that I am guilty?"

Natasha threw her hands up in frustration. "You will do what you will do."

Ulric took the sheet and set it on his desk without cracking the seal. "You will forward the arguments for the charges?"

The Loremaster nodded. "I will. You have one month before trial."

"Very well," Ulric said calmly.

Phelan frowned. "Wait a minute. What are the charges?"

"The charges are confidential, Khan Phelan."

Ulric laid his hand on Dalk's shoulder. "You may tell them. They will know soon anyway."

Dalk grinned coldly. "The charges are most grave," he intoned. "For his collusion with ComStar in the battle of Tukayyid and for elevating a known Inner Sphere agent to the position of Khan within the Wolf Clan, ilKhan Ulric Kerensky has been accused of high treason."

7

> This maiden she lived with no other thought
> Than to love and be loved by me.
>
> —EDGAR ALLEN POE, ANNABEL LEE

Marik Palace, Atreus
Marik Commonwealth, Free Worlds League
15 June 3057

As Thomas Marik opened the door to the chamber where his wife lay, strains of Mozart's *Requiem* drifted toward him. The soft music muted the serpentine hiss of oxygen flowing to her mask, almost permitting Thomas to ignore her malady. As a concession to the use of oxygen, the candles surrounding Sophina's canopied bed were electric, their little glowing filaments flickering in the best imitation of fire they could manage.

Thomas let the door close slowly behind him and recognized instantly the effect she'd intended. The gentle music and gentler light combined with the sheer netting wafting down from the canopy to make Sophina look as she had ten years before, on their wedding night. Though it had not been their first night of intimacy, she had never seemed more beautiful to him.

Thomas knew she wanted him to remember her as she had been then—beautiful and vibrant, full of life and love and joy, but the illusion was not completely successful. The electric candles lacked the warmth and sensuous guttering of real flames. The *Requiem*, though beautiful, could not be mistaken for the more romantic strains of the *Moonlight Sonata*.

And on their wedding night Sophina had neither an oxygen mask over her face, nor a needle in the vein of one arm.

Thomas had come tonight hoping he could talk her out of ending her life, but seeing how spent and exhausted she looked made him surrender silently to her wishes. Every breath was torture for her, yet he knew that if he asked, she would continue that torture for days or weeks or years. The fierceness of her love for him had not waned over time, nor had his for her.

And because I love her, I must free her.

Thomas smiled and approached Sophina from her left to keep his scarred profile hidden. "I have come, my love, as you bid."

Sophina's eyes opened slowly. "I had no fear ..." The oxygen mask muffled her words, and her breathlessness silenced the rest of her thought. Her bluish lips still formed the words, but the fog on the inside of the mask made it impossible to make out what she was saying.

Thomas parted the gauzy curtain that separated them and sat on the edge of the bed. Opposite him he saw the saline sack that dripped into the tube leading to the needle in her right arm. Connected to it through two electronically controlled switches were two more polymer sacks, one colored yellow and the other filled with a green liquid. The device that controlled the switches lay clutched in Sophina's trembling right hand.

Thomas took her other hand in his, nearly flinching at the coldness of her fingers. "You are the passion of my life. The mother of our son and the keeper of my heart. Before you I had no hope of knowing the peace and security of love. After you ..." His voice trailed off as a lump rose in his throat to strangle his words.

Sophina gave his hand a feeble squeeze. "After me will come others ..."

"No. No one will take your place."

"Dear, dear Thomas, you are strong." Her chest labored, rising and falling abruptly beneath the thick coverlet as she struggled to catch her breath. "You are virile. You will have women."

"No. Coupling with another would mock what we had and defile our bed."

"Thomas, do not be blind. I was not the first ..."

"Perhaps not, but by God, you will be the last." Thomas gripped her hand more tightly. "You are the only one I wished to wed, and the only one I ever shall. I shall be faithful to you beyond death."

Sophina smiled, then coughed. Thomas leaned down to cradle her against his chest, which, to his relief, calmed her coughing. He stroked her limp hair and tried not to think about how wasted her poor body had become.

A painfully thin hand came up and stroked his smooth cheek. "Thomas, my love, I was but a mistress to you."

"How can you say . . ."

Fingers pressed against his lips silenced him. "You have been wed to your nation since before I met you." She fell back slightly, gathering the strength to continue speaking. "That I had you this long is the joy of my life. But I know you took me, in wonderful passion . . . because your wife, the state, required an heir that it could not give you."

Thomas began to protest, yet knew her words contained a seed of truth. Passion had influenced his choice, making it a very happy one, but it was true that he had chosen to marry to provide the Free Worlds League a legitimate heir to the Captain-Generalship. By the time Isis had reached the age of ten it was readily apparent that she was too flighty and taken with herself to provide the leadership the nation needed. The shadow of illegitimacy surrounding her birth would also work against her. Having an heir who could replace him became vital, and Sophina had provided him with that heir.

His wife looked up at him. "I wish I had done a better job."

"Hush, woman, you speak nonsense." Thomas gave her a brave smile. "Our son has faced his trials and suffering as bravely as any grown man could. He has the heart of a lion. The doctors tell me that Joshua knows more about his disease than they do and that he does not complain even when the treatments are painful."

"But he will never reign, Thomas. You know that." Sophina shook her head slowly. "Here, at the door to death, I feel as if many light years no longer separate me from my son. Mark me, Thomas, it will not be long before Joshua and I are together again. It pains you, I know. But you must face the truth."

"Our son is strong."

"But not as strong as you must be, my love." A cough wracked her. "You must take another wife."

"I cannot."

"For your nation."

"I will not."

"For me."

"What?" Thomas leaned down and kissed her forehead. "How can you ask that?"

"I am your wife, but I am also your subject. Your lot is to put your personal desires second to the needs of your nation. That I once served both is the crowning achievement of my life." The darkened tip of her tongue wet cyanotic lips. "I would not have my death harm my nation."

"Your death wounds your nation's leader to his heart."

"Better his heart be hurt than his brain, for his brain must prevail in this." Tears pooled in Sophina's eyes, but could not spill free until she turned her head and looked away from him. "You must choose a new wife ... for your nation."

"I do not want for a wife."

"But your nation wants for you a consort." Her fingers traced their way around his left ear, as they had done many times in the languor after lovemaking, when he had held in her his arms as he did now. "The Duchess of St. Ives has daughters, as does the Coordinator of the Draconis Combine."

Thomas tried to push the words from his mind, yet he had become too used to coolly evaluating anything that had bearing on the welfare of his nation. Cassandra and Kuan-Yin Allard-Liao stood behind their brother Kai in the order of succession. Though they were identical twins, Thomas knew the sisters were very different. Cassandra had become a MechWarrior like her mother Candace and was vivacious and outgoing. Kuan-Yin had a quiet spirituality about her that Thomas had noted when the Inner Sphere's leaders had gathered on Outreach to lay their plans to meet the Clan threat. Marrying either of them would forge a link between the Free Worlds League and the St. Ives Compact, leaving Sun-Tzu's Capellan Confederation sandwiched between and making him much easier to control.

Omi Kurita, daughter of Theodore Kurita, would never inherit the throne of the Combine, but her influence with her brother Hohiro meant she would no doubt help shape policy in the future. Marriage to her would renew the old alliance between the Free Worlds League and the Draconis Combine, creating a powerful force to counter any aggression by the Federated Commonwealth.

"And then," Sophina whispered softly, "there is Katrina Steiner."

Thomas started at the name. Katrina, who he had once dismissed as being no more responsible than Isis, had lately shown herself very capable in handling the Skye crisis. Her efforts alone had prevented the eruption of civil war in the Isle of Skye. Victor Davion obviously trusted her enough to turn the Lyran half of his nation over to her regency, and who could know her better than her brother?

Marrying her would secure two-thirds of his border as well as render unnecessary any alliance with Sun-Tzu Liao and the Capellan Confederation. Her dowry would likely include all the worlds lost to the Federated Commonwealth in the Fourth Succession War. The opportunities for trade and especially the exchange of intellectual properties and research with the F-C would mean a renaissance in the Free Worlds League and a strengthening of its position among the nations of the Inner Sphere.

Thomas again stroked his wife's hair. "And there are many, many more women in the Inner Sphere. Now I wish only to think of one."

"But what of all those in your nation who depend upon you."

"To this I say 'No.' For now. While I mourn."

"But you will think on it?"

"I can gainsay you nothing, Sophina."

"Hold me, Thomas."

As he drew her closer, she pushed the plunger in her right hand. With a little whirring, the switches opened stopcocks, changing the mixture of liquid flowing into her arm. First, from the yellow bag, a sedative began to enter her bloodstream, gently letting her drift off to sleep. Within five minutes the second stopcock turned, and the emerald liquid infused the intravenous line. It was a neurotoxin that slowly stopped her tortured lungs from laboring and stilled her pounding heart.

Thomas continued to clutch his wife's limp form to his chest beyond the point when he felt her spirit flee her body. His tears wet her face as well as his own and sobs wracked his chest as coughs had hers. Finally he loosed his embrace and lay her down against the pillow. He straightened her limbs, removed the oxygen mask, and pulled the needle from her arm. Then he backed away and let the gauzy bed curtain float down between them.

Wiping at his tears, Thomas Marik spoke to his wife one last time. "I shall not forget the wisdom of your words, but neither shall I act upon them. For now our son lives, and you live in him. I will not deny our nation the service of our child and the selfless wisdom that comes to him from his mother."

Daosha, Zurich
Sarna March, Federated Commonwealth

The knock at his door surprised Noble Thayer. He was expecting no visitors, and his landlord, Kenneth Fox, had left Daosha for a weekend at his lakeside cabin in the rain forest. Opening the door slightly and peering around it, he found a slender, pretty young woman in an oversized work shirt, old jeans, and older canvas sneakers standing on his doorstep. "Can I help you miss?"

She smiled and extended her hand to him. "I hope so. I'm Cathy Hanney. I worked with Dr. Lear, and she asked a few of us come over to clean out her things from the basement."

"Noble Thayer. Mr. Fox mentioned something about that."

"Deirdre cleared it with him through ComStar messages. I think you have the key to the locker."

"That's right. Please come in while I get it," Noble said, turning from the door as the young woman stepped over the threshold. "I take it your friend left rather unexpectedly?"

"You could say that. About a year ago Tormano Liao whisked her away to Solaris where she and Kai Allard-Liao decided to get married."

Noble smiled as he pulled on a gray sweatshirt bearing the logo of Stevenson Military Prep. "A real Cinderella story, isn't it?"

"The strangest part was that she never talked about him to any of us, but it turns out that he's the father of her son."

"That would be David?"

Cathy nodded, though her blue eyes narrowed suspiciously. "How did you know?"

Noble opened a drawer and pulled out a large plastic tyrannosaurus and tossed it to Cathy. "When I was moving in, I found a loose section of floorboard back in the small bedroom. I thought maybe I was going to unearth somebody's buried treasure, but all I found was this."

Cathy laughed. "I'm sure to David this *was* a treasure."

"Sounds like any normal boy."

"Sure, except now he's in line for the throne of the St. Ives Compact."

"Or," Noble smiled, "destined to become the Champion of Solaris. Here are the keys. Let's go."

Cathy looked puzzled. "What do you mean?"

"I'll help you."

"That's very kind. But I don't want to put you out."

Noble ushered her through the door and locked it behind them. "Look, I don't mind. I need the exercise. And, well, I've been here on Zurich for almost a month and the only people I've met are Mr. Fox, his daughter, and her half-wit husband. Maybe with you I can chat about something more than old wars, new holovids, or how many mips a new computer can perform."

"Well, I get the part about a little occupational therapy, but I wouldn't say you're in need of any exercise at all." Cathy led the way down the stairs and around to the back, then down another flight to the basement. A doorway leading to the rear parking area had been opened, letting sunlight flood the basement. Cathy signaled to a little group of three standing next to a jeep with a trailer attached to it, then made the introductions when they walked over.

"Noble Thayer, this is Dr. Richard Bradford and his wife, Carol. He's the director at Rencide Medical Center and Carol runs our child care and community outreach programs."

The smallish, dark-haired man shook Noble's hand firmly. "Call me Rick."

His wife, who stood a little taller than him, likewise gave Noble a firm grip. "Please to meet you, Mr. Thayer."

"Noble, please."

Cathy pointed to the apple-cheeked woman who completed the trio. "This is Anne Thompson. She, Deirdre, and I all started at Rencide at the same time."

"A pleasure." Noble shook her hand.

"Noble has offered to help us," Cathy said, touching his shoulder lightly.

He shrugged agreeably. "Many hands make short work."

"Happy for the help," Rick said heartily. "We'll load the trailer, then ship it off to St. Ives. After that, we were thinking of getting dinner. Like to join us?"

"Yes, do," Cathy added.

"Well, let's see if you still want me when we're done. You'll want to see whether I pull my own weight, right?"

Carol patted her husband's back. "As the person who would have been massaging the back of someone who would claim for himself all the heavy lifting jobs, you're very welcome here and at dinner."

"Thanks." Noble held the keys up. "Let's go. The sooner we start, the sooner we're done."

Cathy smiled at him. "That will give us more time to get to know you over dinner."

"Ah, even more incentive to get started." Noble ushered them all toward the basement door. "I'll have to send a message of thanks to your Doctor Lear. I've never met her, but I'm certainly grateful for her role in introducing me to some interesting folks here in my new home."

8

Soldiers in peace are like chimneys in summer.
—Lord Burghley, *Advice to His Son*

Tamar, Wolf Clan Occupation Zone
21 June 3057

Phelan sat back and rubbed his hands over his face. His eyes felt like burning coals set into their sockets, and his head like someone was pounding on the inside of his skull to get out. "These charges are all groundless, but the indictment has been worded in such a way that it does appear like treason."

Though he'd really been talking to himself, Ranna leaned heavily against the doorway into their bedroom. She yawned, tugged up at where her nightshirt had slipped off one shoulder, then smiled sleepily at him. "Phelan, you would do better going over that material when you are rested."

"You're probably right, but I want to know what they're going to bring against Ulric. I'm not too tired for that."

Shaking her head, she clucked at him. "You are fatigued enough to be using contractions, my love."

"That is your grandmother's influence, Ranna."

"Maybe so, but we have both just returned from ten days in the field where Natasha's unit had us running around in circles. I am exhausted and all I did was command a Cluster. You had the whole Galaxy to worry about. You must be dead."

"I'd be dead—sorry—I *would* be dead if I had let your grandmother take the city. Losing the industrial zone to her was bad enough." Phelan went from the table to take a seat in the living area. Stretching his legs out, he sighed. "I much prefer real combat to the war we will have to wage in the Clan Council."

"I gather the people who were behind the charges would prefer real combat to the mock combats we have been waging."

Phelan's head came up quickly. "How much do you know about the investigation and the indictment?"

"Vlad asked me to help him with the investigation."

"He what?" Phelan's jaw dropped open. "He did that to get at me."

Ranna shook her head, then combed her fingers through her short white hair. "No, he may hate you, and you him, but the reason he asked is because we were raised in the same sibko."

"Growing up together in the same batch of babies doesn't mean you'd support him in this, does it?"

"No, Phelan. I love you too much to be a party to this charge of treason."

"But you didn't tell me he'd asked you to participate."

"It was an investigation initiated by the Loremaster. Even though I knew the charges were spurious, I could not tell you about it." Ranna crossed to where Phelan was sprawled out, then sat down when he pulled his feet away to make room. "The issues at stake deserve to be discussed, but perhaps they have chosen the wrong method for addressing them."

Phelan smiled at her as she rested her arms on his drawn-up knees. "You're saying you think the treason charges have merit?"

She shook her head. "No, but the questions about the truce and the difficulty of advancement within the Clan warrant attention."

"I'm not certain I understand."

Interlacing her fingers, Ranna rested her chin on her hands. "Take me, for example . . ." she began.

"After ten days in the field I'd like to take you for a lot more than an example."

"You had your chance before you started reading through the legal briefs the ilKhan had delivered in our absence."

"Touché."

"Indeed." She smiled at him, then focused a frown on her face. "This *is* serious, Phelan. I turned twenty-nine a month and a half ago. I am a Star Colonel, which is an excellent position, considering the fact that I have no Bloodname. Without one I can go no further, and if I do not earn one in the next five years, the chances of my ever getting one drop off precipitously—as do my chances of maintaining my rank."

Phelan nodded. Unspoken was the fact that if Ranna did not earn a Bloodname, the chances of her genes ever becoming part of the Clan genetic program were next to nil. Phelan had chosen to withhold his own DNA against the day Ranna's was eligible for breeding, but that was an option he had as a Clan Khan. House Kerensky was known as ultra-conservative in deciding which of its blood to breed, and Ranna had yet to make the list.

Phelan reached out and stroked her smooth cheek with the back of his hand. "Do you think unseating Ulric and renewing the war will let you progress?"

"No, Phelan, I do not, but that is not the point. Clan Wolf has many warriors who have proved their worth in the invasion, but who cannot move up because war is no longer killing off the older warriors or forcing them to retire. Of all the Clans, only the Wolves did well on Tukayyid, but it has hobbled our young. They see themselves as part of the Wolf Clan, and reveal in its glory, but they do not believe they will ever be allowed to add to or increase that glory."

"Thus speaks the gospel according to Vlad."

Ranna reached over and gave Phelan's shoulders a shake. "If you focus on him as the core of the problem, you will miss the larger issue. We Clans are a warrior people. We have been breeding warriors for three centuries for the express purpose of becoming the most efficient fighting force ever created. The Wardens held sway for a long time because they promised we would one day fulfill our destiny of defending the Inner Sphere against some external threat. When that threat did not materialize, the Crusaders won the day and the invasion was begun to conquer the Inner Sphere.

"When you have a people bred for war, how can you expect them to adapt easily to peace? Our whole social structure was designed to permit advancement through combat. We are not even allowed to reproduce unless we have proven that our genetic material will also advance the whole breeding program. To hold to such a social organization while simultaneously denying combat to three generations of warriors is guaranteed to produce the pressure from below we are now seeing."

"But we *have* warfare. We carry out raids against the other Clans. Was it not that way before the invasion, back on the Clan homeworlds?"

"Those are but simulator battles after taking part in the real thing." Ranna's blue eyes sparked with excitement. "Against the Inner Sphere and ComStar we held back nothing, neither asking nor giving quarter. We were tested to our utmost and proved ourselves and our war machines better than those of the Inner Sphere."

"Not always."

"No, not always. We lost battles to valiant warriors and clever tactics, but there is no denying that we now hold sway over almost a quarter of the Inner Sphere."

Phelan frowned. "And, if the Red Corsair is any example, we could have much more."

"Which is exactly the point Vlad and his people want to make." Ranna smiled carefully. "To them war means conquest, and conquests mean a future in the Clans."

"And this indictment is a ranging shot to get the ilKhan to modify his views concerning the truce?"

"That is how it seems to me, but you must remember that Vlad may be playing me one way because of our connections. His true motives—because of his sentiments toward you—may be far more dangerous."

Phelan nodded. "I *do* take the treason charged based on my elevation rather personally."

"I can understand that." Ranna stood and took Phelan's hands in hers. "And I think you will understand the charges and how to deal with them better after a good night's sleep."

Phelan let her tug him to his feet, then he took her in his arms and kissed her pert nose. "I would agree, but I think I am too keyed up to fall asleep immediately."

"Is that so, my Khan?" She kissed him quickly on the lips, then slipped from his arms. Taking his right hand in her left, she led him toward their bedroom. "I know of ways to relax you."

"And then I'll be able to sleep?"

"I should think so," Ranna said, reaching for the wall tab that would extinguish the lights. "Eventually."

Avalon City, New Avalon
Crucis March, Federated Commonwealth

Victor Davion did not hit the pause button on the holovid viewer's remote control until his intercom had buzzed at him a second, insistent time. Victor stared for a moment at the frozen image of Omi Kurita's face and smiled. *This interruption better be worth it.* His finger paused above the intercom button as he tried to imagine what could justify leaving Omi's message unfinished. Drawing a blank, he keyed the intercom.

"Cranston here, Highness. I have the results of the polls you asked to see."

"Bring them."

Victor continued to study Omi's serene visage and replayed a sequence of the holovid in his mind. Her peaceful expression had not changed even as her monologue began to diverge from pleasant remembrances of her recent birthday and the gift conveyed to her by his ambassador. From there she had carefully shifted the subject and relayed to him a message from his brother Peter. *She seems to hear from him more than I do.*

She and Peter had apparently formed a solid bond of trust during Omi's visit to Solaris the previous year, and that made Victor very happy. Omi had been the one to tell him that his brother had traveled with her from Solaris to Zaniah. Once there, according to Omi, he had voluntarily entered St. Marinus House, a religious retreat for warriors. That solved the mystery of where Peter had gone after vanishing from Solaris, and in getting the news from Omi, Victor trusted that he was learning all he really needed to know about the situation.

What amazed him was how well Omi truly knew and understood him. She had told him where his brother was, then added that Peter wished information on his whereabouts be restricted to Victor, Kai, and Omi. She added nothing by way of excuse or explanation to mollify an angry reaction from Victor. Because the news came from her in such a frank and open manner, it didn't anger him. Under any other circumstances his reaction would surely have been very different.

Peter had definitely defied him in leaving Solaris without

permission. Victor should have been furious, but the fact that Peter had been aided and abetted by Omi changed everything. Had Peter been in danger, or had Peter posed a danger to him, Omi would have said as much in her message. That she did not meant that she believed Peter was acting responsibly. Victor knew where his brother was and that he would be safe, so—as Omi's casualness indicated—there was no use in pursuing the matter.

She knows me better than I know myself, this woman I have grown to love. Though they had met only three times, and had never consummated their relationship, Victor could not imagine being more tightly bound to anyone.

Even so, he knew that Theodore Kurita would never allow Omi to marry him. Theordore already had his hands full with the many nobles in the Draconis Combine who viewed his various reforms as serious breaks with tradition. For Theodore to make peace with the Federated Commonwealth by marrying his daughter off to Victor could easily trigger a civil war. Traditionalists would battle reformers in a bloody conflict that would cripple the Combine's ability to fight the Clans when the truce expired.

If Victor had believed he had any chance of successfully winning Omi's hand, he'd have gone to Theodore Kurita long ago. Perhaps it was just as well that their union was impossible, for it would be equally troublesome to him here at home. Until recently Victor might have expected the most potent threat to his realm to come from the lord of the Draconis March. The people of those border worlds would have feared being awarded to the Combine as some sort of bride price. Victor was sure he could deal with them easily enough, but the new threat made theirs seem insignificant.

Both halves of the Federated Commonwealth had long suffered from Combine predation. A thumb of F-C worlds thrust up into the Combine above the Terran corridor, many of them seized only thirty years before in the Fourth Succession War. Because of the Clan threat, large numbers of troops on either side of the Combine/Commonwealth border had been rushed to the Clan front, leaving the border world peoples nervous and defenseless.

More important, those worlds had more in common with the Isle of Skye than with any other part of the Federated Commonwealth. Now that Katherine was exerting her influence in Skye, she also controlled those worlds. Should she have viewed Victor's marriage to Omi as a threat, or chose to use the threat as a way to alienate the people from him, she could split the Federated Commonwealth in half without firing a shot.

Victor didn't think for a second that was what Katherine wanted. By conspiring with Ryan Steiner to murder their mother, Katherine had removed the next to last obstacle between her and becoming Archon Princess of the Federated Commonwealth. She was in a strong position because she had the Lyran half of the Commonwealth as a power base, but the threat of the Clans meant she would always be dependent on the other half of the Commonwealth for firepower and defense.

With ten more years left in the truce, Victor had that much time to find hard evidence proving that Katrina had killed their mother *or* to somehow rebuild the confidence of the Lyran people. No matter how difficult the latter, he imagined it would be the easier to accomplish, but he could not abandon hope that his sister had made some crucial mistake in covering up her connection to Ryan and the assassination.

A gentle knock prefaced Galen's entrance and gave Victor time to turn off the holovid viewer. Looking up from his desk, he set the remote down and smiled at Galen. "Well, Mr. Cranston, what have you got for me?"

The bearded man returned the smile. "The scandal-vid pieces about Joshua and his double have been very popular. The girl, Missy Cooper, has been given a modeling contract to tout clothes that look like designer fashions, but cost considerably less. The fact that she has a cousin who is also suffering from leukemia has made the whole saga even more poignant. Because the cousin has now been flown to Avalon City for treatment at the NAIS—both the trip and treatment at your personal expense—the polls show your approval rating rising nicely. Surveys indicate the people see you as more compassionate than they did six months ago. This is significant because of the reputation for cold-heartedness you picked up for missing your mother's funeral two years ago."

Victor nodded. "At the time I thought Katherine had decided to proceed quickly with the funeral because the way my mother died made it difficult to have her lie in state. Now I wonder if Katherine scheduled the services so speedily to embarrass me."

"I don't know, but I wouldn't be surprised by malice anytime your sister is concerned."

"So, have we begun distribution of the scandal-vid material to the Lyran districts?"

"Yes, Highness. We will saturate them over the next two weeks with packages including enough material for each local media conglomerate to edit together its own presentation. The exception is the Isle of Skye. They'll get the more precise and compact version that will also be released to the Free Worlds League, the Capellan Confederation, and the Draconis Combine."

"Good." Victor opened a desk drawer and pulled out a holovid disk. "I recorded this message of condolence for Thomas Marik. Please see that it gets to him at the highest ComStar priority."

Galen nodded. "Consider it done."

Victor thought for a moment. "What do you think are the chances of Thomas Marik discovering our little deception? Now that his wife has died, he could ask for the return of Joshua to Atreus, and our whole plan might unravel."

"We've had no such requests yet and Sophina died a week ago. The funeral is scheduled for two weeks from now, which is not enough time to get Joshua there. I don't think it's something we need be concerned about." Galen shook his head. "I also don't think we need to worry about the League running any intelligence operation here. We're fairly certain SAFE has sleeper agents on New Avalon, but they don't have the resources to snatch Joshua and prove he isn't genuine. Our security at the NAIS is pretty tight and we've also got a ready-response team in place to stop any violence against the boy. Always have had one there just in case Sun-Tzu decides it would be better if Isis inherited her father's power."

Victor raised an eyebrow. "Aren't you selling SAFE a bit short?"

"Perhaps so," Galen said, "but not as much as some other folks in the Intelligence Secretariat. SAFE has reported, and Thomas believes, that the Clans used nuclear weapons when the Smoke Jaguars destroyed the city of Edo on Turtle Bay in thirty fifty. They even seem to believe the planet is now a lifeless hulk. If they're that far off on events commonly acknowledged to be otherwise—I'm afraid they don't generate much concern among our people."

"It's hard to believe they're quite that backward, but that doesn't mean they can't get lucky. Make sure the hospital staff is given a security refresher, and don't let the people of the Secretariat get too complacent."

"Yes, sir," Galen shook his head. "I think part of the problem is that Thomas, being such an idealist, believes spying is beneath him. As nearly as our people can determine, SAFE's budget hasn't grown much, especially since the formation of the Knights of the Inner Sphere. Our counter-intelligence people have been asking for transfers to the Capellan Confederation desk so they can see some action."

Victor sighed heavily. "Well, see if you can stir them up a bit. We're using a double to buy us some time. Like most of my father's other plans, it's solid. We have to make it work to our best advantage. Let's do what we must to be sure we get all the time we paid for."

"It shall be done."

"Good." Victor picked up the remote control. "Thanks for all you're doing, Ga—Jerry. Learning to be a leader is difficult enough. Without your help, it would probably be impossible."

"Impossible just takes a little longer, sir."

Victor Davion's face and expression were suddenly somber. "A little longer may be far more than we've got."

9

An ally has to be watched just like an enemy.

—LEON TROTSKY

Tharkad City, Tharkad
District of Donegal, Federated Commonwealth
26 June 3057

Katrina Steiner-Davion kept her eyes focused at the far end
of the vast throne room as the doors slowly opened. The
man and woman who appeared looked tiny against the im-
mensity of the room's high vaults and the sheer massiveness
of the stone columns. As they marched toward her, she noticed how first one and then the other tried to gain a step in
walking down the thin red ribbon of carpet. Such antics
might have drawn a smile, but Katrina was determined that
the two ambassadors understand the solemnity of the occa-
sion.

As their pace slowed, she knew they had begun to analyze
the clues to her mood and disposition that she had so carefully put in place. Her clothes were a conservatively cut
black suit over a high-necked blouse of white silk. The skirt
fell to mid-calf, but her knee-high boots hid any glimpse of
leg. A simple string of pearls and matching earrings were the
only jewelry, and her make-up was equally subdued.

Three thrones were set regally on the stepped dais toward
which the ambassadors marched, and Katrina had taken a
seat on the one to the right, as viewed from the entrance.
Above it hung the armored-fist banner of the old Lyran
Commonwealth. Because she was regent over the Lyran districts of the Federated Commonwealth, this was an appropriate choice, but she knew her two visitors would be quick to

mark the fact that now she had her grandmother's throne in addition to her name.

Even more significant would be the sight of two envelopes sitting on the cushion of the centermost throne. That was her brother's place as Archon Prince of the whole Federated Commonwealth, yet her visitors would see that she was using his throne as a side table. Katrina knew that would surprise them, which was exactly what she intended.

Behind the thrones, dwarfing her as easily as the architecture dwarfed the ambassadors, two BattleMechs stood as sentinels. Behind her throne was a *Crusader* painted in the red and black colors of the Kell Hounds, but black garlands were wrapped around its wrists. The visitors would know that the *Crusader* had belonged to Galen Cox, a connection that would explain why she was dressed in somber mourning clothes.

The other BattleMech, the one standing behind the distant Federated Suns throne, no longer sported the black and gold color scheme of the First Kathil Uhlans. The bird-legged *Marauder* had been painted the light powder blue long known as Steiner blue. Before the integration of the Lyran Commonwealth with the Federated Suns, Steiner blue had been the color of Lyran military dress uniforms. Katrina had no doubt that the choice of paint color would also be well remarked upon back on Atreus.

The ambassadors stopped at the foot of the dias, and each one bowed to Katrina. She returned the bow with her head while remaining seated, then opened her mouth as if to speak. As the ambassadors leaned forward to hear, Katrina closed her mouth, looked away for a second and made a show of being unable to talk as she struggled with tearful emotions.

Confident she had their full attention, she looked back at them. "Forgive me. There has been much turmoil and death of late."

Clark Tsu-Chan, the stocky, balding ambassador from the Capellan Confederation, nodded slowly. The smaller, flaxen-haired representative from Atreus, Luise Waskiewicz, tugged at the black armband on her left arm. "Highness, we of the Free Worlds League now understand even more deeply the tragic loss of your mother. Perhaps we must recall what Jerome Blake noted so long ago: 'Death shall have no dominion, and love shall not be lost'."

"Your words bring me comfort, Ambassador Waskiewicz." *Even if they are a butchered plagiarism of Dylan Thomas' poem,* And death shall have no dominion. *I wonder how many other pearls of wisdom from antiquity have been attributed to poor Jerome Blake in the effort to deify him?* Katrina glanced down to make it difficult for the other two to read her true emotions. No matter how good her control, one could never be too careful.

Looking up again, she let a single tear roll down her cheek. "My mother's loss has deeply affected me, as have the deaths of my friend, Galen Cox, and my cousin, Ryan Steiner. Much responsibility has been thrust upon me. Were it not for the need to care for my people, I fear I would have been paralyzed by grief."

The Capellan representative kept his voice low. "Mourning is healing and, as such, is a process that requires time."

"And a process that does not need other concerns pressing in upon it." Katrina brought her head up, then set her shoulders. "But, now, to the matter at hand. Perhaps you wonder why I have requested a joint meeting with you. To forestall any misunderstanding, let me say now that I thought it would eliminate any suspicions about my motives or what had been said."

"You are most considerate, Highness."

"As was your Captain-General, Ambassador, in the condolences he sent me upon the death of my mother and again on Galen's death. You are fortunate to have a leader who is compassionate and wise."

"You are too kind, Highness."

It would be good for you to continue thinking that. Katrina permitted herself a faint smile. "As your intelligence agencies have doubtless begun to report, the news from New Avalon last month contained a bit of confusion concerning a sighting of Joshua Marik outside the NAIS hospital where he is undergoing treatment for his leukemia. It turned out to be nothing but a case of mistaken identity—a young woman was mistaken for Joshua. Here and now, I give you my solemn word that Joshua is safe and continuing his treatments at the NAIS, and I refute any dire or baseless rumors that might intrude upon the Captain-General during his time of grief."

Waskiewicz's face had paled a bit as Katrina spoke, but her color returned by the end of the little speech. "I will convey this message to Atreus."

"I would have you do more." Katrina stood slowly, then

stepped over to pluck the twin envelopes from the Federated Commonwealth throne. "These envelopes contain holovid disks of the original programs concerning the incident, as well as many of the raw images that were used to put them together. My brother is sending you only finished programs, which means you would have to exert great efforts and resources to obtain the preproduction materials I am giving you. Though I realize this may cause a bit of a recession for those of my subjects who pass information to you, I trust you will employ them in verifying that what I have given you is genuine."

Tsu-chan blinked his eyes as he accepted one of the envelopes. "I do not think I have ever heard bribery and treason described so circumspectly."

"Nor will you again, Ambassador, for our nations have secrets that we dearly wish to keep one from another. However, Joshua is not and should not be made a point of contention between our nations. He is but a child and far too important to be a pawn in the games nations play." Katrina stood beside her throne with one hand resting on the high back.

"Joshua is on New Avalon for treatment of his cancer, but I have always hated the impression that he is a hostage."

The Free Worlds League ambassador shook her head. "My people have never held any illusions about Joshua's status in the Federated Commonwealth."

That could be taken two ways, in fine diplomatic style. Katrina let a hint of a smile twist her lips. "Then your people are far more generous than are mine, or, at least, more generous than some members of my family."

That comment struck home with both ambassadors, and neither fully hid a shocked reaction.

Good, then my task here is done. "Please, Excellencies, return to your embassies and dispatch this material without delay. If we can uproot suspicions before they grow, we need not fear any distrust growing in their wake."

Charleston, Woodstock
Sarna March, Federated Commonwealth

Larry Acuff held his hands up toward Phoebe Derden. "There's no way I can win this discussion, is there?"

Clasping her hands behind her head, the blond commander of the Woodstock Militia leaned back and laughed. "You can deny being miffed at all this news about Joshua bumping your presence here on Woodstock from the local newsvids all you want, but I'm not going to believe it."

Larry's brown eyes narrowed. "And why not?"

Phoebe shook her head. "You're a vid-hound, Larry. Last week, when you, George, and I went over to the Neon Club, you used your celebrity to get us in."

"I think you were the one who said she didn't want to wait in line."

"Guilty, but I wasn't the one who spoke to the doorman and got us waved in ahead of everyone else." Phoebe sat forward, a wolfish grin on her face. "That wasn't what keyed me, though. The fact was that when we came into the room, you paused in the doorway so everyone could see you make a grand entrance."

"I was just letting my eyes adjust to the dark."

"Sure, and it wasn't dark outside or in the corridor leading to the bar?"

Larry hung his head. "All right, you win. I wasn't letting my eyes adjust to the light." As Phoebe's laughter began to echo through her office, Larry brought a hand up and pointed at her. "But it wasn't to make an entrance either. It was different."

"How so?"

"I'm not sure you'd understand."

Phoebe frowned at him. "I may not have my face and my 'Mech plastered all over T-shirts distributed throughout the Federated Commonwealth, but I didn't get these Kommandant's bars by being dense. Try me."

Larry leaned forward with his elbows on his knees, knowing how boastful all this was going to sound. "I was trying to figure out if I was going to be ambushed or not. On Solaris there are places where MechWarriors—professional fighters like me—can go and not be in the public eye."

Phoebe arched an eyebrow at him. "Is this going to be some sort of 'it's tough to be a celebrity' speech?"

"That may sound funny to you, Phoebe, but it isn't easy. Sure, it's fun, and brings a lot of advantages—like being able to get yourself and friends into a club without a wait of an hour or two. But you also get a lot of trouble."

"Like the twins who wanted to have a tug of war with your earlobes that night?"

Larry blushed. "No, like guys deciding you don't look so tough and wanting to take a poke at you. And worse." He frowned. "When you're a public figure, everyone who's ever put a bet down on you or bought a ticket for one of your fights or has bought a product you endorse thinks he owns a piece of you. People complain about how much we make and how little we work. They don't think it's right that teachers and nurses make so little when their contribution to society is so great by comparison to ours."

His head came up and he noted that the mirth in Phoebe's gray eyes was muted. "Do you know what the average career for a fighter is on Solaris?"

She shook her head.

"Three *months*! Not *years,* months! And it's not because warriors get killed in the 'Mech duels, it's because the training and the stress are nothing short of bonecrushing. It's worse than I ever experienced when fighting with the Tenth Lyran Guards."

Phoebe glanced down at her blotter. "Worse than the camp on Alyina?"

Larry shook his head, unable to speak for a second. "Alyina puts it all in perspective, which is why I've been able to go on so long. That and the fact that Kai shields his fighters from a lot of pressure. My fights are broadcast and are viewed by billions and billions of people. They see the profiles and little news stories about what I'm doing, and they think they know me. And they do, a little, but they really only know the face I'm showing the public."

Larry laughed for a second. "At the Neon, a guy who had recognized me followed me on the way to the bathroom. Then he started talking to me as I was standing there. He wanted me to go back to his table with him, to 'ditch the losers' I was with and talk to him and his buddies. He said he had the Crucis-R hovercar franchise here in Charleston and would cut me a deal on one if I'd do a holovert for him."

Phoebe's expression darkened. "Was his name Buddy Korren?"

"Sounds right. Know him?"

"He's on the Charleston Municipal Militia Liaison board. He wanted to make an ad showing some of our 'Mechs tearing apart hovercars made by his competitors. When I explained that we couldn't do that, he offered me a bribe. A real winner, that one."

"Well, then, you know the sort of slime I run into. I mean, there are plenty of great people out there who want to shake my hand or ask for an autograph, and that's fine—especially when it's youngsters. But I have to admit that a little ice rolls through my guts when I hear a voice say, 'Hey, you, buddy, you're Larry Acuff, aren't you?' I immediately start to wonder what they want and then start looking for a way out of there.

"And, in answer to what started all this, I don't mind being out of the public eye. Until this thing with Joshua broke, we had holovideographers camped out on my parents' front lawn. Now that it's dying down, I'm afraid they'll be back. Drives my mother crazy because they tromp all over her flower beds."

Phoebe's smile brightened and Larry feared another comic jab at him. "Maybe I can help you with that."

"How so?"

She gestured to the computer console on her desk. "Bachelor Officers Quarters has a suite open. I can put you in there."

"Thanks, but you can't do that with civilians without getting into trouble, right? You were always by the book, Phoebe. George can't have changed you that much."

"He hasn't." She tapped the screen. "According to the books, Reserve Hauptmann Acuff, you've not reported for your duty assignments over the last three years. That means you've got six weeks of reserve duty coming. I can shift you over to the Militia here and put you on public relations duty. That'll square your commitment *and* give you a place to stay where the vid-leeches can't get at you."

Larry hesitated for a second, then nodded. "Thanks. You've got a deal."

"Good."

"I appreciate how you're taking care of me here. Not just this, but introducing me to all your friends. I wasn't sure I was going to fit in back here, and there are still some rough spots, but you've helped make them smoother."

"I owe you, Larry."

He frowned. "You would have met my cousin anyway. In fact, I don't remember introducing you."

"You didn't, and that's not why I owe you." Phoebe bit at her lower lip. "You got left behind on Alyina and I've always thought that was my fault."

"Hey, Phoebe, no, don't go thinking that at all. My *Warhammer* had lost a leg *and* an arm. You and the others got called back to regroup and hold the landing zone so the DropShips could come in and get Prince Victor out. I knew what you were doing, and I was there with you in spirit. You'd have come back if you could have."

"I would have, but you didn't deserve the camp and all that."

"No one deserved the camp, but it didn't kill me."

"So it made you stronger?"

Larry thought for a second, then nodded. "Stronger and wiser. It made me realize that life's a lot more basic than most folks think it is, and that's been worth a great deal to me."

"Makes it easier to tolerate guys like Buddy?"

"No, nothing could do that." He smiled at Phoebe and was happy to see the smile return to her face. "What it did teach me is that nothing is more important than friends. Thanks for confirming the lesson."

10

Do not repeat the tactics that have gained you one victory, but let your methods be regulated by the infinite variety of circumstances.

—SUN TZU, THE ART OF WAR

Marik Palace, Atreus
Marik Commonwealth, Free Worlds League
1 July 3057

From the disgust boiling up in his belly, Sun-Tzu Liao knew instantly he was locked inside a dream. He seldom remembered his dreams and even less frequently found himself walking through one. His disdain for dreams came almost entirely from how his mother and now his sister found such great and mystical relevance in the images parading through their brains while they slept. Neither woman had ever shown much grasp of reality, and their penchant for interpreting reality through dreams guaranteed that they would never truly function in the same universe as the rest of the Inner Sphere.

Sun-Tzu knew, from reading and research, that dreams occurred during sleep to allow the brain to integrate recently learned facts into the sleeper's memory matrix. The few dreams he did recall seemed to provide sufficient evidence to believe that was all the brain was doing. With that as his foundation, Sun-Tzu looked at the symbolism of his dream and tried to decipher what was being integrated and where it would reside.

He found himself in a long hallway—very long as it stretched off into infinity—fashioned from plates of hand-beaten gold. Though no light source was visible, highlights glinted from every surface. Creatures from mythology, scientific symbols, and other icons of life in the Inner Sphere had been carved into or out of the panels. Though fascinating, and annoyingly difficult to identify if he looked directly at them, he knew they were insignificant to his quest for information.

Hanging along the left-hand walls was a series of portraits. Most were dark and old, with cracks forming in the paint as if there were ancient renderings by Terran masters from long before humanity had discovered the secrets of interstellar travel. He even recognized some of the styles: Van Gogh, Rembrandt, Whelan, Parkinson, and Matisse, yet he knew none of those artists had created the portraits. He knew this because all of the portraits were of individuals who had lived long after those masters had died.

Sun-Tzu slowly started down the corridor and saw that his grandfather, Maximilian Liao, was the first subject. Sharp-eyed and sharper-faced, Maximilian looked vital and full of defiant fire. Certainly that was the man his mother had always described, but not the one Sun-Tzu remembered. Of course, he had been only a child when he knew his grandfather, and by then his grandfather had been broken by Hanse Davion and Justin Allard.

Glancing to his right Sun-Tzu saw that a tall silver mirror had been added to the previously bare wall across from the portrait. Looking up he noticed that all the portraits faced mirrors, further intensifying his desire to fathom the mystery. He did not see himself in the mirror, but instead saw a bent old man, his unkempt hair falling in greasy hanks onto the soiled shoulders of a threadbare robe. The old man's eyes burned with madness. Yes, Sun-Tzu thought, *that* was the Maximilian Liao he had known.

He pushed on and next saw Van Gogh's portrait of Thomas Marik. Bold strokes and bright yellow paint traced every scar on Thomas' face. His eyes seemed dull, and exhaustion oozed from the gaunt face. Sun-Tzu thought it also an accurate image of Thomas since Sophina's suicide.

Looking toward the mirror to see what transformation it would work on Thomas, he was surprised at the strong image reflected back. Here was Thomas clad in a silvery suit of armor, a shining sword raised high. A halo of stars surrounded his head, and the scars on his face had became faint. His expression showed the same one worn by the fanatical Word of Blake adherents whenever addressing Thomas at court. And that let Sun-Tzu see how most people in the Free Worlds League viewed Thomas: a reformer who had created the Knights of the Inner Sphere to restore noble ideals to modern life.

Already a theory had begun to form in Sun-Tzu's mind concerning what he was experiencing, so he rushed forward to gather more data. In the next portrait he found himself rendered as a foppish harlequin, with his mouth hanging open in a lopsided, dimwitted grin. His body was twisted just enough for him to show a big yellow stripe running down his spine.

Ah, me as I wish others to see me. On Outreach, when all the young royals had gathered together to train while their parents discussed strategies, Sun-Tzu had purposefully whined and squirmed, shirked duty and run when confronted. He knew well that every one of his peers thought his mother insane, so he played the spoiled, petty fop they expected of him.

Spinning, he saw himself reflected and was surprised to note how much the mirror's image looked like his cousin, Kai Allard-Liao. *This is a caution.* He had noticed enough about his cousin to suspect that Kai played his cards close to his chest and did not expose his full potential. At least that was the conclusion he drew from the fact that his brain was presenting his own image close to where it kept Kai's image stored. *Perhaps I am underestimating Kai.*

Sun-Tzu forced himself to travel yet further down the corridor. Hanse Davion's portrait confronted him next, sending a thrill down his spine. Hanse Davion, displayed in all his tall, robust, and ruddy glory, had well earned his nickname of 'the Fox.' First he had managed to trick Maximilian Liao into clutching to his bosom the asp named Justin Allard, then he'd launched the assault that gobbled up half the worlds in the Capellan Confederation, creating the Sarna March for the newly formed Federated Commonwealth.

To his right the mirror showed him a gauze-swathed mummy. Sun-Tzu peered more closely at it, then an eye opened and he recognized it as the same piercing shade of blue as Davion's eyes. The body seemed trimmer and younger than the Hanse displayed in the portrait, and while Sun-Tzu was puzzling over that, a doorway into his past opened.

He remembered being awakened one night when very young. He didn't see his grandfather at first, just smelled his breath and felt his clawlike nails through the cloth of his sleeping shirt. The little nightlight's feeble luminosity glinted from Maximilian's eyes, making them glow like a cat's.

"Don't worry, don't worry." Urgency filled the voice, but the words were spoken in a harsh whisper. "He is *my* Hanse Davion. This is all a ruse. It is really ours."

Sun-Tzu's door opened and men came to drag his grandfather away, then his father came and comforted him. He told Sun-Tzu not to worry, that his grandfather was confused. He said that Maximilian's doppelganger of Hanse Davion had been discovered, and that had been the reason for the war. "This has just been a bad dream, son. Think no more of it, and never mention it to your mother."

Before his eyes the mummy fell to dust, then more than half of it blew away, just as half the Capellan Confederation had been blown away. Trembling, Sun-Tzu looked away from the mirror and pressed on, even though each step felt as if he were trying to move forward through invisible concrete.

After what seemed to be an eternity during which a palsy shook his limbs, Sun-Tzu came to a portrait of Joshua Marik. Seeing it gave him the solution to his dream: his mind was filing away all of the images he had seen when reviewing the material Katrina Steiner had sent. Sun-Tzu had watched it intently, hoping against hope that something would indicate that Joshua was dying, but he got nothing of the sort. In the portrait the boy looked as he had in the holovids—sickly, but far too healthy for Sun-Tzu's taste.

He turned toward the mirror and saw nothing. His own body shook, then he sat bolt-upright in bed and peeled the sheets from his sweat-slicked chest. Pushing himself up to sitting, he rested against the headboard and licked sweat from his upper lip. *What did it mean?*

For a half-second he started to hear his sister's voice as it began a rambling, nonsensical explanation of a dream, but Sun-Tzu silenced the mental noise, forcing his brain to think clearly. *My mind was correlating data and found no match for what I saw of Joshua. This is not surprising, given he was much younger when I saw him on Outreach. Children change a lot in six years. No correspondence exist, hence no mirror image.*

He nodded and smiled. That was a logical answer. Had this been his sister's dream, she would have come to him burbling on about how Victor Davion had slain Joshua and substituted his own agent in the Marik heir's place. He would have been forced to explain to her that Victor would never do any such thing—he simply wasn't devious enough. Kali wouldn't grasp any of his explanation and would continue to believe her dream and its hidden message.

As sleep drained out of him, his mind passed into a new level of clarity. *Indeed, Victor would never make a duplicate for Joshua. To do so, and to employ the double would be stirring up the pot too much.* Sun-Tzu smiled as inspiration struck. *But just because Victor would never do that, there is no reason I cannot accuse him of it. Victor, with his inflated sense of honor, would be furious.*

Second by second a plan built itself up in Sun-Tzu's mind. He decided that he did not want to make any accusations directly. Drawing Victor's anger could be suicidal for his nation. Instead, if he could fashion a plan to make Thomas believe that Victor had slain his son and substituted another, then Thomas might give Sun-Tzu free reign to step up activities in the Sarna March. If Thomas were outraged enough, he would demand concessions from Victor—possibly even the return of worlds taken from the Capellan Confederation.

Sun-Tzu threw back his bedclothes and padded across the floor to his desk. His body wanted to return to bed, but his mind was too busy and full to let him sleep. Switching on his computer terminal, he began to draft a plan and prepare the messages that would start it running.

"Poor Victor," he laughed softly to himself, "I have a dream and it becomes your nightmare."

O! what a fall was there, my countrymen;
Then I, and you, and all of us fell down,
Whilst bloody treason flourish'd over us.

          —WILLIAM SHAKESPEARE, *JULIUS CAESAR*

Arc-Royal
District of Donegal, Federated Commonwealth
4 July 3057

"I don't know what I'm trying to say, Chris." Caitlin Kell tucked a lock of black hair behind her left ear. "A lot got said on Tharkad, things I can't reveal because they were told to me in confidence. Still, it got me thinking. I tend to process information while I try to explain it to someone else, so I guess that's what I'm doing now."

Christian Kell smiled at his cousin. "So, are Dan and I sounding boards, or do you want reactions to your ideas?"

Caitlin nodded to both Chris and the white-haired man also sitting on the couch with her cousin. "I don't think I can expect you not to comment."

Daniel Allard, leader of the Kell Hounds since Morgan Kell's retirement, gave her a sympathetic smile. "Especially when you start by asking if there's been a coverup of the identity of Archon Melissa Steiner's assassin. You obviously have questions about the official story, or you wouldn't have brought it up."

Chris nodded. "*I* have questions about the official story. I'm not buying the idea that a lone lunatic could have fashioned the sort of bomb used to kill the Archon and your mother, Caitlin. I've heard our special ops guys talking about what kind of training someone would need to pull it off. Aside from the fact that we'd like to string up whoever did it, the skill involved was impressive.

"I'd agree that it was a little too convenient that the assassin committed suicide shortly thereafter, and the lack of a body is less than satisfying. But I think the recent murder of Ryan Steiner shows that assassins do kill themselves after acting."

Caitlin's green eyes shrank to hard slivers. "Coincidental, isn't it, that two assassinations requiring incredible skill end in suicide?"

Chris frowned. "You think the kid who shot Ryan because he thought he was Ryan's bastard child also killed Melissa? Did he think she was his mother?"

"No, that's not it. Look, Ryan was Victor's mortal enemy, and he died at a very fortuitous time for Victor. His death took all the pressure off in the Skye situation." Caitlin opened her hands. "Cross Victor and you pay."

"That's drawing a lot of conclusion from one instance, Caitlin," Dan Allard said, shaking his head. "And the implication is that Victor killed Melissa, which I don't buy."

"Dan, no disrespect intended, but is that something you *think* or something you *feel*?" Caitlin walked from her small living room and ducked into the kitchen for a glass of water. "Your family has worked closely with the Davions."

"Meaning?"

"You have a vested interest in seeing someone other than Victor be the killer."

Dan nodded. "Ah, and the fact that you're related to the Steiner household means that you don't want Ryan suspected as Melissa's killer?"

Ouch. Caitlin frowned and picked up her glass for a sip of water. "We're related to Victor and Katrina through their grandfather, so we're not kin to Ryan Steiner. I just don't trust the official verdict in Melissa's murder, and I think the story of Ryan's death stinks just as much of fraud and cover-up."

"Okay, Caitlin, just so we understand each other. I met Melissa Steiner long before your father and mother got together to bring you into the world and I considered her a dear friend as well as a wonderful woman. I'd like to get my hands around the throat of the fiend who killed her *and* whoever hired him to do it. And I'll agree that the official report on her death is not the most solid of cases, but projecting a conspiracy when there is no evidence is a very dangerous game."

Was that the sound of your mind closing, Dan? Caitlin looked up over the rim of her plastic cup at Christian Kell. "You're quiet all of a sudden."

Chris shifted his shoulders slightly in lieu of a verbal reply. Through his shirt's open collar, Caitlin caught a glimpse of the blue and green dragon tattooed on the left side of his chest. *He has become so much a member of the Kell Hounds that sometimes I forget he was raised in the Combine and once belonged to a yakuza gang.* His upbringing would provide him a unique perspective, yet the societal value given silence in the Combine would make him reluctant to share it.

Caitlin's unwavering stare made him squirm, as she knew it would, but she did not relent. "I really do want to know what you think, Chris."

He ran a hand back through his dark hair, then nodded. "I think you're making some mistakes in your analysis. The first is one of which you may not be aware, and that is lumping Ryan Steiner into the same category as Melissa Steiner."

"I would never . . ."

"Ah, but you did. You see them both as victims of the same assassin, but you have no proof. And even if the same person did kill them, it doesn't mean the assassin was employed by the same person. In fact, if Ryan had retained the assassin to kill Melissa, the assassin might have killed Ryan to cover his own tracks. Ryan might even have tried to get rid of the assassin to cover himself, but got a bullet in return for his trouble instead."

Perched on the arm of the couch, Chris' dark eyes focused distantly. "I'd also point out that you're being very selective in the evidence you're using to build your case against Victor."

Caitlin started. She wanted to say he was wrong, but she knew he was on target. "For example?"

"For example, there are currently three stories concerning Ryan's death. The first is the one advanced by Federated Commonwealth authorities that says a lone gunman shot Ryan over an imagined grievance. They have forensic evidence to back that up and they seem satisfied with the conclusion. The second story is yours, that the suicide was a set up and someone else, a phantom, pulled the trigger, then killed the kid to cover his trail. And the third is that Sven Newmark, Ryan's aide, shot him at close range with a handgun that he was able to discard before authorities arrived."

Caitlin shook her head. "The Newmark story is nonsense. Only conspiracy nuts buy that story."

"But they believe it because it makes sense to them. His motive, if you will recall, is supposed to have been revenge for the attempted kidnapping of Prince Ragnar by Ryan's people from Arc-Royal *and* retaliation for your mother's death and your father's maiming in the attack that killed Melissa. After all, Newmark was a Rasalhague expatriate, and we have a sizable Rasalhagian community here because your grandfather and father made it easy for them to emigrate. Others go further and suggest Newmark was in your father's employ."

"But that's preposterous."

"Why?"

"Because my father wouldn't do that sort of thing."

Chris smiled. "So, you reject that theory based on specialized knowledge of parties involved."

"Yes."

"Then if we return to Melissa's murder and we look at specialized knowledge of your suspect, Victor, I shall plead specialized knowledge." Chris looked up at her. "I trained Victor. He would not order a murder."

"You're wrong, Chris."

Dan eased forward to the edge of the couch. "What are you saying, Cait?"

She took a deep breath, but found it did not lessen the pressure building in her chest. "I know I can trust you. Katrina told me that Victor admitted to her that he gave the order for an assassin to kill Ryan."

Chris slumped back, stunned. "I don't believe it."

Dan nodded. "I do."

Caitlin looked wide-eyed at the older man. "You do?"

"Yes." A weariness entered Dan's voice. "Victor is enough Hanse's son to use such direct methods to eliminate Ryan. He wouldn't have done it because Ryan was a political enemy, though. It must have been because he'd linked Ryan to his mother's death or some other heinous plot."

Caitlin set her glass down on the table. "Do you know that, or are you conjecturing?"

"Conjecturing, but I know I'm right."

Chris still shook his head. "That could be the only explanation, but I still don't believe it. And I don't believe he killed his mother."

"Why not? Just like Ryan, she stood in his path to power. He killed Melissa to take power, and killed Ryan to keep it. On top of that, it's *his* people who conduct the investigations into the deaths and then pronounce Victor innocent."

Dan massaged his temples. "I don't like it."

"I don't like it, either." Chris stood. "And I don't believe it. I don't doubt that you're telling me exactly what Katrina—or Katherine—told you, Cait, but that bit about the assassin is hearsay."

Caitlin frowned. "Katrina wouldn't repeat it if it weren't true."

"No? Victor is all that stands between her and the Federated Commonwealth's throne, if you'll recall."

"She doesn't want the throne. She's having a hard enough time picking up after Victor."

"Specialized knowledge, Cait?"

"Specialized knowledge, Chris."

Dan stood and went between them. "I think, as special knowledge cases go, one or the other of you is wrong."

"Worse yet," Chris whispered, "we could *both* be wrong."

Caitlin felt her stomach tighten down into a knot. *If that's true, then I've been way off in reading Katrina.* That thought made the knot even tighter. "I'm sorry, Chris. I don't want to fight with you about this. It's just that I'm worried that the next time the Federated Commonwealth offers us a contract, we might be used for political reasons, not to defend the nation."

Chris smiled gently. "It's a disturbing subject, Caitlin, and I don't wish to fight with you about it either."

"Good," said Daniel Allard, "because your disagreement is not the most disturbing thing about this."

Caitlin turned to Dan, her brow wrinkling in puzzlement. "What is?"

"That people out there are able to manufacture evidence and rumors that have intelligent, sensible people in a quandary about the Federated Commonwealth's leadership. Face it, we know everyone involved on a personal level." Dan's expression turned grim. "If *we're* this confused, imagine how the ordinary people feel. Without much more effort, things could get very bad, and I don't like the future that paints for me at all."

Tamar
Wolf Clan Occupation Zone

Standing impatiently between Natasha and Ulric on the left side of the auditorium stage, Phelan folded his arms as Loremaster Dalk Carns stepped through the curtains downstage. The Loremaster bowed his head to the ilKhan and his party, then accorded the same respect to the others standing opposite them. Finally he acknowledged the Clan Council members seated beyond the footlights.

"He plays at this as if he expects a review in the morning newsfax."

Natasha cracked a smile at Phelan's whispered remark. "I considered printing up programs, but the list of people under the 'village idiots' section became unwieldy."

Her comment trailed off to silence as Dalk strode to the podium in the center of the stage. While both the Khans and their accusers had chosen to wear gray woolen uniforms, Dalk had again donned the Clan Wolf ceremonial leathers. He set his enameled wolf's-head helmet on the podium and stared out at the audience from between the two ears.

"Trothkin, I am the Loremaster. I call thee, one and all, to stand as jury and judge in the matter here come before us." Dalk kept his voice low and full of import. "By this conclave all will be bound until they are but dust and memories, and then beyond that until the end of all that is."

"Seyla," Phelan breathed in a kind of chant with all the other Wolves gathered here today. He'd uttered the sacred oath automatically, almost without having to think, as though it were the most natural thing in the world. Though raised in the Inner Sphere, he had given himself over to his adopted people fully, accepting without question their system of justice and honor. All things being equal, he would normally have been confident of the defeat of this attempt embarrass and discredit the ilKhan.

If doubt assailed him, it was because he knew all things were *not* equal. He knew the case against Ulric was without merit, but that did not mean a jury couldn't be swayed by politics. The ilKhan was showing no concern about the charges and this also gave Phelan pause. He had seen him navigate through more dangerous political situations than this without incident, but Ulric's fierce determination was what had always won the day.

Ulric's nonchalance could be taken as contempt, which would doom him.

Phelan glared across the stage at the two people who would serve as the prosecution. The woman was small for a MechWarrior, but was nonetheless attractive in spite of her slight height. Honey-blond hair, thickly curled, framed her face and fell forward over her shoulders. When she looked up Phelan saw a white webwork of scars on her throat—the result of wounds taken in the fighting on Tukayyid. Her amber eyes and sharp, vulpine features always reminded Phelan of a wild animal, and her reckless bravery in combat had earned Marialle Radick the nickname of "Death's Vixen."

Standing next to her, Vladimir caught Phelan's gaze and held it unflinchingly. With his black hair slicked back to emphasize a widow's peak, Vlad might have been handsome but for the jagged scar running from eyebrow to jaw on the left side of his face. Pure hatred burned in his brown eyes, and Phelan knew Vlad would have preferred to die of the injuries that had scarred him than live knowing that Phelan, the *freeborn* from the Inner Sphere, had saved his life.

Phelan smiled at Vlad, then scratched his own left cheek. Vlad's eyes narrowed as his nostrils flared. Marialle spoke to Vlad once, then again more sharply, but even her resting a hand on his shoulder did not calm him. More insistent pressure finally did it, and Vlad reacted by looking down and shuffling the papers in his hands.

The Loremaster looked at Marialle, then smiled. "This conclave has been called to examine charges of treason brought against ilKhan Ulric Kerensky as a result of a Loremaster's Inquiry. Marialle Radick, who has standing here in the Clan Council, has agreed to act for the council in bringing these charges. The counts are . . ."

Ulric strode forward imperiously and waved the man to silence. "End your charade now, Loremaster. Embarrass yourself no further."

"What?"

"These changes are groundless. I, in my capacity as ilKhan, order you to dismiss them."

Marialle lunged forward. "You cannot do this. This is improper." Her voice sounded hoarse, but Phelan heard no nervousness in her words. "I object to your actions."

Ulric shook his head slowly. "I am certain you do, child, but we have no time for these games. Because we exist under a truce with ComStar, and have not truly ended the hostilities, we all still live under the rule of martial law. Martial law permits the ilKhan to expedite problems by challenging any charges he believes are spurious, and to order their dismissal if, after consideration, he finds them to be false. I have considered these changes, find both to be false, and here exercise my option to order their dismissal."

"You cannot."

Ulric's head came up. "Are you challenging me to a Trial of Refusal over this matter, Star Captain Radick?"

Radick's eyes widened for a moment, then she looked down. "I meant no disrespect, ilKhan."

Phelan smiled as Dalk looked taken aback. "I believe the ilKhan is correct in this procedural matter. I . . . I will adjourn the conclave for fifteen minutes to review the regulations."

"If you do that, Dalk Carns, *I* will demand a Trial of Refusal of you." Ulric smiled cruelly. "I have spoken. I am not in error concerning our laws. I am waiting."

The Loremaster nodded stiffly. "For the record, you must state your reasons for dismissing the charges."

"For the record, Loremaster, I am under no such compunction, but I shall do so, nonetheless. I will do this because these charges have slandered valuable and honored members of our Clan." The ilKhan kept his voice barely above a growl, clearly playing to the members of the Clan Council. "I will first address the charge of treason based on Phelan Ward's election as Khan. I am aware that among my peers are those who believe that no *freebirth* should have been allowed to become a Khan. They believe it is inconceivable that such could happen.

"These people are fools."

Ulric turned and pointed toward Phelan. "Phelan Ward is a freebirth. This has never been a secret. It has always been acknowledged. He was taken in combat by our forces. He was made a bondsman, as some of you were. Because of service to Clan Wolf, he was eventually adopted into our warrior caste. This is in keeping with our tradition, and many of you pledged on your honor to accept him as one of us.

"Once he became a warrior, genetic typing determined that Phelan had claim against House Ward for a Bloodname.

Cyrilla Ward nominated him as her heir. But that only permitted him a place in the Trial. He earned the Bloodname the same way he earned his rank in our military: by fighting and besting his foes. He is as qualified to stand in this Council as any of you.

"After Tukayyid, Phelan was nominated by Conal Ward to replace our dead Khan. He was elected by acclamation. That election was ratified by the Grand Council and Phelan was granted a seat in that august body."

Ulric clasped his hands at his back. "It has been charged that Khan Phelan is an agent of the Inner Sphere. That rumor has no merit. He was cast out of the Nagelring—their premier military academy—and sent out to hunt bandits. If he were a valued member of their society, they would never have assigned him so menial a task."

Phelan suppressed a smile. Among the Clans, bandit-hunting and other such activities were considered the lowest form of mission for a warrior. To be assigned to a solahma unit was a disgrace from which few recovered. In the Inner Sphere, bandit-hunting had a different reputation. Mercenaries like the Kell Hounds saw it as relatively easy duty, but felt no stigma attached to it. It might not have the glory of a major battle, but it was much safer and even a bit romantic because the chase might lead to all sorts of exotic worlds far from the core of the Inner Sphere.

Ulric continued pounding point after point into his audience. "Phelan followed accepted practices in attaining his rank. To question his *right* to that rank is to question the foundation of the Clans themselves. Nicholas Kerensky and the others from whom all Bloodnames derive were all originally natives of the Inner Sphere. All had been members of the Inner Sphere military, *ergo* they were Inner Sphere agents. They were all *freebirths*. They created the traditions that allowed for *freebirths* to be adopted as warriors, to claim Bloodnames, and to win election to the post of Khan. Since they allowed these things—*intended* such things to happen—following their wishes cannot be treason."

Eyes narrowing, Ulric paced the stage like a predator trapped by the bars of a cage. "As for the charge that I committed treason when I bid against ComStar's Precentor Martial before the battle of Tukayyid, I point out that such a charge was also leveled against me in the Grand Council shortly after that battle. I was exonerated in the Council. That charge is equally without merit."

The ilKhan spun and stared at the Loremaster. "I believe, Dalk Carns, that this conclave can be brought to an end."

Watching Marialle and Vlad, Phelan thought they looked like two people twelve days into a fortnight's artillery barrage. In presenting their case to the council, they'd obviously hoped to use the conclave as a bully pulpit to win converts to their Wolf supremist position. Ulric had ambushed them, and they didn't like it. Neither did Dalk, but Phelan thought that was less because he supported Vlad than because he didn't like losing control of the conclave.

As Dalk's head came up, Phelan realized he was wrong. Where he'd expected to see anger and embarrassment, he saw sinister confidence. Somehow, somewhere, while Ulric was ripping the supremists' case apart, Carns had found something to use against him.

"I am afraid, ilKhan, that I cannot call a close until we address the third charge in the indictment."

Natasha's eyes blazed. "Third charge?"

"You heard me, Khan Natasha. If you will, ilKhan, please explain how you could order that charge dismissed out of hand."

Ulric hesitated for a second and Dalk began to smile. *Ulric took control by surprising Dalk, and now Dalk has turned the tables on him. Ulric exploded the other charges, so he will be expected to do that with this one as well. He cannot avoid dealing with it.*

The ilKhan slowly shook his head. "There was no third charge in the indictment I was given."

"No?" Dalk's oily smile broadened. "Clerical error, then. I suppose a Trial of Refusal is in order with my clerk."

"And this charge is, Loremaster?"

"That you willfully entered into a conspiracy to destroy a Clan's genetic heritage."

Natasha gasped out loud and even Marialle and Vlad looked aghast. Phelan, having been raised outside the Clans, did not react so viscerally, but he knew why the others had. The Clans engaged in a complex program of selective breeding to create their future generations of warriors. Ova and sperm from warriors were stored by the scientist caste and held until the contributors either proved themselves or took themselves out of the breeding program because of lackluster performance.

Of the original twenty Clans created three centuries before, two had been absorbed by other Clans that had defeated them in a protracted war. The third missing Clan—Wolverine by name, though no one spoke of it willingly—had been hunted down and slain to the last in a genocidal war without compromise. The Wolverines had committed the greatest crime the Clans could imagine: they had used a nuclear device to destroy another Clan's genetic repositories.

When the Grand Council had tried them, everyone knew the charge, but the indictment had remained sealed because the people of the Clans found the crime so abominable. To even hint at repeating such an act was enough to end a career, and rumors of a Clan planning to do so would be enough to trigger war with other Clans. Dalk, in speaking those words, was accusing Ulric of being as treacherous as Judas, as evil as Hitler, and as mad as Stefan Amaris.

Ulric looked speechless, so Phelan marched over to the podium and seized Dalk's shoulder. "Explain that charge now, Loremaster, or I will challenge you to a Trial of Refusal immediately, and I guarantee the ilKhan's honor will be cleansed with your blood."

Dalk slapped his hand away and Phelan felt a trap closing around him. "It is simple, my Khan, diabolically so: Because of the truce, we will have three generations of warriors who know nothing of warfare beyond exercises and the occasional raid. When the truce ends, our command structure will be full of untested, untried, and inexperienced warriors. They will lead our young into combat and, as Ulric intends, they will die, and the way of the Clans perish with them."

═══ 12 ═══

Better a known enemy than a forced ally.

—NAPOLEON BONAPARTE, *POLITICAL APHORISMS*

Daosha, Zurich
Sarna March, Federated Commonwealth
4 July 3057

Noble Thayer pushed his empty plate away from the edge of the table and smiled at Cathy Hanney. "I'm glad you talked me into taking you to the Mandrinn's Dragon. I've never been much on Chinese cuisine, but this was good."

Cathy reached out and gave Noble's hand a squeeze. "Thank you for taking me. I like this place, but I can only really afford it a couple of times a year. I save it for special occasions."

"I hope this one lived up to the billing."

Her blue eyes flicked up to meet his gaze. "It did. You're a very special man, Noble Thayer."

Noble shook his head. "Not really. It's just easy to treat you very specially."

"That's sweet of you." Cathy sipped her tea and when she placed the empty cup on the table, he refilled it. "You're a listener—a trait that tends to be rare among folks with that pesky XY chromosome pair."

"You're easy to listen to."

"Oh, I'm sure you found hearing all the superstition about the locals and our medicine absolutely scintillating."

He smiled expansively. "Actually, I did. And as for being a listener, I'm trying to cultivate that. I think it's what a writer has to be."

Cathy stirred some sugar into her tea. "I knew a writer

when I lived on Wroclaw. The only thing he ever listened to was the sound of his own voice. He used to write historical novels set in the Fourth Succession War and then the Clan wars. I only read one—it was awful."

"What was so bad?"

"Characters with the depth of tissue paper and the most purple prose when it came to the battle scenes. The combat was pretty boring—boom, boom, BOOM—I'd rather have a box score at the end. I didn't really read those sections, just skipped past them."

"I don't think *anyone* reads the combat parts of those novels, really."

"You're probably right." She cupped her tea in her two hands. "Now I think he's writing some sort of political thriller dealing with Archon Melissa's death."

Noble's eyes widened. "Really? That's what I'm doing."

"I'm sure your book will be a lot better than his."

He frowned. "I guess I should have figured plenty of other people would decide to write about it. Maybe I should think about shifting things around."

The waiter appeared and looked down at the half-filled dishes on the table. "Shall I wrap this up?"

Cathy nodded emphatically. "Yes." She turned to Noble. "The kung-pao beef is excellent right out of the refrigerator for breakfast."

"If you say so."

Her pale brows drew together as she looked at him. "I'm sorry if mentioning that other writer and his book was discouraging."

He smiled. "No, it wasn't, really."

"I'm glad you told me about your book. It's one of the few things I know about you."

"I haven't told you that much about the book, but you know a lot about me."

She shrugged her shoulders and waggled her head a bit. "Not really. I know you were a teacher at a military academy on Hyde, and that you're here to write a novel, thanks to an inheritance, and I know you don't usually like Chinese food."

"You know much more than that, Cathy."

"But nothing of real significance."

"Like?"

"Religion, politics, favorite holovid show." She smiled at

him. "With most other men I'd know too much at the end of the third date, which is why there wouldn't be a fourth."

"Ah, so my strategy is working."

She slapped him gently on the arm. "My mother warned me about strangers, and I might not go out with you again if I still think you're a stranger."

"All right, you win." He held his hands up and leaned closer to her in the red leather booth. "Religion: I'm agnostic. The chaplain in the hospital where I went after breaking my leg was a real hawk. I had a hard time with a Christian preacher advocating going to war. I figure God's a lot smarter than his employees, especially since he doesn't do the hiring interviews himself."

"I can live with that. Favorite holovid series?"

Noble squirmed a bit. "I'll watch pretty much anything, but what I like is varied. I've enjoyed a number of the docudrama series dealing with the Clan wars." He shrugged. "I watch the fights from Solaris on Wednesday nights, but I'm not addicted to them. They give me a view of warfare so I can put it into my book."

Cathy's expression became very serious, and Noble couldn't tell whether or not she was joking as she asked her question. "Ah, the most important thing—who do you think killed Melissa Steiner-Davion?"

He began slowly, trying to read her reaction to his words. "Well, the government says a mentally disturbed person killed her." The frown on Cathy's face told him she didn't believe that. "Of course, only an idiot would accept that solution to the mystery."

Remembering that she had mentioned having lived on Wroclaw, a world at the edge of the District of Donegal, he assumed she had less love for Prince Victor than most people in the Sarna March. "The obvious person who might want the Archon dead is her son, Victor."

"My thoughts exactly."

Noble nodded. "That's who I had pegged until I started to research my novel. Because I'm inventing some things, I'm playing a bit fast and loose with what few facts are known in this case, but I see another solution to the identity of the person who was behind the killing. And I mean whoever hired the assassin because I don't think anyone will ever know the actual killer's identity."

Cathy watched him warily, but he saw curiosity flash in

her eyes. "Victor, I think, is a little too sharp to kill his mother. He might have wanted power, but Ryan Steiner and the unrest in Skye presented him a problem that his mother was more than capable of handling. With the Archon still alive, he had someone to insulate him from the anger of the Lyran people. You lived on Wroclaw—how bad could Victor be if his mother still loved him?"

"Some son, when you don't show up at her funeral."

Noble smiled. "Exactly. I think something else went on there."

"Such as."

"Okay, follow me. If Victor didn't kill Melissa, someone else did. I think that person was Ryan Steiner. But Ryan couldn't have been working alone because he needed allies to help loosen Victor's grip in the Isle of Skye. These allies needed to be powerful enough to force a rift between Victor and Katrina."

"The only people who could do that are ComStar."

Noble smiled triumphantly. "Or Word of Blake."

"But they're in the Free Worlds League."

"Who better to drag into the Isle of Skye? If Skye joined the League, Victor couldn't attack without triggering a major war. Better yet, Thomas marries his daughter Isis off to Ryan and cuts Sun-Tzu out of the picture."

"But Ryan was married to Morasha Kelswa."

"If Ryan could shoot Melissa, he could become a widower equally fast. Word of Blake could have intercepted the message Victor sent to Katrina concerning the funeral arrangements, making Victor look bad, and, boom, you have Ryan free and clear and charted for a beautiful future."

Cathy blinked her blue eyes, then smiled. "Well, that's a better plot for a novel than any I've read recently. Do you think that's what happened?"

"I don't know, but I can't fully discount it. The point is, though, that anyone with half a brain can concoct something and have it make sense."

"So in your book, who kills Ryan?"

Noble smiled. "Well, I have the same assassin killing both of them, but the second time he's acting to prevent Ryan from taking the Isle of Skye out of the Federated Commonwealth. In my book, he was duped into killing Melissa, and Ryan tries to kill him after the attempt, so the assassin gets his revenge." He shrugged. "It's probably not good enough to sell, but I have my Victor character doing things that parallel the assassin's activities, so I guess it's kind of like literature."

"Sounds fascinating. I'd love to read it."

The waiter arrived with the foamplas carton and the check. Noble gave him a hundred kroner bill and waved away change.

"All I've got is a first draft—not even a complete book—but I'd love for you to read it. I can give you a disk."

Cathy sat back in the booth. "You'd let me read the first draft? You trust me that much?"

"Sure. Maybe we haven't been friends long, but I believe you're someone I can trust." He glanced down at the table. "I hope you trust me as well."

"I do, Noble, I do." She tapped the carton. "In fact, I trust you enough to suggest we head back to your place and put this away. And in the morning, I can introduce you to the pleasures of cold kung-pao for breakfast."

Marik Palace, Atreus
Marik Commonwealth, Free Worlds League

Standing on the balcony overlooking the palace gardens, Thomas Marik heard the door in the room behind him open. He waited a few moments before turning to face his visitor. Though the robe Thomas had chosen was made of velvet and silk, its simple lines matched those of the Word of Blake Precentor entering the room. From the balcony, Thomas regally beckoned the man to join him, then turned away again to stare out at the dark garden and drink in the perfume of its night-blooming flowers.

He did not recognize the Precentor, but even just that first quick glance caught the urgency in the man's eyes. Thomas refused to turn toward the man even after hearing the first, crisp footfall of boot on balcony. He waited until the steps stopped, then counted the seconds until the man cleared his throat.

Instead of turning, Thomas pointed to the stars twinkling coldly in the night sky. "Did you know that our ancestors once believed that the positions of planets in the sky and the very stars themselves had messages for us? They let superstition and fear guide them, as if their lives were not in their control." Thomas turned to his right, letting his scarred profile precede him, then asked, "Do you believe we control our own lives?"

The Precentor, a young man with a full head of brown hair, brought his head up. "I believe Jerome Blake's vision for humanity offers a part for me to play, and my life is dedicated to functioning in that role."

Very good. You personalize the argument to avoid having to debate theology with me. "I understand well your belief, and I applaud your willingness to accept your place in the universe." *Validate him, and he will be your friend.* "You have a message for me, Precentor?"

"I am Precentor Malcolm, Captain-General." The man bowed his head in a silent salute. "I do not exactly have a message, sir. I've come about a delicate matter that has arisen, and I bring it to you because it pertains to your minor child."

Joshua! Thomas nodded. "Go on."

"As you know from your time with the heretics before our split with ComStar, when we are entrusted with a message, we deliver it without tampering or modifying the contents at all."

The Captain-General smiled enigmatically. "I served in a hyperpulse generator station. I know how messages are sent between planets, Precentor Malcolm. I take it you've had something suspicious crop up?"

"Yes, sir. A message was encoded and encapsulated and married to another message heading out from Atreus. We picked it up because of a size-error checking program we've been using to cut down on illegal messages and contraband imagery being encoded within messages."

"And when you decoded it to help SAFE track down the perpetrator, you discovered?"

"We discovered plans for agents of the Capellan Confederation's Maskirovka to make a raid against your son Joshua."

Sun-Tzu, what game are you playing at? Thomas fought the anger rising in his heart. "How serious was this attempt?"

"That is the curious thing, Captain-General. The Liao agents being activated had been inserted onto New Avalon thirty years ago, with the original wave of Sarna refugees. Two were in their sixties, the other one even older."

Malcolm frowned deeply. "Upon receiving this data we initially assumed the whole thing was a ruse by Davion intelligence to drive a wedge between you and the Liao."

Thomas wanted to smile because he had always appreciated the way any Word of Blake member made the words *the Liao* sound like a curse. "I applaud your thinking. Did you uncover the true author of the message?"

"We did, sir." Malcolm took a deep breath before starting. "It appears the author was actually Sun-Tzu."

"What?"

Malcolm held his hands up. "We do not think he intended to harm your son. The men were ordered to gain access to Joshua and to draw a sample of Joshua's blood for the DNA verification test commonly known as a Patmat screen."

Why would Sun-Tzu want to verify Joshua's paternity? A blood screen will prove beyond a doubt that he is my son, but if Sun-Tzu could get a test to cast doubt on that, Isis' position as heir would be strengthened. Casting doubt on Joshua's paternity would get Sun-Tzu nothing unless . . .

Thomas smiled with new appreciation for his daughter's betrothed. *If Sun-Tzu could make me believe Victor had somehow slipped another child into Joshua's place, with the object of carrying off a bloodless coup when I died, then he could get me to support him in worrying the Davion border. Sun-Tzu is making good use of these stories about a double for Joshua. Very good, and very dangerous.*

Thomas shifted his smile to one that was more apologetic. "So, Precentor, are you giving me the option of preventing the transmission of this message, thereby saving my gravely ill son undue stress?"

"I am, Captain-General. Precentor Blane has been informed of the situation and that is the solution he advocated."

"Very well."

The Precentor turned to leave, but Thomas stopped him. "Would it be an undue hardship to ask you to return here in an hour?"

"No, sir, it would be my pleasure."

"Good. As Sun-Tzu tends to be tenacious, I think I'd best have my own plan to block any similar efforts in the future." *Won't Sun-Tzu be surprised when I produce my own Patmat scan of Joshua's blood to refute his doctored results?*

Thomas smiled. "An hour then, Precentor. May the peace of Blake be with you."

13

They say soldiers and lawyers could never thrive both in one shire.

—BARNABY RICH, *THE ANATOMY OF IRELAND*

Tamar, Wolf Clan Occupation Zone
4 July 3057

Phelan swallowed his anger and fear and gave the Loremaster his best sneer. He kept his voice low, but filled it with menace. "This charge is heinous, Carns. It seeks to speculate about what is in the ilKhan's mind, then use it against him. Is there a witness that has heard the ilKhan expound upon his plan?"

Dalk's composure did not crack. "His plans and his guilt in this matter are self-evident."

"So you say." Phelan turned and looked toward the assembly. "Are we not the Clan that defeated ComStar?"

"You speak of the past."

"No, Dalk, I speak of the present. Does not Clan Wolf have the most highly trained, highly experienced leadership among the Clans today?"

"But will that leadership be here in ten years?"

"Do *you* think it will not?" Phelan forced himself to laugh, then pointed back at Natasha. "Look at Natasha Kerensky. She is more than eighty years old—well past the lifespan of a Clansman, yet well below the average years of the people of the Inner Sphere. We have concentrated upon creating better and better warriors with each succeeding generation, while prematurely retiring many able people."

Dalk shook his head. "Natasha Kerensky is an aberration."

"And if she is not?"

The Loremaster's eyes narrowed. "I do not follow your thought."

"No, clearly you do not. If she is not an aberration, then every one of us has more time in which to serve and prove ourselves. Yet a Clan warrior suffers tremendous pressure to prove him or herself in only a short time, or risk being discarded. A pressure I understand keenly because I would probably be dead had I not won a rank and a Bloodname within the Wolves." He glanced over at Vlad. "It is well known the depth of the hatred harbored in Crusader hearts for me."

Vlad rose to the challenge. "What you are suggesting is an expansion of time in which to prove our worth as warriors, but doing that would also require slowing the breeding program or severely limiting the size of sibkos. In effect, you would give us more time, but hand us fewer chances. There is no gain there."

Marialle stood beside him. "And your plan would destroy the Clans from within."

"But you and the other Crusaders are already doing that here and now." Phelan ignored the angry denials and protests from the Loremaster and the prosecutor. "Before the invasion, our vision as Clansmen held that everything—every fight, every agreement to exchange DNA, *everything*—was done by the Clan, *for* the Clan, and with the intention of forwarding the aims of the Clan. The goal was to produce the best warriors possible. Even the Clans that had been defeated and absorbed were preserved. Through their genetics they enrich the Clan that defeated them.

"And what was the reason we were trying to produce superior warriors? We wanted to become the greatest warriors the Inner Sphere had ever seen—not to enslave it, but to protect and lead it through our example. Nicholas Kerensky wanted us to rise above the vicious squabbling that tore the Star League apart. The Clans were formed to promote the glory of mankind, not the glory of a man."

Phelan thrust a finger at Ulric. "The ilKhan clung to that ideal. Yes, our Clan raced toward Terra along with the rest, but not so Ulric could take the world and become the First Lord of a new Star League. He wanted to win the race for the power it would give him to stop the other Clans from destroying the Inner Sphere. He wanted to preserve Nicholas Kerensky's dream. Because the other Khans became blinded by a desire for personal glory, they lost sight of their true mission, and they faltered. This is why ComStar defeated them—moral corruption weakened them and sowed the seeds of defeat within their ranks."

The young Khan turned to face Dalk. "Now you wish to sow those same seeds in our ranks with this charge."

"No, Khan Phelan, I merely seek to preserve the way of life that has made us what we are. And I choose to represent a path that will allow us to continue our way of life instead of destroying it—as the ilKhan obviously intends."

"But you cannot pretend to know what goes on in his mind." Phelan's green eyes blazed. "Again I ask, is there a witness against him?"

"And again I say that his guilt is self-evident. Did he not send you on a mission in which you trained the Kell Hounds in methods to be used against us? Can you deny that they will oppose us when the truce is ended?"

"That was no training mission, Dalk." Phelan hesitated as the importance of Dalk's questions hit home. *Dalk is anxious to show that Ulric has a hidden agenda, but so does he.* "But if you protest a lack of training, I imagine we could arrange a fight with the Jade Falcons."

"And dilute the strength of the Clans with internecine battling?"

"In the old days, fighting against one another was the only way Clan warriors had of honing their skills. Those same skills that permitted us to overwhelm the Inner Sphere. But now you assert that a return to our most time-honored training methods would weaken us?"

"We should press the Inner Sphere now," Dalk barked. "They are the ones we are destined to fight. Let us stop wasting time and fight them."

"So you do not deny that training against other Clans would sharpen us?" Phelan smiled for the audience. "I know I do not want to fight against the Ghost Bears because they have ever been our allies. The Jade Falcons, on the other hand, have always been our enemies—unless one reveres them for their Crusader philosophy. You claim our troops will be green, Dalk, but I think you would prefer them to be *jade* in their leanings."

"*That*, Khan Phelan, is a foul slander."

Phelan opened his arms. "Then challenge me to a Trial of

Refusal and let us decide in a Circle of Equals whose claim has more weight."

"No!" Ulric stalked forward and inserted himself between the two men. "There will be no Circle of Equals to decide this slander, nor this last charge."

Phelan took a step back and folded his arms. "It would be my pleasure to slay him."

"And it wold be mine to see him slain." Ulric pointed at the podium. "Loremaster, this final charge is the most grave known to the Clans. Were I to refute it here, it would only be taken up again by the Grand Council. That being the case, I direct that you refer the charge directly to the Grand Council."

Phelan stared at Ulric. "What are you doing?"

"I refuse to delay the inevitable, Khan Phelan."

Phelan was speechless. Ulric sounded defeated, and Dalk's smile showed that he drew the same conclusion from the ilKhan's words. Phelan finally found his voice and started to protest, but Ulric held his hand out for silence.

The conclave was quickly adjourned, then Dalk left with Marialle and Vlad in tow. The only consolation Phelan drew from any of this was that their little trio looked as bewildered as they were happy at the turn of events. They had obviously hoped to win, and rejoiced that they had done so, but Phelan would have bet that not one of them could have figured out how it happened.

The lights in the auditorium died, leaving Phelan, Natasha, and Ulric alone on the stage, bathed in the bloody glow of exit signs. "What can you be thinking, Ulric?" Phelan slapped the top of the podium. "Here, among the Wolves, we could have defeated that charge. But in the Grand Council the Crusaders predominate. Four of the Clans that invaded the Inner Sphere are dominated by Crusaders. The non-invading Clans can use this charge as a pretext for resuming the invasion so that this time they can join in, reaping the glory they were denied before. You gave up and put everything at risk."

Natasha looked crossly at Ulric. "The pup is right, Ulric. By passing up a battle, you must now win a difficult war."

"I know that, Natasha." Ulric slowly shook his head. "There is a very ancient saying that a good general not only sees the way to victory, he knows when victory is beyond him. It was beyond me here today. I underestimated Dalk and the desperation of the people behind him."

"But we had him."

"No, we did not. We know he invented that third charge on the spur of the moment, but it was a burst of inspiration that was fatal for us. The charge is sufficiently serious that even if the Clan Council had not judged me guilty, the Grand Council would have resurrected it against me. The Crusaders are hoping to make this whole thing seem like a movement from within Clan Wolf to discredit me."

"And your move has allowed that to happen."

Ulric nodded. "You are correct, Phelan, but shifting the battle to the Grand Council means I do not have my own Clan pitted against me. The attack now comes from outside the Wolves, which should help bind us together. What we have done is open the way for a rift between the Crusaders and the young Wolf supremists. Now that Crusaders must take their fight to the Grand Council, the Wolf supremists will feel used and abandoned."

Phelan frowned. "That's fine, but the Wolf supremists will only be useful if we are forced"—he broke off at the look on Ulric's face, which told him the ilKhan had already figured out what Phelan was about to say.

The enormity of the situation also shocked Natasha. "You want them with us for a Trial of Refusal when the Grand Council removes you, *quiaff*?"

"Aff, Natasha."

Phelan looked sharply from one to the other. "You're talking a total war between the Wolves and another Clan."

"Or a coalition of Clans." Ulric smiled coldly. "I rather think the Jade Falcons will claim the right to fight us, though."

Phelan's eyes narrowed. "And that is not a bad thing?"

Natasha nodded, then smiled in a way that sent a shiver down Phelan's spine. "It is, Phelan, very bad. The Crusaders have accused the ilKhan of undermining our way to force him to resume the war with the Inner Sphere. Now, why do they want that?"

Phelan shook his head. "They hate the Inner Sphere?"

The ilKhan let warmth creep back into his smile. "That, yes, Phelan, but they also believe that if we do not fight outsiders, we will fight against each other. The last thing the Jade Falcons want is to see Wolf Clan JumpShips showing up in their systems. That is their greatest fear because they know that even if they defeat us, it will cost them so dearly that they will never be able to profit from a renewed war with the Inner Sphere. Other Clans will come from the homeworlds and take their place in the invasion—and take our place, too. The Jade Falcons' dreams of glory will end forever."

"But if we go to war with the Jade Falcons, we could be destroyed as well. A war between Clans would be suicidal."

"Which is exactly why the Grand Council expects me to repudiate the truce. They believe I will see the wisdom of renewing the invasion over destroying my Clan." Ulric pressed his hands together as if in prayer. "If I comply with their wishes, they have no reason to try to taint my Clan with the charges against me, so the Wolves will live. They might even be allowed to join in the new invasion."

"But if we go to war and do serious damage to a Crusader Clan, then that Clan would be in no position to benefit from the invasion. The Crusaders would be split against themselves in voting on that matter." Phelan shook his head. "They think they have you trapped, but they are not on solid ground themselves."

"You have hit upon the key, Phelan—my plan works *if* we can do enough damage to whomever we fight. Guaranteeing that will take some time."

Phelan smiled. "Time I can buy by preparing to defend you before the Grand Council?"

"If you will accept that task, impossible though it might be, Natasha and I can begin arranging some nasty surprises for the Crusaders."

"Bargained well, Ulric, provided my troops and I get our chance in the fighting."

The ilKhan nodded. "Bargained well and done, Khan Phelan. Yours will be a very special role indeed."

14

The devil can cite Scripture for his purpose.
 An evil soul, producing holy witness,
 Is like a villain with a smiling cheek,
 A goodly apple rotten at the heart.
 O, what a goodly outside falsehood hath!
—WILLIAM SHAKESPEARE, MERCHANT OF VENICE

Avalon City, New Avalon
Crucis March, Federated Commonwealth
15 July 3057

The nurse smiled at Francesca Jenkins as the young woman smoothed the back of her candy-striped skirt. "It looks as if you were a tonic for those kids, Fran. They really didn't want you to go."

Francesca smiled. "I like reading to them, but I could see they were getting tired. It's sad for youngsters to be so sick."

Connie Whynn typed a quick note into the computer, then looked up. "Very sad. And depressing for many people. That's why you're one of the few volunteers willing to work the pediatric cancer wards."

"I'd never thought of volunteering before, but after seeing that program about Missy Cooper and her cousin Raymond, I guess something kind of clicked inside my heart."

Connie narrowed her eyes and pulled back dramatically as if comically skeptical. "Oh, sure, you saw Raymond and he tugged at your heartstrings. Are you certain you're not another golddigger here trying to meet Joshua Marik?"

The petite, black-haired volunteer laughed aloud. "He's not quite my type, being barely into the double digits of age. Besides," she added, smiling devilishly, "there are laws against that sort of thing."

"Well, be that as it may, you're about to meet him." Connie held her noteputer up to the dataport on the desk terminal, downloaded Joshua's chart into the handheld device, then gestured for Francesca to follow her down the hall. "You aren't squeamish about blood, are you?"

"Only my own." Francesca smiled, then blushed. "As long as I'm not going to be drawing it out of him."

The other woman waved that concern away. "The Intelligence Secretariat has poked, prodded, and probed me just about every way they can just so I can have the right to poke, prod, and probe Joshua. I've been pulling so much blood out of him over the last six months that he calls me Nurse Dracula, and I can't blame him. He's really a dear little boy."

Francesca followed the older woman down the hall, past the elevators and lobby, and around the corner to the area of the pediatric ward that had private rooms. Two huge men with rifles stood on either side of the hallway. Before anyone could enter what had to be Joshua's room, they had to go through a small barrier that led past a metal detector. One guard waved them toward the metal detector with his rifle while the other moved slightly away and prepared to shoot if anything untoward began to happen.

Connie handed the noteputer to the guard near the detector, then walked through the magscanning unit. The guard examined the noteputer, then returned it to her. Francesca he blocked with one hand held up. "Is she cleared?"

Connie nodded. "Call it in. I got notice at the start of my shift that she'd passed a screening three days ago.

The guard used a radio to connect with his superiors. He read Francesca's ID number aloud from her volunteer badge, then nodded. "She's not doing anything medical with him, right?"

"Right. Just helping clean up after me."

The guard silently waved Francesca through and she passed without setting anything off. The guard checked their nametags again, tapped something into his own noteputer, then knocked on the door to Joshua's room. Two deadbolts drew back with a click and then the heavy, bombproof door opened slowly.

Aside from the armed guard opening the door, Joshua was the only other occupant of the room. His bed was set with the head against the left wall, and on it sat a bald boy staring intently at the holovision monitor set near the ceiling in the far corner of the room. Francesca saw that the set was play-

ing an old holovid—one of the *Immortal Warrior* series—
but she couldn't identify the mud-covered star nor clearly
make out who he was fighting this time. The series was little
more than a live-action cartoon, but Joshua was, predictably,
engrossed in it.

"Good evening, Joshua."

The boy's head came around quickly and the bright smile
he wore eroded at the edges. "Nurse Dracula, the sun hasn't
even gone down yet."

"I'm wearing sunblock eighty-eight."

"Foiled again!" the hollow-chested boy announced and
bared his left arm. "Be careful. Last time I had bruises."

"Yes you did, but they cleared up faster than before,
which is very good." Connie unlocked a small cabinet and
drew from it some cotton balls, a bottle of rubbing alcohol,
and a vacutube blood-sampling device. These she placed on
a small tray that she set on Joshua's bedside table.

Joshua peered around Connie at Francesca. "Hello. I'm
Joshua Marik."

Francesca bowed her head. "I'm pleased to meet you,
Duke Joshua. I'm Francesca Jenkins, but you can call me
Fran. I'm helping Nurse Dracula."

"She'll be straightening up your room and changing your
bed linen while I give you your bath." Connie raised an eyebrow at her young charge. "Perhaps I should bathe you first,
then take your blood—or do you promise there'll be no
splashing around this time?"

Joshua said nothing, but looked up at Connie with huge,
sad, puppy-dog eyes.

With a wink at Francesca, the nurse took up a cotton
ball, pressed it against the top of the alcohol bottle several
times, then liberally swabbed the crook of Joshua's left elbow. Discarding the cotton ball in the basket, she took up
the vacutube assembly and pressed it against the boy's arm.
Adjusting the constricting strap around his upper arm gave
her a nice choice of veins.

The vacutube system worked simply. A needle ran
through a stopper and collar assembly to end up protruding
from the back. Connie took a test tube containing a vacuum
and inserted it into the stopper assembly. The back part of
the needle pierced the thin membrane, keeping the vacuum
in, then Connie pushed the needle into Joshua's arm. The
vacuum sucked the blood up into the test tube.

When the first tube was almost full, Connie depressed a button on the stopper, shutting off the blood flow. Twisting the test tube free, she set it on the bedside table. The membrane over the top resealed itself, preventing spillage. Connie plugged a second tube into the collar, released the button, and drew a second tube of blood.

Joshua looked up at her, concern on her face. "How many today?"

"Just two." Connie glanced over at Francesca. "I'll run these down to the lab if you think you can handle the swab and bandage detail."

Francesca nodded. "Got it." She crossed to the small table and picked up two cotton balls. One she soaked in alcohol while keeping the other pressed against the palm of her right hand with two fingers. Holding the wet ball up between the thumb and index finger of her right hand, and displaying a bandage in her left, she nodded to indicate her readiness to Connie.

The nurse pulled the whole vacutube assembly from Joshua's arm and Francesca stepped in. Using her body to shield her movements from view, she deftly switched cotton balls, pressing the dry one to the wound. She held it there for three seconds, being sure not to exert enough pressure to close off the blood flow. When Connie turned toward the door, Francesca took the opportunity to switch cotton balls. With her left thumb she kept the alcohol-soaked ball on the needle-hole while her right hand sank into the pocket of her smock.

She reached through the rip she'd made in the seam and stuffed the bloody cotton ball into the top of her stocking, making certain it was secure against the flesh of her thigh. Drawing her right hand out again, she dabbed at the wound with the wet cotton ball, then tossed it into the basket. Applying the bandage to the hole in the boy's arm, she gave him a big smile.

"There, all done," she told him, and it was only half a lie.

Four hours later Francesca Jenkins left the New Avalon Institute of Science Medical Center, ten days into her mission for Marik intelligence and a mere seventy-two hours from completing it. The Intelligence Secretariat had investigated and cleared her for volunteer duty at the NAIS and for contact with Joshua Marik because of her exemplary record.

Except for a trio of four-month periods, the twenty-six-year-old, computer graphics supervisor had lived her whole life on New Avalon. During that time she had collected a half-dozen parking tickets and one tax audit.

Because she had been born on New Avalon, of an Avalonite and his war-bride from Castor, Francesca had started out in life as a low security risk. When she was fourteen, her parents divorced, and her mother went back to her maiden name of Jenkins. Francesca's name was also legally changed. Mother and daughter clung tightly to each other, Francesca being an only child and her mother far from home and family in the distant Free Worlds League.

In the meantime, Francesca's father had become obsessed with gaining custody of his daughter, going so far as trying to abduct her on two occasions. Both attempts failed, and Francesca's mother got a restraining order to keep her ex-husband away from them both. On her sixteenth birthday, Francesca came home from school to find her mother lying on the kitchen floor in a pool of blood and her father sitting slumped over at the table, dead from a single, self-inflicted gunshot wound to the head.

Orphaned, she was taken in by her father's sister. Though her new family was kind and treated Francesca very well, they believed her mother was somehow responsible for the whole tragedy. The fact that Francesca decided to keep the Jenkins name did not help matters.

The next summer the maternal grandparents she had never met sent her tickets to visit them on Castor. Francesca jumped at the chance even though the round trip would take three months and only give her a month with her grandparents. Once on Castor she met Stefan and Adrianne Jirik—the name her mother had changed to Jenkins in an attempt to fit in better on New Avalon—and was welcomed into the Jirik family fold.

The Jiriks, she was told, had a grand tradition of service to the League. In that one month Francesca was given a history and family roots and a tradition on which to base her self-image and self-esteem. After hearing all this she told her grandparents she wanted to remain with them instead of returning to her aunt and uncle, but they cautioned her against such rash action. They reminded her that New Avalon was a world of great learning, and that the Jirik family valued education highly. They also knew that her aunt had been good to her. To return that kindness with ingratitude would, they said, be dishonorable.

Reluctantly the girl agreed to return to New Avalon.

On the two subsequent visits to Castor the Jiriks completed Francesca's subversion into an agent for the Free Worlds League. On Castor they addressed her as Frantiska, the version of her name more commonly found in the League. They taught her simple but nearly unbreakable ciphers, how to create and work dead-drops, how to employ a cut-out, and even how to maintain and shoot a variety of pistols. They assured her that as a mole on New Avalon she would never be asked to harm anyone, only gather information in areas where the Federated Commonwealth was strong and the League weak. They strongly intimated that this meant only industrial espionage, again promising their granddaughter that she would never be asked to do anything truly dangerous.

Ten days ago the fateful message had arrived in a piece of electronic mail at her office. On her lunch hour she went to a dead-drop she'd established—a small envelope fastened to the underside of a kneeler in the first confessional in St. Andrew's Church—and from it retrieved a computer disk. She did not know who put it there, but that didn't bother her. Not knowing was the purpose of a dead-drop; it was part of the game and she was determined to play it as well as she could.

At home the computer had easily decoded the message, which outlined a simple task: obtain a sample of Joshua Marik's blood without attracting attention, conduct a genetic typing on it, and report if it matched the datafile on the disk.

Francesca immediately began to research her problem. In refreshing her memory of basic biology, she discovered that the amount of blood needed to obtain a gene match was relatively small. A discarded bandage or other similar item would never be noticed, whereas a purloined vial of blood would surely attract attention.

That meant she had to get close to Joshua. It was not long before she thought of volunteering at the hospital to gain admittance to his floor and his room. She started talking to friends about how her life felt incomplete, that something was missing despite her success at work. She hinted at a desire to get pregnant and raise a child on her own. Deflecting her from that course of action, her friends suggested she volunteer to work with children at the hospital. As though simply following her friend's advice, she made a call to the hospital.

The two Intelligence Secretariat agents who'd investigated her also spoke with her friends. They reported trying to help Francesca by suggesting volunteer work with children, which made her cover even more viable. Within forty-eight hours Francesca had clearance for contact with Joshua if her duties so required.

Three days after that, she had her blood sample.

There were plenty of private labs that could do a full genotyping of the sort commonly used in a paternity/maternity suit, but they were costly and time-consuming. They would also create a paper trail that Francesca definitely did not want. Instead she went to an educational supply house with the story that she was tutoring a neighbor child in the sciences and needed a genetic experiment kit intended for secondary school use. She paid in cash.

The basic tools for genetic manipulation had been around for centuries, but their availability had not resulted in the explosion of genetically altered lifeforms many bioethicists had railed against a millennium before. It was one thing to identify a string of nucleotide base pairs and yet another to swap known genes one for the other. Even that was still worlds away from being able to play God and make life up from scratch. As one of the kit's booklets noted, the science of genetics was at the point where it could recognize the shapes of jigsaw puzzle pieces, and could even switch some pieces from one puzzle into another. It was another thing to combine twenty million puzzles into one cohesive picture while drawing pieces from yet other puzzles. It was a feat no one had yet accomplished.

At home she took the cotton swab and soaked it in a test tube into which she poured some distilled water. After squeezing it out, she had three ccs of pinkish liquid. Into this she dumped three ccs of the kit's DNA amplifier solution. Following the diagrams in the instruction book, she placed the test tube in her oven and programmed it to heat and cool the solution over the next thirty hours.

The amplifier was a chemical solution rich in the nucleotides needed to recreate bits and pieces of the DNA double-helix. It also included some special chemical strings designed to isolate specific genetic sequences. For identification purposes the chemical concentrated on two chromosome pairs: X, Y, and the pair number 1. The X and Y sequences would allow matching by sex while the number 1 pair samples would provide a contrast of contributions from each parent on a chromosome both contributed. By the end of the thirtieth hourly cycle, a million copies of the particularly selected sequences had been manufactured.

After the DNA content of the sample had been enhanced, Francesca drew off one cubic centimeter of fluid into each of five test tubes. She poured the last cc of fluid in the original test tube into a plastic bag and tucked it back in her freezer in case she needed to repeat her tests or her controllers wanted her to pass the material on. Simply by repeating the step with the DNA amplifier solution she could create as many samples as needed.

Into each of the five test tubes she added a single drop of each of the five different cutter/trimmer solutions provided in the kit. These droplets contained chemical cutters that looked for a specifically repeated pattern of nucleotide pairs within the duplicated samples. Because all DNA is made up of only four nucleotides: adenine, cytosine, guanine, and thymine, and because they only bond adenine to thymine and cytosine to guanine, a fair amount of sequence repetition is common. The cutters looked for specific sequences, about sixty base pairs long, and snipped them out of the duplicated chains.

In the five hours the chemicals took to prepare the samples, Francesca boiled up the banding gel and poured it into the shallow pan that looked like an electric pancake griddle. The gel cooled and hardened into a translucent film over a black background. It reminded her of ice on the roadways during particularly bad Avalon City winters.

She put one drop from a marking dye bottle into each test tube, thoroughly mixed it in, then used a pipette to draw a drop from the first tube. She sunk the pipette's end into the gel at a spot about ten centimeters from the top of the sheet and deposited the droplet there. Using individual pipettes for the other solutions, she repeated the procedure until she had five drops in the gel. She placed the cover on the incubator, plugged it in, turned it on, and left it to do its work for two hours.

While she waited, Francesca washed out all her experimental glassware, then boiled it, and finally crushed it before sweeping it into a bag. In her fireplace she burned the box and instructions—save the last two pages, which gave procedures for completing the experiment—stirred the ashes and swept them up for later disposal. The plastic chemical vials were emptied down the sink, then washed and melted down. The melting, which she did in her fireplace, did not work terribly well and she ended up scraping plastic from the bricks after the mess had cooled enough.

Two hours later the incubator shut itself off. It had not been cooking the solution in the gel, but had been separating it. Electric current ran through the gel from left to right. In two hours it drew the clumps of sequences along from the starting point toward the other side of the gel. The larger the separate segments in the clumps, the further away from the starting point they moved in the electrical field.

The marking dye had stained the segments so they would fluoresce. Francesca removed the cover of the incubator and subjected the gel to a strong light for five minutes. She placed the overlay grid on the gel, then turned out all the lights. Once her eyes had adjusted, she saw glowing lines at certain points in the grid matrix and she faithfully recorded the grid coordinates: X, 3, 25; Y, 12, 24; 1.1, 2, 9, 20, 31; 1.2, 4, 15, 37, 43; 1.3, 7, 16, 30, 42.

Returning to her computer, she pulled up the record for the match sample and compared the two of them side by side:

Chromosome	Joshua	Match Sample
X	3, 25	2, 18
Y	12, 24	15, 45
1.1	2, 9, 20, 31	3, 7 23, 39
1.2	4, 15, 37, 43	12, 17, 31, 33
1.3	7, 16, 30, 42	2, 14, 19, 37

Francesca smiled. Though she was only twenty-six and had led a normal life on New Avalon—save for being recruited as a spy by her grandparents—she had not led a sheltered one. All the while she cooked the solutions and tended them and stained them and incubated them, she had been thinking about why her superiors in the Free Worlds League might want someone to do a genetic match on Joshua. About the time the plastics started dripping all over the bricks in her fireplace, she hit upon the reason: with the recent death of Sophina Marik, someone must have come forward and claimed to be Joshua's real father. Wanting to prevent the media having a field day with a trumped-up scandal, the Captain-General would need some way to refute this foul claim. Thus had she been chosen to collect a blood sample and conduct this simple test.

Francesca studied the results. There was no correspondence between the two samples. There was no way the two of them could be related. The man claiming to be Joshua's father was a fraud. With a cotton ball, a school science kit, and some patience, she, Frantiska Jirik, had saved the Free Worlds League from the greatest threat to its sovereignty it had ever known.

Confident in this historic contribution to the nation of her people, she encoded her data and prepared the cipher sheet she would leave in the dead-drop for pickup and delivery back to Atreus. That done, she destroyed the rest of the science kit equipment and threw it away in scattered dumpsters well away from where she lived.

Then, stopping only to have an abridged confession heard at St. Andrews, she returned to the hospital and continued her volunteer tasks. It made her feel good to be so close to Joshua, to help him if he needed it. And though she never spoke to him when their paths crossed again, she believed he instinctively knew that in her he had a loyal friend.

$$=== 15 ===$$

Let who desires peace prepare for war.

—VEGETIUS, DE RE MILITARI

Charleston, Woodstock
Sarna March, Federated Commonwealth
21 July 3057

Riding high in the cockpit of his *Warhammer* 'Mech, Larry Acuff felt as if all was right with the world. Despite being tightly strapped to the command couch, with medical sensors stuck to his bare flesh and a heavy neurohelmet grinding down on his shoulders, he felt free enough to fly. Gloved hands manipulated the joysticks on either arm of the couch, bringing the 'Mech's twin crosshairs together over the computer-generated image of a *Crusader*. A gold dot pulsed to life in the center of the crosshairs, indicating a target lock, and Larry jammed his thumbs down on the firing buttons for the PPCs mounted in the *Warhammer*'s arms.

Though humanoid in shape, the *Warhammer* had PPC muzzles where other 'Mechs had hands. From each of these a jagged blue beam of energized particles sizzled free. The particle projection cannon's synthetic blue lightning stabbed in at the *Crusader*. As the beams neared the target, they united and cored into it. The holographic image in Larry's cockpit showed the beams converging on the *Crusader*'s left hip, boring their way in through armor to melt the ferrotitanium leg bone and amputate it.

The targeting image had been painted by the computer over an old powerline tower, and the twin beams sliced through its supports as if they were no more than spider webs and tissue paper. With a shrieking groan, the tower wa-

vered, then slowly toppled to the ground. As it hit the external microphones picked up the resounding thud and transferred it to the speakers in Larry's helmet. The computer
image likewise fell, and the real-world dust cloud served as
a dissolve matrix for the computer to use in erasing it.

"Nice shooting, Deuce." Phoebe's congratulations broadened the smile on Larry's face. "You learn how to fuse those
beams on Solaris, or was that luck?"

"Pure luck—one in a million. In keeping with everything
else on this run, too."

"Four ninety-five out of a possible five hundred ... I
don't think that was luck."

"Had to be luck, Ace. I never did that well back when I
was training on this course."

"Larry, that was seven years ago." He heard Phoebe laugh
gently. "You've fought the Clans and you've been dueling
on Solaris since then. It's all the practice that's made you
better, not luck."

Larry thought about that for a moment. It was true that he
had seen a tremendous amount of combat since the last time
he was in a 'Mech on Woodstock. The learning curve for
BattleMech combat was fairly steep, and all the training in
the world couldn't prepare a warrior for the utter chaos of
the battlefield. Those who couldn't handle it became casualties, while those who could went on to the next battle.
"You're probably right, Phoebe, but I wouldn't mind a little
luck from time to time."

"I'd trade a ton of armor for a dollop of luck. Ready to
wrap it up?"

"Are we done already?"

"Larry, all you needed to requalify was to shoot three
seventy-five. You were done on the tenth target. These other
five have been for the range record."

"Really? Did I break it?"

"Yeah, with target group thirteen, the Savannah Masters.
You smoked them."

Blake's Blood! Back when he was still in training on
Charleston, a recruit had needed a score of three twenty-five
to qualify for duty. The Clan War had raised the standards a
bit, hence the fifty extra points he'd needed today. His skill
had improved, but Larry hadn't really known how to measure the improvement because his matches on Solaris were
one-on-one 'Mech bouts. Compared with his best score of

seven years before, he'd progressed from a status of adequate to that of an elite warrior, and the thought started a warm fire burning in his belly.

"I'd never have expected to break the record. As PR officer, I don't have to publicize this, do I?"

Phoebe laughed. "I thought we'd do a press release and send it to the Clans. That would make them think twice about going back to war, don't you think?"

"I think fighting computer simulation targets has little resemblance to fighting the Clans."

"I was there, remember?"

"Sure." Larry frowned as he turned his *Warhammer* around and followed Phoebe's *Marauder II* back toward the hangar. "Would you want to fight them again?"

Larry heard nothing but the static of dead air over his headphones for a moment or two before Phoebe came back tentatively. "I'd fight them again, but I don't know that I *want* to fight them again."

"I saw some Elementals on Solaris," Larry said, referring to the giant, genetically bred infantrymen of the Clans. "Taman Malthus, the one who helped Kai free us prisoners, came to Solaris to watch Kai defend his championship. They're still pretty frightening, even when they're friends. Even so, I'd be first in line if the truce ended tomorrow."

"It's marriage that's got me thinking differently. Before George, my future was in the army. Now it's *our* future, not just mine."

"Makes things complicated, doesn't it?"

Phoebe's nervous laugh resounded through his neurohelmet. "Which comes first, self or the state?"

"In the Draconis Combine it's the state, definitely. Ditto the Clans, I gather. Elsewhere in the Inner Sphere, though, I think that question gets answered on an individual basis. Of course, the way you put it makes it sound cold and impersonal."

"Larry, the state generally *is* cold and impersonal."

"Without a doubt, but only if you see the state as an institution. We've both met Prince Victor. He's not cold or distant." Larry's *Warhammer* moved from the hilly precincts of the targeting course and started across the ferrocrete to the Reserve's hangar. "To me the state is everyone and every place I know and love. If duty calls me to defend them to the point of death, well, I'm willing."

"Easy for you to say. You don't have a wife."

"And you've refused to give me the visiphone number for your best friend. How can I give her a look if you won't?"

"Larry, she's happily living in sin with one of George's buddies."

"So I'd call when he wasn't home."

"You're incorrigible."

Larry brought his *Warhammer* around to the hangar stall designated for it. He initiated his shutdown procedure, then picked up the thread of their talk. "I think you'd be out there fighting again, Phoebe. Once it's in your blood, there's no cure."

"I used to feel that way, Larry, but now I think there is an antidote."

"And that is?"

"True love. Something about love and life makes playing around in death's domain a lot less tempting."

"Doesn't mean you wouldn't be there, Phoebe." Larry unbuckled the straps holding him to the command couch. "Having George just means you have one more thing to fight for. No greater reason to fight than to protect your family."

"Wars have been fought over less."

"And likely will be again in the future." Larry undid his helmet's chinstrap. "But if we're lucky, it won't be during our lifetimes."

Marik Palace, Atreus
Marik Commonwealth, Free Worlds League

Thomas Marik felt empty. Like a hollow terra cotta figure, fragile and vulnerable, as if he'd shatter into a billion pieces if he breathed. Everything inside of him had torn loose and been crushed down into the black hole of dread and despair centered just below his heart.

He didn't even feel pain.

Standing alone on the balcony, he did not need to glance again at the slip of paper Precentor Malcolm had brought him. The message had been as simple and eloquent as it had been brief: *No match.*

My son is dead, and Victor Davion has killed him. A

those words linked themselves into a sentence, the rational part of him fought that verdict. He knew as well as anyone that Joshua had been as good as dead the instant the doctors diagnosed the leukemia. Only sheer desperation had made him accept Hanse Davion's offer of treatment at the New Avalon Institute of Science. It had been the only shred of hope.

Sophina had urged Thomas to make a second child with her, one who could provide a marrow match for Joshua, but he had refused. His father, Janos Marik, had produced ten children. Two had died of leukemia at ages twelve and eight. The rest—except for Thomas, his brother Paul, and his sisters Theresa and Kristen—had died in the various internal struggles and wars that had plagued the Free Worlds League. The strife ended only in 3036 when Thomas appeared before a stunned Parliament to reveal that he had survived the bomb blast that killed his father and brother a year and a half before. Janos Marik's family proved that large families and sibling rivalries caused significant problems.

he had feared giving Joshua a brother or sister. If that child was unsuitable for donating marrow, she would forever be in the position of having failed the task for which she'd been conceived.

The alternative, a child who did provide the marrow needed to save Joshua's life, would have been worse. If that child had been the least bit proud or ambitious—and what child would not be when, just by the fact of being born, he had saved his older brother's life?—he would resent the fact that Joshua stood to inherit the throne. If the cancer returned, would the new child refuse his brother more marrow to deny him the chance to become Captain-General? Isis had done so when approached to save Joshua's life, then laughed in Thomas's face when he found himself in the absurd position of threatening to punish the person who would become his new heir if she did not help his current heir.

And now she is my heir and in the thrall of Sun-Tzu Liao. Thomas knew he had other choices: Paul, Kristen, Theresa, or their offspring, but he knew they did not share his goals. Though seeming to favor one or the other of them—Paul's daughter Corinne, for example—might upset Sun-Tzu Liao, events had moved to a point where Thomas could not indulge himself in such a game, no matter how much pleasure it would give him to throw a scare into Sun-Tzu.

Victor Davion did not kill my son, but he has denied him the dignity of death he would have been accorded here. This act, substituting another for my dead boy, is beyond barbarism. It is a profane deed that mocks my son and his life. For this, Victor will pay, and pay dearly.

Bits and pieces of a plan began to build itself inside the emptiness in his soul. Each element was like an ultra-thin membrane settling into place in a matrix growing inside Thomas. Though any one strand was too delicate to stand up to pressure, and even though arranged like a house of cards, the structure did not collapse. On this Thomas could build his vision of the future.

Behind him, hovering like a shadow in the entrance to his office, Precentor Malcolm cleared his throat gently. The sound irritated Thomas so much that he wanted to turn and throttle the man, but doing so would have upset the crystalline lattice coming to life inside him.

"If I may, Captain-General, I would like to express my own sorrow at learning that you have lost your son."

"Thank you," Thomas replied faintly.

"I also wish to say that I stand ready to help you relay the orders that will visit justice upon the malignant dwarf seated on the throne of the Federated Suns."

Thomas's head came up, though he still did not turn to look at Malcolm. "You believe I should avenge myself on Victor Davion?"

"There is a saying—'Revenge triumphs over death.'"

The Captain-General came around slowly, his shoulders hunched. "You are a fool, Malcolm."

"Pardon me, sir?"

"Do you know who you quote?"

"The Blessed Blake."

Thomas angrily waved that answer away. "That quote is from Francis Bacon, and your use of it is out of context and inappropriate. It is wrong. You are wrong."

The Precentor's brown eyes became ringed with white as Thomas's fury backed him into the door jamb. "I did not mean to offend," he stuttered.

"No, no, of course you did not, but you did offend. If you know what this message contains, then you have also read the messages I sent out. How many other people know what I have sent and what I have gotten back?"

Malcolm shied from the question. "There are things I cannot . . ."

"*Tell me?* I am Thomas Marik, Precentor. *I* am the man who Precentor Blane has hinted at naming ComStar's Primus-in-exile. You might have secrets from others, Malcolm, but certainly not from me."

Thomas pulled himself to his full, considerable height. "This is not information I want just for its own sake, but vital information I must have. I do not know how far this story has traveled, or how likely is the chance of a security breach. Without knowing that, I cannot prepare to repay this unkindness done to my son."

"But you just said I was a fool for thinking you would revenge yourself on Victor Davion."

"And you were." Thomas opened his arms toward the night sky, to its billions of worlds and stars, including those of the Federated Commonwealth. "It was not Victor who visited this indecency upon my son, but the Davion arrogance that nurtured him. His father, Hanse Davion, held my son hostage to win my assistance in producing materiel for his war with the Clans. How could someone raised by such a man understand the pain a father feels at the loss of a child? I blame not Victor, but the man who sired him."

"But you will punish him."

Thomas nodded slowly. "I cannot punish Hanse, but Victor must learn from his father's mistake. This punishment will take time to engineer, however. Border raids and demands for reparations will not suffice. My first duty is not to salve my wounded soul by killing FedComs—my duty is to liberate my countrymen from the yoke of a nation that could permit this obscene behavior. That liberation will take time and planning."

Thomas saw the light of comprehension come on in Malcolm's dark eyes, but he knew the Precentor couldn't guess at even a fraction of his plans. "You are now my liaison with Word of Blake, Precentor Malcolm. Send a message to Blane over my signature—he will ratify this decision. You will bring me the information I want, when I want it, without question. It will be complete and you will not comment upon it unless I so request. Everything you learn will be in these reports."

"But you have SAFE and the rest of your intelligence apparatus for preparing reports like that."

"Yes, but they have resources you do not, and vice versa. Each of you will verify the other." Thomas smiled and barely felt the scars tugging at his mouth. "And the first thing you will do is prepare me a dossier on my enemy."

"Victor?"

Thomas shook his head and remembered his own family. "No, Victor I understand fairly well. The person I want to know now is Katrina Steiner."

"Katrina Steiner. I understand." Malcolm bowed his head to Thomas. "Do you require anything else of me?"

Thomas was about to dismiss the man, when another crystalline thread slid into place. "Yes. Sun-Tzu's message to his operatives on New Avalon. Do you still have a copy?"

"I do."

"Could you still send it?"

Malcolm thought for a moment, then nodded his head tentatively. "Davion intelligence compromised the code sequence used to create the message. The Maskirovka agents on New Avalon never actually got the key to the cipher."

"You could send it to them again, yes, in lieu of whatever key they are supposed to receive in a given week?"

"The Maskirovka only changes codes on a monthly basis, but, yes, we could make the substitution."

"Good. Be prepared to send the key and the message out quickly." Thomas clasped his hands together in satisfaction. "My plans may require providing a distraction for Victor Davion, and employing Sun-Tzu in that capacity may just kill two birds with one stone."

══ 16 ══

Diplomacy without arms is like music without instruments.

—FREDERICK THE GREAT

Tamar
Wolf Clan Occupation Zone
8 August 3057

Phelan Ward, Khan of Clan Wolf, stood beside Natasha Kerensky as the ilKhan took his place at the high bench in the Grand Council chamber. Neither Phelan nor Natasha wore their enamel wolf masks, though they did wear Clan leathers in gray and black, respectively. Ulric also wore gray and his helmet, which he solemnly removed and set beside him on the bench.

"I, Ulric Kerensky, being ilKhan in this, the sixth year of the Truce of Tukayyid, do hereby convene this meeting of the Wolf Clan Grand Council. As was determined at our conclave of twelve June thirty fifty-two, we are yet governed under the Martial Code handed down by Nicholas Kerensky. This matter will be despatched in a manner fitting."

"Seyla," chanted each Clansman and woman present. Their voices came almost in unison, the ancient oath uttered with an accent completely foreign to normal Clan speech.

Had the Grand Council been called in time of peace, it would have been convened in the Grand Council chamber on Strana Mechty, the Clan home world far from the boundaries of the Inner Sphere. Each of the thirty-four Khans of the seventeen Clans would have been required to attend in person. Because the Marital Code required the speedy resolution of important questions, twenty-two of the thirty-four

Clan Khans only appeared via video monitors. The twelve other Khans, all from the Clans that had participated in the Inner Sphere, had come in person.

Phelan shook his head. Even though he knew the both the charge and the trial were a sham, in the six weeks of preparing his argument he'd begun to hope it might be possible to sway his peers by dint of a logical and rational presentation. Looking at the expressions ranging from bored to eager on the faces of the gathered Khans, he sensed that almost all had either prejudged Ulric, or would vote for whichever outcome seemed most favorable to their own Clans. *I could be the personification of eloquence today and it would make no difference.*

Ulric looked out over the assembled Khans. "Brothers and sisters, near and far, this *rede* binds us now and forever and beyond that until the end of all that is. We are gathered to judge the truth of a serious charge made against me. It is said that I plot genocide against the Clans and have done so by entering into a truce that will leave us unable to defend ourselves against the Inner Sphere."

Vandervahn Chistu, the younger of the Jade Falcon Khans, rose at his place. "I stand today before my brother and sister Khans in this Grand Council and accuse Ulric Kerensky of genocide."

"Then it begins." Ulric typed something into the computer console on his bench, then looked up. "The Martial Code, in the interest of brevity, allows for each side to field only one speaker. Who comes forward before this conclave as prosecutor?"

The other Jade Falcon Khan rose. "That honor is claimed by Elias Crichell, ilKhan."

Crichell's willingness to go after Ulric surprised Phelan. He had expected Lincoln Osis, the Smoke Jaguar Khan, to demand the right of prosecution. The Smoke Jaguars were just as vociferously Crusader as the Jade Falcons, and their Khan, Leo Showers, was originally the ilKhan leading the invasion of the Inner Sphere. The death of Leo Showers called for the selection of a new ilKhan and Ulric's successes during the invasion made him the logical choice as new Khan among Khans, the leader of all the Clans. For one of theirs to present the case against Ulric would have given the Smoke Jaguars a chance to regain some of their lost prestige, but the fact that matters did not so proceed meant that either a deal had been made or a shift in power had occurred somewhere.

As Phelan mulled over the situation, he began to see the larger picture. The Falcons had conquered more worlds than the Smoke Jaguars in the invasion, giving them a bit of an edge, a claim to moral superiority. The Jaguars had lost the battle for Luthien, the Draconis Combine's capital world, and their defeat had come at the hands of two mercenary units—a shameful fact that cost them even more respect. It was also significant that Lincoln Osis had been the one to raise the charge of treason against Ulric four years before, a bid he lost in the Grand Council vote after Phelan's defense of Ulric.

The younger Khan found it mildly disconcerting that he had not expected the challenge to come from the Jade Falcons, but he really should not have been surprised. As Ulric had noted, none of the Crusaders expected intra-Clan war to result from the verdict, so the ease with which the Wolves could strike at the Jade Falcons along their mutual border did not concern them. Phelan guessed that the Jade Falcons already had forces poised to strike at Terra the instant the truce was repudiated. To be prosecutor of a trial that deposed Ulric would give Elias Crichell an inside track to become the new ilKhan.

Elias Crichell rested one hand on top of the green enameled Jade Falcon helmet that sat on his bench. With the other he flipped his feathered cape back from his shoulders before beginning to speak. At sixty, he was quite old by Clan standards, yet he was so astute a political manipulator that he had maintained a steel grip on the reins of power within Clan Jade Falcon.

"ilKhan Ulric Kerensky, my brother and sister Khans both present and distant, the charge against Ulric is as grave as any ever raised against either an ilKhan or a Clan. And it is more than that because Ulric has not plotted to destroy the genetic heritage of *one* Clan, but of *all* our Clans. In his eccentric view of the universe, *we* Clans have apparently come to embody all that is evil. He has changed black for white, pushing us beyond the looking glass, so that everything we think we know is reversed, and every action he takes in accordance with our traditions is really meant to destroy those traditions."

Crichell's blue eyes sparked as he looked around the

chamber, then fixed his gaze on one of the cameras sending his soliloquy out to the remote Khans. "The truth of this charge cannot be doubted because the proof of it lies in our very existence. When the Truce of Tukayyid ends after fifteen years, everything we have learned in fighting the Inner Sphere will be forgotten. Not only will our troops lack that experience, but the Inner Sphere armies will have modified their tactics so that we have no way to counter them. There you have it—we will be without experienced commanders and they will lead inexperienced troops. The enormity of Ulric's crime is self-evident.

"You must ask yourselves, as I have, *why* would Ulric wish to destroy his own people? What in him has so changed? Why does he betray us? Were there signs we should have seen long ago?"

Crichell smoothed the bristle-brush gray hair at the back of his head, then continued. "The Wolves have ever been willing to revise the traditions begun by our founder, Nicholas Kerensky. They have claimed the right to do so because Nicholas was one of them, and we have long let them hide behind this claim. We might have been blind once, but none of us now doubts that what they call flexibility is really only another name for revisionism and revolution.

"With this predilection for change, Ulric fell under the spell of three individuals. Two have been elevated to stations well beyond their worth. Natasha Kerensky, *if* she is the same woman who left the Clans half a century ago, has been seduced by the Inner Sphere and wields undue influence over the Khan. With Phelan Ward, Ulric sold his soul in return for intelligence that allowed him to progress quickly in the invasion. Through Phelan, the Inner Sphere had one of its own anointed among us—one they knew they could control—and the truce was their reward."

The elder Jade Falcon Khan paused to let all see his withering look of disgust. "Ulric's third collaborator was the individual from whom he sought counsel during the invasion, and with whom he negotiated this truce. Precentor Martial Anastasius Focht was rewarded with a victory that has made him, in the eyes of the Inner Sphere, a warrior equal in stature to the legendary Aleksandr Kerensky. Were that obscenity not enough, Ulric kowtows to Focht, seeking his permission to move people into and out of the Inner Sphere.

For a Clansman to be reduced to such groveling is sheer blasphemy.

"These four, Ulric, Focht, Phelan, and Natasha, have entered into a secret alliance, the purpose of which is nothing short of forming a new Star League. Phelan is cousin to Victor Steiner-Davion, who will take the throne of First Lord if this plan succeeds. He will wed Omi Kurita, and their realms will unite. His warlord will be Kai Allard-Liao, the Butcher of Twycross, and their first move will be to engulf the Capellan Confederation and press Kai Allard-Liao's claim to rule that realm. Kai will marry Katrina Steiner-Davion. The Free Worlds League will fall after that, with Thomas Marik's daughter being forced to marry Peter Davion, brother to Victor."

Phelan shook his head, despairing at the utter lack of reason in Crichell's words. It was probably true that Victor Davion and Omi Kurita were in love, but they were not lovers nor did either one harbor the illusion that they might one day marry. Kai, according to a rumor traced back to Taman Malthus—a Jade Falcon—had found himself a wife, and it wasn't Katrina Steiner. The rest of Crichell's statement was pure fantasy, yet it seemed vaguely plausible and might even prove terrifying to the other Khans.

"What is the role Ulric sees for himself and the other Clans in this new order, this new Star League?" Crichell held up a single stubby finger. "He seeks to make himself the new Aleksandr Kerensky. He will subordinate us to this Victor Davion. We will be *used* to subdue the Capellan Confederation. We will be *used* to bring the Free Worlds League to heel. We will be *used* to hunt bandits and support corrupt rulers and to reinforce the evils of the Inner Sphere that drove our ancestors from it so long ago.

"None of us would ever willingly submit to becoming puppets of Victor Davion, but Ulric's truce will give us no choice. As we look forward ten years into the future, with the clock of the truce ticking away, he would begin to point out that we cannot win against the Inner Sphere. He would undermine us and promise us glory, but in a role more closely aligned with the aims of the Inner Sphere. He would argue for fusion with the Inner Sphere, and where could that lead but to our *absorption*!"

Phelan hissed as Crichell hit on the word "absorption." Of the original twenty Clans, one had been destroyed and two had been *absorbed*. Clan Widowmaker had been absorbed by the Wolves, and the red hourglass Natasha used as her personal crest spoke to Widowmaker blood running in her veins. Clan Mongoose had been absorbed by the Smoke Jaguars, but of them nothing remained, not a hint, not a symbol. The complete death of a Clan through absorption was the greatest fear of all Clan leaders, and Crichell had just used it to drive a stake through Ulric's heart.

Crichell nodded slowly. "We know what Ulric intends by reading his actions and understanding their true meaning. The only way to prevent our own destruction is to remove him from his office, to repudiate the truce, and to resume the sacred war he has prevented us from completing."

Ulric looked to Phelan. "Your response?"

Phelan nodded and stood at his place. *Not in a million years could I have anticipated defending Ulric against such an attack.* He set down the note cards he'd printed out, then shook his head. *We always knew I couldn't win, but Crichell may have done himself some harm. What I must do here is narrow the margin of his victory, and the paranoid fantasy he has presented might just allow me to do that.*

"I know not how to counter Kahn Elias' case, for his argument lacks cogency. I *am* compelled to *review* it, for that is what one does with fictions. The scenario he has constructed is not without some interesting points, but it lacks any grounding in reality. He assaults you with concepts with which he intends to inspire you with *fear*. Clearly, in doing this, he underestimates the minds and gifts of more *youthful* generations.

"I urge upon you caution as you evaluate his remarks. Khan Elias has played a very subtle trick upon you. He exhorts you to realize that you are in a mirror-world, a place where anything Ulric has done, he has, in fact, *not* done. Following this thinking then, we know that the Khan who has taken the most worlds has taken the *least*."

Phelan paused, letting the contradiction sink in. "In asking you to change how you view everything, Elias drives you away from what makes you the Khans that you are. He is destroying your command and control over your own minds. He is asking you to let him usurp your judgment. He wants you to trust him, this man, this Khan whose troops were slaughtered on Twycross by a *single* warrior from the Inner Sphere."

Phelan sharply rapped the desk with his knuckles. "Do not abandon reason. Use it. Look at his scenario. He offers no evidence to place Anastasius Focht, Khan Natasha, and me in a conspiracy with ilKhan Ulric. He has invented that by himself.

"He distorts evidence. He neglected to tell you that Victor Davion and I, despite being related, have despised each other for years. During the time Khan Crichell says I was conspiring with Victor to create a new Star League, Victor's father, Hanse Davion, ruled the Federated Commonwealth. Victor was so far out of power at that time that he had been sent on a suicide mission deep into the Smoke Jaguar Occupation Zone. Since I was here, among the Wolves, the conspirators obviously never had a chance to conspire.

"Except in Khan Crichell's fertile, febrile imagination."

Phelan opened his arms wide. "It is no secret that the Jade Falcons hate the Wolves. It is no secret that they are Crusaders and they hate the fact that a Warden has beaten *all* of the Crusader Clans in their efforts to conquer the Inner Sphere. Especially galling to the Jade Falcons is the fact that the Wolves accomplished their triumph with troops trained in the same way we train troops now. The Jade Falcons, quite rightly, do not trust the effectiveness of their own training methods. In fact, I would not doubt Khan Crichell fears the Inner Sphere is training cadres consisting of single warriors to slay whole Jade Falcon units in seconds. Were *I* a Jade Falcon, and had *I* such fears, I would seek refuge in a looking-glass world where defeat is victory and success is to be condemned as failure."

Phelan pointed to the ilKhan. "You all know Ulric has led us to victory against the Inner Sphere. You all know it was the hunger for personal glory that doomed the Clans on Tukayyid, not some phantom treachery by Ulric. That is reality and we all know it.

"With your votes, you can deny the truth and join Khan Crichell in a mirror-maze of paranoia and fantasy. Do that, destroy Ulric and you will destroy the Clans. Vote with Ulric and the reality of our future glory will be yours to share."

Phelan sat down and Natasha leaned over to him. "Good work, Phelan. You've given the video-Khans something to think about."

"No chance we can win?"

"You were good, Phelan, but no one could have been *that*

good." Natasha smiled. "I think you did reduce the odds against us rather substantially, though, and that may make all the difference in the long run."

Ulric called for a vote. Four of the invading Clans—Jade Falcon, Smoke Jaguars, Nova Cats, and Steel Vipers—voted solidly for a finding of guilty. The Ghost Bears and Wolves voted for innocence. The rest of the Clans split along Warden and Crusader lines, with some Khans canceling out their partners' vote. The net result was nineteen guilty votes and fifteen for innocence.

Ulric stood as the last vote was cast. "The motion carries. I am no longer ilKhan, but I inform you immediately that I demand a Trial of Refusal concerning this vote. The ratio of guilty to innocent votes is one point two-six to one. You have one month to decide who will face me and my forces to ratify this vote."

Khan Elias Crichell stood and let a big smile spread over his face. "Ulric, withdraw your challenge of the verdict. Let us resume the invasion we began eight years ago. Let us select a new ilKhan—I am certain he will allow your Wolves to join in the renewed invasion. Surely you can see there is no reason to fight among ourselves when there is so much more to fight for."

Ulric looked surprised. "Are you *afraid* to meet the Wolves, Elias?"

"No, of course not." Crichell smiled benignly. "I just want you to be reasonable."

"I am being quite reasonable." Ulric smiled too, but more like a wolf. "It is reasonable to expect you will bid among the other Clans to win the right to defend your victory, *quiaff*?"

"Aff, if there is no other way. I did not support this charge out of a vendetta against you or your Wolves."

"I had never assumed, Elias, that personal *hatred* was your motive." Ulric shook his head. "I, on the other hand, do harbor hatred against the Crusaders and even your Jade Falcons. I have brought matters to this point precisely so I *could* fight you and your Jade Falcons. You may have known you would win this vote here in the Grand Council, but *I* decided what you would win."

The ex-ilKhan let his laughter fill the room. "What you won was the Wolves and all the real combat your troops can handle."

Marik Palace, Atreus
Marik Commonwealth, Free Worlds League

Sun-Tzu Liao fought to keep his expression neutral. It had been five weeks since he'd given the order for his operatives on New Avalon to strike. It had never mattered to him that their chances of success were minimal. If they succeeded in getting a blood sample and doing a Patmat scan on it, Sun-Tzu would alter the results and present them to Thomas to show that a switch had been made. If they failed and died in the attempt, he would tell Thomas what he suspected and convince his future father-in-law to support him in his efforts against Victor.

It had been a no-lose proposition, but the waiting had eaten at him like a disease. When no word came at first, he'd feared his agents had been uncovered and his plot exposed. Then he'd suspected that the agents had decided the task was impossible and simply abandoned it. He found that humiliating and cursed his mother for not having maintained better intelligence assets in the Federated Commonwealth.

Then the summons had come from Thomas. The instant the Word of Blake Precentor showed Sun-Tzu into Thomas' office, the younger man saw from Thomas' expression that his operation had succeeded. He marveled that Victor Davion maintained so tight a control over his media that no word of the raid had leaked out, but Thomas obviously knew something. And from his worried look, it was not good.

"I thank you for coming so quickly, Sun-Tzu."

Sun-Tzu bowed to Thomas. "It is always a pleasure to be called to your presence, Captain-General."

"I could hope it were thus, Chancellor Liao, but I fear it will not be so." Thomas slumped back in his chair and sighed heavily. "I foresee difficulties ahead and I require of you a number of favors. I do not know if I have the right to ask them, but ask them I must."

Use of his title had surprised Sun-Tzu, but he recovered himself as Thomas went on. He definitely found the Captain-General distracted, which caught his attention like a field mouse running through the grass attracts a hawk's sharp eye. "I would be honored to be of any service to you, Captain-General."

Thomas nodded, but as though he only half-heard the reply. "You maintain and support a variety of subversive groups and revolutionary forces in the Sarna March, do you not?"

"I do. My Zhanzheng de guang are active on a number of Davion worlds. I also have ties to certain tongs and Liao loyalist groups."

"Good," Thomas said. "A situation has arisen that will require me to enter negotiations with Victor Davion. I would like to use your agents in his Sarna March to pressure him in a way that will incline him to speak in good faith with me. To do this, I wish to create the impression that we have had a difference of opinion on certain matters. You will leave immediately and return to your capital on Sian."

Sun-Tzu arched an eyebrow. "I know you do not intend this, Captain-General, but some might interpret what you have suggested so far—a feigned split and my forces stirring up trouble in the Sarna March—as an attempt to force me away so you can conspire with Victor Davion to split my realm. I do not think this of you, but there are those who might."

Thomas' mouth opened, then hung open for a second with no sound coming out. Finally Thomas closed his mouth and concentrated before deciding to speak again. "It could seem that way, I agree. What sign would you have of me to prove I do not intend to throw you to that rapacious wolf?"

"There is the matter of setting a date for my wedding to your daughter."

"Yes, Isis." The Captain-General nodded thoughtfully. "Six months from now we shall announce that the wedding will take place roughly another six months hence."

"That is acceptable, but covenants are easily broken. Not that I would accuse you of such a thing, but if there were a coup . . ."

"You are correct. Take Isis with you to Sian. You may hold her hostage as Victor has my . . ." Thomas' words trailed off and he covered his face with his hands.

There is something else going on here. Did my operation actually discover that Victor had *substituted a double for Joshua? Could Davion have been that stupid?* Sun-Tzu kept the elation off his face. "She would not be a hostage, Thomas, but cherished as my bride-to-be."

"Yes, I know you would keep her safe." Thomas sniffed, then looked up at Sun-Tzu. "I will cover your expenses for creating this added pressure, and my troops will stand by to repel Davion invaders if they decide to strike at you. I will also coordinate with the Capellan military to move troops around to make life more difficult for Davion intelligence."

"Very good." Sun-Tzu nodded. "When do I leave?"

"Within the week. Precentor Malcolm can help you send out orders to your subversives so their activities can begin before you arrive in Sian. You should be there by mid-September, I would think, but I need matters underway before then."

"It shall be done, Thomas." Sun-Tzu smiled proudly. "Together we will teach Victor lessons his father never learned."

17

> ...Self-preservation, the first law of states even more than of men; for no government is empowered to assent to that last sacrifice, which the individual may make for the noblest of motives.
>
> —ALFRED THAYER MAHAN,
> *THE INFLUENCE OF SEA POWER UPON HISTORY*

Zurich
Sarna March, Federated Commonwealth
18 August 3057

The way Cathy's look of utter surprise melted into one of total relief told Noble Thayer he had made the right decision to head out to the Rencide Medical Center in spite of the emergency situation. He set the box full of Chinese food cartons down on the counter and gave her a quick hug. "You look like you could use that, kid."

She threw her arms around his shoulders, but kept her body and the bloodied surgical gown she wore away from his white shirt and blue jacket. "When I had someone call and tell you I'd have to miss our date, I didn't expect to see you today."

Noble disengaged himself enough to give her a quick kiss. "It's tomorrow already, darling." He shrugged. "I had to come out. I knew you and the others would be hungry and the Mandrinn's Dragon doesn't delivery, so . . ."

"It was a zoo, but we came out of surgery ten minutes ago and everyone's in the lounge. Come on." She let him heft the box again, then led him from the Emergency Room lobby, past some bloody gurneys, and around a corner to the staff lounge. The scents of coffee and sweat competed with each other, but blood offered a pungent undercurrent for it all. Anne Thompson and Rick Bradford sat staring at the sugar container in the middle of the round table as if they could make its contents boil by willpower alone.

Noble slid the carton onto the table and into their lines of sight as if fearful it would combust. Both of them blinked, then looked up at him. It took a few seconds more before they recognized him, then both broke into smiles.

Rich peered in over the edge of the box. "Definitely what this doctor would have ordered if he'd been strong enough to punch a number into a phone."

Noble shrugged. "It was the least I could do. The news was full of reports about the Zhanzheng de guang attack on that New Syrtis branch bank. I gathered you got the serious cases while the superficial stuff went to Daosha Public."

Anne nodded as she helped Cathy pull smaller cartons from the box. "Daosha Public is really a clinic with limited in-patient space. Our trauma center is better than theirs, and we have the new magnetic-resonance imaging center. The only chance the bus driver had was our ability to pinpoint shrapnel with an MRI scan and pull it out."

Bradford sat back in his chair. "If Deirdre had been here, she could have saved him."

Noble walked over to the lounge kitchenette and pulled down a stack of plates. "The vid reports said the bus driver threw himself on the grenade the Zhanzheng de guang tossed into the midst of those school children. Catch a blast like that in the belly and I'd say you'd be lucky to survive evacuation to a hospital."

"You're right, but he *did* survive long enough to get here. He was a fighter and I really wanted to give him a chance." Rick shook his head and stared down at his hands. "Then again, he was so ripped up inside that he'd never have walked again and I'd have had to resect his bowels into a colostomy. And with the kidney damage, he'd have been on dialysis for the rest of his life."

"I can't understand how someone could do that." Cathy opened a steaming carton of lemon chicken, filling the room with its sharp, sweet scent.

Noble handed her a serving spoon. "He felt it was his duty to protect those children."

"No, I meant how could the Zhanzheng de guang people do that—toss a grenade into a crowd of children? They were only second-graders."

Anne snapped a pair of chopsticks apart and rubbed them together to remove the splinters. "They do those things because they're terrorists."

"They robbed the bank to get themselves some operating capital. It was also a statement, because attacking banks makes people feel less secure. That breeds anxiety and instability." Noble spooned a bit of General Tso's chicken onto his plate. "They want to expose the local government's inability to protect its citizenry. They expose the hollowness of the government's claims that they represent security and it bleeds over into other areas. Then they offer themselves as a logical alternative to the government."

Anne looked up at him. "But killing seven-year-old school children hardly makes them seem an appealing alternative."

"Well, they don't see it that way. The act only proves that children are not safe away from home. Families would pull their children from schools if they thought there was a risk of bombings or other attacks. This increases discontent. If the parents back the terrorists, their children won't be targets anymore."

Noble held his chopsticks poised over his plate. "I've done some reading about the Zhanzheng de guang and their leader, Xu Ning ..."

Rick Bradford looked up. "Research for your next Charlie Moore novel?"

Noble blushed. "Well, yes." He glanced over at Cathy.

She shrugged. "It's a good book. I was just drumming up business for you."

Anne wiped her mouth. "I'll buy it."

"Me, too." Rick pointed at Noble with his chopsticks. "But you were saying about Xu Ning?"

"Xu was a student of political science here on Zurich when the Federated Commonwealth took the world. He went on to become a professor of polisci, but became more and more disenchanted with the feudalistic government of the F-C. His writings, all of which were brilliant, became increasingly anti-Davion. About the time Hanse died, Xu was connected with a bombing on the campus of Zurich University up on Quayloon. He fled here, to the southern continent, and started up the Zhanzheng de guang with Capellan funding and Sun-Tzu's full support."

Cathy wiped her mouth. "So you're saying Xu Ning knows what he's doing?"

Noble shook his head. "He *thinks* he knows what he's doing. From one of the things he's written I gather his solution to our very stratified society is the abolition of all rank and class differences. And he wants it to be more than just a cosmetic change—he wants everyone equal. That means we'll all have to start from scratch and be educated in the proper ways of thinking."

"Do you mean re-education camps, like ComStar tried to establish on Clan-occupied worlds?"

"I don't know anything about that, Rick, but I wouldn't bet against it." Noble caught a piece of chicken up in a tight chopstick grip. "I don't even want to think about what Zurich would be like if Xu Ning's revolution succeeds."

Rick looked up, back toward the emergency room. "If it's more of this, I'll be too busy to care."

"Well, with any luck, it will never happen." Noble shook his head. "And, if it does, let's hope somebody out there decided to fight fire with fire."

Tharkad City, Tharkad
District of Donegal, Federated Commonwealth

Katrina used the holovid viewer's remote control to play Thomas Marik's message again. She did so automatically—the information delivered in the first playing had stunned her. So much so that she could barely believe what she'd heard and hoped, in viewing it again, that she would hear a different message in Thomas' words.

A weary Captain-General stared out at her from the monitor. "It is with the utmost respect that I have recorded this message to you, Duchess Katrina. Your kindness and personal message to me at the time of my wife's death touched me deeply. It also revealed to me how different you are from your father or brother, and so much more like your mother. For this I am thankful.

"It is difficult for me to communicate the following to you, but I must because without this information, you cannot properly judge this situation. I have incontrovertible proof that your brother has substituted a double for my son Joshua. As I have not been informed of the reason behind this exchange, it leads me to conclude that my son is, in fact, dead. This means your brother's action is a threat to my internal security because replacing Joshua with an imposter would allow your brother to one day place a Davion dupe on my throne in order to enslave my nation to his will."

Thomas' face tipped up, as if the man hoped gravity would keep the tears trapped in his eyes. When he looked again at the screen, a single tear did roll down his scarred cheek and toward his ragged ear. "I will be presenting my evidence to your brother and will demand from him political and planetary concessions in the form of reparations for what he has done. He must be punished for his inhuman activity—in this I believe you would agree. The nature of his punishment will depend upon his response to my inquiries, but punished he will be."

Katrina shivered at the adamance in Thomas' voice. *He is actually considering going to war with Victor over his son's death. He doesn't want to, but he can be pushed that far.*

"In formulating my demands upon your brother, it has come to my attention that I might end up asking him for the concession of worlds in which you have a proprietary interest. As I do not view myself in conflict with you and, indeed, see us as friendly neutrals, I do not want to cause you any hardship. I am aware that the Federated Commonwealth is an alliance governed from two worlds by two different people, but I remember the days before the union. You make it easy to imagine that it is your grandmother, Katrina Steiner, who is again guiding the Lyran Commonwealth. My father knew better than to provoke her anger, as I do not wish to provoke yours.

"That is why I am contacting you to ask which of the Sarna March worlds you consider part of your realm so that I do not include them in my demands on your brother."

Thomas looked down at his folded hands, then back up again, obviously choosing his words carefully. "Being born into my family, where brother set himself against brother, and son against father, I have come to especially value family loyalty. If you feel you must relay this message to your brother, I will understand. In many ways it might be best were you to do so, for it would absolve you of any wrongdoing.

"I have no desire to create a rift between you two, and I will not play you off, one against the other, but I do not consider you two of a kind. Your actions have shown you to be benevolent where your brother's are nothing short of cruel. So, though you may seek to present an united front against me, know I bear you no malice for the actions of one you cannot control.

"I bid you farewell, Katrina, and extend my fondest wishes for your health and prosperity."

Katrina killed the holovision monitor, then returned to her desk. Punching a few buttons on her computer, she brought up a holographic map of the Inner Sphere. She narrowed the focus to the border the Federated Commonwealth shared with the Free Worlds League and the Capellan Confederation.

With this overlay, the corridor of worlds connected the Lyran districts with the old Federated Suns narrowed considerably. Though the vastness of space and the ability of JumpShips to traverse thirty light years in the blink of an eye made frontiers meaningless, the laws of a nation-state did extend into the void. If Thomas convinced Victor to return to him worlds lost in 3030, the Free Worlds League would hold sway over some of the shipping lanes carrying commerce between the Steiner and Davion halves of the Federated Commonwealth. Ships could still get through easily enough by passing through the Terra system, but that would make some routes longer than necessary.

Still, nothing that cannot be overcome. She studied closely the worlds of the Sarna March—old Capellan Confederation worlds her father had conquered—and evaluated each of its worth. The few that had value in terms of industry or strong export economies, like Woodstock and Nanking, were too far from her borders for her to lay claim to them. Besides, Victor would contest her claim, and she did not want a direct confrontation with him.

Other worlds that had value for her were located up near Terra. In her role as ruler of the Sarna March, Melissa had often visited New Home and Keid, worlds whose people had revered her like a goddess. They'd transferred their devotion to Katrina upon Melissa's death, which was reason enough to keep them. Caph traded heavily with both planets, so it too had to be kept in the package.

Katrina knew that if she were to somehow wrest control of those worlds away from her brother, she would need military force to hang on to them. The planet Northwind stood between Victor and her trio of worlds. Home to the feared Northwind Highlanders, the planet had been hotly contested for years. Katrina knew that if she took it under her control, then released the various Highlander units from their assignments on other worlds so they could return home to see to their own affairs while Thomas and Victor sorted things out, she would win their loyalty. The Northwind Highlanders would be a sharp needle to jab at Victor if he tried to bring her into line.

Katrina also realized that these would be the first steps in pulling her half of the Federated Commonwealth out of the alliance formed when her father and mother had wed. That thought filled her with dread for a moment, then she saw with calm clarity that the breakup was inevitable. So inevitable that Katrina had long viewed her route to power as via the role of conciliator and peacemaker. By being the one to bring the realms back together after Victor had torn them apart, she would supplant him.

This new move would be a variation on that theme, but a risky one. Should Thomas and Victor negotiate a settlement, her brother could then use his military strength to bring her to heel. It was true that he had transferred most Davion loyalist troops out of her Lyran districts, but he still commanded enough forces within it to make her life difficult. Such armed tactics might also set off the Skye separatists again, and she would face the dilemma of trying to put them down if her realm were to survive.

Victor's weak point, she well knew, came in terms of JumpShips. When their father had invaded the Capellan Confederation in 3028, more than eighty percent of the Federated Suns' JumpShips had been dragooned into service for the invasion. That had wreaked havoc upon interstellar commerce, but it had also made the invasion possible. If Katrina were to issue orders diverting ships away from her brother's portion of space, he would be harder pressed to move against her militarily. Once denied to Victor, those same JumpShip assets would let her move troops to counter his advances.

Katrina knew full well that Victor's military strategems were not the only ones she must consider. Thomas' message made that abundantly clear. If she chose to ally herself with Victor, her Lyran districts were at risk. Thomas could decide to reignite the Skye Rebellion by supplying the separatists with capital and equipment, and use the Skye March as a big cork to keep Victor from getting troops to Katrina to repel a Free Worlds League invasion. If she remained neutral toward Thomas, and he went to war with Victor, that struggle would occupy all of Victor's attention, freeing her to continue weaving her own designs.

What Katrina wanted, ultimately, was whatever was best for her people. She knew it would have surprised Thomas if he knew her true thoughts on Victor's use of a double. It horrified her, of course, but not because it was cruel to hide Joshua's death from his father. The use of the double disgusted her because Victor had committee such a gross blunder where no blundering had been necessary. Had he simply announced Joshua's death, Thomas might sooner or later have initiated the attempt to regain the former League worlds, but his demands would have been far less than they were likely to be now, and the results far less dire.

Such lack of judgment made her wary of her brother and his ability to guide the Federated Commonwealth into the future. Most disturbing was that Katrina would not have expected Victor to make this kind of mistake. It was out of character for him, but if he could err that gravely, close association with him was a troubling prospect.

"Perhaps I've given you too much credit, brother, but no more." Sitting at her desk, Katrina began composing the script for her reply to Thomas. "Win Thomas over if you can, Victor, and I will still appear to be your friend. Fail, and you will stand alone in facing his wrath."

Marik Palace, Atreus
Marik Commonwealth, Free Worlds League

Thomas looked up when Precentor Malcolm entered his office. "You have something for me?"

"Word has come back from Tharkad that Duchess Katrina Steiner has received your message." The Word of Blake official opened his hands to show they were empty. "We have no word yet of her response, but neither have we heard that she has forwarded your message to her brother."

"*That* is something, then." Thomas thought for a moment, then nodded in satisfaction. "The longer she takes to reply, the better for our case. Sun-Tzu is still two weeks away from Sian?"

"Yes. He is expected to arrive on the seventh of September."

"You have the coding and message he earlier sent to his agents still available?"

"Yes, Captain-General." Malcolm smiled easily. "We have even identified the agents' back-up vector for receiving orders. By using it we should allay suspicions if there are any irregularities in the message."

"You have outdone yourself, Malcolm. Send the message to New Avalon, routing it through Sian. If the agents take action on or about the fifteenth, I would be pleased."

"Consider it done, Captain-General."

"No, Precentor," Thomas said. "With that act, I consider it *begun*."

18

No plan survives contact with the enemy.

—HELMUTH VON MOLTKE

Avalon City, New Avalon
Crucis March, Federated Commonwealth
14 September 3057

Had it not been for the training by her grandparents, Francesca would never have noticed the men. Four hours into he shift in the pediatric cancer ward, she was busy keying in the charts of those children who needed medication during the night. With visiting hours just ended, it was her first chance to get behind the desk without having to attend to anxious parents and relatives needing various kinds of assistance.

Studying the trio of older men, at first she thought they were confused or lost. The general cancer ward had an extra two hours of visiting time in the evening and these were not the first people to mistakenly get off on the sixth floor instead of the seventh. The fact that all were dressed up in suits and carrying flowers made her to want to help them.

The little group smiled at her as she came out from around the desk, and she reflexively returned their smiles. Politely averting her eyes to avoid staring, she glanced down at the floor. Something in the back of her awareness told her something was amiss, but she couldn't place it immediately. It was only when her white shoes squeaked on the floor tiles barely a dozen paces away from them that she realized what was wrong.

Their shoes! The three men all wore nicely cut suits that were a bit out of date, but on their feet were brand new, soft leather shoes with rubber soles. The footwear would have been perfectly appropriate had the men been dressed less formally. With suits, the shoes were incongruous. Instantly her mind flashed to a memory of her grandmother talking about how such noiseless shoes were perfect for covert operations.

Francesca didn't really think the three men before her were agents, but their furtive, darting glances and their whispered conversation as she approached kept her on edge. Despite looking far too old for covert ops, the three men seemed alert and less nervous than most disoriented visitors. Aside from the shoes, they looked the part they were supposed to be playing. They just didn't *feel* right.

"May I be of assistance, gentlemen?" Francesca forced her voice to be friendly and polite. "You were looking for the cancer ward, yes?"

One of them, the beefy man nearest her, nodded. "Yes, but it looks like we've stumbled into the wrong one. Isn't this where the news showed Joshua Marik being treated?"

Involuntarily Francesca glanced down the corridor toward Joshua's room. The instant she did so, and saw the beefy man register her eye-motion, she realized how easily they'd duped her into giving them the clue they needed to find Joshua. She had betrayed the boy despite wanting to protect him. Yet even as she came to that alarming conclusion, Francesca also realized that the man's question was a natural one for anyone who'd followed the story of Joshua and Missy Cooper over the last year.

Careful, Francesca, *try not to overreact.* "Yes, it is. I believe you gentlemen must be wanting to visit someone one more floor up. Let me call you an elevator." As she moved behind the beefy man to get to the wall panel, Francesca let her left hand brush across his body. Under his left armpit she felt the compact hardness of a gun.

Time slowed for her. The instant she felt the gun, she knew these three men had to be agents—assassins—sent to kill Joshua. Liao agents, sent by Sun-Tzu Liao to eliminate Thomas' legitimate heir. Her innocent glance toward Joshua's room had doomed the boy, and she had to act to save him. Joshua was *her* responsibility.

Reaching up and over the beefy man's shoulders, she grasped the lapels of his blazer and pulled back. She stripped the coat halfway down so it trapped his arms, then reached out and tugged the Mauser & Grey P-17 needle pistol from the man's shoulder holster. Sweeping her right leg around, she toppled the beefy man onto his back, then snapped the pistol's safety down with her left thumb.

"Stop! Don't move!" she commanded the other two. "Guards!"

The other two men reacted instantly. The nearer one turned, and as he tossed his bouquet of flowers at her, Francesca pulled the trigger. The cloud of plastic flechettes mulched the flying bouquet, reducing it to botanical confetti, and hit the man in the shoulder. Her second burst struck him in the center of his chest, shredding his shirt and tie.

Her first target slowly spun and fell as the next man dropped the flowering plant he had been carrying. He cut to the right as he reached for his pistol, so her first shot only tugged at the hem of his jacket. Francesca tracked him to the left and, fighting the pistol's recoil, started snapping shots off in double-tap pairs.

Her second and third shots also went wide. One exploded the holovision viewer in the waiting lobby while the next reduced the floor map *on* the wall to a crater *in* the wall. Her target had no more luck, his first shot sending a bullet clanging into the elevator doors.

Instinctively Francesca moved to her right while continuing to track left. That saved her life because her target overcorrected, his bullet blowing by on her left. Fighting his own momentum, the agent tried to aim at her, but even as he had her staring down the barrel of his gun, Francesca shot back and kept her aim on target.

Her first shot opened the man's belly. The cloud of flechettes ground through his midsection, perforating his bowels, stomach, and kidneys, as well as shredding major blood vessels and severing nerves. The second shot caught him in the face. The ballistic-plastic rain stripped the flesh from his bones more efficiently than a sandstorm. Falling back, the agent looked to Francesca less like man than a personification of death, and she took that as a dire omen.

The first bullet took her in the left hip and began to spin her in that direction. As she came around, she saw that the man on the floor had freed his right arm from the coat and filled that hand with a snub-nosed revolver. *Must have been at the small of his back.* She triggered a shot at him at the same moment he fired at her.

His second shot punched her right below the breastbone and sent her flying backward. Francesca never saw what her shot had done to him, but as she slammed into one of the waiting room couches, flipping it over, she saw Joshua's guards running down the corridor with their guns at the ready. She knew they would get the last man.

She also knew Joshua would be safe, and her joy in that knowledge held off the pain for as long as it took for her world to dissolve into peaceful oblivion.

Tamar
Wolf Clan Occupation Zone

Phelan Ward nodded to Khan Elias Crichell. "Please follow me, Khan Elias. I will take you to the holotank." Intent on irritating the Jade Falcon Khan, Phelan made no attempt to keep his contempt for the man from his voice. In return he got a satisfactory tightening of the man's blue eyes and considered it a battle won in what would surely be a long war.

Phelan led Crichell through the maze of offices shared by the Wolf Clan's Alpha and Beta Galaxies. The offices themselves were ominously quiet. Coffee cups sat steaming on desks and the water level in water coolers still undulated, as if ghosts had been drawing it down. The whole complex felt like a place that had been abandoned in haste, as if a fire alarm had gone off, but the eerie silence canceled the chances of that explanation.

From the corner of his eye Phelan could see that Crichell was feeling uneasy. The Jade Falcon Khan had visited the Clan Wolf command center before and knew well the place where they had erected their holotank. He also knew they were not heading toward it. They were, in fact, heading away from it, toward the back of the building and the vast 'Mech hangars there. Phelan had no doubt Crichell was wondering if he was being led into an ambush that would take his life.

When they finally reached the red fire-door leading to the hangar, Phelan opened it and waved Crichell through. The building's air cooling system surrendered to the humid, sweltering air of the hangar, but Crichell was sweating even before he stepped through the door. Phelan followed closely, bumping Crichell forward with his body, then pulling the door hard shut behind him.

"After you, my Khan."

Crichell stared forward at the smoked lucite panels of the holotank, which had been arranged in a large oval on the hangar's ferrocrete floor. Little lights around the holotank's rim showed it to be operational, but nothing of the interior could be seen from where they stood. A gap between panels at one end provided a point of ingress but, as obvious as it was, Crichell did not move toward it.

No physical barrier barred Crichell from crossing the short space to the holotank, but Phelan knew it would take a tremendous act of will for the man to take even one step in that direction. Lining the path, both on the flat and up on the various levels of catwalks, and standing throughout the hangar on anything that gave them a vantage point, were members of Clan Wolf all staring soundless hatred at Crichell. They watched him with the disgust and resignation professional warriors reserve for someone who rushes head-long into a war that need not take place. Foremost among them, Natasha Kerensky stood by the entrance to the holotank and defied Crichell to approach.

Phelan remained behind Crichell until he saw sweat bead up on the back of the man's neck, then he nodded once. In conjunction with the signal, all the Wolves—save Natasha—turned away from the Jade Falcon. They did not speak, but the sounds of warriors preparing to fight filled what a moment before had been a soundless void. Stepping out from behind Crichell, Phelan waved him forward.

After a moment's hesitation, the Jade Falcon began to walk toward the holotank. His pace slackened slightly as he drew abreast of Natasha. "Theatrics? The old Natasha Kerensky would never have stooped so low."

Fury blazed in Natasha's eyes, but she somehow refrained from exploding. "The only reason you are alive, Elias, is because the old Natasha Kerensky was marauding through the Inner Sphere before you were ever allowed inside a 'Mech. Had I remained with the Wolves, even a freebirth wouldn't have wanted to acknowledge carrying your blood."

She turned away from him and stalked into the holotank. Crichell stiffened, a retort frozen on his lips. Phelan again waved Crichell forward, then followed him, taking up a place beside Natasha just inside the doorway of the holotank.

Crichell stared at the man standing in the center of the holotank, then turned to Natasha. "What is this? A Khan only negotiates with his equals."

The Black Widow smiled cruelly. "Then you are fortunate Ulric has deigned to descend to your level. He speaks for me and for the Wolves."

Ulric gave Crichell no chance for further protest. "I have reviewed the data you sent concerning the world where you wish to fight this Trial of Refusal. As defender of the Grand Council's vote, you have the right to choose the place you will defend. Computer, display the Jade Falcon data."

At Ulric's command, the dim holotank interior filled with color, the computer using lasers to project both the Clan Wolf and Jade Falcon occupation zones into a three-dimensional display. Brightly colored spheres filled the tank. Reaching up to a world located near his heart, Ulric touched it and transformed it into a data window through which scrolled troop data. "I concur that Colmar should be the first battleground."

"Good." Crichell nodded, then stiffened. "Excuse me, did you say the *first* battleground?"

"I did."

"But the combat on Colmar will decide matters."

Ulric slowly shook his head. "You and I both know it will not. Were you to win on Colmar—though I assure you that you will not—the Jade Falcons would immediately break the truce and begin a drive toward Terra."

"We would do no such thing. That is a decision for the ilKhan to make."

Ulric squatted down and touched a golden world near the floor. "I have noticed that here, on Quarell, you have stockpiled incredible amounts of munitions—enough for a Galaxy-size force to wage a campaign through what is left of the Free Rasalhague Republic. That would put your troops sixty light years closer to Terra than any other Clan. Another hundred and fifty light years of space would still be left to cross, but having crushed ComStar's troops in Rasalhague, the way would be open to you."

The leader of the Wolves straightened up again, giving Quarell a kick to close the data window. "You have your Peregrine Galaxy down there, *quiaff?*"

"You are no longer ilKhan, Ulric. I am not obliged to answer your questions about my troop dispositions." Crichell tugged at his tunic to straighten it, but sweat had already begun to darken the green garment beneath the Khan's armpits. He turned to glare at Natasha. "We will stop you at Colmar, then a new ilKhan will be elected."

"Which you expect to be you."

"That may be."

Ulric folded his arms across his chest. "Then I will challenge the election, and you will have to defend again."

Crichell frowned heavily. "Have I misjudged you Wolves?"

"If you thought us interested in power, yes." Ulric smiled coldly. "I am ten years your junior, Elias Crichell, and that means I am two generations your superior in breeding—apart from the fact that the Crichell bloodline is innately inferior to the Kerensky bloodline. I am a warrior, not a politician. But I think you have forgotten how a warrior thinks, Elias, and in doing so, you have most certainly misjudged me. In doing so, you have misjudged us Wolves, one and all."

Crichell hunched his shoulders, then looked up. "What do you want? What must I concede to you, for I see where you are going with this. If I win on Colmar and am elected ilKhan, you challenge me again and again we will fight. If I win a second time and announce the resumption of the invasion of the Inner Sphere, you challenge me once more. And again and again, on every world, at every turn. What do you want?"

"What do I want?" Ulric's eyes grew distant for a moment. "I want an end to any efforts to resume the invasion."

"Impossible."

"Then I want the truce respected and maintained."

"Not possible."

"Ah, but it is." Ulric reached out and touched four worlds in the Jade Falcon occupation zone. "I am going to hit you on Colmar, Dompaire, Sudaten, and Zoetermeer. After I have beaten you there, I will push up and through your occupation zone. To defend your position, you will have to defeat me throughout your zone."

"And I will attack back into your zone."

"Go ahead. What use will our worlds be to you when I have destroyed your Galaxies?"

"You are telling me you will turn this contest into a Trial of Absorption!"

"No, it is a Trial of Refusal—a refusal to let you destroy the Clans. If the Wolves must perish to save the rest, so be it."

Crichell's face began to turn red. "This is madness, Ulric. It is suicidal."

"Just as suicidal as resuming the invasion."

"You are wrong."

"No, Elias, you are blind." Ulric pointed toward Phelan and Natasha. "These are the two best commanders the Wolves have, and both have come to us from the Inner Sphere. Why are they the best? Because, in addition to being formidable warriors, they are flexible and sensible. They plan for victory, and consider the consequences of defeat. For them warfare is about more than winning enough glory to breed; it is about the way of the Clans and how we will pass that way of life down to future generations.

"When Nicholas Kerensky founded the Clans, he envisioned the creation of the greatest warriors the human race had ever known. He accomplished that, and the soul of our being as Clansmen is the drive to perfect ourselves and our equipment beyond that of all others. Improving our ability to wage war has become, perversely, our reason for being.

"The advantage Nicholas Kerensky had over all of us is one Natasha and Phelan share. They know that the purpose of life is to *live*, not to make war. They cherish life and are willing to fight for it and die for it. That is the reason for their superiority as warriors. And it is also the reason ComStar's army was able to defeat us at Tukayyid and impose this truce upon us. And it is the same reason I am willing to use all my troops and all my resources against you."

"You cannot win."

"Nor can you."

Natasha stepped forward. "Phelan, please escort Khan Elias from this place. He has not bargained well, but the bidding is done. We choose to bid everything Clan Wolf has to stop him, and the Jade Falcons must bid just as high if they hope to survive."

19

I am more afraid of our mistakes than our enemies' designs.

—PERICLES

Avalon City, New Avalon
Crucis March, Federated Commonwealth
14 September 3057

Stepping from the elevator, Victor looked past the sheet-shrouded lump on the floor at the feet of Curaitis. "What happened?"

Curaitis stepped past the forensic holovideographers, moving far more easily across the bloodslicked floor than anyone should have been able, as far as the Prince was concerned. He waved Victor around the corpse on the floor and past two others, then stopped in the small waiting lounge. "You should not be here, Highness."

"I *had* to be here, Curaitis. Someone has tried to kill Joshua Marik." Victor took off his cap and almost used it to brush holovid monitor fragments from a chair. "May I? Has it been holographed yet?"

"Don't. The area is not secure yet." Curaitis' icy blue eyes sparked with anger. "You should leave."

"I'll leave after you tell me what happened." Victor stared defiantly up at his security chief. "And don't omit any details."

"As you wish, my Prince." Curaitis clasped his hands together at the small of his back. "At approximately seven-ten PM, three individuals entered the elevator lobby area through elevator number two. Shortly after their arrival, a volunteer, Francesca Jenkins, approached them. We do not know what was said, but she must have realized they were no ordinary visitors. Apparently she got a Mauser & Grey needle pistol away from one of them and killed the other two. The man whose gun she took had another pistol. He fired two shots that knocked her into this overturned couch here.

"Ms. Jenkins had called for help when she took the gun from the first man and that brought Joshua's guards running. They saw her get shot by the man down by the elevators there. They killed him."

"No one got near Joshua?"

"He slept through the whole thing."

Victor glanced past Curaitis at the overturned couch. "What happened to the woman?"

"She's undergoing emergency surgery right now. One bullet pulverized part of her left hip. The other one nicked her heart and punctured both lungs. Had the assassin been using a needle pistol, she'd be dead. As it is, her chances of survival are very small."

The Prince exhaled audibly. "Spare no expense for her, Curaitis. Whatever she needs, let the NAIS give it to her. She probably saved Joshua's life."

"The staff is aware of that, Highness." Curaitis pointed off toward the location of Joshua's suite. "The two guards who killed the last man have been pulled out for debriefing, but they wouldn't go until they'd donated blood for her."

"An excellent idea, I'll do the same. She's a hero and we'll make certain everyone knows it."

Irritation shot through Curaitis' voice. "Your office would be a better place to take care of such information-management problems."

The man's tone stung Victor, but he reined his anger back. *He's right. I'm thinking about the chance for good press when this attack represents a major security breach. If Joshua had been killed—murdered—there would be hell to pay.* He looked up at Curaitis. "Any identification on the men?"

"Nothing solid. They carried no IDs, no labels in their clothes, though the shoes are sold fairly exclusively in uniform shops and places catering to ex-military or police types. Specialty surplus shops mostly. We might get lucky there. Edgars was here earlier—he worked in Regional Ops for New Avalon before coming over to Internal Investigations. He thought he remembered the fat one on the floor from the Justin Allard murder investigation." Curaitis frowned. "Edgars is good, so I take his comments seriously, but it's too soon to know."

"If that man was connected to Justin Allard's murder, then he was an agent of the Capellan Confederation." The full import of that realization made Victor slump back against the wall. "Is Sun-Tzu stupid enough to try to kill Joshua? Something that would anger both me and Thomas? With his realm wedged between us, that is hardly a wise move."

"So it would seem, Highness."

Why would Sun-Tzu do it? What could he gain? The most he could have hoped was that the return of Joshua's body to the Free Worlds League might lead to discovery of a double. But Sun-Tzu would have needed to know about the double in advance to come up with this plan, and he couldn't have known about the switch.

Victor's jaw dropped open. *My father got the idea of substituting a double for Joshua because Sun-Tzu's grandfather once plotted to replace my father with a double, and almost succeeded in putting his own puppet on the throne of the old Federated Suns. If Sun-Tzu guessed at the possibility of a substitute, or even intended to manufacture evidence to prove to Thomas that I'd put a double in his son's place . . . Thomas's gratitude to Sun-Tzu would have firmly cemented their relationship.*

"Curaitis, check the bodies for syringes or scalpels or anything they could have used to take tissue or blood samples."

The dark-haired security man paused for the briefest second, then nodded. "Another wrinkle."

Victor almost laughed out loud. *Another wrinkle!* He hadn't had a full night's sleep since the day they'd actually begun Project Gemini. Victor also suddenly realized he didn't even know the name of the boy who was risking and enduring so much for reasons he couldn't possibly understand. The whole operation could blow wide open if the scandal vids got wind of any of it. And now, with Sun-Tzu running operations against Joshua, the pressure over the situation was building to a point where Victor could only expect the worst.

This cannot continue. We need time to let this story die down, then we'll let Joshua die and return his body to

Thomas. If it costs me worlds, then it costs worlds, but this stops now.

The Prince tapped Curaitis on the shoulder. "I think I know what happened here."

"Yes, Highness?"

"I think you will find these three were tied, covertly, to a fledgling Zhanzheng de guang cell here on New Avalon. Like their Zhanzheng de guang comrades on Zurich, these desperate men did not balk at carrying out attacks against children. Before they could act, a hospital volunteer bravely and selflessly opposed them to save Joshua and the other children on the ward, then our guards gunned them down."

Curaitis nodded slowly. "Your ability to read a crime scene is impressive, Highness. It probably also tells you that we are not certain whether these three acted alone or in concert with other confederates in the area. Caution would dictate that you leave immediately."

"Good point, Curaitis. The Zhanzheng de guang are known for their tenacity." Victor tugged his cap on and headed for the elevator. "As soon as I give blood, I'll be home again safe and sound."

20

Wars are caused either by women or priests.

—CZECH PROVERB

Marik Palace, Atreus
Marik Commonwealth, Free Worlds League
16 September 3057

Thomas Marik, Captain-General of the Free Worlds League, ignored the teleprompter and looked directly into the lens of the holovid camera. He wanted to project himself through the camera to all of his people. Intellectually he knew the limitations of the medium, but he wanted this holovid to be more than just the message. The people might not understand why he was doing what he must, but he wanted them to know that he *did* understand why it was vital to go to war with the Federated Commonwealth.

"Fellow citizens, were there another course open to me, I would never have led you into a war in which we are the aggressor. There is nobility in defending one's homeworld against invasion, but naked aggression is without honor and boasts no defense.

"Our aggression is not naked, however, but is clothed in righteousness. Perhaps it would more rightly be called an aggressive defense of our future. Our way of life, our traditions, have been threatened by a crime so foul, so hideous, so shameful that I would deny you knowledge of it, had I a choice. Because of the nature of my response to this crime, I must reveal it to you, in all its sordid detail, and those facts will be made public within the next twenty-four hours. Until then, a briefer explanation must suffice."

Thomas consciously hesitated, reinforcing the impression

of his reluctance to share with them the information he possessed. He softened his expression, then swallowed hard and only allowed his sorrow to show in the tightness at the corners of his eyes.

"I have evidence, incontrovertible evidence, that the Joshua Marik under care in the Federated Commonwealth is not my son. He is, in fact, a minion of Victor Davion. Davion's purpose in substituting this other child for my son is obvious: he wishes to put his puppet in the Captain-General's place at the helm of this nation.

"The evidence was obtained at great risk by a noble agent of the Free Worlds League. It consists of a blood sample from the imposter, which was then compared to my blood sample in a DNA match. The procedure was simple enough to perform that my agent used a science kit to do it. It is simple enough that, using blood supplies at hand in the New Avalon Institute of science, Victor Davion himself could duplicate the results. The simple results of this simple test tell me simply that the Joshua Marik on New Avalon is not my son."

Again Thomas stopped, but this time the pause was not planned. He bit back the pain of his loss, then pushed on. "I am forced to assume that my son is dead. Given the nature of his illness, such an outcome was not unexpected. What was unexpected was Victor Davion's cold and cruel and calculated attempt to take advantage of my loss, *our* loss, to further his own political ends. Unable to govern the realm his butchered mother left to him, he dabbles in the internal politics of his neighbors, desperately hoping to absorb them into his faltering empire."

Thomas' face became a steely mask of controlled anger. "At best Victor Davion is a kidnapper, an extortionist, and an abuser of children. At worst he is the most diabolical leader in the Inner Sphere since Stefan Amaris destroyed the Star League. I find it inconceivable that any person would be content to live under the dominion of such a monster, but that is not a judgment I can make.

"What I can do, and what I have done, is decide that no one who wishes to be liberated from the Davion yoke need endure his oppression any longer. Toward this end I have begun the re-occupation of former Free Worlds League planets taken by the Federated Commonwealth a quarter of a century ago. In addition, I will support self-determination movements in the similarly occupied Capellan systems of the Sarna March. With my Knights of the Inner Sphere, I will back those who wish to determine for themselves who will rule them and what their future will be."

Thomas took a deep breath. "I know this means war, and war means hardship, privation, and death. As Sophocles said, 'War prefers its victims young.' Before the first shot was fired, this war cost me my youngest child, so I already know the pain and fear you, my people, will face as this campaign unfolds. I would never ask of you what I would not be willing to do myself, and I know you join me in the depth of my commitment to freeing people and planets from Davion subjugation.

"This is not a war of conquest to capture worlds or industries. It is a war of ideals and a collision of philosophies that cannot abide one another. To Victor Davion, everyone exists to feed his nation's hunger for power. For us, the people are the only source of power and we hold their future in trust. It is for that future that we fight."

"It is for that future we *must* fight." Thomas Marik nodded solemnly to his people. "And it is in the name of that future that we *will* triumph."

21

It is the fashion these days to make war, and presumably it will last a while yet.

—FREDERICK THE GREAT IN A LETTER TO VOLTAIRE

Charleston, Woodstock
Sarna March, Federated Commonwealth
16 September 3057

Having already packed his clothes and other personal effects, Larry Acuff sat back in his Bachelor Officers Quarters' suite and flicked the holovideo monitor on. He left his bags sitting next to the door and dropped himself onto the couch. Phoebe Derden-Pinkey said she'd call before leaving her office to drive him over to a farewell dinner with his parents. Two days later he'd be back aboard the *Starbride*, heading back to Solaris.

Using the remote control, Larry switched up to the 'MechWar Network broadcast through Recital City Cable. He'd be back on the Game World just before Christmas, with plenty of time to enter the Grand Tournament that would decide the new Champion in January. With Kai opting out, Larry knew there would be a major scramble for the top spot. He wasn't sure how well he'd do, but he figured a low teens, high single-digit finish was not out of his reach. *And if a few other warriors eliminate one another, I could sail into the finals.*

Larry instantly recognized the two fighters going at it on the screen. Liz O'Bannon in her *Marauder II* stalked after Adam Wiley's *BattleMaster* through the jungles of the Liao arena. He'd fought Wiley back in his Class Three days and could see old Adam was getting the worst of the fight, despite being in the Jungle—a venue Wiley preferred. The li tle color bars on the edges of the images showed that both 'Mechs were running hot, but even more significant was that Wiley was running *away*.

Suddenly the image dissolved into boiling static, then slowly faded into the image of an amateurish stage set. Larry hit a button, but the next channel and the next showed the same image. On the screen were two men in dark green paramilitary fatigues seated behind a folding table. Over their faces were red bandannas and perched on their heads were red berets. A hand-lettered banner behind them read "Woodstock Eco-Liberation Force Alliance to Restore Equality."

"This has got to be a bad joke." Larry leaned forward and punched the remote button a few more times. The channel number changed, but the image remained the same. "What the hell is going on?"

He heard a hoarsely whispered, "Go, action, start!", then the man on the left lifted a trembling sheaf of papers and began to read.

"People of Woodstock, we have taken control of the satellite broadcasting facilities to inform you of our intent to liberate you from the destructive, chemo-terrorist regime led by Victor Davion. With his criminal complicity, the interstellar corporations who control the agro-combines here on Woodstock have poisoned our water and soil for the express purpose of raping our world. They exploit Woodstock's fecundity, reaping profits from what we sow and selling it to people on other worlds ..."

The visiphone bleated at him, and Larry reached over to answer without looking away from the holovideo. "Acuff here."

"Larry, are you watching the holovid?"

"Yes, Phoebe, I am. What is this?"

"I don't know, but it's coming over all the radios, too."

He looked over at the visiphone and saw that Phoebe was obviously worried. "You mean this isn't a joke?"

"I wish it was." She held up a blue sheet of paper with a red stripe running across the corner. "This just came in through ComStar. We're all on alert now. Leaves are canceled and you're back in the AFFC."

Larry's jaw dropped open. "What the hell's going on?"

"I don't know, but it appears we're at war with the Free Worlds League."

"Oh, my god." Larry glanced back at holovideo. "Then who are these clowns?"

"I don't know that either, but this call-up is for real." Phoebe shook her head. "Whoever these Eco-Liberation people are, a Free Worlds League JumpShip has just shown up in system, and the first message they broadcast says they're here to support WELFARE's war of liberation against tyrannical Davion rule."

Avalon City, New Avalon
Crucis March, Federated Commonwealth

Victor Davion sat in reverent silence as he stared at the holographic display of the Inner Sphere. The computer always showed the Federated Commonwealth as a broad swath of gold that narrowed somewhat near Terra, but now numerous worlds in the central area were flashing purple and green, indicating incursions by Free Worlds League and Capellan Confederation troops. Yet other worlds had the intensity of their golden color muted, indicating various levels of civil unrest, from demonstrations to outright rebellion.

Above the map, Thomas Marik's scarred visage hung trapped in a box two and a half centimeters square. His mouth moved, but Victor heard nothing. He'd killed the sound during his second viewing of the message that had been broadcast throughout the Free Worlds League. His own intelligence network had gotten him a copy of it before the Marik ambassador could deliver one, but that was the only good news he'd had that day.

"Well played, Thomas. Very well played." Victor looked through the holo map at Jerrard Cranston and Curaitis. "What is the soonest landfall of his troops, Jerry?"

Galen looked down at his computer console. "The League brought their troops in at pirate jump points at Callison, Denebola, Marcus, Talitha, Van Diemen IV, and Wasat. They'll achieve planetfall in two to four days on each of those worlds. We estimate they're hitting each target world with at least three regiments. Every other place they're hitting they're coming in a bit lighter and will take a week to ten days to land."

Victor nodded slowly. "And the Liao attacks?"

"Pirate points and five regiments going into the planet Liao in two days; everything else is a week or more."

"Five regiments, and all I have is a virgin militia unit protecting that world."

Galen shook his head. "Liao is well away from Capellan worlds. We no more anticipated Thomas letting Sun-Tzu ferry troops up to Zion to attack Liao than we anticipated the attack."

"How could we have missed it? These must have been signs." Victor wished for an instant that the display before him was glass, not glowing light, so he could smash it to bits. His hands tightened into fists, but he controlled his rage and forced his hands open. "We were aware of his troops building up on the borders, weren't we?"

Galen nodded emphatically. "We were, but the build-ups were carried out as if they were normal Marik redeployment exercises. It's standard procedure for the league to bring troops from the interior to the border, then rotate the border troops back to the interior. We were able to obtain the normal redeployment intelligence we always get when they do this. For all we know, the troops themselves thought they were heading back to the interior before they jumped out into our systems."

The Prince slid his chair back from the black lucite table in his briefing room and stood. "I can see how that happened, but we're obviously working too much off assumptions, and not enough off known facts. We assumed, for example, that even if Thomas did learn of Joshua's death he, being a man of peace and reason, would bargain for worlds, not take them."

"Agreed, that was a lousy assumption." Galen shrugged. "It was based on what we know about him. He has ever been a conciliator. Even the formation of his Knights of the Inner Sphere was seen as a philosophical event, not a military one.'

"Is this philosophy, too?"

"I don't know, Highness. I'm not certain what we know."

Victor almost shouted back at Galen, but stopped himself again. *He's only been my security advisor for four months. This is not his failure. It's mine and the system's.* "Let's concentrate on what we do know." Victor turned and looked at Curaitis. "Thomas says he has a blood sample from our Joshua that proves they are not father and son. Possible?"

Curaitis nodded. "It is possible he could have obtained blood from Joshua. It would have had to be someone in the hospital, and most likely someone working on that ward."

"You checked everyone, correct?"

"We did a basic security check on everyone, yes." Curaitis frowned. "It's possible that the person who obtained the sample did not realize how it would be used. They might have sold it as a souvenir."

"Blood?"

"A bandage, a syringe. Something that was used on Joshua would go for good money in the collector market."

Victor didn't try to hide his surprise. "People collect things like that?"

Galen nodded slowly. "The oxygen mask used when paramedics tried to revive your father recently sold for ten thousand Kroner."

"Thomas also says we could perform the same blood tests and get the same result with stored blood. Is that true?"

"It is."

"Do it."

Galen frowned. "Highness?"

Victor stared back at him. "Do it. I want to know what Thomas knew when he made his decision."

"Highness, you'll forgive me if I point out that this is a small detail compared to an attack on your nation." Galen's eyes narrowed. "DNA identification is not really a key issue here."

Victor looked from Galen to Curaitis and back again. "This is not the same as when I thought I could unlock the identity of my mother's assassin all by myself. I'm going to have to make a broadcast similar to Marik's to explain to my people why we're at war. I need to understand how this sort of thing is done so I can explain it, if necessary. I will have to reveal that Joshua is dead and that we did put a substitute in his place. I have to tell them why I did it. I've got to be sincere and convincing and so forthcoming that I won't fragment my people. Thomas has painted me as a monster and I have to show a nation why I'm not—because their sons and daughters are going to be dying to defend me and my honor."

Curaitis folded his arms.

Victor looked at him. "Do you have a comment?"

"I think you're looking at disclosing something that need

not be disclosed. If you admit what we have done, you will validate Thomas' justification for the invasion. Deny everything. Brazen it out. That is exactly what your father would have done."

Victor hesitated for a second. *He's right, my father would have called Thomas a liar, and he would have gotten away with it, too. In admitting we used a double for Joshua, am I showing weakness? Or am I countering a strong move on Thomas' part with a stronger one of my own, by coming clean? As a warrior, I would counterattack, but as a politician I still don't know the rules and angles that well.*

Looking up, he found both Galen and Curaitis waiting for his answer. "Were I my father, I would do what you suggest, Curaitis, but I am not Hanse Davion. Some of my people already think I've lied to them about my mother's death, and I *have* lied to them about Ryan Steiner's death. I think I gain more by telling the truth now."

Galen nodded. "It seems a workable strategy to me."

Curaitis looked unconvinced, but made no further comment.

Victor pointed to him. "I want to know who was the person that supplied the blood sample to Thomas' agent. I want that agent and I want his organization. Period. *And* I want all of Sun-Tzu's people swept up. He's got rebellions brewing on over a dozen worlds out there, and I don't want any bombings or unrest to break out here."

"We've already begun the latter operation and the former is being organized now."

"Good. I want Joshua's double put into hiding *now,* and I want extra security on the Jenkins woman. She's a hero—someone who was willing to lay down her life for Joshua Marik. If we play up her role in stopping Sun-Tzu's terrorists, we'll focus some outrage away from me and back onto the enemy."

Galen pointed back to the map. "Highness, though I've been the loudest voice saying that you need to think more politically, I really think right now it's Victor the warrior who's needed."

"I know." Victor sat back down in his chair and scooted it up to the table. The worlds that had been taken from the League at the end of the Fourth Succession War were doomed. Thomas was hitting them hard with troops, and the Federated Commonwealth had insufficient garrisons there to repel the invasions. Most of Victor's best troops were on the lines in Clan areas or over in the Achernar Command area near Tikonov for war games.

Games designed to convince Sun-Tzu to reduce his activity in the Sarna March. "It's rather ironic that the reason we didn't garrison the worlds Thomas is hitting hardest is because we had Joshua and knew Marik would never strike at us while we did. Now he will take them and win a big victory over us—albeit a temporary one."

"I think the irony will be lost on the troops on the ground, Highness."

"No doubt about that." The Prince rubbed a hand over his jaw. "Sarna March troops are going to have to hold their own worlds and remain at their stations in case Thomas has another wave on the way. We'll have to bring reinforcements in from the border with the Draconis Combine. I'll need time/arrival reports for all the units we have in the area."

"I'll have those for you as soon as possible."

"Thanks." Victor's blue eyes narrowed as he looked at the map. "The big question is this: how much of what he's going after does Thomas want to keep? Under the guise of supporting independence movements, he has employed mercenaries to extend his reach beyond worlds he once owned. That means we'll have to fight on our own worlds before we ever fight on his. Is it a buffer zone he wants, or does he actually hope to hold the captured worlds?"

"Of the worlds in the Sarna March that he has attacked, only Nanking has 'Mech production facilities." Galen glanced down at his display. "Neither Styk nor Sarna have been attacked, and Tikonov is garrisoned so solidly right now that his whole invasion force could be swallowed up there."

"Nanking is going to be one of our primary objectives when we bring our reinforcements in. I'm not going to lose it." The Prince frowned. "Zurich and Hsien have big JumpShip recharging stations, don't they?"

"Yes, Highness."

"And recharging there will give his JumpShips significantly greater range. He might indeed have another wave coming." Victor nodded appreciatively. "Well planned and well executed, and most of it learned from my father's invasion of the Capellan Confederation thirty years ago. Impressive actions for someone who isn't really a warrior."

Galen frowned as he studied the map. "Thomas appears to have made damnably few mistakes."

"You see mistakes? Name one."

"Why hit Woodstock?"

"Troops have to eat, Galen, either his or ours. And if not for that reason, well, one more world falling to him means one more we have to take. No, Woodstock is not a mistake." Victor raised an eyebrow. "However, there is one *big* mistake he did make, and that will win us the war."

"And that is?"

"Thomas is fighting against us as if we're only the Federated Suns." Victor pointed to the long border between the Lyran districts and the Free Worlds League. "He decided to fight on our territory, but when I have his troops tied up in the Sarna March, I'll show him that two can play at that game. He'll learn plenty about waging war from a Davion, but it's a lesson he'll never have a chance to use."

22

A little rebellion now and then is a good thing, and as necessary in the political world as storms in the physical.
—THOMAS JEFFERSON, WORKS, VOL. VI

Tharkad City, Tharkad
District of Donegal, Lyran Alliance
18 September 3057

Katrina Steiner narrowed her eyes as the bright lights in the media center went on. She made her way to the podium and paused behind it as the hubbub in the room died slowly. A couple of scandal-vid reporters shouted questions at her, but their brethren in the legitimate press quieted them with stern glances.

"I have a brief statement to make, and I will not be taking questions afterward. By tomorrow morning you will have full information disks filling in the details of what I will allude to in my statement. At some future point I will address you again, as needed, depending on events."

She glanced down at the small monitor built into the podium. The blue screen showed the text of her statement in white letters. It would scroll along as she spoke, but Katrina would not need it. She had practiced her statement enough to deliver it from memory, and she intended to do just that.

She inched her right hand up and touched a button that shifted the monitor picture from her speech to an image of her standing there at the podium. Had she not wanted to maintain the weary, subdued look on her face, she would have smiled. The silk of her gown was Steiner blue, but the cut of the dress in no way suggested militarism. Her golden hair had been brushed out and draped around her shoulders as if she'd had insufficient time to prepare for an appearance in public. Her makeup was equally understated.

Good, the image is right for the message. "My fellow citizens, I speak to you now about a situation that is most grave because it involves the security of our realm. As you know, the Free Worlds League has, in conjunction with the Capellan Confederation, launched an offensive against the Sarna March of the Federated Commonwealth. This assault appears intended to retake worlds lost by the League nearly thirty years ago and to liberate worlds taken from the Capellan Confederation in the same conflict.

"Many of you will remember that conflict. Our people made gallant sacrifices in that war against Maximilian Liao. Much blood was shed and many lost their lives."

She paused for a moment as if unable to go on, then swallowed and continued. "Thomas Marik says he launched this attack because my brother, Victor Davion, killed his son Joshua and installed a double in his place. Thomas says my brother's intent was to put his own puppet Joshua on the Marik throne, and thereby gain control of the Free Worlds League.

"As you all know, I have tirelessly championed my brother against accusations that he murdered my mother and my father. Nor have I ever believed, as some suggest, that he had Galen Cox slain. Neither do I believe he had Duke Ryan Steiner executed. I have refused to believe such charges because the Victor Davion I know could never have done these things."

Spreading her hands to the edges of the podium to brace herself, Katrina let sorrow wash over her face. Taking a deep breath, she looked out at the dumbstruck reporters and thought, for the briefest of moments, how they reminded her of rabbits transfixed by the headlights of an oncoming hovercar.

"The evidence Thomas Marik has supplied to back his claim has me wondering if I ever knew Victor at all. If he could do this, if he would willfully kill a child and substitute another child for him, Victor could do anything. My brother has not answered these charges, in public or in private to me, so I do not know his side of the question. I suppose it is possible that he does have an explanation, and that it might mitigate in some small way the gravity of these charges. I do not know, and I wait to hear from my brother.

"For the good of you, my people, however, I cannot afford to wait passively for Victor to account for his actions. He has broken faith with you, and I will not have you suffer while I cling to the faint hope that my brother can justify himself. To guarantee that the Lyran people do not suffer, I have given the following orders:

"First, I have decided to declare our Lyran districts in a state of crisis. This gives me greater powers under the regency, which include the right to sever the connection between Lyran agencies and their Federated Commonwealth counterparts. We will function in the interim as an independent political unit, which I have designated the Lyran Alliance. Lyran, because we have a long history that traces back to the Steiners' origins on Terra itself. Alliance, because that is what I feel we are. The term Commonwealth has a taint to it now. I want all my people—from Northwind to Poulsbo, Loric to Barcelona—united and allied together, for we must work hard to safeguard ourselves in these dangerous times.

"Second, any Lyran military unit serving in the Sarna March or elsewhere in the Federated Commonwealth is invited and urged to return here to the Alliance. As long as Lyran forces offer no resistance to Free World League troops, they will be considered noncombatants and allowed to withdraw.

"Finally, any and all Lyran expatriates who wish to return to their homes are encouraged to do so. This is not a time for our families to be split apart. We need to stand together, for only unity and spirit will enable we Lyrans to endure the hardships we will face as a nation."

Letting her head droop a bit, Katrina stole another glance at her image and was pleased. She looked harried and exhausted, but still vital and strong. It was a fine line to run, but she ran it as if it were a kilometer wide. *Now the sprint to the finish.*

"My brother, the warrior, has taken his half of the Federated Commonwealth into war. I will not bleed my people to defend his actions. It is my sacred duty to ward you welfare—the same duty my mother honored before she was so cruelly cut down. I hereby lay claim to her mantle, though aware of the dangers inherent in doing so. Anything less would be to deny my heritage as a Steiner and my responsibility as your Archon."

Daosha, Zurich
Zurich People's Republic, Capellan Confederation

Noble Thayer knew that his uneasiness came from being unable to exercise control over his life. Things were moving too quickly on Zurich—not too quickly for him to understand, but too quickly for him to find comfortable. Within two hours of Thomas Marik's announcement, Xu Ning and his Zhanzheng de guang had declared open war on the government. The government had responded by declaring martial law, as was to be expected.

What no one on Zurich, save the revolutionaries, had expected was the extent to which the local militia and constabulary had been won over to the Zhanzheng de guang position. Five out of six militia and police units had turned on the government, and, within twelve hours, the revolution was over. Xu Ning ruled Zurich as the Chairman of the People's Liberation Party.

That the revolution took place so smoothly and without opposition frightened Noble, but did not surprise him. Only a generation ago Zurich had been part of the Capellan Confederation, and been a pet project of then Chancellor Maximilian Liao. When the world was lost to Davion in the Fourth Succession War, the population barely noticed the change in ownership. The fighting had not been fierce, resulting in almost no collateral damage, and because Hanse Davion used Tormano Liao as a conduit for funneling aid to the world, the people simply shifted their allegiance from one Liao to another.

And now, with the revolution, the world had become the Zurich People's Republic and the population shifted loyalty again to a third Liao. Xu Ning had already begun erecting huge portraits of himself and Sun-Tzu in public places. The militia had become the People's Army and the constabulary had traded their white uniforms for olive drab, calling themselves the People's Committee for State Security. A whole host of social and cultural programs had been announced, for the express purpose of getting the people back in touch with Capellan history and traditions.

As he reached the doorway to his apartment house, Noble shifted his sack of groceries from his right arm to his left so he could punch in the lobby security code. With food prices already beginning to shoot through the roof, he'd loaded up on rice, sugar, flour, and salt as well as simple medical supplies. Anything more potent he could get from Cathy.

He took the first six stairs almost oblivious to his surroundings. Then, with the seventh step he noticed light pouring into the stairwell, and knew it could only be coming from one source: his apartment. Chances were that it was only Ken Fox getting around to fixing the sanitation float. And, though he'd not yet given Cathy a key to his place, Fox would have let her in if she'd asked.

At the top of the stairs he did stop and looked with surprise at the two Security Committee officers sitting in his living room. "Excuse me, this is my apartment," he said, coming through the open door. "Is there something I can do for you?" He closed the door behind him. "Is there a problem?"

The lieutenant, a small, dark-haired woman with a hatchet face, wore her hair pulled back so tightly into a bun that Noble half expected her flesh to split down her nose. She stood up, tugging her belted tunic into starched order. "You are Noble Thayer, yes?"

He nodded and set his net bag on the floor. Keeping his hands in plain view, he looked from the woman to the silent giant standing to his right. "I'm Noble Thayer. Is something wrong?"

"Should there be something wrong?"

"No, ma'am, not at all." Noble tried to smile, hoping she would soften as a result. "I don't want any trouble."

"Have you done anything for which you should be in trouble?"

His smile had been utterly lost on her, so he abandoned it. "No, ma'am. How may I be of service to you?"

The woman withdrew a noteputer from the side pocket of her trousers. "This apartment belonged to Doctor Deirdre Lear. Did you know her?"

"No, ma'am."

"But you sublet the apartment from her."

Noble read in her brown eyes that she did not believe him. "I didn't know her. I arrived on Zurich after she left. My landlord, Mr. Fox, let me sublet through her lease so he wouldn't have to redecorate or something. He said it would also avoid paperwork."

Neither the lieutenant nor her companion seemed inclined toward mercy. "You had possession of her things, yes?"

"No, the apartment was empty when I moved in." Noble pointed to the futon and the other furnishings. "I'm not much of a decorator, but I've been working at it. I have receipts."

"I'm certain you do, Citizen Thayer. You had access to Dr. Lear's possessions before they were shipped off Zurich, yes?"

"No, well, yes, but it was only because I helped move them to the spaceport."

The woman's eyes narrowed and Noble sensed a trap. "So everything here is yours? Nothing belongs to Doctor Lear?"

"To the best of my knowledge, yes, everything here is mine."

"Then perhaps you can explain this." The lieutenant led him back toward the small bedroom he'd made into his computer room. She stepped to the center of the hardwood floor and her aide took up a position beside the door. Spread out on the canvas army cot he'd been using as a table for computer manuals, Noble saw two packets of Kroner bound with K5,000 bands, a moneybelt from which two gold K10 coins had slipped, and an M&G P30 flechette pistol with four extra blocks of ballistic polymer. "Are these yours?"

"That's a fortune in Kroner." Noble stared incredulously at the woman. "Where did you find this?"

"In the floor, under the loose floorboard."

"A hideaway?" Noble dropped to his knees and started to feel about like a blind man. The aide tapped a board with his toe. Noble slipped his fingernails into the crack and pried it up. "I'll be damned!"

The lieutenant drew her head back and crossed her arms over her chest. "You're saying you know nothing of this?"

Noble lifted the long section of board away with his right hand, then stared down at the hole. He opened his mouth as if to speak, then stabbed upward with his left hand, smashing his fist into the giant's groin. A second later, without rising from his knees, he backhanded the board edge against the lieutenant's right knee. Legs buckling, she started to go down.

Reaching back beneath his jacket with his left hand, Noble pulled out the slender dagger he'd clipped to his belt at the small of his back. The blackened blade slid from the sheath as effortlessly as its six inches penetrated the wilting giant's chest just below his breastbone. Noble angled the cutup, then cocked his wrist to guarantee a fan-shaped wound that would get heart and both lungs.

Looking back at the woman, he cracked the board down on her right hand as she clawed for her pistol. She screamed, but a blow to the head with the board stunned her enough to reduce the wail to a whimper. Another blow shattered her other wrist. "The money, the weapons," she gasped. "You're a Davion agent."

"Could be." Noble stood as he picked up the needle pistol. "but then, if I told you, I'd have to kill you." He pulled the slide back and charged the pistol. "But what the hell, I'll kill you anyway."

He fired two shots into her chest, then shot the giant once as well. Satisfied that they were dead, he stripped them of their weapons and tossed the guns on the bed along with the money. He also took their identification papers and her noteputer. After wiping his knife clean on the giant's uniform, he returned it to the sheath on his belt.

Noble debated for a moment whether or not he should try to move the bodies to the storage room in the basement, but the chances of getting caught grossly outweighed any benefits from hiding the corpses. Given that flechette pistols make little noise when fired, and that he'd shot them in the interior room of his apartment in the early afternoon, the chances that anyone had heard the gunshots were low, and of being reported even less. Though the Xu regime was only a day and a half old, Zurich's citizens had already learned to mind their own business and avoid attracting attention.

Noble stripped out of his bloody clothes and washed the blood from his hands in the bathroom. Knowing he could never return to this apartment, he dressed warmly and even pulled on the parka he'd bought for the winter from Fox's son-in-law. From his closet he took a rucksack and packed it with the security officer's pistols, his spare polymer blocks, and a heavy sweater. In the kitchen he would add to that some tins of stew and chili and a bottle of water. In the side pouches he put all the optical data disks from his computer.

He fastened the money belt containing the gold Kroners around his waist and tucked his shirt in over it. He broke the K10,000 into packets and distributed them in various pockets and the tops of his all-weather boots. After pulling on his parka and picking up his grocery sack, Noble Thayer took one last look around his apartment.

Blood had flowed out into the hallway. He shook his head. "Sorry to leave you with such a mess, Ken, but that's what a cleaning deposit is for." Locking the door behind him, Noble Thayer left his home for good and let the streets of Zurich swallow him up.

23

> To delight in war is a merit in a soldier, a dangerous quality in
> the captain, and a positive crime in the statesman.
>
> —GEORGE SANTAYANA, *THE LIFE OF REASON*

Avalon City, New Avalon
Crucis March, Federated Commonwealth
19 September 3057

Victor Davion, First Prince of the Federated Commonwealth, sat behind the huge desk his father had always used when addressing the nation. He had no prepared text, only notes, and these he had transcribed onto index cards. He laid them out at the top of the blotter and folded his hands so he would not fiddle with them while speaking.

Despite protests from Galen and warnings about an anti-Lyran backlash from his pollsters, he had chosen to dress in the blue and gold uniform of the Tenth Lyran Guards. The Tenths was his unit, and Victor knew that after all they had been through in service with him, they would remain loyal. He would never wish to dishonor them by shifting to the uniform of a unit more closely associated with the Davions.

He also knew that even if Katherine had decided to split away from the Federated Commonwealth, he could never relinquish his claim to that territory. It would be simple to use her action—*betrayal,* as others had termed it—to bolster support for himself, but he didn't want to see the situation polarized any more than it already was. Victor wanted to focus his people on the problems of greatest immediacy without doing anything that would make his long-term goals more difficult.

The lights went on and the director pointed at him.

"My fellow citizens," Victor began, looking straight into

the camera, "we are at war. It is not the Clans who have broken the truce, but old enemies who have decided to exploit our fight against the Clans to their own gain. While neither of those two nations possess fighting forces as brave or tenacious as the Clans, they are even more dangerous foes. This is, quite simply, because their leaders are not warriors, they are statesmen.

"Statesmen do not understand war. They see war as a legitimate arm of national policy. To them it is a tool, like a law or a treaty. They do not realize that war is a great bloody business that destroys people and worlds, families and lives. They only know that war can gain them worlds and build coalitions to oppose an external threat. In this our old enemies see value, so they have started their war."

Victor made no attempt to keep the anger and outrage from his words or his eyes, but neither did he allow himself to rant. He needed to infect his people with his anger, but also show them that he was in command of the situation. His other concern was not to stir them so deeply that their emotions would run rampant. That could rekindle factional fights within the Federated Commonwealth and create further divisions.

"Thomas Marik has accused me of substituting another boy for his dead son. He confirmed this fact by having a spy steal a blood sample from Joshua, then test it and determine that Thomas and Joshua were not father and son. Were I the sort of monster Thomas paints me to be, I would deny the validity of this test, and produce other proof that Thomas was either mistaken or misled by an agent.

"I am not a monster, even though this charge is true. I come before you today to offer an explanation for *why* a double was put in Joshua's place. At the time Joshua came here for treatment at the NAIS, the antidotes being prescribed by his father's own physicians were killing the boy. I remember meeting him on Outreach, where all the leaders of the Great Houses had come to consult and plan our response to the Clans. Despite his illness, Joshua was a happy boy, and a surprisingly quick one as well. To have met him was to like him—and no one I know ever pitied him, because he was not the sort of child to be pitied.

"My father, Hanse Davion, knew that the NAIS was Joshua's only hope of survival, and he was ready and willing to make treatment here available to the boy. Though Thomas

Marik participated in the Outreach meetings on how to oppose the Clans, he was at that time reluctant to contribute to the defense of the Inner Sphere. Though my father and Theodore Kurita's grand plan for stopping the invasion included gifting the Free Worlds League with the fruit of years of research to bring his forces up to par with ours in the blink of an eye, he balked. And yet, Thomas knew that only his realm, untouched as it was by the Clans, could supply our troops with the equipment needed to defeat the Clans.

"As would any statesman, he saw an advantage in this, and he pressed it. He demanded territorial concessions. He demanded material concessions. He demanded payment, all before he would give us the things we needed. The Federated Commonwealth and the Draconis Combine had their backs to the wall. They needed that materiel, and the League was their only supplier."

Victor paused for a moment. He'd built to a dramatic climax, and wanted to give his listeners time to fully absorb what he'd said. Satisfied that he had done so, he lowered his voice. "My father offered Thomas something he would have given him under any circumstances: the life of his son. Hanse Davion offered to take Joshua to the NAIS, where the finest physicians in the Inner Sphere would try to cure him. We all knew Joshua's chances of survival were slim—as slim as those of any line unit facing the Clans—but Thomas had to give his son that opportunity. In doing so, he enabled many others to live, to return home to our loved ones, to stop the Clans, so that we would still have homes to which we could return.

"My father knew Joshua's life hung by a thread. He knew his prognosis was poor, so he found a child who resembled Joshua and groomed him to be Joshua's replacement. Without Joshua at the NAIS, there was no way to guarantee the supply of weapons we needed to stop the Clans.

"Of course, this was all before Tukayyid and the signing of the truce. Had I known of the double program, or had my mother been informed of it, it would have been stopped right then. I did not learn of it until after my mother's death, at which time I had a rebellion in Skye and Sun-Tzu Liao's agents terrorizing the Sarna March to occupy me. It was about that time that Joshua took a turn for the worse, and I chose to use the double to buy time. I wanted to calm Skye and cool down Liaoist activity in Sarna before having to deal with Joshua's death."

Victor frowned. "Those were my intentions. Joshua's body was preserved and has been treated with the utmost of respect. He also gave our researchers a chance to get another step closer to curing leukemia. Because of Joshua, countless children will live."

His voice became cold. "And because of his father, the statesman, countless children will die. Had Thomas thought more about his realm than himself, he would not have dishonored his son's memory by launching attacks into our territory. Though no material gains could replace his son, the fact is that I would have agreed to negotiating a settlement with him because of Joshua's death. Even though our people at the NAIS did their best to save his son's life and even though we all knew Joshua would have been dead four or five years ago had he not been brought here to New Avalon."

Victor glanced down for a second, then lifted his head again with a look of serious concern. "Many of you will wonder that your leader could hide the fact of a boy's death from his father. I can only tell you that I did so to prevent exactly the sort of slaughter that will take place when Thomas' troops land. And I would do it again had I to relive those decisions because I still believe they were the best choices facing me under those circumstances.

"We have no need to feel shame about the kind of people our society produces. The Federated Commonwealth is a nation that creates heroes. Lying in the NAIS Medical Center right now is a woman, a volunteer at the hospital, who is just such a hero. She worked in the ward where Joshua was being treated. Five days ago, when a terrorist group in the employ of Sun-Tzu Liao—a group akin to the one that threw a grenade into a group of school children on Zurich—came to the hospital to kill and maim, she intervened. Bravely, selflessly, she stopped them and was shot multiple times. Her assailants died and she was the only casualty because she acted in defense of the children in her care—including the youth she believed to be Joshua Marik."

Victor nodded toward the cameras. "Her name is Francesca Jenkins and I hope you will all remember her in your prayers."

Again he hesitated briefly, but brought his head up and let

the solemn concern drain from his voice, leaving only a bleak firmness in its place. "Many of you have heard it reported that my sister Katherine has withdrawn what she now calls the Lyran Alliance from the Federated Commonwealth. You fear this means civil war, but it does not. Katherine is doing what she believes she must to preserve her half of the Commonwealth. Unlike Thomas and his minion Sun-Tzu, Katherine realizes that war should be a last resort, and she wished to keep her realm out of this conflict. Unlike Thomas and Sun-Tzu, she also realizes she must be ready to hold the Clans at bay, and if making a deal with the lesser of two evils will enable her to cope with the larger, I cannot, in good conscience, oppose her.

"Thomas, as a statesman trained in governing and mystical philosophy by ComStar, does not understand war. If he did, he would order his DropShips back to the Free Worlds League. He would cease supporting illegal revolutions in the Sarna March. He would stop supplying Sun-Tzu with equipment and materiel for his invasion. He would get out while he can."

Victor drew in a deep breath and slowly shook his head. "I understand war. I have had my 'Mech destroyed under me. I have watched brave men and women die around me. I have lost friends in battle and even in the aftermath of battle. Worst of all, I lost years fighting in the field, far from my family, not seeing them, not speaking with them, and to return only to greet my father's death.

"At this point, it is not within my power to say we will not fight. As we saw with the Clans, we cannot surrender to or compromise with aggression. We cannot reward aggression with acquiescence. Like a child who must learn for himself that fire burns, Thomas has reached his hand into the fire of war, and it is our duty to teach him the dangers so he will never again be so eager or willing to write his bold philosophy in the blood of innocent people."

Victor continued to gaze straight at the holovideo camera. "I will mourn those we lose in this fight as I mourned my parents and even Joshua Marik. I will mourn them as I mourn all who lose their lives to the rapacious ambition of a man who should look beyond himself and his concerns to those of his people. And I will fight such a man in the hopes that someday, someday soon, ambition's thirst will no longer be slaked with blood."

=== 24 ===

The art of war is simple enough. Find out where your enemy is. Get at him as soon as you can. Strike at him as hard as you can, and keep moving on.

—ULYSSES S. GRANT

Colmar
Jade Falcon Occupation Zone
24 September 3057

Phelan Ward stood beside Natasha Kerensky in the battle bridge of the DropShip *White Fang*. Within the lucite walls of the holotank was projected a ten-to-one scale representation of the battle being waged in Colmar's Marakaa Valley lowlands. The BattleMechs of the 352nd Wolf Assault Cluster sat in the center of the smoke-filled valley using the dry river that snaked its way through the terrain as cover. The Twelfth Falcon Regular Cluster, despite enjoying an advantage in numbers of BattleMechs and the amount of fighter cover they had available to them, had paid dearly for having come up and over the ridgeline from the south.

Even so, they'd done serious damage to the Wolf Clan forces. Phelan, his arms crossed over his chest, shook his head as a Falcon *Turk* wheeled wing over wing through the holotank. Its tail assembly disintegrating, the aerospace fighter arced toward the ground, then exploded upon impact. "If the Silver Wolves' pilots were not having so hot a day in the air, things could have been much nastier for our side."

"Star Colonel Oriega got what he deserved." Natasha said. Her voice seethed with angry delight. "I offered him the honor of battling against my own Thirteenth Wolf Guards, but he opted to fight the 352nd."

Phelan smiled at the older woman. "I'd have made that choice. The 352nd was rebuilt after Tukayyid and has a lot of young Wolf Supremists in its ranks. Even Star Colonel Serena Fetladral is relatively inexperienced."

"Yes, Phelan, you would have made the same choice, but not out of cowardice or refusal to fight someone of my age. Imagine him calling the Thirteenth Guards a solahma unit."

"Your Wolf Spiders *are* more seasoned than most other line unit members."

Natasha's blue eyes glittered devilishly. "Is that pique over the fact that you're too young to be one of us?"

"I wasn't too young on Tukayyid, Khan Natasha." Phelan held his hands up to forestall further discussion about his age or the unit. "You did make the right call on the Falcons here, though. By having the 352nd go through the Marakaa, you've brought them in at the Falcons' position at Bright Basin from the south. That *is* their weakest side in that place."

Natasha nodded. "Oriega knows as well as you and I that a defender in a covered position takes a lot of killing. As opponents of the Grand Council verdict, we had to bid *under* what he was using to defend, which made it difficult to force him from his position. He made me underbid him on Elementals and on aerospace fighters, though he did allow me an edge in BattleMechs. When I sent Serena and her troops through the Marakaa Valley, it gave Oriega a chance to come over the hills and hit them in the flank while they were traveling in a column."

The younger Khan had applauded the strategy when Natasha first suggested it. The steep walls of the valley made it difficult for the Jade Falcon aerospace fighters to make strafing runs that didn't bring them straight in at the 'Mech column. While fighters could be devastating to BattleMechs, the 352nd used cover and spread their formations while firing back at the fighters. They only tagged one or two, but the fighters decided it was a more hostile environment than they wanted to play in, and they withdrew to engage the Wolf fighters.

The Falcon BattleMechs, now without air cover, came in anyway. They had the high ground, but the ridge was too far away for them to engage the Wolves down in the valley. Oriega started his troops heading down in a line, but the steep slope forced the 'Mechs to pack together as they descended. While some did use their jump jets to get down quickly and in good order, the ridge mostly served to split the force and let the Wolves pick them apart. And, unfortunately for the Falcons, a slope that is difficult to descend is often even tougher to ascend.

Phelan winced as the holographic display sent parts of an exploding Falcon *Daishi* flying at his face. "The Falcons are down to a Star and a half of 'Mechs."

"Those eight will die shortly. Their fighter have abandoned them and their Elementals have run. It was not unexpected."

"You lost half your fighters and half your Elementals." Phelan moved around in the tank so that he stood like the Colossus of Rhodes, with one foot on either side of the dry riverbed. "From here it looks like you'll come out of this with about four Stars of 'Mechs."

"That may be, but I've lost only five of my Mech-Warriors. That's one Star's worth out of a dozen Stars in the Cluster." Natasha nodded confidently. "Most of these fighters were pups who had never seen real combat. This, Phelan, is how we sharpen the teeth of or pups. I can repair 'Mechs and have them ready to go again, but turning a green kid into a veteran warrior is not so easy."

Two Wolf 'Mechs, a squat *Adder* and a notorious *Timber Wolf,* combined to savage a Falcon *Gladiator.* Red laser darts from the pulse lasers in the *Timber Wolf*'s left breast stormed over the humanoid *Gladiator*'s right arm. Ferro-fibrous armor bubbled off as greasy vapor, exposing the twisted myomer fibers and ferrotitanium bones making up the limb. The artificial myomer muscles contracted, swinging the quartet of lasers mounted in that arm toward the *Timber Wolf.*

The *Adder*'s twin particle projection cannons each sent an azure bolt of lightning in at the *Gladiator.* One blue beam of accelerated particles scourged smoking armor from the *Gladiator*'s torso while the second bit into the naked arm. It sliced myomers apart, leaving the ends whipping back and forth or twitching. The beam's energy filled the ferrotitanium bones with enough energy to change it from a dull silver to an incandescent white before the metal vaporized, cleanly amputating the *Gladiator*'s arm.

Natasha stabbed a finger at the *Gladiator* as if her intervention in the holotank could somehow finish it off. "There, Phelan, that's a lesson *our* people have learned, but the Jade Falcons have not. The Falcons still cherish the idea of individual combat. That might have been fine in the day of the samurai of ancient Japan, but it has no place on the battle-fields of the thirty-first century."

Phelan shook his head. "It had no place on the battlefield of ancient Japan, either. Though the typhoon known as the Divine Wind destroyed most of the Mongol invasion fleet, some of Kubla Khan's troops did land. When they faced sa-murai, one lone samurai would ride out and announce his lineage, then challenge a Mongol to combat. The whole *company* of Mongols would feather him with arrows—killing the samurai on the spot. The samurai had won a moral victory, but he was still dead."

The elder Khan smiled at him. "Very good, Phelan. The Jade Falcons made the mistake of assuming that we would prefer engaging the military of the Inner Sphere to fighting our own fellow Clansmen. No doubt they take our Refusal as ill-mannered and dishonorable, but they will be dead."

"I have no doubt, Natasha, that the Jade Falcons were as surprised as I was to learn that you and Ulric had managed to shift all of our front-line units around into these two spearheads without anyone noticing." While he had been spending his time preparing a defense of the ilKhan, the other two Khans had gone about planning the offensive against the Jade Falcons. Even though their plans were bril-liant, and they had given him the special role Ulric had promised, Phelan felt left out because they had not consulted him. By the time they revealed the plan, the Clan's various Galaxies had been formed and task forces given assign-ments. Phelan realized his input probably would not have changed things much, but he still would have wished to par-ticipate in the decision-making.

Get over it Phelan, you know they told you what you needed to know when you needed to know it. "That said, you can't be thinking the other fights are going to be as easy as this."

Natasha shook her head grimly. "No, of course not. I had a full unit, albeit a green one, going against a garrison unit. That's like taking my old Black Widows company against some raggedy militia unit. The Falcons were taken by sur-prise, but they were supposed to be. They'll be shifting units around to deal with us, but they're at a disadvantage because they have to protect everything, whereas we only have to at-tack targets we want to hit."

"Case in point: Dompaire. The Falcons have no garrison there."

Natasha smiled coldly. "But they do on Sudaten. More garrison units, but two full Clusters. I shall enjoy bidding against you for the honor of taking the world."

"That's the problem with you *seasoned* warriors, Khan Natasha—no grasp of reality." Phelan winked at her as the last Jade Falcon BattleMech crashed to the ground in the holotank. "I will win that bid, which means you'll get no enjoyment out of it at all."

DropShip Lair, *Assault Orbit*
Zoetermeer
Jade Falcon Occupation Zone

Star Captain Vladimir of the Eleventh Wolf Guards brought himself to attention as the cabin door slid shut behind him. "You sent for me, Star Colonel?"

"I did, Vlad. At ease."

Vlad's posture did not relax, nor did the severe expression on his face soften. Though most of the other Wolves in Task Force Delta still addressed Ulric as "ilKhan," Vlad refused to do so. The Grand Council had stripped him of his title and, because the Wolves already had two Khans, the only rank Ulric could claim was Star Colonel. "How may I be of service, sir?"

The older man smiled at him with a casual air that angered Vlad, but Ulric gave no sign of noticing the flush starting to burn the tips of Vlad's ears. "You may be of service, Star Captain, by remembering you are a Wolf before you are a Crusader."

"Star Colonel, I remember that I am a Clansman before I am a Wolf."

Ulric rose from behind his desk, his blue eyes tightening. "Your tone is insubordinate and your statement is treasonous. I would watch that, were I you. We are under martial law and entering a theater of war. I could have you executed."

"But you will not."

"No, I will not." Ulric gestured toward Vlad. "You have permission to speak freely. Air your grievances against me."

Vlad shook his head. "I bear you no ill will, Star Colonel. You have done nothing to me."

"No?" Ulric again smiled, but this time his expression was not neutral, only cruel. "You are aware that I prevented House Ward from holding a Trial of Bloodright for Conal Ward's Bloodname. Of course, very few people would want that Bloodline, soiled as it is, but you hunger after it, *quiaff*?"

Vlad ground his teeth. "I knew you had asked that no Trial of Bloodright be held for that name and that Khan Phelan, acting as the leader of House Ward, agreed with you." He knew he should say nothing more, but the hatred boiling inside him eroded his discretion. "It is not surprising that Conal Ward's murderer would agree to further dishonor Conal's Bloodright by leaving it uncontested."

Ulric arched an eyebrow. "Murderer? Conal Ward died in a Circle of Equals. He was not murdered."

"He was unarmed and Phelan shot him."

"He is lucky that *Khan* Phelan granted him so simple a sentence for his crimes."

Conal was not criminal. He was doing what had to be done for us to remain true to what we are. "As *Khan* Phelan's report on the whole Red Corsair mission has been classified to the level of Khans and above, I will have to assume you are telling the truth."

"Yes you will, Star Captain." Ulric blue eyes sparked like charging coils. "You take it as an affront that I have assumed personal command of Delta Galaxy, the Galaxy Conal Ward used to command."

"I do not take issue with that. It is the transfers in this unit that I question, especially as they came without request by the individual MechWarriors moving into or out of the unit."

"And, requests like your, to transfer out, were specifically denied." Ulric opened his arms. "I thought you would appreciate a Galaxy full of your Crusader companions. I thought being of like minds concerning the future of the Clans would give you a cohesion that other units lack."

"It would, sir, and might yet still." Vlad frowned sharply. "I have noted that the youngest of our soldiers have been transferred en masse to units headed by Khan Phelan and Khan Natasha."

"Younger warriors have much to learn."

"And we do not, *quiaff*?"

"Aff. You need learn only one thing."

Vlad's head came up. "And that is, sir?"

"Solon's maxim: Learn to obey before you command."

"I do not know what you mean, sir."

"That's why you're here."

"I might remind the Star Colonel that using debased language to speak with me is not necessary."

Ulric laughed and clapped his hands together. "You surprise me, Vlad. I had not thought you could do that. This might prove to be an interesting venture after all."

"And what might that be, sir?"

"Getting you killed."

Getting me killed. Vlad blinked with surprise. "But you could have me executed whenever you wished, Star Colonel. Accuse me of treason and have me shot."

"No, I think not, Vlad." The white-haired Wolf lowered himself into his chair again. "You want to know why I have assembled a task force peopled almost entirely with Crusaders? You gave me the idea. The Red Corsair, in her raids on the Inner Sphere, captured a number of MechWarriors. She forced one of them to go to war against his own people. She coerced him into acting against his nation with promises that she would free his comrades.

"By setting Crusaders against Crusaders, I will destroy you."

Vlad swallowed hard. "Now you are the one uttering treason."

"Am I? Can you show me anything about Crusaders or Wardens anywhere in the writings of Nicholas Kerensky or any other great leader of the Clans? Can you show me where it says they intended for one philosophy to be dominant over another? Can you show me how those philosophies are tied to the way of the Clans or our continued existence?"

"You are foolish, Star Colonel Kerensky, to believe that destroying the Crusaders among the Wolves and the Jade Falcons will destroy the desire to conquer the Inner Sphere. We are but six Clans in occupied territories. There are eleven more, and they too have Crusaders among them."

Again Ulric opened his hands like the doors of a treacherous pitfall. "Have you forgotten how we Wolves earned the right to be among the Clans who invaded the Inner Sphere? We bargained for our positions. We fought those other Clans. We are the best the Clans have to offer. The others might come, but they will not be the juggernaut we were. Some have still not recovered from the battles they lost in trying to compete for a place in the invasion. You expect them to be able to finish the task, *quineg*?"

Vlad's own images of the other Clans, the ones left behind in the den worlds, were as full of contempt as Ulric's voice in speaking of them. "Perhaps you speak true about that, but not about the willingness of Crusaders to destroy other Crusaders."

"I think not."

"It is an unwise general who does not know his troops."

"Oh, I know my troops, Vlad. I know them very well. Think of the Jade Falcons." Leaning forward, Ulric snapped his fingers. "There, the sneer on your face tells me how you feel about them. They may be your philosophical kin, but they are inflexible to the point of being brittle when challenged. You may hate Khan Phelan, and you have been defeated by him in personal and 'Mech combat, but at least *he* was adopted into *our* Clan. The warriors of the Inner Sphere who have defeated the Jade Falcons were not even as fine as Khan Phelan. The Falcons are not the best of the Clans."

Vlad frowned, as if that would banish his discomfort at Ulric's words. Ulric was right. He had always thought the Jade Falcons were too much like their totem animal, a preening creature with a piercingly loud scream but yet so very fragile. When the Wolves wanted to accustom their younger warriors to combat, they would send them against the Falcons. When they wanted to test warriors in a real fight, they pitched them at the Smoke Jaguars or Ghost Bears.

Ulric slowly nodded his head. "I can see it in your eyes, Vlad, as I have seen it in the eyes of all my warriors. Crusaders the Falcons may be, but the only way we will lose to them is if we surrender. Crusader you may be, but no Wolf will surrender to a Falcon. We would rather die than do that."

Vlad nodded solemnly. "You speak true."

"I know. I am a Wolf, and I am your commander, and so you will follow me into war with the Jade Falcons." Ulric sat back. "And even if we all should die, what a glorious death it will be."

25

The steady operations of war against a regular and disciplined army can only be successfully conducted by a force of the same kind.

—ALEXANDER HAMILTON, *THE FEDERALIST*, 1787, XXV

Sian
Sian Commonalty, Capellan Confederation
26 September 3057

Seated behind the desk at which Justin Allard had once plotted the betrayal of the Capellan Confederation, Capellan Chancellor Sun-Tzu Liao permitted himself a smile. "Thirty years ago this was the cradle of destruction. Now it has whelped our revenge." He nearly laughed aloud, almost wishing the ghosts that inhabited the room were yet alive to see his triumph. Almost but not quite, for he knew, better than anyone else, that did Justin Allard and Hanse Davion still live, they would very likely have anticipated and blunted his action.

Victor's big mistake, Sun-Tzu concluded, had been in viewing the Clans as his greatest enemy. It made sense, of course, because Victor had fought against the Clans, had almost lost his life against them. Then he'd been too distracted by political unrest within the Lyran districts of the Federated Commonwealth—culminating in his sister's repudiation of him and the creation of the Lyran Alliance. Distracted enough that Victor had not been ready for the Free Worlds/Capellan invasion against him.

As battle reports scrolled up the screen of the antique terminal on his desk, Sun-Tzu shifted his shoulders uncomfortably, but not in reaction to the data he was reading. It was universally wonderful. His commanders had used regiments to confront lone Davion battalions and trios of regiments to oppose single regiments of Federated Commonwealth troops. It was the same three-to-one advantage the Capellan forces had learned to hate when Hanse Davion had used it against them decades before. Victor's focus on protecting the Clan front, and then his need to pull troops for use in quelling the rebellion in his Lyran districts had left the Sarna March woefully undermanned.

The use of overwhelming force had been successful beyond Sun-Tzu's conservative dreams. he had launched nine planetary assaults in his invasion zone, all of which had resulted in Capellan victories. On eight other worlds he had stepped up his revolutionary activity to the point where his forces were engaging Davion garrison troops in hit-and-run attacks that did no real damage, but did seriously fatigue the Davion soldiers. After his regiments had secured their initial targets, then began the second wave of attacks, the weary Davion defenders were easier prey than before.

Up in the Zurich Theater, things had gone equally well. Thomas had supplied mercenaries to support local rebellions. The only Liao units being used up there were the Warrior House battalions that dropped as a single unit onto the planet Liao to liberate it from the Davions. The planetary militia had revolted and deposed the Davion governor. The Liao dynasty's home world again belonged to the Capellan Confederation.

But for all this, Sun-Tzu's spirit did not rest easy. He'd not been surprised by how well the invasion was going but by the competence and drive Thomas had shown in organizing the assaults. In the time it took Sun-Tzu to travel from Atreus to Sian, Thomas had sent him plans for the invasion that were complete down to the least detail. The sham of the supposed rift between them had been abandoned. Thomas had wanted Sun-Tzu on Sian so the assault would look like a concerted effort on the part of both nations to recover occupied territory the Davions had taken almost three decades before. Moreover, with Sun-Tzu on Sian, his troops would not view him as a puppet being directed by Thomas or vice versa.

Thomas' quick and forceful leadership was responsible for the successes they now enjoyed, but it had taken Sun-Tzu completely by surprise. He had always considered the Captain-General to be as meek as he was idealistic. Even the creation of the Knights of the Inner Sphere had seemed to him more an attempt to show the Inner Sphere that idealism and war could be wed, that warriors could rise to a high code of conduct. It was Thomas' attempt to reintroduce chivalry to the Inner Sphere—though Sun-Tzu thought chivalry as much a myth as the much-vaunted nobility of the ancient Star League.

Sun-Tzu's computer beeped twice, alerting him to two messages that demanded his attention. The first was a response of sorts to his declaration of the planet Outreach as an independent barony of the Capellan Confederation, which he granted to the mercenary Wolf's Dragoons in perpetuity. The Dragoons, according to a spokesman, appreciated Sun-Tzu's ratification of the grant originally made them by Hanse Davion. The message also said that the Dragoons would maintain their major focus against the Clans, and that they would only involve themselves in the current conflict if attacked.

The Chancellor frowned. He had hoped, in vain, that the Dragoons might show some gratitude by sending at least one regiment to smash a Davion unit. It was true that Victor was still their employer, but Sun-Tzu believed the Dragoons' refusal to help was intended to punish his own audacity.

The second message, a terse and short "Continue as planned" from Thomas, proved more disappointing than the Dragoons' ingratitude. Because of the invasion's initial successes, Sun-Tzu had pushed for an accelerated attack schedule, but Thomas balked. Had Marik agreed, it would have made him look like just one more greedy leader intent on reestablishing the old Star League with himself on the throne. Sooner or later Sun-Tzu could have taken advantage of that.

Leaning back in his big, overstuffed chair, Sun-Tzu swiveled it around and looked at the dappled green camouflage of the ivy leaves that had overgrown the French doors of the office. *Hanse Davion and Justin Allard would never have been daunted by an ally's reluctance to act. I need something that will prove I am more than a junior partner in this, but not something so great that it will draw all the military retaliation against me. I need a symbol worth going after and a reward that will strengthen me if I obtain it.*

Sun-Tzu nodded as an idea burst into his brain. Thirty years before, Hanse Davion had successfully subverted the

Northwind Highlanders—one of the Capellan Confederation's prime military units—by returning to them their homeworld of Northwind. The loss of that planet to the Davions years earlier had left the Highlanders feeling somewhat orphaned. With his generous gesture, Hanse Davion had won the Highlanders away from the Capellan Confederation, robbing House Liao of some of its best warriors.

Sun-Tzu had established a network of agents on Northwind, but had not used them as he had used the Zhanzheng de guang on other worlds where he was funding its cells. He intended to use his network there to threaten or kill Highlanders or their kin should Victor ever decide to employ the unit against the Capellan Confederation. His success on Northwind had resulted in the creation of similar secret networks on Caph, Keid, New Home, and Epsilon Indi.

"If I activate those networks to stage coups, Thomas will be inclined to expand his umbrella and push the war further." The Chancellor steepled his fingers. "Thomas will see that I am not without resources in all manner of places. We can take this war further than he imagines, and win back worlds lost to the Davions from before even *Thomas* was born. This shall be done."

Charleston, Woodstock
Green Harmony Republic, League Liberation Zone

Climbing in through the hatchway in the back of the *Warhammer*'s head, Larry Acuff shrugged himself out of the hooded great coat he had worn while waiting to move. He pulled the hatch shut behind him and spun the wheel to lock it into place, then punched the button that would bring the 'Mech's engine to life. Vibrations as the engine ignited the fusion fire bled up through his heavy boots and started his cold toes aching.

He folded the coat up and stuffed it into the locker behind his command couch, then squirmed into a seat on the couch's padded surface. As he plugged his cooling vest into a socket alongside him, the first burst of coolant circulating made him shiver. Larry knew he'd relish the coolness once they engaged the first regiment of Smithson's Chinese Bandits.

He drew the heavy neurohelmet from an overhead shelf and settled it down onto the padded shoulders of his cooling vest. Hanging down from the helmet's chin like a wispy beard were four biomed leads. Larry threaded each one through their loops on his cooling vest and clipped them to the monitor patches on his thighs and upper arms. He snapped on his restraining belts, then tightened his helmet's chinstrap, securing the neurosensors against his skull.

Computer monitors came to life all around him in the tiny cockpit. One reported on engine performance and another fed him all kinds of weather data, but the primary monitor, the one that gave him weapons status and condition remained blank. Dropping his jaw to key his microphone, he said, "Computer on, initiate cross-check."

"Voiceprint identification complete. Welcome aboard, Hauptmann Acuff. Please proceed with phrase identification and verification."

Because voiceprints could be faked, BattleMech security was maintained through a two-step process. Each pilot's voice was verified, then he was asked to repeat a phrase that he personally had programmed into the 'Mech's memory. Torturing the pilot or extensive probing of the 'Mech memory might elicit the phrase and make the 'Mech vulnerable to theft, but to actually steal a 'Mech would require an operation of such sophistication that the theft of actual line-unit 'Mechs was a thing possible only in holovid dramas.

"War can look for its victims elsewhere."

"Verification obtained. Weapon systems coming up now." The primary monitor filled with an outline of his *Warhammer*. The extended-range PPCs, one in each arm, reported operational. Next the short-range missile launcher on his 'Mech's right shoulder came on line, followed by the medium lasers, machine gun, and anti-missile launcher in the 'Mech's torso.

Again he keyed his radio. "Trey Battalion leader all green. Company commanders report."

All three of his leftenants reported in with fully operational companies. Including his command lance, Larry had forty 'Mechs in the battalion. Though the troops were all militiamen who had seen little actual combat, they were well drilled and better skilled than most militia pilots. This was because most had grown up piloting AgroMechs on the large farms for which Woodstock was known. They might not know the deep jungles near the core of the southern continent as well as they did the fields around Charleston, but they were certainly more at home in them than the mercenaries Thomas Marik had dropped onto the world to support WELFARE's revolution.

"Let's move out slow, Trey Bat. Don't pull your heat sinks on line until given clearance. Slow and steady wins this race."

When Kommandant Phoebe Derden-Pinkney learned, through a WELFARE broadcast, that Smithson's Chinese Bandits were incoming, she moved quickly to set up her defense. The Bandits were known as a formidable unit, but they had undergone changes since their early days of fighting for the Lyran Commonwealth. Thirty years before, attrition had reduced them from two regiments to one, with their aerospace fighters only a memory. Under Thomas Marik they'd been brought back up to two regiments, but still lacked fighter cover. The newness of their recruits also somewhat diluted their talent.

Leaving transport of the Woodstock Reserve Militia Regiment to the continent's interior to Larry and her other battalion commanders, Phoebe had decided to learn all she could about Colonel Ada Gubser, the Bandits' commander. Doing that had turned up what she felt was the key to beating the mercenaries. "You kill soldiers, you *defeat* commanders," she'd told Larry.

Back when the Federated Commonwealth had first taken Zurich, Ada Gubser had been a MechWarrior in the first battalion of Trimaldi's Secutors. The Fourth Deneb Light Cavalry Regimental Combat Team had hunted the Secutors down and finally trapped them in Ling's Cusp, a rocky stronghold that was the shell of an extinct volcano. Gubser had been captured but released after the war. She joined Smithson's Chinese Bandits and rose to command of the first regiment.

Ling's Cusp was the only truly defensible position for a whole unit on the southern continent, though the uneven land around it made for some excellent tactical fire zones. The Reserve had headed into the interior and vanished, leading everyone to believe they had taken up a position in the Cusp to wait for the Bandits to attack.

The Bandits, working from Gubser's antiquated memories of the Cusp area and conditions, moved in slowly. Gubser wanted to position her troops in a way that created enough pressure to deny the Reserve units their supplies. That would create a need for the Reserve to break out of the Cusp, at which point she could engage them on a battlefield of her choosing, instead of trying to ease them out of the Cusp. Even the Davion forces back in the Fourth Succession War, with their nine-to-one advantage over the Secutors, had been cautious about charging into the Cusp.

Gubser had set her Bandits up in a formation that made it difficult for the Militia to attack. Her forward force was about five kilometers ahead of a line of hills that was to be the real line of defense for her camp. This put the forward troops a little over ten kilometers east of the Cusp's opening. The forward force was a tripwire unit that would fall back to the line of defense, delaying the Reserves enough to let the rest of the Bandits come up to their line and pick the Reserves apart.

The Bandits' actual camp was another five kilometers due east behind their hills, around the settlement of King's Down. The Bandits had cut all communication lines out of the town and set up checkpoints on the roads leading into and out of King's Down. Believing themselves secure, the mercenaries were spending most of their time in carousing and otherwise enjoying themselves in King's Down.

What the mercs failed to realize was that the agrocombines had laid out a fiberoptic communications network of their own that independent of the old communications system the Liaos had installed. Also unknown to the Bandits, the Reserves had allies in town who were reporting on their activities through agricultural field stations. Updates on Bandit activity came in so reliably that most of the Reserves were more hooked on listening to what was going on in King's Down than the politically correct soap operas WELFARE was broadcasting from the capital, Recital City.

The Bandits' whole position had been oriented toward the Cusp and relied on sophisticated devices to help warm them of the approach of the Reserve 'Mechs. Foremost among these were small electronic sniffing units. Similar to smoke detectors, they picked up on the presence of 'Mech coolant in the air. Where there are 'Mechs, there's coolant boiling off or being pumped into heat sinks. Pick up on a concentration of coolant and you've located your enemy.

The problem for the Bandits was that the presence of coolant did not always mean 'Mechs were about. While Deuce Battalion of the Reserves had taken up residence in the Cusp, justifying the defense in depth Gubser had used, One and Trey Battalions had gone to ground in the jungles to the southeast of the Cusp, roughly ten kilometers southwest of King's Down. Because the prevailing winds of September blew in from the northwest, they carried the scent of coolant to the monitors from the Cusp, but blew away the coolant scent from the two hidden battalions.

And leaving open buckets of coolant hanging in the trees and dripping near the sniffers also produced readings sufficient to convince the Bandits they had a full regiment of 'Mechs trapped in the Cusp.

Moving those same buckets to a position more northerly also convinced the Bandits that the Reserve had sprung loose and were trying to flank their position to the north. The Bandits reacted immediately, as did the Reserve allies in King's Down, and by the time the Bandits had begun to push north, One and Trey Battalions had started their own march north.

Off to the northwest Larry saw hellacious flashes of light illuminate the sky, then he heard Phoebe's voice coming through his earphones. "One Lead to Trey Lead, Deuce has engaged. Go hot. Good luck."

"Roger, Lead." As per the plan, Deuce Battalion had come boiling out of the Cusp as the Bandits moved north. Either the tripwire force would try to hold so the other Bandits could wheel and come in through the north, or they'd pull back and hope the rest of the Bandits made it to the defense line in time to make the plan work. Trey Battalion's job was to get to the Bandits' defense line first and use it against them.

"Bring your heat sinks on, Trey." Larry hit a switch on his command console that set his *Warhammer*'s heat sinks working. He caught a faint whiff of coolant and saw the heat levels reported on his auxiliary monitor begin to dip. Another switch brought up the holographic display that stuffed a three-sixty view of his surroundings into a one-sixty-degree arc in front of him. A gold crosshairs floated in the middle of the display, responding to his movement of the joystick on the right arm of the command couch.

"Move it, people. We want to get to those positions before the Bandits do." He smiled as his *Warhammer* began to pick up speed. "They invited themselves to our dance, now it's time to make them pay for having so much fun."

I have never met or heard of troops who can withstand a night
attack from the rear.

—BERNARD NEWMAN, *THE CAVALRY CAME THROUGH*

Daosha, Zurich
Zurich People's Republic, League Liberation Zone
26 September 3057

All around her on the crowded hoverbus, Cathy Hanney
saw other people who looked the way she felt. The revolutionary government had wasted no time in instituting the
regimentation of society. Fuel and food were rationed and
power allotted on an as-needed basis that forced Daosha's
civilian population to turn their lights out by ten o'clock at
night. The hospital had already seen casualties from two in-
cidents of fire caused by people using various portable
stoves and other dangerous means to heat their homes after
the power was shut down.

The physical privation was tolerable, but Cathy knew it
was the reason she felt so tired and dull. Rick Bradford had
tried to suggest that sleep, a hot shower, and a cup of es-
presso would straighten her out, but the latter two were nowhere to be found on the planet, and sleep refused to come.
She knew that was partly because of the depression into
which she'd sunk, but possessing the clinical knowledge to
diagnose her condition did nothing to cure it.

She knew the depression had begun when Noble Thayer
had failed to call her on the eighteenth. They'd had no special plans, but they usually stayed in touch by phone. When
Cathy tried to call him, she got no answer.

The next day Ken Fox had come looking for her at the
hospital. "If you see Noble, tell him not to go back to the

apartment. Seems like he really made some people mad." He wouldn't say more than that, only that she was better off not knowing, then he'd vanished as well.

Noble and Fox weren't the only ones disappearing. People who came to the hospital gossiped in the waiting room, and a lot of tears were shed over stories that sounded horribly similar: a knock at the door, People's Security Committee officers asking for someone in particular, then carting him or her off for a "debriefing" from which that person never returned.

Every time she began to think Noble might have been arrested by the security forces, she felt a vise tightening on her heart. *It's like they say, you never know what you have until it's taken away from you.* She hadn't realized how attached she'd become. She and Noble had been intimate, but the fact that they didn't live together had given her an illusion of independence—an illusion that his disappearance shattered. Looking back she could see how she had gradually fallen into his orbit—and enjoyed every minute of it.

She leaned back in her seat, glancing idly at the placards riding above the hoverbus windows. Xu Ning, looking stern as rendered in stippled grays, glared down at her. "State Security begins with YOU!" the advert told her. Those posters had chilled her when they'd appeared overnight in the buses, but Cathy noticed that in the next one over some street artist had given Xu Ning floppy bunny ears. She would have smiled or laughed except that the hard stare of a woman in the olive drab uniform of a revolutionary bureaucrat killed the mirth in her heart.

The bus fishtailed slightly as the driver reduced the speed on the forward fan and bumped the vehicle against the curb at Cathy's stop. She got up and descended from the bus through the back door. She turned away quickly as the bus powered up, but most of the debris had been blown away when the bus came to a stop, so her legs only got pelted with a little sand.

Cathy glanced up the street toward her apartment house, giving a little sigh as she tried to decide what to do next. She could go straight home and hope to find a message from Noble on her digital answering service, or she could head back up the street to the corner grocery and see if they had anything approximating fresh fruit for her to take to the hospital. The fact that a derelict sucking on a bottle sheathed in a paper sack had taken up residence in the shade alongside her building almost sent her toward the store, but the bottle reminded her of some returnable ones she had waiting to go back. They wouldn't get her much, but with inflation running rampant, *anything* was *something*.

Pulling her sweater tight around her against the first cool breeze of evening, Cathy started toward her apartment house. At first she paid little attention to the gleaming black limousine that had silently pulled up at the corner. Then she smiled to herself, thinking that Noble might somehow be a passenger in the vehicle, but the smile died when the doors opened and two Security Committee members stepped out.

The one from the driver's side, a man with a crooked nose, pulled his cap on and smiled at her. "Excuse me. Are you Cathy Hanney?"

Cathy nodded. "I am. Is there something I can do for you?"

"We hope so, ma'am." The man's tone would have been casual enough to put Cathy at ease had not his partner been fingering the butt of the gun on her hip and moving around toward Cathy's back. "We need your assistance in a investigation."

Cathy glanced back at the woman standing between her and the stairs to her apartment, then turned to the man again. "What sort of investigation?"

"I can't tell you that right now, Ms. Hanney. We have to discuss this down at headquarters."

"No, I don't think so." Cathy looked back the way she had come. "Leave me alone."

"Can't do that, ma'am. You're coming with us. Don't try to run." He shrugged easily. "If you do, we'll shoot you in the legs. You're going to tell us what we want to know anyway, so why get yourself crippled first?"

Charleston, Woodstock
Green Harmony Republic, League Liberation Zone

This is nothing like Solaris. Standing with his 'Mech's feet about five meters below the crestline of the hill, Larry Acuff brought the crosshairs around and dropped it onto the outline of one of Smithson's Chinese Bandits *Shadow*

*Hawk*s. A gold dot pulsed in the middle of the crosshairs, but he refrained from triggering his weapons. He glanced at his secondary monitor and waited until the computer reported that most of his company's 'Mechs had target locks.

"Fire at will!"

With the words of that command he tightened up on the triggers beneath his index and middle fingers. Heat exploded in the cockpit as he fired both PPCs and his lasers. Like bright blue lightning the PPC fire burned through the darkened distance between the two 'Mechs and drilled into the *Shadow Hawk*'s right flank and chest. Fluid gobbets of melted armor flew from the 'Mech as the sudden evaporation of a ton and a quarter of armor unbalanced the war machine. The laser's ruby lances skewered the turning 'Mech in both the left and right flanks, carving into the right side of its chest down to eggshell-thin armor.

The pilot was obviously struggling to keep the 'Mech upright, but the attack had taken him by surprise as much as it had hit him hard. The *Shadow Hawk* listed toward the left, then overcorrected to the right, crashing down on its hands and knees. The autocannon on the 'Mech's left arm gouged up a huge divot from the killing field the Bandits had prepared and prevented the 'Mech from falling entirely prostrate.

Up and down the line, the Bandits coming in from the north took fire from Trey Battalion. BattleMechs, in the dark and distance looking much like men in armor, waved their arms to show the people in their lines that they were not the enemy. All that did was make those 'Mechs better targets, and Trey Battalion needed no encouragement to shoot up the Bandits.

Their swift return to the south had caused a serious problem for Smithson's Chinese Bandits. Eager to get into their defenses, the faster and smaller Bandit 'Mechs had outdistanced the heavier 'Mechs in their formation. That meant the least powerful and most vulnerable 'Mechs ran into Trey Battalion first, and Trey's first volley proved devastating.

Larry's target heaved itself up off the ground and staggered forward. Larry covered it with the crosshairs again and fired. The first PPC lashed armor from the *Shadow Hawk*'s right arm, stripping away more than half its armor. The second PPC's azure needle pierced the remaining armor on the 'Mech's right flank and sank deep into the *Shadow Hawk*'s chest. Glowing structural supports dropped through the gaping wound and even more fell when the *Warhammer*'s left laser enlarged the hole.

The *Shadow Hawk* pilot brought the 'Mech's left arm up and triggered his autocannon at the same time his right-arm medium laser stabbed out at Larry. The laser's scarlet bolt sliced nearly a quarter of the armor off the *Warhammer*'s right arm, but Larry easily corrected for the loss of weight.

The *Shadow Hawk*'s autocannon projectiles hit the dirt plug that had caught in the barrel. Though the first depleted-uranium round had more than enough kinetic energy to blow through the plug, doing so slowed it ever so slightly. That meant the slug following it, and the one following that one all slammed together. Three rounds trying to occupy space meant for one made the autocannon's barrel burst. The expanding gases in the barrel behind the bullets jetted out of the breach in a fiery flare that spun the *Shadow Hawk* around like a toy and dropped it onto its right flank.

The 'Mech's ruined side collapsed. The *Shadow Hawk* slowly fell onto its back, leaving its smoking right arm on the ground. The canopy of the 'Mech's cockpit exploded upward and the pilot rocketed out on his command couch. His arc was carrying him back toward King's Down, but Larry knew he'd land well short of the town and would spend the night in the jungle.

Off in the distance, Larry saw silhouettes moving at the edge of the cleared fire zone the Bandits had created. Punching up magnification on his holographic display, he started tagging the images. With the flip of a switch he opened the frequency he shared with Phoebe. "One Lead, I have the heavies coming in. ETA two minutes."

"Roger, Trey Lead. One has the flank."

"Roger." Larry switched back to his battalion's tactical frequency. "Keep firing and hold steady. We're omelet chefs and the Bandits are eggs. Those Humpty-Dumptys are going to have a long walk home, and it starts right here."

Daosha, Zurich
Zurich People's Republic, League Liberation Zone

As the male security officer reached for her, Cathy backed away. At the same moment the derelict suddenly staggered to his feet, then reeled forward straight at the female officer. The woman tried to get out of his way, but the drunk lurched at her and grabbed at her shoulder.

The security woman slapped him away with her left hand. "Away, dog!"

The bottle came up, shattering as it caught the security woman in the face. The rumpled bag tore and dark wine mixed with darker blood. Fragments of the bottle hung in the air, spinning like tops, and the rest of it went careening off into the sky like an errant missile when the man released it.

The male security officer's eyes widened in surprise, but he reacted quickly, reaching out to grab the man in the ratty woolen coat. That was when Cathy saw the gun. The derelict's trigger finger tightened twice, instantly transforming the security guard's neck and face into gaping, bloody wounds.

Clutching at his ruined face, the security man fell to the ground, making strangled gurgling sounds. The derelict instantly spun away from him and back toward the woman. Firing his gun twice more, he hit her in the stomach and the hip. The woman fell heavily against the steps, then tumbled down to the sidewalk where she lay in an ever-expanding pool of blood.

Acid bubbled up from Cathy's stomach, searing her throat, as the derelict turned toward her. "Please don't hurt me," she begged.

He pulled off his cap and smiled at her through the grime of his face. "Hurt you? I don't think so. Let's go."

Cathy's jaw dropped. "Noble? How?"

"It's a lot to explain. But not now. We've got to go. If they're after you, they're probably after Rick Bradford and Anne Thompson, too." He fished in his pocket and tossed the joker from a deck of cards onto the woman's body.

"How did you—?" She stared down at the bodies, confusion and exhaustion threatening to swallow her. She'd thought Noble was dead, but he wasn't. He was back and so . . . so violent.

He grabbed her left arm. "Let's go. We've got to get out of here. I can explain later."

"But . . ."

"No buts, Cathy." He gave her a weary smile. "Look, I wasn't going to let them get you, and I'm not going to let them get our friends. Are you with me?"

Cathy shook herself. *He's just saved my life! Pull it together, girl, and go.* "Yes, yes, let's go. Let's help the others."

"Good." Noble smiled and led her off down the street. "And after we do that, maybe we can see about the rest of the world."

27

> Never, never, never believe any war will be smooth and easy.
> —WINSTON CHURCHILL, *A ROVING COMMISSION*

Avalon City, New Avalon
Crucis March, Federated Commonwealth
2 October 3057

Seated at his desk, Victor frowned at Galen. "There are revolts on Northwind, Caph, New Home, and Keid?"

"Yes, sir. It appears that Sun-Tzu had guerrilla organizations on all those worlds. Moves were also made to set off a revolt on Epsilon Indi, but that fizzled. Tormano Liao had apparently infiltrated his nephew's organization with his own people and they refused to act. The rebellion was put down quickly." Galen shook his head. "I don't know how we missed picking up on these guerrilla activities before."

"Don't worry about it now. Spilled milk."

Galen looked surprised. "Are you so certain you want to let the existence of subversive enemy networks pass so easily?"

"No, but those networks weren't established on your watch. I'm sure you're doing all you can to uncover others." Victor leaned back in his chair and smiled. "We mustn't forget that Sun-Tzu is also fomenting rebellions on worlds my sister has claimed. I don't like losing Northwind, but most of the Highlanders are stationed in her Lyran Alliance, so their defection won't hurt us much right now. We had troops on New Home, but I think it was the Thirtieth Lyran Guards RCT, and their devotion to me is questionable at best. Let them chew on Sun-Tzu's bandits for a while."

Galen sat in the brown leather chair facing Victor's desk

and frowned slightly. "If you don't mind my saying so, you're behaving very differently than during the Clan Invasion. That Victor Davion would have been hopping mad. He'd have been frantically shifting troops and directing strategy to meet the invasion. But you seem so calm. I don't understand it."

The Prince shrugged. "I'm hamstrung by circumstances, so all the fury in the world won't do me any good. First and foremost, we can't possibly begin to predict when, where, and with how much the League or the Capellans are going to attack. Being the defender might have a tactical advantage on the ground, but on the strategic level the advantage is with the attacker. He hits where we're weak and we can't stop him. That's a fact we have to live with."

Galen nodded. "True enough. We've got troops on the key industrial worlds, so we're still holding all of them saving Nanking. Smithson's Chinese Bandits' second regiment broke the militia at Xuanji. The mercenaries are mopping up, but reports suggest they also got hit fairly hard in the fighting."

Victor opened his hands. "Ah, now there is a situation I could exploit. We know where one of the League units is, we know it's hurt, and we could deliver troops enough to crush it, but I don't have the ships I need to do it. Katherine's refusal to return my JumpShips to me is the most damaging thing she's done. I'd consider attacking her except that, one, I don't want to kill my own citizens and, two—I don't have the damned ships to get at her!"

Galen and Victor shared a nervous laugh. "I suspect, Highness, that your sister has considered that fact."

"No doubt. We could try to shift mercenaries around to try to cover things, but very few of them have the necessary JumpShip and DropShip assets either. Group W, the Legion of the Rising Sun, Wolf's Dragoons, and the Kell Hounds all have the transport, but they're either too far away—or pledged to neutrality—so I can't use them. Besides, in this fight, I'm not sure I want to."

"Why not?"

Victor exhaled slowly. "Thomas has been very conservative in his assaults. He hit the six old League worlds where we had troops, and though he captured two without a fight, he hasn't reassigned those units to launch new attacks."

"To the best of our knowledge."

"True—and with Word of Blake taking over communications on the conquered worlds, our 'best knowledge' is pretty weak. But he's used mercenaries to support Sun-Tzu's revolutions. I may be reading him incorrectly—and this whole war is confirmation that I haven't read him right before—but I don't think he's going to push his own Free Worlds troops beyond the borders of what was once the League. If he has to, he can always pass his mercenary contracts over to Sun-Tzu, turning the war into us versus the Capellans. He sues for peace, has the Capellan Confederation back as a buffer between us, and he's won an incredible victory. Thomas set his sights on limited gains, executed a war to obtain them, and succeeded. He'll be stronger than ever at home—which would justify the Word of Blake declaring him Primus in Exile.

Victor frowned. "But, this is all speculation, and worth exactly nothing. Is there any good news?"

"I have JumpShips available to move the Third Royal Regimental Combat Team to Northwind. With everything in such an uproar, we might be able to get that world back."

"Good. Do it. What else?"

"On Woodstock the Reserve Militia crushed the first regiment of Smithson's Chinese Bandits. They're mopping up the small remaining bands of resistance now, and Woodstock should be back in the fold inside a week."

"How badly was the Militia torn up?"

"They apparently escaped with surprisingly modest damage. Out of a hundred twenty-five BattleMechs only thirty-five are down with damage, but they expect to return to full strength by salvaging Bandit 'Mechs. Most of the Militia's pilots survived the battle. Two of their officers were in the Tenth Lyran Guards with you, so they've got some experienced leadership there."

That softened Victor's frown. "Who's commanding?"

"Kommandant Phoebe Derden is the unit commander and Hauptmann Larry Acuff is the Third Battalion's leader."

"I remember Derden. She had four kills on Teniente. And Acuff, wasn't he one of Kai's stable on Solaris? What's he doing on Woodstock?"

"He was visiting family. He's still in the Reserves, so he got activated when things began going to hell."

The Prince clapped his hands in applause. "Well, send them a congratulatory message over my signature. Tell them that we've very proud of their success." Then he laughed, but it was a sound of frustration. "And tell them that the other half of Smithson's Chinese Bandits is waiting for them on Nanking, anytime they can get over there to clean that up, too."

Galen smiled. "Oh, they'll love that. Want me to make a note to move them to Nanking when we get ships in the area?"

"By all means—they earned it. We'll send them in with the First Davion Guards and the First Kathil Uhlans. They'll be part of the task force taking the world. It'll make them happy and won't get too many of them shot up. Who would have thought a militia would beat up the Bandits?"

"Miracles do happen."

Victor's eyes narrowed. "Speaking of which, have we learned the identity of whoever did the blood test on our Joshua?"

"Not yet, but we're still checking."

"What's taking so long?"

"The New Avalon Criminal Investigations Bureau has been investigating the connection between organized crime and the cartage firm that hauls medical waste from the NAIS. They're claiming we shouldn't be working on domestic crime, even if it does tie in with espionage."

The Prince's nostrils flared as his temper began to boil. "You tell Director Harrison that his career at the CIB is perilously close to over. He'll tell you that he can't be fired and you can tell him I said he can sue the government and that I guarantee the case won't be heard until his grandchildren are the age he is now. He's to cooperate fully with this investigation."

Galen smiled. "Ah, Prince Victor has returned."

"Then I want you to have Harrison get hold of Christopher Wobbe."

"I'm not certain the head of the NACIB is on speaking terms with the Godfather of New Avalon."

"Well, if Harrison can't reach Wobbe, then he *does* deserve to be sacked. You have him tell Wobbe that Wobbe's son Thorinn is going to be moved from the country club prison where we put him for his little confidence games to a prison on a very cold moon orbiting Perdido or Nagel or some other world so far away you can't even see the star it orbits from here. If Wobbe's organization had anything to do with this and Wobbe doesn't comes clean now, he'd better appeal to my sister for asylum because New Avalon will become very unfriendly to him."

"Consider it done," Galen said. "And to think I thought there'd be no fun in this job."

The Prince shook his head. "There is, but not often enough."

While Galen made notes on his noteputer, Victor thought about Galen's comment that the old fire had returned. Being fiery was easy when it came to the domestic situation, because the necessary actions were obvious. There were things that had to be done and it made him angry that they weren't being done.

The war, on the other hand, was not as clear-cut. Besides not knowing where Marik's forces would strike next, and not having the ships to move troops to counter those strikes, something else bothered Victor. He couldn't put a finger on it, but it left him ill at ease.

Before he could further analyze any of this, Galen looked up and unknowingly interrupted him. "Another bit of good news is that the Jenkins woman has turned the corner. She'll have to remain in intensive care for a bit, but she's regained consciousness. It looks as if she'll recover, with therapy of course. She'll probably need a hip replacement once she's more stable, but Dr. Allard and her team are ready to do the job."

Pushing his dark thoughts aside, Victor smiled. "Good. She's to have anything she needs. We've taken care of her medical and living expenses, correct?"

"Yes, sir, she'll be able to pick her life up where she left off. There's been a groundswell of support for her. Even a trust fund set up through donations."

"Cut the red tape and make it all tax-deductible."

"Yes, sir."

"Anything else?"

"One more thing, Highness." Galen glanced at his noteputer and back up. "Just got a note here that the Draconis Combine ambassador would like to speak with you."

"Any idea why?"

Galen shook his head. "Not really, but I saw the abstract of an analysis of Combine media reports about the Lyran Alliance that suggests Theodore Kurita might be worried about the militarization of the worlds in the Lyons thumb. With Katrina claiming Northwind, it could look as if she might try a drive to take Dieron."

"That's not good." Because of Victor's relationship with Omi and the pact Hanse Davion had made with her father, the Federated Commonwealth and the Draconis Combine had agreed to suspend hostilities until the Clans were no longer a threat to the two realms. Victor would not have minded seeing Katherine have trouble governing the worlds in the thumb that bulged into Combine space, but if war should break out between Katherine and the Kuritas on the Combine border, he would be forced to intervene against Theodore.

"I can't give Theodore Kurita my blessing to invade the Lyran Alliance." The Prince thought for a moment, then smiled. "However, I could suggest to Theodore, through Omi, that if the Combine wanted to arrange with ComStar to station 'peacekeeping' troops on those worlds, I would not object. In fact, given that Katherine mouths a pacifist line, neither should my sister."

"It could backfire."

"Not if the troops used as peacekeepers come off their border with us. That relieves pressure on me and frees up more troops to move into the Sarna March." Victor massaged his temples, hoping to chase away the first hints of a headache. "I think that's the best I can do right now. Do you agree?"

"It will frustrate your sister while reassuring the Combine." Galen made another note on the device in his lap. "There might be a better solution somewhere, but this is workable for now."

"I agree, but if there's a better solution I can't figure it out." The Prince shrugged. "Probably something simple, something I'm overlooking. I think I'm finally reading Thomas accurately, but my track record on that doesn't inspire confidence."

"You'll see what you're missing soon enough."

"I hope you're right, Galen. I don't even want to think about what will happen if you're not."

Wotan
Jade Falcon Occupation Zone

Khan Vandervahn Chistu of the Jade Falcons slowly paced around the column of figures the computer was projecting inside his holotank. The image moved with him, keeping the data readable as he walked. Another commander might have hoped vainly that the numbers would somehow change as they shifted position, denying the disaster they reported.

But not Chistu. He did not want them to change. He studied them hard. Those numbers, ugly and devastating as they were, supplied a key to Khan Natasha Kerensky and the young *freebirth* Phelan Ward. Once he had it puzzled out, had fit all the clues together, he would have them.

They had been generous with clues, but that only made him suspicious. On Colmar, Natasha's 352nd Assault Cluster had crushed the Twelfth Falcon Regulars, then opened the armories and armed the populace. Natasha had proclaimed Colmar "free" and told the people she would take their status up with the Falcon Khans on Wotan.

Chistu laughed as he recalled the fury in her voice on the holovid report about the fighting. Elias Crichell had taken her threat seriously, but Chistu had managed to convince the older man that Natasha would never survive to fight on Wotan.

The results of the fighting on Sudaten convinced him that his judgment had been right. The Eighth Falcon Regulars and Dorbeng Garrison Cluster had both fallen to Khan Phelan's Fourth Wolf Guards Assault Cluster and the Sixteenth Battle Cluster. Though the Jade Falcons had lost the planet and their force been destroyed, it was estimated that the Wolves had suffered 'Mech casualties of thirty-five percent or more. The Wolves' road to Wotan was going to be littered with 'Mechs, leaving them only a skeletal force for the actual attack.

Chistu believed the Wolves would never make it to Wotan, but Crichell's fearful reaction to Natasha's boasts had underscored the one thing that made growing old so ruinous in a warrior. Crichell had begun to worry about his own mortality. Such concerns had no place in the way of the Clans—Crichell had ample progeny guaranteeing the immortality of his genetic material. For him to fear death was an abomination.

Such a coward cannot be a Khan of the Jade Falcons if we are to achieve greatness, and cannot be the ilKhan if we are to take the Inner Sphere.

Chistu smiled as all the pieces of the puzzle came together for him. Natasha's pride meant she would go for Wotan, and on as straight a line as she could. Her next target would be Baker Three, then Devin, Denizli, and, for symbolism's sake, Twycross—the site of the Jade Falcon's most humiliating loss. Then to Wotan she would come.

Just as Twycross was a symbol of worth to her, Natasha was a symbol for him. He would let her come, tossing garrison units at her to bleed her with each step. He would let her win each victory and wear them as banners of her greatness. Then to Wotan she could come—with his own Peregrine Galaxy arriving right behind her—and on Wotan she would die.

By his hand she would die and all her glory would pass to him. And when it did, he would be the logical choice for ilKhan, not Crichell. And when he became the Khan of Khans, the Inner Sphere would fall as fast and as hard as did that solahma, Natasha Kerensky.

28

How different the new order would be if we could consult the veteran instead of the politician.

—HENRY MILLER, *THE WISDOM OF THE HEART*

DropShip **White Fang,** *Assault Orbit*
Baker Three, *Jade Falcon Occupation Zone*
5 October 3057

Phelan Ward stopped halfway across the docking bay deck and turned back toward Natasha Kerensky. "We can change the plan, you know."

Natasha laughed gently, something she'd been doing of late far more than he'd ever seen before, then shook her head. "No, Phelan, we can't. Ulric and I talked long and hard about this. We must do things the way we outlined them."

The younger Khan jammed his fists against his hips. "Sending me away with half your spearhead, over a third of our total line forces, is not going to win us this Trial of Refusal."

The redheaded woman snorted. "I don't think I'm going to need your troops to handle the Nega Garrison Cluster."

Phelan looked sternly at her. "Natasha, you know as well as I that this little war of attrition is going to destroy you. Taking me out of it, taking my people out of it, isn't going to make it any easier."

"But, Phelan, you know that having you there would not guarantee a victory either. We constantly fight with a handicap, so we will lose. We are meant to lose, and we know that. We're just making the Falcons pay a heavy price for winning."

"But with me and my troops, we *could* win!"

She shook her head, then draped an arm around his shoulders. "Son, I really do understand what you're saying, and you might be right."

"Then I should go on with you."

"But you can't." Her voice dropped to a whisper for a moment and she flashed him a brief smile. "If we beat the Falcons, another Clan will bring up the same challenge. And if we beat them, another and another will challenge us until we are no more. You're a hell of a warrior, Phelan. I've always thought that about you, but you believe too much that when your ferocity is wedded to the righteousness of a cause you will prevail. There are times when that doesn't work, and this is one of them."

"Dammit!" Phelan protested. "Dammit, dammit, dammit!"

"Don't you hate it when someone else is right for a change?" Natasha laughed.

"Yes, but that's not it. I hate when I can't change something that shouldn't happen." He looked at her, green eyes snapping. "Together we'd give Chistu and Crichell nightmares."

"You'll be able to do that on your own, Phelan." Natasha half-smiled. "Hell, that's enough of an incentive to make me consider letting them live."

They shared some laughter over that, yet with an undercurrent of melancholy. The sound echoed from the docking bay's metal walls, coming back to them distant and alien. It mocked them and sent a shiver through Phelan.

"I guess this is goodbye, then."

Natasha nodded. "Look, Phelan, I've never been good at farewells. And, well, I have a reputation to uphold, the Black Widow and all that, so I can't let myself get all weepy. Even if I did, I wouldn't tell you that if I'd had a son, I'd have wanted him to be like you. As you know, I had a son—a number of them actually—and they'd likely have kicked your butt in a fight."

"Sure, Natasha, right after all the Crusaders decide they're wrong and leave the Inner Sphere."

"What a smart-mouth. I wonder where you learned *that!*" Natasha stood before Phelan and rested a hand on each of his shoulders. "The fact is I *am* proud of you. I *started* in the Clans, won a Bloodname, and became a Khan. That's tough, very tough. You did it too, but came from being a freebirth of the Inner Sphere."

"Couldn't have done it without your help."

"I appreciate that, but you already had what it took." She poked a finger against his chest. "You have the heart and the brains and the soul of a warrior. Don't ever forget that, Phelan. You're a warrior, and with that comes a lot of responsibility."

He nodded. "Which is why you're sending me away, *quiaff*?"

"Aff. And that's why we're entrusting the future of the Wolves to you." Natasha gave him a wink. "Just so you know, on a personal level, I'm glad you and my granddaughter have each other."

"Ranna *is* very special."

"Better remember that, because she's a Kerensky and will have your head if you forget it." Pulling back, Natasha fixed Phelan with a serious stare. "She's my choice to win my Bloodname."

"You can tell her that later, when you're ready to die of old age. You know the plan. We'll be waiting for you."

The woman nodded solemnly. "I know you will, but I also know I won't make it to the rendezvous. You've got to see to the future, Phelan, and I'll take care of the problems of the past. Besides, once I've killed a Khan or two, there'll be nothing more to live for."

"Perhaps after I've done that too, we can compare notes." Phelan gave Natasha a brave smile. "If we get out of this, Ranna and I will marry. The universe is going to need more Wolves to keep the Kerensky bloodline going."

Natasha reached into the pocket of the jacket she wore and held a slender aluminum tube out to Phelan. "In case you want to go into mass production."

Phelan looked puzzled as he took it from her. "What is it?"

"My DNA. Should be enough there to create a galaxy of Black Widows."

"Without you to lead them . . ."

"You and Ranna will do fine." Natasha pointed to the shuttle. "Go on, Phelan, do your duty. Your people are waiting at the jump point, and I've got an appointment with the Nega Garrison down there on Baker Three."

"Goodbye, Khan Natasha. Fight hard. Give 'em hell."

"Give 'em hell?" Natasha waved as Phelan boarded the shuttle that would take him to his fleet. "I don't think I'm inclined to let them off that easy."

Tharkad City, Tharkad
District of Donegal, Lyran Alliance

Katrina Steiner clenched her fists in outrage so tightly that it was a second or two before she felt the pain of her nails digging into her palms. "How dare Sun-Tzu foment revolts on any of *my* worlds!"

She stared at the holographic map of the Inner Sphere hovering above her desk. Everything looked normal, just as she wanted it, except where Steiner blue and Liao green alternated in painting four worlds. The fact that the computer made the image green for longer than it made it blue meant Sun-Tzu's forces were winning. The Thirtieth Lyran Guards had left New Home, taking her invitation to return to the Alliance at face value. Without their presence, there was no one to oppose Sun-Tzu's revolutionaries.

And after Sun-Tzu took Northwind, he granted the world similar status to that of Outreach. The Highlanders got their world back *and* were reunited with the Capellan Confederation. The unit was returning home, and Sun-Tzu had brought their homeworld back into his fold. It was a bold move on his part, not one she would have thought him capable of pulling off, and it was one she could not let stand.

Her initial impulse was to crush Sun-Tzu somehow, but she rejected that as impractical and, worse yet, damaging to her image as a conciliator and peacemaker. The Free Worlds League blocked her path to the Capellan Confederation, and she did not think Thomas would let her ferry troops through his space to strike at Sun-Tzu. Bringing direct pressure to bear on Sun-Tzu was, for the moment, impossible.

So was the idea of letting Sun-Tzu get away with seizing her worlds. Since she had claimed them for herself, she knew Victor would never try to retake them. As long as Thomas did not reinforce the worlds, all of them save Northwind would be vulnerable to reconquest. Sun-Tzu would certainly know that, and had to be pressuring Thomas to support him by pushing his mercenary units deeper into Federated Commonwealth territory.

"I shall have to make certain Thomas does nothing of the kind," Katrina said softly, pressing the button on her desk to summon her secretary. "And if he can't curb his little Liao pit bull, I might have to teach him why they say blood is thicker than water, and why better nations than his have stood in fear of the united Federated Commonwealth."

29

War is much too serious a business to be left to military men.
—Attributed to Tallyrand

Recital City, Woodstock
Sarna March, Federated Commonwealth
10 October 3057

Larry Acuff, his breathing slightly restricted by the tightness of his ballistic armor, looked to the left side of his helmet's faceplate and saw a postage-stamp size image of a WELFARE spokesman ranting and raving about Davion cruelty. The rebels still claimed to control the planet, though the defeat of Smithson's Bandits had driven them back underground.

He smiled as the two eco-terrorists promised more surprises for the Davion forces on Woodstock. "You've got the surprise part right."

He signaled Sergeant Collins to start the raid. As she and Kerrigan hauled back on the portable ram, Larry glanced at the countdown clock clicking down the seconds on the right side of his faceplate. Precisely as the time hit 00:00, the ram broke through the warehouse door and the Reserve's close assault team burst into the WELFARE studio.

The two men seated behind the table stood abruptly as four troopers in black fatigues shoved submachine guns at them. Others poured in around Larry to bring the camera crew and control room staff under guard. A spontaneous cheer went up from the Reservists as Kerrigan tore down the WELFARE banner.

"This is not over!" shouted one of the WELFARE men. Larry saw from the image on his faceplate that the broad cast was still going out to all of Woodstock. He handed his shotgun to Collins and pulled off his helmet. With a smile, he stepped before the camera and waved the terrorists out of the shot. Seating himself casually on their table, he gently set his helmet down, then picked up a microphone.

"It's over, Woodstock. This was a test of the Emergency Terrorist Suppression Network. This was only a test." He kept a straight face despite the laughter starting among his people and the low moans from the terrorists. "In the event of an actual emergency, we would have faced more than has-been mercenaries and the Bean-Sprout Liberation Army. We now return you to your regularly scheduled lives."

Marik Palace, Atreus
Marik Commonwealth, Free Worlds League

Thomas smiled with the left side of his face. "I suppose you are correct, Precentor Malcolm. It is time I answer the missive from Duchess Katrina Steiner."

"Archon Steiner," the man smile apologetically.

Thomas nodded slowly. "Thank you, Precentor. I would not want to offend Katrina."

Looking up from his computer console, Malcolm frowned. "Begging your pardon, sir, but her message to you threatened hostilities—in veiled terms, of course—if you did not make Sun-Tzu return worlds she claims for the Lyran Alliance. If you do that, you will anger Sun-Tzu. If you do not, Katrina could bring considerable force to bear against our border. She might even reconcile with her brother."

Thomas slowly shook his head. "You will find, Precentor, that familial rifts do not heal themselves without a great deal of scar tissue." He brushed his right hand over the twisted, ruined side of his face. "I have certain knowledge of this."

"Yes, Captain-General."

"Katrina is not a warrior, which means she would have to turn control of her troops over to Victor to coordinate operations. That would leave her without weapons once our threat was ended. She cannot afford to do that, so she will not. That was a bluff."

The Captain-General's eyes became brown crescents beneath heavy lids. "Having taken the position of peacemaker, she will have a hard time ordering troops into action, especially House troops. She has invited them home in the name of peace. Sending them forth again will hurt her. Since she is only a politician, and appearance means more than substance to her, she cannot do this."

An idea blossomed in Thomas' head. "The trick here is to refuse her, while also providing her a hint about how she can still get what she wants. Katrina often shows herself intelligent and thoughtful, but in this instance a tendency to impulsiveness has betrayed her ability to think clearly. Otherwise she would have made her Lyran Alliance neutral in order to negotiate a settlement between her brother and me. That would have gotten her what she wanted without any fighting while raising her status in the Inner Sphere. She did not, and now she is a bystander hemmed in with no strong way to respond to Sun-Tzu's threat."

He looked over at Malcolm. "Please take this dictation and send it out immediately."

"As you wish, Captain-General."

"Good. It begins: Dear Archon Katrina, I, too, was dismayed by the bold advances Sun-Tzu made against worlds you have claimed as your own. I have told him that I will not send my mercenaries to sanction his revolutions. I have done this despite the fact that my daughter and heir, Isis, is with him on Sian. Though this makes her a hostage much the way my son was to your brother, I cannot support Sun-Tzu's action against you.

"I am aware that you do not wish to see your people die in battles, and so you do not truly wish to deploy your forces against these disputed worlds. I understand your difficulty, for I wrestled with it myself. It is the very reason that I am employing mercenaries instead of regular Marik troops in the occupied zone, and why I have decided to deny Sun-Tzu the support of same . . ."

Belsen, Leskovik
Wolf Clan Liberation Zone

Though he resisted seeing anything positive in Ulric Kerensky, Vlad grudgingly admired the way the man looked every inch the military leader. Still clad in cooling vest shorts, and heavy boots, Ulric straightened up from a basin of water and wiped his face dry on a towel. The fact that his makeshift washstand stood in the center of a building the Wolf 'Mechs had reduced to rubble and that water fountained up from a ruined pipe in the corner, seemed not to matter.

Ulric's blue eyes sparkled as he saw Vlad. "Star Captain, a most glorious performance by our troops today, *quiaff*?" The broad smile that came with the question almost infected Vlad. "The Ninth Provisional Garrison gave us a much better fight than the Tenth did on Zoetermeer."

Vlad stepped over a pile of bricks and heard glass crunch beneath his heavy tread. "Aff, Star Colonel. But they could hardly have done worse, since you used only a portion of the forces the bidding would have allowed you to bring in."

Ulric nodded, then cupped some water in his hands and splashed it over his white hair. "The forces I used were sufficient to take the world, *quiaff*?"

"Aff, but insufficient to prevent us from taking undue casualties. A wise commander would have called for more troops when the garrison retreated into Belsen. We were not well chosen for urban fighting."

The Wolf leader shrugged. "We won."

"And more of us died than needed to." Vlad folded his arms across his chest. "But that is your stated goal, *quiaff*?"

"Provided you take more of the enemy with you than you lose, yes." Ulric's smile froze into a parody of itself. "But your irritation is not with losing people, *quineg*? It is another question you wish to ask, *quiaff*?"

The accuracy of Ulric's words took Vlad by surprise and he almost blurted out a denial just to prove the other man wrong. His head came up and he clasped his hands at the small of his back. "You view all of us Crusaders as your enemies, *quiaff*?"

"Aff."

"And you see me as one of the worst of them, *quiaff*?"

"Among the Wolves, aff."

Vlad drew in a deep breath. "Then if you wish to kill us all, and I am one of the most dangerous to you, why did you not let me die when that Garrison Star ambushed me?"

"The answer is simple, Vlad," Ulric said slowly, looping

the towel around the back of his neck. "I am not of a mind to be deprived of my Phelan in this invasion."

"What!" Vlad's mouth dropped and he felt his face flush, the long scar burning like a white-hot wire. "How am I your Phelan? He and I are nothing alike."

"No? You are both passionate and convinced of your own superiority. You both bear grudges. You fight fiercely, and when you are not blindly rushing off into trouble, you can be intelligent.

"In the last invasion, Phelan was invaluable because he knew the enemy. This time you are the one who knows the enemy best. You are my Phelan against the Crusaders."

Vlad shook his head violently. He knew he was nothing like Phelan. Though the humiliation of having suffered defeat at Phelan's hands still scourged him like a barbed-wire whip, he refused to acknowledge Phelan's superiority over him in any way, shape, or form. Yet, in that thought, he found the first tiny scrap of resonance with what Ulric had said. *Neither of us would ever compromise on anything where the other was concerned.*

But his mind still revolted against the idea. *We are different because Phelan is a Warden, and in that he is wrong. I will never see things the way he does, and I know he will die before he would admit I am right. That difference forever separates us.*

Ulric went on as if he had not noticed Vlad's angry silence. "When you were ambushed, you merely reported the situation. You did not ask for help, you simply warned those coming behind you of what had occurred. That is what Phelan would have done. I would not have let him die as a consequence of his action, just as I chose to rescue you."

"It was a mistake to exempt me from the death sentence you passed on our task force."

"I did not exempt you, Vlad. I merely postponed the time of your death."

"Perhaps I should thank you for that, but it will not win me over to your side."

"I know that, Star Captain, and rest assured it was not the reason I saved you." Ulric shook his head slowly. "I will see you dead, but just not yet. We have many worlds to visit, you and I, and much killing to do before our mission is ended."

Recital City, Woodstock
Sarna March, Federated Commonwealth

Seated in a rear corner of the ballroom of the Grand Woodstock Hotel, Larry smiled in spite of himself when the holovid projection unit splashed his face across the wide screen at the front of the room. He saw himself as billions of people had seen him earlier in the day, setting his helmet down on the table to announce the liberation of Woodstock. The cheers of the other Reservists drowned out his voice and his words, but he remembered clearly every syllable he'd uttered. He cringed a little at the corniness of it.

So much for spontaneous brilliance.

He took a swallow of the Woodstock Private Reserve lager someone had set before him, then shook his head. "They going to run that every hour on the hour, Phoebe?"

"What's the matter, can't you stand the star treatment? I'd have thought you were used to it from Solaris." She laughed at his obvious discomfort. "It's big news here, and you're big news, too. Definitely no waiting in lines now!"

Larry frowned playfully at her. "At least on Solaris, if my face were on the holovids so much, I'd be hyping some product and be getting paid for it."

"Pity that your AFFC agreement doesn't have an endorsement rider in it," Phoebe teased. "Relax. Your heroic declaration got us all put up here in this hotel and there will be the parade tomorrow. You may be bored with all this hero treatment, but why not let the rest of the plowboys and harvester-girls bask in a bit of glory?"

Larry was about to make some witty riposte when the appearance of a yellow-robed ComStar courier at their table instantly made him forget everything else.

"Kommandant Phoebe Derden?"

"Yes."

"I have a message for you from New Avalon." He held a folded slip of yellow paper out to her.

Phoebe took the sheet and began to read, a smile blossoming on her face at first, but dying quickly as the color drained from her face. She seemed to re-read the message, then slid it across the table to Larry.

He turned it around so he could read it, but her reaction made him hesitate for an instant. Even so, the beginning made him smile as well.

"To: Kommandant Phoebe Derden, Woodstock Reserve Militia," it began, with instructions for forwarding from Charleston to Recital City.

"Dear Hauptmann Derden," it went on. "You have my hearty thanks and sincerest congratulations on your recent victory over Smithson's Chinese Bandits. I knew, from your action on Teniente, that there was little chance the invaders would prevail, but the efficiency of your success exceeded even my wildest dreams and has been the sole bright spot in the past month of conflict.

Your unit's spirit and ability have not gone unnoticed. In fact, the other half of Smithson's Chinese Bandits are on Nanking, waiting for you to complete their destruction. I look forward to a reunion in which you can introduce me to your Reservists and give me a first-hand report on our exploits.

Knowing we have such reliable commanders and troops in our armed forces keeps up my hopes for the future of the Federated Commonwealth.

With sincere thanks, your friend, [signed] Prince Victor Davion."

Larry looked up with a big smile on his face. "Phoebe, this is great. You should read it to the troops. They'll love it."

"I'm not good at that sort of thing." Her uneasiness showing, she handed the note back to the ComStar courier. "Perhaps you would be good enough to read it to my people?"

"It would be my pleasure, Kommandant Derden."

As the courier headed toward the front of the big room, Larry leaned forward. "What gives, Phoebe? That was a great message."

"Sure, but what about the other half of it?"

Larry frowned. "Am I missing something?"

"Victor wants us to go to Nanking and liberate it." She sat back and squared her shoulders. "I know we can do it, but how are we going to get there? The Reserves don't have either DropShips or JumpShips."

Larry leaned heavily forward on his elbows. "I don't think any Militia unit has DropShips or JumpShips assigned to it."

Phoebe shrugged. "Victor's always been big on personal initiative, and he obviously expects us to get to Nanking.

There are DropShips here on Woodstock, and JumpShips coming in to pick up shipments of grain, but our budget isn't big enough to charter any of them."

Larry smiled ruefully. "I do have a corporate card from Cenotaph Stables, but I don't think Kai's credit limit is quite high enough for us to hire an invasion fleet."

Phoebe glanced at cheering troops, who had begun shouting even before the ComStar courier finished reading the message. "We can't let Victor down, but what am I going to do? We can't very well have a bake sale to raise funds, can we?"

"Limited return on a bake sale, though we'd probably get a lot of food products donated for it." Larry stopped, then smiled at Phoebe. "No, dammit, that's the key."

"A bake sale?"

"Not exactly." He winked at her and drained his beer. "Trust me, Phoebe, we're going to Nanking. I have a plan and it's going to work like a charm."

30

Force, and fraud, are in war the two cardinal virtues.
—THOMAS HOBBES, *LEVIATHAN*

Tharkad
District of Donegal, Lyran Alliance
13 October 3057

Katrina Steiner allowed herself a small smile as she reread Thomas' reply to her message to him. *Well played, Thomas.* She did not like having been outmaneuvered, but she had to admire how he'd done it. By citing the fact that Sun-Tzu had Isis, he appealed to her for sympathy while vilifying Sun-Tzu. By noting that he feared his daughter might suffer the same fate as Joshua, he beseeched her not to put the girl into jeopardy by pressuring him. He also made it clear that he could easily strike at her were Isis to die and he able to blame her for the death.

Thomas' mention of mercenaries had seemed at first read to be a threat, since he still *could* decide to use them to back Sun-Tzu. On her second reading she took his words in a different way. *Is he suggesting I use mercenaries as opposed to House troops?* The subject had been approached obliquely enough that the attempt to influence her might have seemed clumsy, but she knew Thomas did not make such mistakes. It must have been intentional, she decided, which meant he was offering her a solution he could live with.

She smiled. *Great minds think alike.* Katrina had already decided that if intervention was warranted, she would employ mercenaries. She had already been studying Thomas Marik's use of them in the Sarna March, appreciating how it had distanced his nation from the conflict. He wasn't spilling the blood of his people in a foreign realm, but using hired soldiers to take those risks. Mercenaries were an elegant solution to the problem.

For Katrina, there was only one choice of mercenary unit to call upon. The Kell Hounds were without a contract—something her brother had lamented at various times—and were fierce Steiner loyalists. Not only did they owe their existence to bequests from her maternal grandparents, but the Kells were also related to her through her mother.

If she sent for them, they would help her.

Her smile grew as she recalled recent conversations with Caitlin Kell. The groundwork implicating Victor in the death of their mothers had been laid during Caitlin's last visit. Katrina could build upon that in her request, binding the Kell Hounds more tightly to her. If Victor should decide that he wanted a military confrontation with the Lyran Alliance, she wanted the Kell Hounds on her side.

Then another thought occurred to her, and she bit her lower lip in response. Daniel Allard commanded the Kell Hounds, and his father and brother had been devoted to the Davions. Her request might not be so inviting to him.

She shrugged. "I'll simply have to go over his head."

Striding over to her desk, she sat down and tapped the switch that brought the small holovid camera up. It focused tightly in on her, then she punched the button that started it recording. *Earnest but worried should do it.*

"My dear Morgan, I need your help ..."

Daosha, Zurich
Zurich People's Republic, League Liberation Zone

Cloaked in anonymity by the vast throng filling Fengzilusude Square, Noble Thayer stamped his feet to keep the circulation going. Cathy looked over at him, rosy-cheeked and bright-eyed. He smiled at her, then motioned with his head toward the far end of the brick-walled square. "We should pay attention."

"Of course."

Out across a vast expanse of paving stones, beyond the 'Mechs of the Black Cobra regiment of the mercenary Crater Cobras and the olive companies of the People's Freedom

Army infantry, Xu Ning stood at a podium exhorting the crowd. In front of him, in ranks ten deep and twenty wide, two hundred of Zurich's leading politicians, police officials, clergy, academics, journalists, and artists knelt in steamy silence. Each one, regardless of gender, had been stripped to the waist and bound hand and foot. Each had also been made to don a paper tabard with his particular crimes emblazoned on it in scarlet letters.

The crowd was too far away to see clearly, which was why, hung on the south wall, a thirty-meter-tall, forty-meter-wide, flat holovision monitor blew everyone up to heroic proportions. Xu Ning appeared big enough to go one-on-one with a BattleMech, and Colonel Richard Burr looked as stiff and mechanical as the 'Mechs in which his Crater Cobras rode. The screen, as if it were a magic mirror that emphasized emotion, also displayed the fear and humiliation of the two hundred.

Xu Ning, his bass voice somehow incongruous with his nervously slender body, gestured defiantly at the captives. "These are the agents of the counter-revolution. They seek to perpetuate the servitude of the masses to the absentee planet lords who rape us second by second. Hanse Davion took this world twenty-eight years ago, claiming he would liberate us from the fetters that the Liaos had used to oppress us. He lied, and his son has murdered an innocent child to continue the evils of his father."

He half-turned and pointed his right hand at the screen. "Look at them. Look at the enemies of the people. They have preached against the Liaos. They hold themselves to be better than we, the people, are. They defy the revolution because they are afraid of having their true depravity exposed. Theirs is a struggle to delay the inevitable, to deny the single verifiable tenet of reality, to escape the bonds that make us all one.

"They wish to be apart from our great society. In the name of Sun-Tzu Liao, I am the granter of wishes. As I grant you the wish to be truly one with all your brethren, so I grant them their release from the human compact that binds us all. Liberators, do your duty."

The ranks of the Liberators behind the prisoners parted. Two troopers from each company came running forward, automatic rifles held high above their heads. Clad in quilted olive green uniforms, only a scarlet collar and cuffs distinguished the Liberators from their comrades in arms. Twenty in all came to the front, and each one stood at the head of a column of state enemies.

"Ready!" Xu Ning shouted.

The soldiers charged their rifles.

Many of the prisoners began to cry and curse.

Cathy turned to Noble. "Do something."

"Aim."

The solders brought their rifles up to their shoulders.

Several prisoners tried to get up, but managed only to hop a step or two before falling over.

"We cannot save them," Noble whispered harshly, but the wind whipped his words away. "The world has to see this. They're lost, but their sacrifice might save others."

"Fire!"

Bright flashes and glittering brass cartridges filled the air before the podium. Gunshots combined into a rumbling roar that echoed off the walls and swallowed the screams of the dying. White paper and red letters vanished in an ocean of blood. Bodies writhed and spun, slamming into one another and collapsing limp and motionless in heaps and piles.

Cathy cried out and clung to him, her voice just one among the sounds of outrage and fear rising from the crowd, a defiance immediately dampened by gunshots. Noble slipped his arm around Cathy's shoulders, holding her tight and comforting her, but did not turn away from the slaughter in the square or its spectacular depiction on the electronic mural.

Reaching into the right side of his jacket, he thumbed the square button on the remote device hidden deep within the pocket.

The image on the monitor dissolved into a field of bright blue. Then up through it came the image of a white square. As the corners rounded, a capering harlequin appeared in the center of the card. In Chinese at the top and English on the bottom was the legend, "Lord, what fools these mortals be!"

Rising through the thunder, and gaining volume as the shooting stopped, a sinister, cruel laughter filled the square. It built until all the spectators were staring up in disbelief at the image of the Dancing Joker filling the screen. Off to the right, Xu Ning pointed frantically at the holovision monitor, and officials scrambled around as if they could somehow change what was there.

This time, Noble hit the device's round button.

The laughter trailed off, but the voice returned after only a moment of silence. "For they have sown the wind, and they shall reap the whirlwind!" The harlequin, stark in black and white, slowly grinned and a single drop of bright blood ran languidly from the corner of his mouth.

Two seconds later, four small explosions along the top of the screen shattered the silence. The screen shook and the image wavered, then the massive monitor started to tip away from the wall. As it fell, gathering speed, a cry of triumph went up from the crowd.

One of the Black Cobra 'Mechs, a small *Commando*, reached its hands up to catch the screen, but the pilot miscalculated, the monitor crashing down on him, exploding in sparks and shards of glass. The 'Mech, its hands still upthrust, punched through the screen and out the other side. Electricity crackled and sparked over the war machine's surface. Victorious for an instant, the humanoid machine then wavered and toppled over onto its face.

The smoke from the screen rose thicker than the steam from the bleeding bodies.

Noble turned Cathy away from the scene and guided her away amid the other fleeing spectators. "We have to go."

She gave the center of the square one last glimpse. "All those people . . . I wish we could have done something . . ."

"We have," he whispered to her. "They'll rest easy now. Our opposition won't, and that's comfort enough."

31

> An army is of little value in the field unless wise counsels
> prevail at home.
>
> —CICERO, DE OFFICIIS

Old Connaught, Arc-Royal
District of Donegal, Lyran Alliance
20 October 3057

Because her father sat at his desk, behind her, Caitlin Kell could not see his face nor read his reaction to the holovid message from Katrina. She desperately wanted to see how he was taking her cousin's plea for help, words that were tearing her up inside. The fear and sadness in Katrina's voice pressed in on her heart. On either side of her, Chris Kell and Dan Allard watched without emotion, a reaction she could not understand.

Katrina smiled bravely at them from the monitor screen. "I have endeavored to keep the Lyran Alliance out of war, but Sun-Tzu has brought war to me. The Captain-General of the Free Worlds League has told me he would view it as a hostile action if I send House troops into the chaos of the Sarna March to oppose Sun-Tzu. This leaves me little choice but to appeal to you to bring the Kell Hounds from Arc-Royal to put down the revolts on New Home, Keid, and Caph."

The Archon looked down for a moment and when her face came back up, Caitlin saw that all the hopefulness had been replaced by fear. "You no doubt wonder why I don't ask my brother for aid in this matter, as Sun-Tzu's action against me is merely an expansion of his war against Victor.

"I have not done so because I fear I can no longer trust Victor. I never believed the stories that he had our mother and father killed, but after what he did with Joshua Marik and his sanctioning of the Combine's action in the Lyons thumb, my belief in Victor is shaken. I now think he may have had something to do with my mother's death."

Katrina stopped, sniffed, and wiped a tear from her cheek. "Forgive me the loss of composure, but I feel very alone. Sun-Tzu's attack has disconcerted me to the point where I am no longer certain of my decisions. I know he must be dealt with, and I know my parents trusted you implicitly, so I beg of you, come to the aid of the Lyran Alliance."

The picture froze there. "What do you think?" Morgan asked.

Caitlin turned her chair around to face her father. His long white hair touched the shoulders of his jacket, and only the barest hints of gray running down from the corners of his mouth darkened his white beard. His brown eyes burned with an intensity Caitlin had not seen since before his retirement.

What surprised her even more was the fact that the right sleeve of his jacket was not pinned into place at the shoulder. The bomb blast that had killed Archon Melissa Steiner and Salome Kell, Caitlin's mother, had also cost her father his right arm. Prince Victor Davion had ordered the NAIS to construct Morgan a new arm, but her father rarely wore it.

Caitlin half-closed her eyes. "Does what we think really matter, Father? The message was addressed to you."

"True, but Dan runs the unit, and you and Chris are consulted on contracts. Dan?"

Lieutenant Colonel Daniel Allard frowned. "We've never used the Hounds to suppress civil disorder. I don't think I like the idea of setting a precedent."

Caitlin turned to him. "But, Colonel, the rebellions have been fomented by Sun-Tzu Liao. This would be a military action. You've seen the holovid reports from Zurich and the other rebellion worlds. Someone has to help those people."

Chris Kell nodded in agreement. "Caitlin has a point. Normally warfare is between military units, and the populace at large is unaffected by it. If I remember my unit history correctly, the Hounds destroyed a unit that had been making war on the civilian population of Lyons during the Fourth Succession War."

"Different circumstance, Chris. The unit was the Third Dieron Regulars and they'd invaded Lyons with the specific intention of destroying one settlement on the planet. They slaughtered people wholesale." Dan Allard's blue eyes hardened. "Everyone in New Freedom died save two adults and thirty or so children. In that situation, we were fighting a military unit, not a civilian-based revolutionary movement."

Morgan thumped a black metal finger against his desktop. "Besides that, we're a 'Mech unit. We do have some very good, rapid-response infantry, but not the kind of forces needed to put down a revolution."

Caitlin frowned. "But the League has been using mercs to support Sun-Tzu's revolutions."

"Not so on these worlds." Chris leaned forward, resting his elbows on his knees. "I've been scanning all the reports from the Sarna March area and it's a mess. Katrina called it chaotic, but I'd say even that's optimistic. The second wave of the League and the Capellan invasions are hitting now. They've taken about a quarter of the March all by themselves. Everything else is fragmenting. Tikonov and the worlds in its bulge are staying with Victor, but all the other worlds are either going independent or forming alliances between themselves and other nearby worlds."

Dan smiled. "We've gotten a half-dozen offers from some of those governments to head down there. There are so many pieces I've started logging such requests into a file marked 'Puzzle March'."

Morgan sat back in his chair, but stared straight at Caitlin. "So, you agree that we reject Katrina's offer?"

She knew her father meant that question for her alone, but she hesitated before blurting something out. *Throttle back, Caitlin. He'll listen to reason.* "No, I don't agree. I don't think we should abandon Katrina."

"Why not?"

Caitlin glanced at Dan and Chris. She read no support on their faces, but neither did she read dismissal. That encouraged her. "I think we should not abandon Katrina because I believe she is right: I believe that Victor did kill Melissa and, therefore, also killed my mother. By not helping Katrina, we help Victor, and that I won't do."

Morgan's eyes tightened. "So, you do not trust Victor?"

"No, I don't."

"And you base this lack of trust on what Katrina has told you?"

"Yes, father, that and the feelings and impressions I've

gotten from him. He's distant and stiff. Whenever I've met him I've felt like I'm being rated and tested, evaluated and ranked from some nefarious purpose." She shivered. "I can't warm up to him."

Her father nodded slowly. "So your belief that Victor may have killed your mother comes from Katrina and your feelings about Victor?"

Though someone else might have spoken the same words sarcastically, her father's tone was sincere, letting her know he valued her feelings. She knew he might not give them as much weight as he would hard evidence of Victor's guilt, but he was fair enough not to dismiss them out of hand. "Yes, Father, her words and my feelings."

"Good. Then, if you will permit me, I'll let you know why I *don't* believe that Victor had anything to do with your mother's death." Morgan smoothed his beard down with his flesh and blood hand. "That distance and stiffness you see in Victor I also saw in his father a long time ago. Both men were born strategists, so they do evaluate and rank people. Victor may be a bit harsher about it because, as the heir apparent, he had to sort between true friends and those who cultivated him solely for personal advancement and advantage.

"Key in this is the fact that Victor is a warrior, as was his father. You probably don't remember that Hanse Davion had an older brother, Ian, who ruled the Federated Suns before Hanse did. We were there, Dan and I, on Mallory's World, when Ian was killed in combat. Until then, Hanse had never given a thought to the possibility of ruling a nation. He had always assumed his life would be in the field as a soldier leading his troops."

Caitlin shook her head. "But Victor was groomed to rule from birth."

"No, Cait, he wasn't. Hanse Davion and Melissa agreed to raise him the way Hanse and Katrina Steiner—the original, Melissa's mother—had grown up. Victor was *destined* to rule, but he was *groomed* to be a warrior. Remember, even after Hanse's death, Melissa ruled the Federated Commonwealth while Victor stayed with his unit. Had he wanted the throne, he could have pressed his suit, and Melissa would have abdicated in his favor."

Caitlin sank back into her chair. "You're saying Victor

could have taken the throne three years before his mother's death put him there?"

Morgan nodded slowly. "Archon Melissa told your mother and I that she spoken with Victor about her desire to retire, but he'd asked her to postpone retiring until 3062. He said he wanted to wait until he was at least the age his father had been when he became head of House Davion and the Federated Suns. He also told her he would be willing to wait longer than that."

"Why haven't you told anyone this?" Caitlin asked.

Her father's left hand knotted into a fist and the mechanical one aped the gesture imperfectly. "No one would believe me. The only people who could confirm what I have told you are Melissa and Salome, and neither one of them is alive. Once upon a time my word would have been taken at face value, but now conspiracy-mongers are even tying me into their fantasy schemes, citing as proof the fact that I ducked at the precise moment the bomb went off. They even use the fact that I lost an arm to that bomb as proof I was part of the conspiracy. They say Victor bought me a new arm as part payment of some devil's pact I'd made with him."

Morgan's eyes sharpened. "Caitlin, you've known Victor and Katrina as long as I have. Which of them is the better politician?"

Caitlin's mouth went dry. "Katrina."

"And which of them has managed to expand her holdings to well beyond any she would likely have claimed had things progressed normally?"

She nodded her head slowly. "Katrina."

"And Katrina, by declaring herself neutral, has allowed the Free Worlds League to attack her brother."

Caitlin brought her head up. "Then you're saying you believe Katrina had Melissa killed?"

Morgan nodded solemnly. "I am."

"Then why aren't we on our way to Tharkad to overthrow her?"

Her father hesitated before answering. He forced his hands open and pressed his palms flat on the desktop. "We are not heading to Tharkad for two simple reasons. The first is that while I do believe Katrina had my wife and your mother killed to advance her own career, I cannot prove it conclusively. If I could, I would immediately demand justice. Since I cannot, I am content to let her fret and stew over how to deal with Sun-Tzu."

The anger and pain she heard in her father's voice sliced like a razor through Caitlin's image of Katrina. Behind the facade of the smiling face, Caitlin now saw a monster with a huge maw and an insatiable appetite.

She looked at her father and a wordless agreement passed between them. Somehow, some way, they would find proof of Katrina's crime and make her pay for it. And Caitlin was certain her father knew that if he died first, she would see it through.

Caitlin felt a lump rise in her throat. "What's the second reason we're not going to kill Katrina?"

Morgan picked up a yellow slip of paper with his left hand. "This came at the same time ComStar brought me the holodisk. A Clan unit just jumped into the Alliance. It's up to us to deal with them."

Wotan
Jade Falcon Occupation Zone

"Yes, Elias, I will get her." Vandervahn Chistu succeeded in keeping the contempt out of his voice. "Natasha Kerensky has not survived to be her *age* by being stupid."

Elias Crichell's head snapped around the emphasis on the word *age*. "I never thought she was stupid. On Baker Three she ripped through the Nega Garrison Cluster as if it were not there. She even destroyed the buildings they were using as headquarters. Had you left the 305th Assault Cluster on Baker Three, she would not now be assaulting Devin. You know as well as I do that the Choyer Garrison Cluster will fall to her there."

Chistu clasped his hands behind his back and slowly began to pace around the interior of the holotank. "I do not doubt you are correct, Elias."

"Will you do nothing about it, Vahn?"

"I could call up real-time holovid and let you watch the fighting."

Crichell thrust a finger at him. "*That* is not what I meant. You said she would never get here, but you have done nothing to stop her. And now it looks as if Ulric's column will bring him here as well. You should be scrambling forces to stop them, and instead you have sent your Peregrine Galaxy off into Lyran space. Are you secretly a Wolf, *quiaff?*"

A jolt ran through Chistu. "No, I am not a Wolf." He stopped in the center of the tank. "Computer, project a map of the Jade Falcon Occupation Zone. Include Steel Viper worlds."

In an instant a helix of lights appeared in the center of the holotank. Green marked the worlds the Jade Falcons owned, silver the ones administered by the Steel Vipers, and red burned on the worlds the Wolves had hit. Chistu pointed to the collection of lights as if they explained everything. "I have the situation under control."

Crichell, folding his arms across his thick middle, looked unimpressed.

"Natasha Kerensky's task force hit Colmar. The 352nd Assault Cluster sustained an estimated twenty-five percent casualties. On Baker Three she used the 341st Assault Cluster. They took similar damage. Because of the poor weather on Devin, where she is using the Third Battle Cluster, we anticipate forty percent or higher casualties. Next she will hit Apolakkia or Denizli, where I have enough forces to cripple or kill her."

Annoy her, in truth, but still enough to bleed her. She did bid surprisingly well at Devin, so my casualty reports may be off a bit. Chistu looked over at Crichell. "Any questions, Elias?"

"I notice you have drawn some of your best Clusters here to Wotan instead of using them to kill her."

"I brought them here to calm your worries. I don't expect Natasha to make it to Wotan," Chistu lied. *She'll be here, and this is where I will kill her.*

"What of Ulric?"

"His unit took heavy damage on Evciler. I have troops setting up for him at Butler."

Crichell accepted that statement without comment, though Chistu read in his eyes that he thought the plan flawed. "Why did you send the Peregrine Galaxy into Lyran space?"

"For the same reason I have pulled the Omicron Galaxy from its garrison duties in the Periphery and also sent it into Lyran space."

"You did what?"

"I have two Galaxies operating in Lyran space." Chistu

touched the star representing Baker 3, and it enlarged to ten times its previous size. He touched the star icon about which the planets in that system revolved. The computer opened a window and displayed holovid footage of a large fleet vanishing from the jump point at the apex of the solar axis. "This was Khan Phelan's half of Natasha's spearhead."

He touched one of the silver stars and it expanded to display similar images of a fleet jumping into the system and quickly jumping out again. "The Vipers gave me that little bit of intelligence and have told me that the Wolves have not appeared at any of their worlds. This leads me to the conclusion that they have jumped into Lyran space. I suspect this is an attempt at a flanking attack."

"Where are they?"

"I do not know precisely. There were only two Lyran worlds within range of a jump from Graus: Morges and Babaeski. The Peregrines are on their way to the Babaeski system since it is the one that lies closest to Wotan. The Omicon Galaxy will investigate Morges. If they do not find the Wolves there, those Galaxies will work their way toward the Periphery. We have excellent data concerning those systems from the work Nekane Hazen did on the Red Corsair mission."

Crichell's eyes grew wide. "You must never speak of her. Never."

"Don't worry, Elias, your secret is safe with me. As safe as we are right here on Wotan." Chistu waved his hands through the holographic cloud of stars. "The future ilKhan has nothing to fear."

32

Avalon City, New Avalon
Crucis March, Federated Commonwealth
1 November 3057

Sweat dripping from his nose and his lungs pumping like bellows, Victor Davion rested his hands on his knees to catch his breath. His throat felt a little raw, but he had come to expect that from the gym's dry air. Taking his exercise indoors was one of the few concessions he made to Curaitis' sense of caution. The indoor track, which hung suspended six meters above the gym's trio of basketball courts, was short, but was constructed from wood and covered with a rubber surface supposed to be less stressful to the knees.

And Curaitis likely ordered a layer or two of ballistic cloth run in there in case an assassin should try to shoot up through it at me. Straightening up, Victor began to walk around the one hundred-and-sixty-meter track to the southeast corner of the gym. Galen had broken off three laps earlier to use the wallphone to answer his pager.

A chill draft cut through the thin fabric of Victor's shirt and shorts, bringing goose-bumps to his flesh. Galen was just returning the phone to the receiver and turning to look at the Prince, anger and bewilderment fighting for control of his face.

"Do you want your heart rate to stay up, or shall I save the bad news for the office?" Galen said.

Victor smiled and picked his towel up from the corner platform. "It can't be that bad, Jerry, especially after the news we had this morning. Morgan Kell has refused Katherine's request for help against Sun-Tzu. We might still be slow on organizing our counterattack, but I'm generally satisfied with how things are progressing. Can this news spoil that?"

"Yes. That call was from Curaitis. They've got the agent who did Joshua's DNA match."

Victor's face brightened. "Who was he?"

Galen looked down. "She. It was a female agent."

Katherine? Victor wiped his face on the towel. He looked up. "Who was she?"

"Francesca Jenkins."

Stunned, Victor sat down hard on the track. "She's the one . . ."

"Yes, the one who stopped Sun-Tzu's people."

"But . . ." Victor frowned. He knew that everyone who worked with Joshua had been changed when the double was brought in. If Thomas had decided to put an agent of his close to Joshua, why then? Why not have one there from the start? It made no sense, unless Marik knew, somehow, that Sun-Tzu would attack the hospital.

The Prince looked up at Galen. "What did Curaitis say?"

"He said they'd double-checked *anyone* who came in contact with Joshua, and they all came up clean. In going over the background checks, it occurred to him and some other agents that Francesca was the only person who hadn't been double-checked.

"A forensics team went over her apartment with a fine-tooth comb." Galen smiled. "If you'd not been so generous in making certain her expenses were taken care of, the place might have been cleaned out, and we'd have gotten nothing. As it was, they found a small plastic bag with a DNA sample that matches that of our Joshua double in the back of her freezer. Curates says chemical residue in the liquid indicates she did the matching with a science kit."

Victor shook his head. "How is that possible? She—I remember reading a profile of her—she was an Avalonian. Her father was a MechWarrior."

"Who murdered her mother and killed herself."

"Granted, that's a nasty way to go, but she was counseled, she learned to handle it. How did she become a League agent?"

Galen leaned back against the metal guard rail on the interior of the track. "According to the aunt who took her in, the girl spent three summers on Castor with her 'grandparents.' Her mother was from Castor, and her maiden name *was* Jirik, but her real parents died before your father took Castor from Marik. Curaitis believes League intelligence ran an operation, keyed by the embassy here at the time of the mother's death, in which they persuaded Francesca to become an agent. They recruited her, trained her, and left her here as a mole. They played off her loneliness and gave her a proud, pro-League heritage to counter the hideous one her father represented."

"And that son of a bitch Thomas has the gall to call me evil!"

Galen gently cleared his throat before Victor could continue. "Highness, the creation and turning of agents is rarely a pretty thing."

Victor nodded reluctantly. "I know, I know. I understand the theory, but the practice is repellent when you look at specific cases. How is the women, anyway?"

"Her luck is holding. It appears she'll suffer no permanent damage. The hip replacement worked fine. With a year of therapy, she'll be good as new."

Victor's eyes narrowed. "This information about her *faux* grandparents, that's the kind of data you could use to turn her, isn't it?"

His intelligence advisor thought for a moment. "It would seem so."

Victor glanced down at the track. "See if you follow this: Francesca Jenkins is a problem for me. I've praised her highly and she's become a heroine throughout the Federated Commonwealth. If it comes out that she's a League agent, both I and my whole Intelligence Secretariat will look incredibly stupid. If, on the other hand, she *dies,* and vanishes from sight, she ceases to be a problem."

"You're not thinking of killing her."

"Not at all. Regardless of what she's done to hurt us, her action against the Liao agents was brave, and I'll not reward that with death. In fact, I'd not want her brought to trial because of what she did. At heart she's obviously strong. By pointing out how she was used, we can re-forge her into a powerful weapon against our enemies. She will be allowed to atone for what she did, we will save face, and, if we let her suffer an embolism or something and die, no one will be looking for her to expose her secret."

Galen nodded. "I know of other cases where faking a death has worked wonders in erasing ties with the past."

"Thank you for your expert opinion," Victor said drily. "Speak with Curaitis and get his opinion on this. If he agrees, have her appearance changed—but keep her pretty— and get her trained."

"You think you could use her against the League?"

Victor shrugged. "The League, or Sun-Tzu, or perhaps even my sister. Understand me, Jerry. I don't want an assassin—I don't ever want to use one again. What I do want is an agent who's smart enough to lay a trap for my enemies."

He stood and draped the towel around his shoulders. "I think Francesca Jenkins could be just that."

33

An army of deer led by a lion is more to be feared than an army of lions led by a deer.

—ATTRIBUTED TO CHABRAIS

Denizli, Wolf Clan Liberation Zone
7 November 3057

Natasha refused to let herself curse aloud at the stiffness and pain in her lower back and legs. She gently lowered herself onto her camp stool, then leaned forward to ease the pain in her back. The sharp twinge running down her rump and along both hamstrings made her breathe in sharply. She *had* almost cried out, but her iron will transformed anger into an analgesic.

She looked up at the younger men and women filing into her tent. "You have reports for me, *quiaff?*"

The tall black man nodded, starting the long braids of his hair swaying slowly. "The 341st Assault Cluster obtained its objectives, suffering twenty-five percent casualties. This puts my Cluster down approximately forty-eight percent in 'Mech assets for the campaign and five percent down on pilots. Operationally, the Cluster is running at fifty-two percent and, if given a week for salvage and repair, I can bring that back up to fifty-five percent."

"Good, Ramon." Natasha shifted her gaze to Serena Fetladral. "How is the 352nd holding up?"

"The Silver Wolves have lost fifty-five percent of our 'Mechs and twelve percent of our pilots. I can come back up to half-strength operationally with a week of repair."

"Good. Darren?"

The Third Battle Cluster's Star Colonel, Darren Fetladral, shared his distant cousin's blue eyes, but resembled Serena in no other way except for the weariness slumping his shoulders. "In a week I can have my Cluster at fifty percent as well. I've lost more pilots, but I have good Techs who are bringing my wounded people and damaged 'Mechs on line quickly."

The last man, Marco Hall, slowly shook his head. "Khan Natasha, your Wolf Spiders are down forty percent in 'Mechs, including yours, and ten percent in pilots."

"Is that including me, Marco?"

The man shook his head. "Even if you were dead, cremated, loaded into a shell and launched, I'd expect you to get a kill, so you are not counted in that total."

Natasha settled a grim mask over her face. "And the Falcons' Fifth and Ninth Talons—they are destroyed?"

Ramon Sender folded his arms. "Gone, all of them, gone."

"Excellent. You have a week for repairs, then a week of travel. We'll be at Twycross and down on the ground by the twentieth. Get some rest. You all deserve it. Dismissed."

No one moved. *They waited far longer for this conversation than I ever would have. They're good troops.* Natasha brought her head up despite the pain in her back. "You have permission to speak freely, but not all at once."

Ramon, the senior officer among them, took the lead. "I was informed of the text of the message you sent to Twycross. You told the Steel Vipers they had better move their four Clusters off that rock or you'd destroy them utterly. You included data on our Clusters adjusted to look like they had been generated after the battling here, but actually reflecting our *pre*-campaign strength. While the Eleventh Battle Cluster has not seen action so far, even if we include it in our total, we are still under the Steel Viper garrison strength. Their garrison, as you know, is made up of line units, just as is our assault force, and they are dug in."

Serena glanced at Ramon, then looked at Natasha. "Attacking Twycross could prove to be the fight that breaks us, and we know you want to get to Wotan."

"So are you asking me if I am mad, or do you want to know if I intend to fight the Steel Vipers on Twycross?"

The flesh tightened around Darren's Fetladral's eyes. "We want to know how you intend for us to take our objectives?"

Natasha smiled and her back eased a bit. "Other troops—Jade Falcon troops or most any of the Inner Sphere—would have mutinied by now. You haven't. You're as good a collection of warriors as ever a commander had the fortune to lead. That said, let me answer all your questions.

"I intend my bold boast of our strength to make the Steel Vipers decide they want to stay out of the fight. If they let us use Twycross for another engagement with the Falcons, I will agree not to liberate the planet. I expect that bargain to be offered and done by the time we reach Twycross. I also expect my boast of our troop strength to be sent on to Wotan and for Chistu to be sweating glass splinters by the bucket. We know Crichell will be."

She looked up at Serena. "My goal is to reach Wotan, but my *intention* is to destroy as many Jade Falcon units as possible. In crushing their garrisons, in liberating their planets, we will force them to divert both troops and equipment to reassert their influence over the worlds where we fight. By destroying their garrisons we also limit the number of troops they can send after Phelan."

"Or," Marco asked, "use in launching a new invasion of the Inner Sphere?"

Natasha nodded her head wearily. "Hamstring the lead 'Mech in a formation and the others have no one to follow. Chistu is getting worried—he tossed the Fifth Talon in here to help the Ninth Talon. He has no idea what we have for troops, and that's making him crazy. Even with us bidding in lower numbers than he has in his garrisons, we're chewing his troops up."

Darren nodded slowly. "And with Twycross being a Steel Viper world, the battle will not be part of the Trial of Refusal. Chistu will send troops to oppose us, expecting to enjoy a numerical superiority, but he won't have it. We'll surprise and tear up what he throws at us."

"My hopes and dreams." Natasha folded her hands together and rested her forearms against the inside of her thighs. The fabric of her cooling vest felt rough against the flesh of her upper arms, and it surprised her how that simple sensation somehow overrode her pain. Glancing down she saw where a streak of blood had dried on the vest, but whether the blood belonged to her or one of the Elementals she'd killed after ejecting, she could not tell.

The Black Widow stood slowly. "The one advantage we have over the Inner Sphere is that we have no need to survive a battle for our genetic heritage to be passed on. We can die and still be part of the future. That is enough for a Clan warrior. But the Falcons and the Crusaders want more—power and conquest. They overreach themselves, and I mean to cut their grasping hands off at the wrist."

She pointed up toward the sky. "Our futures are out there, with Phelan. Our destiny is on Twycross and Wotan. Our destiny is to deny the Falcons their future, so *our* future has a chance to sprout and grow."

Natasha smiled, then shook her head. "I must be getting old—I usually leave such speeches to someone else."

Marco winked at her. "Our job is to kill Falcons."

"Yes." The Black Widow squinted one eye and contracted the trigger finger on her right hand. "And I've always believed actions speak louder than words."

Tharkad
District of Donegal, Lyran Alliance

Katrina Steiner gave the ComStar demi-Precentor a withering stare and was pleased to see the effect her icy mien had on him. The smallish, balding man shuddered and bowed his head. *Good.*

"Have you brought me a reply from the Primus?" she asked.

Demi-Precentor Correy held his hands up like a supplicant before a vengeful goddess. "With the events of recent days, the Primus has been inordinately busy."

"Too *busy* to deal with a message from *me*?"

The man wilted beneath her ire. "Please, Archon Katrina, understand that no disrespect is meant by her delay in replying to you."

"Then how would she explain her agreement to let Draconis Combine troops stand as ComStar peacekeepers, *then* allow them to virtually invade the Lyons thumb? My citizens are being made the subject people of an ancient foe, and I will not stand for it."

"Yes, Archon, I know that. You have eloquently comunicated your concern to the Primus on repeated occasions and I have been assured at the highest levels—*First Circuit levels*—that special attention is being paid to your messages. It is just that Prince Victor also has a claim to the Lyons thumb and the Combine action has not brought a protest from him and . . ."

Katrina imperiously waved Correy to silence. "My brother has *nothing* to do with the Lyons thumb. You are sanctioning this violation of my border because there is no protest from a man who intended to use the death of a child to further his own political gains. I had thought ComStar, defender of the Inner Sphere, architect of the Clan truce, would take a higher moral position than justifying greed and treason because a murderer has not complained that a part of *my* realm has been amputated!"

"That is a very good point, Archon Katrina. I will communicate it to my superiors, immediately."

She let her fury flare her nostrils, then studied Correy from under half-closed eyes. "If you did not come today to deliver me the Primus' apology, why are you here?" She let the hint of a smile tug at the corners of her mouth. "Surely you cannot enjoy it when I rage at you?"

"No, Archon, most assuredly not."

"Then?"

The man, cringing still, reached into his red jacket for a folded slip of paper. "I have been asked to intercede for someone who seeks an audience with you." He held the paper out to her and she took some satisfaction in its trembling. "Without diplomatic standing, he had no other way to reach you."

Katrina took the paper from Correy and opened it. She read the name, then thrust the paper back at him. "Why would I meet with *him*?"

Correy took the paper back. "He said he would be sending a representative with a token of his esteem. He begs your indulgence in delaying a decision about his request until after you inspect his gift."

A gift? What could this man give me that I would want? She recalled having met him and vaguely remembered hearing of a serious reversal of fortune he had recently suffered. But she also remembered that he had once been considered resourceful.

Katrina nodded once, curtly. "Tell him I will receive his representative. If I am pleased, I will then see him."

"Satisfactory, Archon. That is more than he had hoped for."

"Good." She looked toward the door. "You might want to

suggest to your mistress that she seriously consider using a similar approach to get back into my good graces. As a gift she can return to me the Lyons thumb, and the timeliness of that gift will be very important. If it misses Christmas, the Primus will have no reason to expect anything good in the New Year."

34

The conventional army loses if it does not win, the guerilla wins if he does not lose.

—HENRY KISSINGER, 20TH CENTURY DIPLOMAT

Daosha, Zurich
Zurich People's Republic, League Liberation Zone
15 November 3057

Noble Thayer could feel the giddy energy coming off his people. It was odd—four ordinary citizens—Rick and Carol Bradford, Anne Thompson, and Cathy Hanney—all glowing with the success of having blown up a Security Committee office. Only Ken Fox showed the sort of noncommittal demeanor that suggested he found the bombing to be business as usual.

Rick looked with suspicion around the bare basement apartment before discreetly raising his wine glass in a toast. "To the Dancing Joker and his punchlines."

The others, except for Noble, joined in. He smoothed his newly blond hair down, then smiled. "That one did go very well. It was an added benefit that Werner Chou had returned to the office to work late."

Carol shook her head. "I'd hoped that setting the bomb for three in the morning would have prevented casualties."

Noble nodded, despite Ken Fox rolling his eyes. "We've agreed, all along, to target assets and not personnel whenever possible, but by now you all realize that every operation carries with it a threat of death—ours or theirs. You've accepted that—at least you said you did when we started. I need to know if it is still true."

Ken Fox's head came up. "Why?"

Noble stood up, his upper body sinking into shadow as he

rose beyond the cone of light produced by the light hanging over their table. "I need to know because we've reached the point where we're going to have to escalate our level of activity."

Rick rubbed a hand over a stubbly beard. "I thought things were going fine."

"They are. We've each got a bounty of more than twenty thousand C-bills on our heads. Graffiti throughout Daosha supports us and there've been a number of copycat operations, even to dropping other playing cards as identifiers."

Cathy smiled. "Jacko Diamond is the only one who's any good. The rest look like they must be kids."

"Agreed. I think I have a line on Jacko and I may try to recruit him." Noble folded his arms. "The thing is this—we started off, as far as the public is concerned with blowing up the screen in Fengzilusude Square. Try as they might, the Zurich Political Directorate can't hide news of things we do. The word is getting out."

Anne laughed lightly. "I heard a joke the other day—one security man is asked by his wife what progress they've made in finding the Dancing Joker. His reply? 'Zip, dear!' "

Noble's voice rode above the gentle laughter in the room. "It's true. We're embarrassing ZPDir, but that's not enough if we want to succeed. Face it, as long as they exist and have greater resources than we do, they'll win and we'll lose. Our only chance at success is to stage a counterrevolution. To do that we have to convince the people of Zurich that ZPDir is limited in its ability to strike back at us. Doing that will cost some lives, so I need a confirmation of your commitment to this movement."

Carol drew back. "When did this become a movement?"

"It's always been a movement, Carol." Rick rested a hand on her shoulder. "A struggle against the government."

"Yes, but this is the first time Noble has said anything about taking over the planet." Carol looked up at Noble. "No offense intended, but being a science teacher in a military academy hardly qualifies you as a planetary leader."

Noble held his hands up to ward off her irritation. "What I want is to remove Xu Ning from power, not power for myself. Look, you know the old saying, 'All that's needed for the triumph of evil is that good men do nothing,' right?"

Carol nodded.

"Well, it has a corollary: the triumph of good requires that good men force evil men to do nothing. We're on that track, but we need to hit harder. Blowing up a security committee office helps, but with enough people, the government can reconstruct everything we destroy."

"Excerpt Werner Chou."

"Valid point, Anne, but do any of us mourn Chou's death? He stood there with Xu Ning when the two hundred martyrs were killed. He could have stopped it, but he didn't. His people rounded the martyrs up and we all know that it was SecCom troops in ZPCadre uniforms who did the shooting, not the troopers themselves."

"Not that they wouldn't have." Ken Fox scratched at the side of his face where a bruise had faded to a yellowed shadow of itself. "I've still got ringing in my ears from the rifle butt I took trying to stop them from hauling those kids off."

Noble nodded sympathetically. "Look, SecCom, the Cadre, and the Black Cobras are the three pillars that prevent Xu Ning's empire from toppling. We've hurt SecCom, but that only buys us time. Going after the others will mean some people are going to die. If you can't or won't be part of that, you can go. I don't want anyone working against their own feelings and ethics. I don't think killing a dictator's warriors is a moral dilemma, but I respect beliefs to the contrary."

He waited, then looked at every one of them in turn. Each nodded—the most enthusiastic being Fox and the least Carol Bradford. Noble knew he could count on Carol, but he decided to give her tasks that made use of her administrative skills but kept her in the background when all hell broke loose.

"Good," he smiled, leaning forward onto the table. "This is what we're going to do: in nine days, we'll attack the Zhongdade Armory."

"What? You can't do that. That's suicide." Ken Fox shook his head. "I know it's got all those weapons, but we'll never get any of that out. It's an impossible target."

"Nothing is an impossible target." Noble kept his voice low, but his words were edged with excitement. "It's true that the Armory is as impossible a target as, say, hitting a DropShip. Both have an incredible amount of firepower to defend themselves."

Fox frowned. "So why are we going to hit it?"

Noble smiled. "What if we don't want the weapons stored there? What if we decide just to deny those weapons to ZPCadre?"

Rick Bradford's eyes lit up. "You mean we blow the Armory up?"

"With the amount of weapons and explosives stored there, an explosion would take out the whole street. ZPCadre has appropriated the area to house their troops, so civilian casualties shouldn't be a real factor." He looked around for reactions and questions. When none came he continued. "I think I have a way to deliver the bomb while minimizing risk to us."

Ken Fox furrowed his brows. "Getting enough explosives to take the Armory down isn't going to be easy."

Noble shook his head. "Trust me. Just find me a garden center and a place to purchase gasoline and I can produce all the explosives we need." As Fox started to speak again, Noble held a hand up. "A second thing we're going to have to do is start working through a cell system. That means two things. The first is that I'll be giving each of you assignments that you cannot reveal to anyone else. *No one*—especially not to the rest of us. That way, it won't blow the whole plan should any one of us get caught.

"Second, we're going to have to start recruiting more people. Our new plans are going to take more of us than we have now. I'll be trying to draw in folks like Jacko Diamond. You four look for people you can trust, people you've known for a while. Just watch them and when you have a likely candidate, I'll help you bring him or her in. Understood?"

Everyone nodded.

"Good. One last thing: in the event any of us gets captured, the rest of us should walk away. We can't pull off a rescue if we're running blind. We'll back off, then find a way to get you out. Everyone got it? Walk away, rescue another day."

Cathy looked up at him. "Xu Ning never tried to rescue any of his people that the government caught."

"That's because he's an animal." Noble tapped the table with a fist. "And it's the same reason I won't let him have any of you for any longer than necessary."

Director's Palace
Daosha, Zurich,
Zurich People's Republic, League Liberation Zone

Xu Ning patted the corners of his mouth with his starched linen napkin, then sipped the last of his Montchartre Bourgogne Blanc '43. *Governor Campbell had such excellent taste in wines. When I try the '39, I'll have to pour some into the urn with his ashes.* Returning his crystal wine glass to the table, he looked over at his dining companion. "So, Colonel, you were saying that it's no surprise that my Security Committee has been unable to find these insurgents?"

Burr, obviously a patrician trying to descend to the level of someone who had upset the social order, slid his half-finished plate toward the center of the table, then pressed his napkin down in the newly vacant place. "I merely meant that you, as the leader of a successfully waged guerrilla campaign, must appreciate the difficulty of trying to ferret out the members of a covert and irregular force. Though I believe the evidence indicates that a Davion agent must be head of the operation, he is clearly using your methods against you."

Ning smiled politely, accepting the man's condescension. "We had speculated, poor Werner and I, that this Dancing Joker might be an agent sent to infiltrate our organization—perhaps even without the knowledge of the local constabulary—and capture us."

"The same constabulary that could not catch you, Mr. Director, will never catch the Dancing Joker. I know you have inserted your own people into the constabulary and subordinated the organization to your Security Committee, but incompetence will out."

Ning raised a slender-fingered hand and waved his man servant into the dining room. "You may clear this. Coffee, Colonel? And dessert?"

"Please."

"Carl, bring the dessert and the Domaine Fiedade Beaumes-de-Venise 3050. And the Colonel will want an ashtray for his cigar."

The servant cleared their plates and the Colonel offered Xu Ning a cigar, but he politely declined. "I never acquired the habit. Tobacco was not easy to obtain while on the run, and the scent of smoke carries incredibly far, as you know, in a jungle. We learned to avoid patrols by sniffing them out."

Burr chuckled throatily. "More proof of the constabulary's idiocy."

"So, then, you are of the opinion that my ability to survive in the field was due to the incompetence of the constabulary, not due to my own skill at evading them?"

"Please, Mr. Director, do not interpret my remarks as any criticism of the feat of survival you accomplished. It was quite incredible, but an organized force could have found you out."

"Your Black Cobras, for example?"

"We've done counter-insurgency operations, yes, but not in an urban area."

"So finding the Dancing Joker would be beyond you?"

Burr smiled and sat back as the servant returned with dessert. "Finding the Dancing Joker would not be beyond me, but it is well outside my mission profile. The Black Cobras are here to secure this planet, defend it, and defend ourselves. The Dancing Joker is no threat to us, I am afraid."

Xu Ning sipped the wine and nodded to Carl to pour for the Colonel. "But the Dancing Joker could *become* a threat to you, yes?"

"Only if he increases the size of his organization." Burr paused as he tipped one of the candles to provide him a flame to light his cigar. "Of course, in doing that, he'll provide you the opening you need to get him."

Xu Ning chose to ignore the splotches of cooling wax splattered over the mahogany table's surface. "You believe he will recruit people with questionable loyalties?"

"His natural allies are the criminal element and the merchant class, neither of which likes your control over the economy. Luckily for you, members of each can be bought."

"So, I need an insurgent *mercenary*?"

Burr lowered his cigar and his voice at the same time. "Mr. Director, *mercenaries* are professionals who are paid to provide a service. What you want is a greedy amateur willing to sell his soul for a few thousand C-bills."

"I see the distinction, Colonel, and I shall heed your advice." Xu Ning savored more of his dessert wine. "Tomorrow I shall start shopping for an informant and see whether, once and for all, I can remove this thorn from my side and reshape Zurich to my will."

35

The unknown is the governing condition of war.
—FERDINAND FOCH, PRINCIPLES OF WAR

JumpShip Werewolf, *Morges*
Tamar Domains, Lyran Alliance
20 November 3057

Phelan Ward adjusted the headset and brought the microphone up to his mouth. "Say again, Morges System Control."

A tired little man stared up at Phelan from the monitor in the *Werewolf*'s communications center. "This is Morges System Control, Tamar Domains. Your ship's transponder has no code recognized in the Lyran Alliance. Please identify yourself and state your reason for being here."

Phelan blinked. *Tamar Domains? Lyran Alliance? What the hell is going on? Did we jump into another universe?* Since splitting from Natasha's task force a month and a half earlier, the *Werewolf* had double-jumped through the Steel Viper system of Antares and then to an uninhabited star system still within the Jade Falcon Zone. There the JumpShips in his task force had unfurled their solar sails and recharged their Kearney-Fuchida jump coils and their lithium fusion batteries, enabling them to make another double jump.

Though the plan was for Phelan to bring his force into Morges, he'd debated abandoning it to strike immediately for Wotan. While the ships were recharging, he'd made battle plans, run simulations, and refined his strategies until he was sure he could beat Chistu and his Clusters. A dozen times he almost issued orders that would have put his force on war footing as it made for Wotan.

What stopped him was the canister Natasha had given him. Of the nine JumpShips in his flotilla, only three carried combat troops. The rest contained support personnel from the other castes within the Wolf Clan. His force was a holographic slice of the Wolf Clan, the cutting from which it could grow again.

His responsibility for them warred with his desire to crush the Jade Falcons. He wanted to rush off and join Natasha and Ulric in the battle that would decide the fate of the Clans. Both knew that tendency in him, a rebellious streak that could send him into a mad dash toward Wotan.

And they also knew me well enough to know I'd not abandon the responsibility they saddled me with. He smiled to himself. *I hope, after all this, you both can tell me how unnecessary it was.*

His silence prompted the man from Morges System Control to become quite insistent. "You *must* identify yourself and your business here. If you do not, you will be considered hostile. We will respond in kind."

Phelan slowly shook his head. "I don't think you want to do anything rash."

"Tell that to the aerospace fighters that scramble to shoot you down."

Phelan took a deep breath. When his fleet had left the uninhabited system and jumped into the Morges system, they'd come in far out on the orbital disk, at a point where a gas giant hid them from observation by Morges System Control. From that vantage point they had noticed considerable activity going toward and away from the planet. The only group they had been able to positively identify was a Jade Falcon task force, but it left again after recharging its JumpShips. Soon after its departure, more ships arrived and headed in toward the planet.

He had hoped that the troops arriving after the Falcons showed up would leave again, but they did not, which left him with a difficult decision. He had chosen Morges for two reasons. The first was that its austral polar continent was uninhabited and, at the tail end of the year, locked in a winter of nonstop blizzards and temperatures that would freeze a man after about ten steps. If he had to fight Falcons, and he knew he would, he wanted to defend that spot—both to minimize civilian casualties and to let the Falcons know his people were playing for keeps.

The second reason was a bit more practical. Morges, despite being on the Jade Falcon border, was only lightly defended. It had no strategic industries or assets. Two battalions of the Fourth Skye Rangers had been assigned to protect it because it was part of the holdings owned by the Duchess of Skye. One battalion of the Twentieth Arcturan Guards RCT brought the garrison up to a full regiment in strength, but the Guards were green and the Rangers' allegiance had been to Ryan Steiner. With his death, their resolve to defend this world so far from their homes would surely have waned.

Or not. Phelan stared back at the man in system control. "You can be a hero today, if you wish. Save your fighters. Keep them on the ground." He turned and nodded to the navigator at his station. "Light us up."

At his command, all six of the DropShips connected to the *McKenna* Class fighting JumpShip turned on their identify Friend/Foe transponders. In addition, the navigator switched the *Werewolf*'s transponder from one found on commercial haulers to that of a WarShip.

Phelan looked at the shocked space-traffic controller. "And, yes, there are more of us out here. I am Khan Phelan Ward of the Wolf Clan. I require the use of your austral continent. I will use it, but before you make any Rangers or Guards die defending a lot of ice, I suggest you send a message to Prince Victor Davion. He will grant me permission to make planetfall there."

The controller's head came up at the mention of Victor's name and a sneer twisted his lips. "Citizens of the Lyran Alliance take no orders from Victor Davion. We've fought you Clanners before." The man's flesh tightened around his eyes. "You're going to want to be bidding your force, aren't you?"

Phelan nodded slowly. "You understand our customs."

"And I'm not alone. I'm transferring you to Planetary Defense."

The screen went blank for a moment or two. Phelan turned from the monitor and looked at Ranna. "Tell all Cluster commanders that we'll be fighting our way in. They should prep bids for engaging two Clusters of the defenders."

"Planetary Defense here, incoming Clan unit. Identify yourself."

Phelan started as he recognized the voice. He turned back to the screen and smiled. "This is the prodigal son. Will you welcome me home?"

Morgan Kell nodded his head slowly. "If you're seeking a have we will welcome you."

"W e, but those who come after us will be fighting."

"I know. They were here looking for you earlier, or so I was told." Morgan smiled slowly. "Internal politics?"

"Lyran *Alliance?*" Phelan shook his head. "Some things I do not want to broadcast."

"Understood." Phelan's father laughed. "We'll speak when you get down."

Liao Palace, Sian
Capellan Confederation

Sun-Tzu Liao reached into the holographic display of worlds hovering above his desk and squeezed Keid as if it were an annoying gnat. The star remained displayed there on the back of his thumbnail, but his moment of anger evaporated as the pressure on his fingers built painfully. He shook his fingers out, a snarl on his face.

Keid's revolution had gone very well. In fact it had gone better than he'd expected because he had not been using terrorist tactics there to create unrest in the population or to undermine their confidence in the government. Roland Carpenter, his agent on planet, had exploited a combination of religious fervor and moral outrage at Victor's murder of Joshua Marik to spark resentment against the local government. Revelations about the planetary Duke's affair with underaged twins who had ties to a known agent of the Draconis Combine had toppled his government and Carpenter been acclaimed as a leader who could defend the world against corruption from within and assault from without.

The whole thing had gone so well that Thomas had rejected entreaties to reinforce the world with mercenaries. Sun-Tzu would have pressed him, but the invasion was going so well enough in terms of his conquests that complaining would have seemed ungracious and mistrustful. The fact that Thomas had suggested that Sun-Tzu foot the bill for any mercenaries he wanted to move to defend his holdings revealed him how quickly Thomas would abandon him. That further convinced Sun-Tzu to ease back on his demands.

After all, they *were* winning and Victor Davion had done

almost nothing to defend his worlds. Because of that, Sun-Tzu told himself that what he had taken, he would keep.

Then Roland Carpenter disappeared from Keid without a trace. A loyalist Steiner counter-revolution put the Duke's daughter on the throne from which her father had been torn. She swore fealty to Katrina Steiner and granted amnesty to those who had risen against her father. Sun-Tzu's agents, however, she ruthlessly hunted down, wiping out more than half the cells. Not only had he lost Keid in one brutal week, but he had also lost his means of contesting it.

Sun-Tzu pressed his hands together, palm to palm, as he sat back in the chair. "I have let Thomas Marik turn my re-conquered worlds into a buffer zone between his realm and the Federated Commonwealth. It is in Thomas' interest to let me consolidate those holdings, but beyond that he will not support me. What I want and what he deems sufficient are widely divergent, but what I have now is better than what I had before. I must work within these constraints to further my ends without destroying my alliance with Thomas."

Of the worlds within the League Liberation Zone, only Nanking had an active Davion presence. The messages coming from Smithson's Bandits indicated they could hold out against the Militia force sent from Woodstock to dislodge them, but reinforcements would be necessary to destroy the Militia. Sun-Tzu wanted Nanking because of its manufacturing capabilities, but snapping up the undefended worlds in the liberation zone had a higher priority. The stalemate could stand until Victor moved to reinforce his own worlds and counter the invasion.

"In this seat, Justin Xiang Allard engineered the loss of all those worlds. In this seat, I engineer their return to the Capellan Confederation." He patted the arms of the chair. "Once I have accomplished that much, I can do more and see how much magic this chair has left in it."

The Great Gash, Twycross
Steel Viper Occupation Zone

Even insulated from the stinging spray of sand and gravel by her *Dire Wolf*'s cockpit canopy, Natasha shuddered when she looked at the Great Gash. "This is the place."

Marco Hall's voice crackled with storm-wrought static through her neurohelmet's speakers. "Yes, this is the place where the Falcon Guards were destroyed."

"That, too." The rocky scarlet cliff-faces rose up some two hundred meters over the floor of the mountain pass. The canyon had once been deeper and more narrow, but it was now carpeted with a layer of the pulverized stone that had tumbled down from the Gash's walls in the last great battle here. Drilled and sown with explosives, the Gash had been blown by Kai Allard-Liao—to prevent Jade Falcon troops from reaching the Plain of Curtains down below. In detonating the explosives, Kai had destroyed an entire front-line 'Mech Cluster and saved Prince Victor and the Kell Hounds from death.

Natasha had still been in the Inner Sphere when news of that spectacular victory was broadcast. Though she'd spent nearly fifty years away from the Clans as a member of Wolf's Dragoons and had all but forgotten the alliances and enmities of the her former life, word of the Jade Falcons' humiliating defeat had made her smile. Before coming to the Inner Sphere, one of her greatest victories had been at the Falcon Guards' expense, so their defeat at the hands of a single Inner Sphere MechWarrior seemed somehow appropriate.

Hall's *Hellbringer* came into view to the right through the swirling sheets of reddish, wind-whipped sand. "It looks as if the Gash is still useful for bringing troops into our rear area. That is, *if* you still intend to fight the Falcons on the Plain of Curtains."

"I do. Any Falcon units sent to oppose us here are going to be thinking about the last time they fought here and how badly they were mauled and humiliated. They'll be afraid of being disgraced again, and that will eat into them. It will help us win this fight, then push on to Wotan."

Static prefaced Hall's comment. "You really think they will come here?"

"They can't avoid it." Natasha shook her head as the storm draped a sheet of red sand across her canopy. "They'll come and, if we're lucky, Chistu will be leading them. History repeats itself and here on Twycross the Falcons will once again know the bitter taste of defeat."

══ 36 ══

I don't know what effect these men will have on the enemy, but, by God, they frighten me.

—THE DUKE OF WELLINGTON,
IRISH-BORN MILITARY LEADER AND STATESMAN

Wotan, Jade Falcon Occupation Zone
27 November 3057

Khan Vandervahn Chistu stood in his holotank looking first at one data window and then the next. On the right he had Khan Natasha Kerensky's unbelievable statement of her strength—relayed to him by the Steel Vipers. He had also seen the casualty reports. His agents had sent him terrabytes of information about how much damage Natasha had taken so far in this campaign. The idea that she still boasted five full Clusters was incredible—in the truest sense of that word.

To his left hovered Khan Phelan Ward's stated strength in the polar wastes of Morges. His Alpha Galaxy had five line Clusters. Of the garrison Galaxy traveling in his task force there was no report, but Khan Phelan had added two regiments of a mercenary unit—the Kell Hounds—to his forces. That put him at effectively nine Clusters in strength—as formidable a force as had yet been mustered in the Wolf campaign.

The Jade Falcon Khan shook his head. "Oh, how foolish you must think I am." He knew better than to doubt the reports sent by his own people about Natasha's strength. Though her command had been badly hammered, it would be so like her to exaggerate her strength in some vain attempt to awe or even frighten him. He knew she expected him to react rashly to punish her for the audacity of trying to intimidate him.

Natasha expects me to stop thinking, but I am not the sort of Jade Falcon she knew in her far-distant youth. Had he been such a retro-thinker, he would have tossed line units at Twycross, stripping away the forces he had brought to Wotan in order to destroy her on Twycross. She would have dodged him, lifting off with her troops into space once his force landed, then jumped out to Wotan.

Were I as old as she is, I would not have seen through her subterfuge. Chistu knew the substitution of a mercenary unit for a Clan Galaxy in Phelan's force was a problem because it left one Galaxy unaccounted for. The Khan might have assumed it was being held in reserve for some purpose, but in that case Phelan would have included it in the roster of his forces on Morges. Phelan did not mention it, but he did not have to.

Its location was obvious.

"You wanted too much, Natasha. You inflated your numbers to get me to send all my best troops to destroy you. Meanwhile you would hit me here on Wotan." Chistu smiled. "And if you cannot trick me into that, then you expect me to underestimate your numbers and send units for you to grind up. You have obviously reinforced your units with Phelan's missing Galaxy. If I do not take the bait that you are stronger than you seem, you expect me to challenge you with fewer troops than I should. I will do neither."

Chistu spoke into the air. "Computer, issue orders for Delta Galaxy to report to Wotan." That brought the number of line Clusters on Wotan to four, which equaled Natasha's self-reported strength. "Report Phelan Ward's position on Morges to Peregrine and Omicron Galaxies and tell them to destroy him and the mercenaries—with no quarter given. Send the following units to Twycross: Fifth Talon Cluster, Sixth Provisional Garrison Cluster, Eighteenth Falcon Regulars and . . ."

Chistu's voice trailed off as he considered the last unit he would send. The first three were second-line troops of the same caliber Natasha had already ground up in her campaign. They would be sufficient to inflict heavy damage, especially in the close-quarters fighting engendered by the endless sandstorms on Twycross. He would have been content to send a fourth garrison unit, but Crichell would wonder at that choice when there were perfectly good frontline units on Wotan. He needed a unit, one he could count on to hurt Natasha. He needed the unit to seem, on paper, a good choice, and an appropriate choice as well.

He smiled coldly. ". . . and the Falcon Guards. Their mission is to destroy the Black Widow's expeditionary force. This will be their final act of redemption. If they succeed, then the Pryde faction will owe their success to me. And if they fail . . . well, another potential rival for power is removed."

Using the Falcon Guards suited his plan perfectly. The Guards were as much a disgrace as Natasha herself, and sending them back to Twycross, the scene of their most mortifying defeat, would undermine their ability to fight. They would soften Natasha up, and he would kill her on Wotan.

And then he would be elected ilKhan, and would lead the Clans to their destiny.

Daosha, Zurich
Zurich People's Republic, League Liberation Zone

Noble Thayer flipped the remote control over and double-checked that it was the one operating on 49mhz before he flipped the On switch into position. The red LED lit up on the toy plane's pilot canopy. "Rick, open the garage door. Cathy, start the plane's engine."

They did as commanded, filling the warehouse with the high-pitched whine of the plane's little motor. The propeller spun into a blur as the blue toy rolled toward the open garage door. Picking up speed it lifted off as it hit the street. Noble punched the Program button on the remote control. The plane, with the image of the Dancing Joker on its wings and tail section, soared up past the streetlights and vanished into Daosha's night-shrouded, concrete canyons.

Cathy turned and smiled at Noble, holding up both hands with her fingers crossed. "T-minus two minutes and counting."

Rick Bradford shivered. "It's weird to be using a toy as a weapon."

Noble smiled. "The Dancing Joker will use any means necessary to do the job. Some might see this as the perversion of innocence, but we are up against people who have butchered their enemies over planetwide video hookups. The

Dancing Joker finds the hypocrisy deserving of punishment." Noble saw Cathy's smile ebb as he spoke. He knew she didn't like him speaking as if the Dancing Joker were a separate person, but Noble viewed the Joker as his own little internal cell system and occasionally indulged himself aloud.

"Better mount up." Noble set the controller down on top of a rusty oil drum, then opened the back of the hover-ambulance. Offering his hand to Cathy, he gave her a broad wink. "Don't want you to get your white uniform dirty going over this dust-skirt."

"You are most kind, sir."

"And you are most gracious to notice." Noble closed the white doors behind her, then went around to the cab and climbed in behind the driver's seat. He keyed in the vehicle's ignition code. All three fans, the one in front and the two in back, came online immediately.

Rick Bradford slid into the seat beside him and patted the vehicle's dashboard. "This baby cost the Rencide Medical Center a bundle and gave us a lot of good service." He shook his head. "If we could have afforded a new one, this would have been long gone. Now it's just as well we're using it for this."

Noble tugged a cap onto his head, then patted Rick's left knee. "Don't worry, Doc. After tonight Xu Ning will regret shutting down the hospital and slaughtering people like your colleagues at Daosha Public. Get the radio, will you?"

Rick flipped it on and set it to the municipal emergency frequency. "Thirty seconds."

"Bringing the fans up." Noble eased all three throttle levers forward. The diagram on the dashboard indicated the vehicle should have lifted up at thirty percent, but carrying this much weight, it did not clear the concrete floor until he brought it up to fifty-five percent of full power. "It's going to be sluggish."

Rick shrugged. "Always did handle like a sow. I don't think we ever had it this full—but close."

Packed into the rear, into every cargo bay, drawer, and even between the interior and exterior hulls, a metric ton of home-brewed plastic explosive weighed the ambulance down significantly. Noble figured it to have roughly half the power of military-grade plastique. When it went up, it would make a big hole and, if things went as planned, would trigger an even bigger explosion.

Rick's watch beeped. "Bingo."

Noble smiled. "The Dancing Joker strikes again."

The plan Noble had come up with had not been particularly inventive or complicated. Anne Thompson had easily managed to purchase a radio-controlled toy plane and controller. The only thing unusual about it was that the plane was one of the higher-priced models that included enough computer memory for a two-minute "course memory." That allowed the user to put the toy plane through a complex series of maneuvers that the plane would remember whenever the program was engaged from the remote control.

The plane had been slightly modified for its part in the mission. The Dancing Joker insignia had been painted on the wings and tail section. The antenna that would allow another control unit to take over and break the program had been snipped off. Once the plane got beyond twenty meters, even Noble's little team could not have called it back.

Once it took off it was locked into a course that would take it from their warehouse to the Armory's front door.

Noble had also provided the plane with an explosive payload. He packed it with four ounces of the homemade plastic explosive he'd rolled in a dish full of 20-gauge shot. As a detonator he used crystals obtained from mixing two chemicals: picric acid and lead oxide. He coated one end of the bomb with these crystals so that when the plane hit the building, inertia would drive the bomb forward, smashing the crystals against the engine, thereby triggering the explosion.

The radio squawked. "All available units, we have report of an explosion at the Zhongdade Armory. Report to the site, code three."

Jamming the throttles forward, Noble started the hover-ambulance moving. Rick reached up and flicked on the lights and siren. Traffic parted before them like magic as they began to race toward the Armory.

Preparing the ambulance to become a bomb had presented less in the way of problems than the others had expected. The only difficulty in creating the explosive itself was the sheer quantity they wanted to make. Fortunately for their effort, reeducation classes had local schools open around the clock and adults could move around freely on the campuses without attracting undue attention. Breaking into unused chemistry labs got them the more difficult to obtain chemical supplies they needed and in sufficient quantities.

Bribing warehousemen to load a truck with close to a ton of petroleum jelly had been simple. The singular nature of the cargo had raised a few eyebrows, but Ken Fox telling them he was catering a Peoples' Party function turned their suspicion into laughter. Noble had watched Ken drive the truck out of the warehouse, then signaled him to take it to their bomb factory after he was certain no one had followed the truck.

Ken's daughter Rose and her husband, Fabian Wilson, had helped mix up the plastic explosive. Noble had not liked Fabian when he bought his computer from him, but Ken said his daughter would be good for the organization and Fabian came as part of the package. Noble did not trust the man, but as long as he had someone keeping an eye on him, he figured any harm Fabian might do would be minimized. As it was, Rose and Fabian only did the mixing and knew nothing about the target or timing of the strike.

Their biggest problem was figuring out how to detonate the bomb, a problem that actually broke down into two parts: how to prime the explosive and how to detonate the primer. The plastic explosive required a small explosion to make it go off. Blasting caps, which were available from Daosha's black market, would normally have done the trick, but with a homemade explosive, Noble wanted something more reliable.

Ken Fox came to the rescue. One of his friends worked in construction in Daosha and, before that, had been a demolitions expert in Ken's AFFC unit. Ken had described the man as being paranoid—which made Noble consider Ken a bit of an optimist—and cited that as the reason why he had a wide range of detonators and blasting caps in his possession.

From this man they purchased a kilo of military-grade plastique, a handful of blasting caps, and three meters of detonation cord. This latter acquisition especially pleased Noble because it virtually guaranteed success in their mission. With the det-cord, a centimeter-thick, fiber-wrapped cylinder of plastique, they could trigger the military plastique and that would make his own explosive detonate.

Still a problem was the ignition system to make the blasting caps blow the det-cord. A timing device was less than satisfactory because the mission had to be quick and they didn't want to risk the explosives being discovered and disarmed. Worse, if they had trouble leaving the site after setting the timer, they would be caught in the blast.

Using a radio transmitter to blow the bomb posed other problems. Because radio-controlled bombs were not uncommon, the Armory and other important buildings in Daosha had been equipped with counter-bombing transmitters. Those transmitters sent out pulses on the most commonly used frequencies, causing the bombs to detonate at a significant and safe distance from their target. Noble had even seen SecCom transmitter trucks roaming through Daosha, putting out signals in the hopes of triggering any bombs being worked on by the Dancing Joker, Jacko Diamond, or other anti-government forces.

Using a cellular phone as the receiver would have worked well and eliminated the hazards associated with less sophisticated devices. Unfortunately Xu Ning had ordered all local cellular networks shut down because calls placed from the devices could not be traced. Until those networks went down, it had been possible for anti-government forces to use cellular communications to plot operations against the government.

Direct-wire detonation was one of the oldest and surest forms of triggering blasting caps. A spool of two-line wire and a common battery were all that were needed. Simple and very effective, but not as safe as Noble wanted. The problem with a simple electrical system was that static electricity might complete the circuit before he was out of the blast radius, which would not let him live long enough to regret his choice.

Luckily, one other method of detonation finally suggested itself to him. With the purchase of two phones and some cable, the last obstacle to the mission was removed.

The ambulance swung right and was waved on past the crowd of spectators lining the street. Noble proceeded forward to a spot directly in front of the Armory, then brought the hover-ambulance up onto the sidewalk and killed the fans. With dust billowing out from beneath it, the hovercraft settled into place and Rick killed the siren.

Noble opened his door and leaned out to address one of the Military Police standing guard. "How many you got down?"

"None, that I know of." The MP pointed at the Armory

door. A big black burn mark showed where the plane had hit. "Looks like that Dancing Joker thought he could blow us up with a fistful of dynamite or something. Could have been worse if the door was open, but it wasn't."

"Bastard. You sure no one is hurt? No one got anxious, had heart pains or nothing?"

"The Director might be having palpitations, but he's not here." The MP smiled and Noble returned the smile. "Looks like you made the trip over for nothing."

"If you say so." Noble shrugged. "We'll batten some things down in back and file a quick report before we head out. You might want to double check, just in case we're needed. I mean, we're here."

"I'll ask around. See you in five."

"Great."

Noble closed the vehicle door, then stepped between the two buckets seats and into the back. Behind him he drew a little white curtain with red crosses on it. Seeing that Cathy had done the same with the curtains over the small windows in back, Noble nodded to Rick. "Go."

Rick Bradford pried up a plate in the bottom of the vehicle's bed and dropped down to the sidewalk beneath it. There he used his prybar to get the manhole cover up and rolled aside. Reaching down into the sewer hole, he pulled up a spool of phone chord and handed it to Noble.

Cathy ducked beneath Noble's right arm and dropped to the sidewalk with Rick. Noble opened one of the equipment compartments and tossed each of them a flashlight. "Get going."

As they descended into the darkness, he turned back to prepare the bomb. From a drawer he took a pair of foot-long loops of det-cord to which had been taped two blasting caps. The free ends of the cord, along with the blasting caps, had been taped together and the leads from the blasting caps had been screwed down onto a little black cube bearing the phone company's logo. These were his fuses.

From another drawer he pulled out the two blocks of military plastique he had created from the kilogram he and Fox had purchased. Shaped like a brick, with a four-centimeter-wide channel running down the length of it, each block had been wrapped up with det-cord. Noble threaded the head of the loops through the channel, beneath the winding det-cord, then pulled the blasting caps through the lead curve of the loop, securing the fuses to the plastique.

In the back of the compartment from which he had taken the flashlights, a brick-sized hole had been made in the homemade explosive. Noble placed one plastique brick in that hole and the other in a similar hole at the back of another compartment. Satisfied they would stay in place, he laughed softly to himself.

Hardly the sort of thing a mild-mannered chemistry teacher should be doing. But, then, the Dancing Joker is hardly a mild-mannered chemistry teacher.

He picked up the phone cord Rick had passed up, and split the dual line cable. Had it been metal wire he would have had to screw it into place in the black boxes, but because it was fiber optic cable, he pressed a button on each box in turn, shoved cable into the hole that opened up, then let the button go. Pressure kept the cable in place, completing the arming of his bomb.

Noble let himself down through the hole in the bottom of the hovervehicle and felt for the top rung of the manhole ladder with his toes. He found it and quickly scrambled down into the stinking darkness of a sewer tunnel running parallel to the street above. Roughly eight meters below the surface he met his companions in a big storm drain tunnel. Without a word, Rick led them back toward the intersection through which they had turned to find the Armory, then immediately took a crosscut tunnel leading north.

Every ten meters the flashlights picked up the reflective tape they had used to fasten the five hundred meters of phone cable to the walls of the tunnels. The floor pitched up as the tunnel started a climb toward the Heights in Daosha, but Rick took another tunnel that ran around the base of the hills. Further up the tunnel, rats squealed at being caught in the light, their eyes burning like binary stars in the night sky.

Finally they reached a large square of reflective tape on the wall of the tunnel. Rick stopped there and wiped sweat from his brow. "Do you need my light?"

"No, I've got mine." Noble reached into his pocket and pulled out a simple laser pointer. "I once did a fiber optic experiment in one of my classes. I used my pointer to send Morse code to a phone. Never thought I'd be finding a *practical* use for that lesson."

He flashed the laser against the wall, playing a red dot

along the moist stone surface. Looking farther into the tunnel, he pointed his laser at two of the glowing eyes and flashed the dot between them.

"Nice shooting," Rick laughed.

"This will be nicer, trust me."

Noble picked up the end of the fiber optic cable. He pressed the laser to one of the two lines and smiled. "Brace yourselves. Remember we may get secondary blasts."

When his thumb hit the button on the laser, the beam flashed to life and shot down the cable. Moving at slightly less than the speed of light, but not so much slower as to make a difference, the photons shot through the cable, along the twists and around the corners where the cable ran and, finally, up and into the ambulance.

Inside the vehicle, the photons hit a simple photosensitive cell within the black box. The influx photons excited atoms, creating a trickle of electrical current that flowed through the cell and out the leads connected to the blasting caps. They went off with a pop barely loud enough for the MP returning to the ambulance to hear.

With that, the blasting caps exploded the det-cord fuse, which triggered both the det-cord through which it had been looped and the military plastique. As the milplas detonated, it sparked the product of Rose and Fabian's labors to explode. Within a second of Noble's hitting the button on his pointer, the entire metric ton of explosive in the ambulance had gone off.

The MP died before his brain could register any threat to him, the incredible energy unleashed by the bomb literally disintegrating him. The force spread out from the ambulance in a sphere and met its first real resistance on the ground. The sidewalk buckled and fragmented. The asphalt of the street rippled as if it were water. The vibrations broke it into chips and rocks and hurled them outward from the center of the explosion.

When the force hit the Armory itself, several things happened. The shockwave slammed into the building with uneven amounts of force. The ground floor, which was nearest the point of detonation, took the brunt of the blast. The force lessened as it hit the second and third stories, and again as it moved further up the block to the half of the building on the far side of the doorway. Yet even as the force of the blast dropped off, it was more than sufficient to wreak incredible damage.

The windows imploded, spraying the rooms beyond them with a razored hail of glass. Several people, partially protected by the heavy desks behind which they sat, did not die immediately as the glass flayed them alive. Blind and screaming, they spent their last moments of life in an eternity of agony.

The walls, which were made of rough-hewn stones mortared together, with polished granite for window casings and trim, buckled as the force of the blast built. Mortar crumbled and walls caved in. The explosion ripped the walls into their component pieces, then drove the debris back through the softer interior walls. The floors undulated like flags snapping in a hurricane. With a crackling and popping, floorboards twisted into splinters that flew up and out with enough force to pierce sheet-rock walls.

The same was true for office equipment. The explosion shattered plastics and broke wooden furnishings into tiny fragments. It twisted chairs and metal desks into unrecognizable lumps and crushed refrigerators like aluminum cans in the hands of a BattleMech.

People in the offices, being somewhat less dense than their office equipment, did not survive collision with pieces of wreckage.

Outside, the explosion penetrated the ground to a depth of nearly ten meters, obliterating the tunnel Nobel and his team had used for their escape. The crater, with all the dirt, asphalt, piping, and wiring in it being cast into the air, spread out to a diameter of roughly fifty meters, undercutting the whole Armory and the buildings on the other side of the relatively narrow street. Those buildings had none of the sturdier Armory's structural integrity. They collapsed as if made of cards, major chunks of them sailing away through the air amid the dirt being blasted up out of the crater.

Oddly enough, there had still been very little in the way of fire in the area. As the apartments around the Armory collapsed gas mains ruptured, sending fireballs up into the sky. Some debris ignited and, when it came down, fell on other flammable materials, spawning a number of fires. The fact that water mains had been cut by the blast would mean a loss of water pressure in the area and that would severely hamper firefighting efforts until the Black Cobra could bring in their 'Mechs to deal with the situation.

When computing how much explosive he would need to level the Armory, Noble had done all the math very carefully. That meant plugging into an arcane formula things like the nature of the materials used in the building, their resistance to force, and compression factors for the explosive itself. Confident that his calculations were correct, he used one last factor that he knew would get him the desired result.

He doubled the amount of explosive his computations indicated were needed.

As a result, when the force from the blast hit the explosive storage lockers in the Armory basement, it was great enough to make the military plastique detonate. This created another explosion in the heart of the Armory—one with roughly four times the power of the ambulance bomb—and the ruins of the building launched themselves into the air.

Three hundred meters away, in a storm tunnel buried inside a hill, bracing for the shockwave was of no use to Noble, Rick, or Cathy. As the initial explosion rippled through the ground, it knocked them off their feet and onto the curved floor of the tunnel. Rick's flashlight smashed when it hit the ground, leaving his section of tunnel drowned in darkness. Cathy's flashlight stayed on, but she cried out as she went down.

Then the second shockwave hit. Noble covered his head with his hands and tucked his head in toward his chest as he felt the ground begin to swell. Suddenly he found himself launched into the air. He saw stars as his head and hands smashed into the roof and he heard something snap. He hoped it wasn't part of himself, but the pain of hitting the ground again kept him from pinpointing any injury. Unsure which way was up, he bounced back and forth a couple of times, then lay still as the ground movement subsided.

He tried to take a deep breath, but the air was so thick with dust that all he could do was cough. Rolling over onto his belly, he pulled his T-shirt up over his nose and mouth to filter the air. He could still taste the dust as he breathed in, but he wasn't coughing now.

"Rick? Cathy?"

"I'm here, Noble. Bruised and beat, but alive. Cathy?"

"Here, ow! Dammit, my ankle!"

Noble turned in the direction from which their voices had come. He saw Rick's silhouette moving through the darkness and realized that was only because the explosion had popped a manhole cover from a spot behind Rick to let a wavering light pour in.

Working his way forward, he found Cathy and scooped her up. "Head for the manhole, Rick. I'll pass Cathy up to you."

The doctor did as he was told and in no time they were once again out in the cool evening air. A little way down the hill a hovercar's lights flicked on and off, and Noble flashed them with his laser pointer. The hovercar rose up on a cushion of air and started toward them.

Beyond the roadway and down the hill, Noble saw the smoking hole that was all that was left of the Armory. For blocks around it in every direction buildings sagged in on themselves. Broken gas pipes ended in little yellow flames. Four different buildings had caught fire. Strobing lights and shrieking sirens filled the night.

Noble took off his baseball cap and from his pocket pulled one of the Dancing Joker cards. He stuffed the card inside the band and tossed the hat back down the manhole.

Rick smiled at him as Anne Thompson stopped the car. "You think they're going to need that to identify who did this?"

"Probably not, but if we don't take credit, someone else will." Noble got into the car beside Cathy, then pulled the door shut behind him. "Xu Ning has himself a problem, and I want to make certain he knows who it is."

37

The soldier, above all other people, prays for peace, for he must suffer and bear the deepest wounds and scars of war.

—Douglas MacArthur

Australarctica
Morges, Lyran Alliance
5 December 3057

Khan Phelan Wolf nodded to the holographic image of the older woman as it materialized in his holotank. "Greetings, Star Colonel Mattlov. I am honored Khan Chistu thought enough of me to send you after me."

Spite flashed through the older woman's eyes. "Spare me, *freebirth*. I am attacking this world. With what do you defend it?"

"Quickly to business, I see." Phelan was uncertain about the source of her urgency, but thought it might have to do with being called away from being the spearpoint for the Jade Falcons' renewed offensive against the Inner Sphere. "Before I make my bid, allow me to say that I always thought the fiction of Chistu stripping Clusters from your Galaxy was transparent. I am glad to see the Peregrine Galaxy together again."

The computer colored Mattlov's cheeks. "I neither need nor desire your commentary on my situation. I am come to destroy you. With what will you meet me?"

Phelan opened his arms. "I have the Wolf Clan's Alpha Galaxy, with the addition of the Sixteenth BattleCluster. I also have two regiments of the Kell Hounds. I will not be employing my battleships in this engagement. We are defending Australarctica and have cleared the area of noncombatants."

Mattlov looked to the side, out of the image frame, then faced Phelan again. "What of the Omega Galaxy? It was reported to us that they accompanied your retreat from Clan space."

The Wolf Khan shrugged. "I do not include them in my bid, so their location is immaterial. Suffice it to say, they are well away from here and will be unable to intervene in our fight. Consider my defense being conducted by nine frontline Clusters."

"You overvalue these mercenaries of yours."

"And the Smoke Jaguars underestimated them at Luthien. Bid against them what *you* think they are worth. With the Omicron Galaxy in tow, you have five frontline Clusters, a solahma unit, and five garrison Clusters. I will be content to wait if you decide to request more troops."

Mattlov snapped to attention as if she'd been hit by lightning. "No *freebirth* Wolf has ever dared speak to me as you do."

"Remember, Star Colonel, I am a *Khan*! You have my bid. You may send as many or as few of your troops as you will against me. Those I do not kill I will make my bondsmen—including you, if it comes to that." Phelan folded his arms. "Are you prepared to bid at this time?"

"Yes." Anger suffused her words. "No WarShips. This will be warrior to warrior. I will bring all of my Clusters, even the solahma. We will land in a day and initiate combat within the week. Mattlov out."

Her image faded and Phelan focused on the people standing beyond where it had been projected. "With the garrison units and the solahma, we're slightly outnumbered, but probably very even on strength."

Morgan Kell nodded, his expression grave. "Why did you make her angry?"

Phelan smiled. *He thinks that was not wise, but instead of criticizing me for it, he asks my reasons. Therein is the difference between a* leader *and a* commander. "The Falcons are probably the most reactionary and hidebound of the Clans. Angeline's willingness to employ a solahma unit—one made up of has-been MechWarriors usually assigned to disgracefully duties such as bandit-hunting—means she has contempt for our troops. By being condescending to her, I reminded her of just how far apart we are. She will demand that her troops prove how much better their ways are than ours. Until Theodore Kurita initiated reforms in the Draconis Combine's military, similar thinking proved a tactical handicap for them."

Daniel Allard scratched at the back of his neck. "With our defenses and deployments, she has to be mad to come at us with equal strength."

"Agreed, but she does not see it that way. If she concentrates on one portion of our positions, she can direct overwhelming strength against it. Her job is to destroy us, while we merely need to survive." Phelan shrugged. "Because loss is not possible in her thinking, visions of victory will always linger just a bit beyond her grasp. If she keeps going for it, and we can outlast her, she'll overreach herself and then it will be our turn."

"A lot of ifs there, son, *quiaff?*"

"Aff." Phelan threw his arm around his father's shoulders. "But if an old hound like you can learn a few Wolf tricks, there's no way a birdbrain could ever beat us."

38

How are the mighty fallen in the midst of battle!
—II Samuel 1.XXV

Plain of Curtains, Twycross
Steel Viper Occupation Zone
7 December 3057

As effortlessly as if the metal flesh she piloted was her own, Natasha Kerensky turned her *Dire Wolf* to the right, a Jade Falcon *Uller* impaled on her crosshairs. She hit the triggers for her two right-arm PPCs and each vomited a coruscating cerulean beam that burned deeply into the *Uller*'s right arm and right flank.

Marco Hall's *Hellbringer* also came around to face off with the wounded Falcon 'Mech. A trio of lasers on his 'Mech's left chest shot volleys of ruby bolts out at the hole Natasha had opened in the squat *Uller*'s chest. His laser fire turned the 'Mech's internal structures into a molten red liquid that gushed from the hole as the *Uller* began to falter. With its next step the 'Mech's right leg punched up through the chest and the right arm fell away. The 'Mech hit the red dust of Twycross face-first, then the cockpit canopy exploded as the pilot blasted free of his dead machine.

"Where are they, Marco?" With so much sand filling the air, Natasha could see barely thirty meters in front of her machine. The conditions had kept the fighting sharp and furious, and conducted at close quarters. The *Uller* had less been looking to attack them than trying to find its way back to its own lines. Had things been going according to plan, the Falcon lines *should* have been as close as the *Uller* had come, but something was wrong.

"They are not coming, Khan Natasha. They are not being drawn in."

Natasha pounded a fist on the arm of her command couch. With Chistu sending so many 'Mechs against her, the Black Widow had worked hard to lure the Jade Falcons into a trap. Star Colonel Ravill Pryde, commander of the Falcon Guard force, had bargained hard and well with her. She smiled. *He was almost Wolfish in his enthusiasm for this fight.*

That enthusiasm she had put down to the fact that Ravill had not been with the Falcon Guards when they were virtually destroyed the last time they had seen the Great Gash. Few of those who had survived that last battle on Twycross were still with the Guards, and these Guards seemed more than anxious to get at her troops. The other units—garrison Clusters—had been more scornful of her force. Natasha decided they would pay for their insolence before she destroyed the Guards.

To frustrate Ravill Pryde, Natasha had put her Thirteenth Wolf Guards in the rear of a diamond formation. The 341st bore the brunt of the assault, but as instructed, they fell back quickly, the Sixth Provisional Garrison of the Jade Falcons hot in pursuit. When that happened the Third Battle Cluster and 352nd Assault Cluster opened up on the Falcons from each flank. Great chunks of the Sixth Provo died on the Plain of Curtains.

The other two garrison units, the Fifth Talon and Eighteenth Falcon Regulars, had come in more cautiously, but the 341st advanced again to hammer them as they engaged the wings of Natasha's formation. Under pressure from the Falcon Guards, the 341st broke and passed through the Thirteenth Wolf Guards and into the Gash. The Third Battle Cluster and the 352nd Assault Cluster also drew back into the Gash while the Thirteenth Guards gave ground until they plugged the mountain gap.

Natasha's last unit, the Eleventh Battle Cluster—the only unit yet to see action in the campaign—lined both sides of the Gash up on the plateaus above it, ready to pour fire into the Gash itself. Natasha intended the Guards to chase her into the trap, but, according to Marco, they weren't coming.

"Have our survivors start loading up in the DropShips, Marco. They're to head out immediately."

"Do we go with the original plan, or do you want them to drop in behind the Falcons?"

Natasha considered that bit of tactics, then rejected it. "We've hurt them here today, but not as much as I wanted." The image of Ravill's face, complete with cocky smile, played through her mind. "We've not killed the bodies, so we must kill the heads."

"Can you please make sense, Natasha?"

She laughed. "They're not coming, Marco. They know this is a trap. Order the Eleventh off the plateaus and to the DropShips. They are to head out, bound for Wotan. Survivors from there and the wounded go to Phelan."

She heard the concern in Marco's voice. "Why are you telling me this, Khan Natasha? You can give those orders yourself."

"Not me, Marco. I'm staying here."

"What?"

"You are now the head of the Thirteenth Wolf Guards. Pull them back, too. Make me proud on Wotan."

"Heat gotten to you, Natasha? That's madness."

"No, it's not. Their fear, the Crusaders' fear, was that their battle-hardened leaders would be *too old* to fight when the invasion began anew. They are wrong, but I can play to their fear." As the plan crystallized in her mind, Natasha felt a sense of rightness that she'd not known since her lover, Joshua Wolf, had been murdered forty years earlier in the Marik civil war. "One by one, I'll challenge the Falcon officers here. They'll die in the Gash, and that'll destroy their morale along with any competent officers they have."

Natasha waved Marco Hall's *Hellbringer* up into the Gash. "Go, Marco, go. Destroy Wotan, then come back and get me."

She expected a quick riposte from Marco, but the man's response came terribly subdued. "They could kill you."

"Them? Not likely. They think youth and new genes will win out. I'll prove to them that age and experience are far superior." Natasha forced bravado into her voice because the twinges in her back and legs told her that she was not at her best at the moment. "Besides, even if I do die, it is better to die here, in combat, than in some nursery, wiping the noses of sibko brats."

Marco's 'Mech pushed on, but the man's voice stayed with her. "If you do die here, Natasha, I will not be coming back. I don't want to be anyplace you might be haunting."

Natasha laughed freely. "Fear not, my friend. There are

countless Falcon ghosts here I can terrorize. Go, Star Colonel, and show Khan Chistu no mercy."

As his 'Mech disappeared among the blood-red sands,
Natasha felt alone, but this time it was different. She had
faced terrible danger by herself before, and in those times
she had always sensed something missing in her. She had
never known what that might have been, but no longer did
she feel the lack.

She felt complete.

She was the Black Widow.

Natasha switched her radio over to the Jade Falcon tactical frequency. She heard pops and squeals from their scrambled transmissions, but paid them no heed. Her words, which
would not be scrambled, would get her message through.

"I am Khan Natasha Kerensky of Clan Wolf. I have sent
my troops away. I wait in the Great Gash of Twycross to
meet and slay any Jade Falcon who thinks more of himself
than he should and prefers courage to wisdom. Come now.
Your time is at hand."

39

Daosha, Zurich
Zurich People's Republic, Capellan Confederation
9 December 3057

Noble Thayer smiled and shook Fabian Wilson's hand as the man joined him and Cathy at the booth in the rear of the Cathay Cafeteria. "Thank you for coming." Beyond Fabian, back by the door, Ken Fox gave Noble a nod before he took a seat at a table near the restaurant's entrance. That meant Fabian had not been followed and their meeting should remain uninterrupted by the reconstituted State Security Committee.

"When I got the word, I knew it would be important."

"You could definitely say that." Noble took Cathy's hand and gave it a squeeze to reassure her, then lowered his voice. "I've spent the last ten days planning a mission and recruiting some new people for it. Because you lack weapons training, I have an auxiliary job for you. It may not seem important at first, and you'll be working with Cathy on it, but it is vital."

Fabian listened intently and nodded his head. "I'm in."

"Don't you want to hear what it is first?"

The man's head came up. He glanced side to side, then leaned forward. "Look, you know me. I sold you a computer and everything. My life was a dead end. I know that. My ship was always coming in next week or the week after that. I was always living in the future. Well, this is *now*, see. Man, it's like having sex for the first time. It's so real. And it helps people. I mean, being a salesman, I always wanted to do the best for my customers, but I had to eat and the commission on nothing is nothing, right? So I don't care if you have me clipping coupons or what. I'm in."

Noble smiled as did Cathy. "This mission is going to be very big, my friend. And everyone will know we struck."

"Like they don't from the Armory?"

"That's old news. This will be big, really big." Noble looked around the room, then sat back and sipped some tea. "The government, in their desire to level society to one class, has killed a number of the people who designed the computer system the government is using. All the computers have a twelve-hour backup battery, but it only works for twelve hours if regularly discharged and recharged. I have learned that this maintenance schedule has been neglected. The municipal backup generators are still offline because of the Armory explosions, so the batteries are it right now.

"If the computers are without power for five hours, they will have to be backed up from CD-WORMs recorded earlier. I've succeeded in inserting a virus into the backup CD-WORMs that will destroy the data State Security uses to find its victims. To force the re-start from back-ups, the Dancing Joker will be taking down the Jihuaide Chumai Power Station on the twentieth."

Fabian's jaw dropped open and Cathy stared at Noble with similar surprise. He felt a tremble run through her hand, so he winked at her. "It will be our biggest operation yet."

Fabian shook his head in disbelief. "The station has its own little garrison unit."

"That shouldn't be a problem, but I can't tell you any more about the plan. It's the cell system. It's for all of us and our safety. Cathy can confirm that she's not known anything about this until now—unless I talk in my sleep."

Cathy took Noble's left hand in both of hers and shook her head. "So, Mr. DJ, what's the plan?"

"There are two roads into and out of the station. You'll be the lookouts on Northstar Drive. If you see anything, you'll radio us at the plant and we'll react accordingly. Reaction time from the Black Cobra facilities at Kaishiling Garrison Base is ten minutes, but only if they're running from a hot start in their 'Mechs. Even if an alarm goes out the second we strike, we'll have more than enough time to do what has to be done."

Fabian frowned. "You have others watching the other road, right?"

"Need to know, for your safety and theirs."

"Right, right, sorry." Fabian shook his head. "I got one question for you, but you'll probably 'cell system' me on it, too."

Noble shrugged. "Ask."

Fabian's voice became a whisper. "Look, you're not really a school teacher, are you? All this stuff you've done here, that's not school teacher stuff. You're really a Davion agent, aren't you, sent here to stir things up."

"You're very intelligent, Mr. Wilson, and you've seen a great deal," Noble told him, "but the last time I answered that question, I had to kill the person who asked it."

Fabian held his hands up. "Enough said."

"Indeed, enough said." Noble smiled, then reached down and gave Cathy's leg a playful squeeze. "Now, shall we eat?"

40

Between a battle lost and a battle won, the distance is immense
and there stand empires.

—NAPOLEON BONAPARTE

Wotan, Jade Falcon Occupation Zone
10 December 3057

Khan Vandervahn Chistu could barely contain his anger.
When Khan Elias Crichell slapped him on the back, he almost reacted instinctively and smashed the older man in the
face. He could feel his fist mashing lips against teeth, crushing Crichell's nose, and blackening his eyes. And the shock
that would register on Crichell's face would be vastly preferable to the unbridled mirth there now.

"It was brilliant, Vahn, brilliant. Keeping line units here
as if you were afraid of her, then overwhelming her on
Twycross." Crichell clapped his hands. "Now Natasha
Kerensky is dead and our plans can go forward."

"Yes, my Khan."

Crichell reacted to the clipped delivery of Chistu's words.
"Is there something wrong? Is it possible the report was in
error? Is it possible that Natasha yet lives?"

Chistu shook his head. "No, my Khan, there is no chance
she survived. She died in single combat with one of the Falcon Guards. Her cockpit was breached, destroyed. There is
no doubt. The Black Widow is dead."

"Excellent. Everything is going as we planned it."

We *planned* it? Chistu was glad Crichell had his back
turned and could not see his expression. An aging pilot had
killed Natasha Kerensky in single combat. He had watched
the gun-camera holovids of the fight over and over again.
The Black Widow was truly and finally dead. He should be

rejoicing because one of the three threats to the Jade Falcons had died so ignominiously, but he could not take pleasure in her demise.

He had wanted to finish her. *He* had intended to bring the Black Widow to her knees. *He* would have made her beg for life. *He* would have broken her and made her his bondswoman. He would have humiliated and ridiculed her and, by bringing her to heel, *he,* Vandervahn Chistu, would have been elected the next ilKhan. And then, to him would have come the glory of taking Terra and restoring the Star League.

But an old warrior on Twycross had robbed him of his victory. Chistu made a mental note to find out who that warrior was and see if she would be useful in the future. She did deserve some sort of reward, and she'd not be getting it for the overall outcome of the fighting there. Aside from Natasha's death, the battle on Twycross had been relatively unremarkable. The Falcons had won—Natasha's troops had fled—but it was a bit of a pyrrhic victory in that the Sixth Provo had been heavily damaged and the Fifth Talon had lost a quarter of its 'Mechs.

Crichell rubbed his jaw with his right hand as he turned back to face Chistu. "You have a similar reception planned for Ulric and his horde on Butler?"

"Ulric?" Chistu frowned as he thrust his anger aside. "Yes, on Butler. I have the Seventh and Eighth Provisional Garrisons and the Seventh and Eighth Talon Clusters on the planet. Ulric's fleet came into the Butler system at a pirate point a good way out on the orbital plane. They are working their way in and have already inquired what forces we will be using to defend the planet."

Crichell raised a bushy gray eyebrow. "You have sent only garrison units to deal with Ulric? Should you not have sent a frontline unit, the way you sent the Falcon Guards to kill Natasha on Twycross? You have four here on Wotan, any one of them more than equal to the job."

Chistu clenched his jaw for a second, then slowly shook his head. "True, but I had hoped I would not need them. You have seen from the damage reports how seriously we have been hurt by this war. We will need time to rebuild, but if we can keep some frontline units intact, it will mean we can strike sooner.

"My plan is to let the garrison units engage Ulric. Since

our units are defending, they will have an advantage over the Wolves and should be able to cripple them even if they cannot kill them. In the event that Ulric wins the fight, I will deploy our line units here to force him to defend his victory." Chistu frowned as his explanation fell on deaf ears. "Is there something wrong, Elias?"

The other Khan nodded slowly. "You say we will have to rebuild before we can renew the invasion?"

Vandervahn Chistu nodded once, emphatically, and took pleasure in the fact that Crichell had paled considerably. "Five years, I should think. Possibly seven."

"Five years, or seven?"

"Yes, Elias, an eyeblink." *Except if, like you, one is a MechWarrior whose skills have long since faded.*

"Do you really think that will be necessary?"

"If you wish the Falcons to take Terra, yes." Chistu's head came up. "Unless ..."

"Yes?"

"I could take the frontline units we have here and form them into a new Galaxy. I would also bring in the Peregrine Galaxy—after they kill the Wolves on Morges, of course. We could stage again on Quarell and then blow through to Terra when you, as ilKhan, repudiate the truce."

As Crichell's smile grew, Chistu made certain to ape it on his face. *I will do no such thing, of course. In fact, if I let it be known in the Grand Council that you had planned such an underhanded drive to Terra, you would be in serious trouble. I will say that I, offered the glory of that conquest, rejected it as unfair. Then I will be elected ilKhan in your place. After my accession, I will be able to control the destiny of our Clan and, through it, the future of humanity.*

"Yes, Vahn, I think that would be superior. Finish Ulric on Butler, then push on toward Terra with our best troops. We have not fought this war with the Wolves just to be thwarted by their Warden strategy. That would mean Ulric won, and I will not have that."

"As you wish it, my Khan." Chistu bowed deeply. *And if I get my wish at the same time, you as well as Ulric will be the loser.*

===== **41** =====

A battle sometimes decides everything; and sometimes the
merest trifle decides a battle.

—NAPOLEON BONAPARTE, LETTER TO
BARRY E. O'MEARA, 9 NOVEMBER 1816

JumpShip Dire Wolf, *Inbound*
Butler, Jade Falcon Occupation Zone
10 December 3057

His eyes burning from lack of sleep and his neck and upper
back muscles aching from hours hunched over a computer
terminal, Vlad stepped into the holotank and looked over at
Ulric. Conflicting emotions warred within him. Though he
wanted to hate the man, and certainly did, Vlad realized he
respected him too. He also felt grateful because Ulric had
entrusted him with planning the assault on Butler.

"I have finished, my Khan. I am prepared to show you my
plans. Though we are reduced to two and a half functional
Clusters, I have taken the best of the garrison pilots from
Tau Galaxy and used them to reinforce our line units. We
have two full Garrison Clusters left over, the Fifth Wolf
Regulars and the First Cavalry, to use as reinforcements."
Vlad allowed himself a brief smile. "Even with the Falcons
using fortifications, I believe we can defeat them."

Ulric nodded slowly, as if giving Vlad's words great
weight, but Vlad had the impression Ulric barely heard him.
"What would be your assessment of the condition of our
troops after this fight? Estimate conservatively—give me the
highest casualties and slowest repair rate you can."

The seriousness in Ulric's voice surprised Vlad and cut
away at his fatigue. "If we are forced to use our reserves, I
would estimate we will come out of this with one and a half

to two frontline Clusters, with a Trinary or two of garrison-level troops to spare. The defenders outnumber us and though they have chosen to defend separate sites on the planet, which will allow us to overwhelm individual garrisons, I cannot imagine they will not band together quickly and pursue us."

"That is my thinking as well." Ulric gave Vlad a cold, blue-eyed stare. "How much of a Wolf are you, Vlad?"

"I do not understand you, Ulric."

Ulric smiled slowly. "How loyal are you to your Clan, Vlad?"

"Have I ever given you cause to doubt my loyalty?" Vlad frowned, the flesh around the scar tugging on the left side of his face. "You have ample time to review my plans in the five days before we reach Butler. If you think I have betrayed the Wolves, you can deal with me before we attack. If I am guilty of treason no punishment would be too harsh."

"Ah, an excellent parry and riposte, Vlad. You remind me that I have been charged with treason—by your investigation."

"That was not my intention, Ulric."

"No, I do not suppose it was—at least not entirely." The white-haired man began to pace the interior of the holotank, circling Vlad like a hungry shark. "The fighting we engage in will be fierce. You will be fighting by my side. If my 'Mech is disabled, what will you do?"

"I will defend you, or do what I must to safeguard you."

"Why?"

That question blasted through the facade Vlad had erected over the months to shield him from Ulric's probing queries. *Why would I save him? I revile him. I want him dead.* Suddenly the answer came to him and he knew he could never repeat it to Ulric. *I want him defeated, but he will never be defeated. The Falcons did not see this—none of the Crusaders saw this. Ulric is a Wolf and more than they will ever be able to break.*

"I will defend you because I am a Wolf and you are a Wolf. I need no other reason."

Ulric came face to face with Vlad. "If I fall, you know what your duty is, *quiaff?*"

"To win."

"To preserve the Clan. If victory will do that, then you

will win. If it will not, you will do what you must to bring as many of the Clan as possible to Khan Phelan."

Vlad stiffened. "Take them to Phelan?"

Ulric shrugged. "That, or surrender to the Jade Falcons and become a bondsman in their Clan."

"There is no lesser of evils in that choice, Ulric."

The older man laughed aloud. "Ah, you might have made a good Khan after all. Perhaps you will find a better option when the time comes."

I may do just that, Ulric. Vlad exhaled slowly. "Phelan is fighting on Morges. You would have me take our survivors to him if he lives?"

"If he lives. If he is dead, if Natasha is dead, then responsibility for the fate of Clan Wolf falls to you."

Vlad's jaw dropped open. "To me?" He shook his head. "Why would you entrust the future of the Wolves to me? I am a Crusader."

Ulric opened his hands. "In the Clans we select which genetic combinations will produce the most superior warriors. This is evolution by choice, but evolution happens on more than just a physical level. The human race has evolved philosophically, and so, too, have the Clans. Once we were all Wardens, but now the Crusaders have risen in power. Perhaps the Crusader philosophy is superior to that of the Wardens. Perhaps it will give rise to something new in our Clan ways.

"As you have a duty to me because you are a Wolf, so I, a Wolf, have a duty to the Clan. If I am wrong, if I am destroyed in this Trial of Refusal, I still wish my Clan to be dominant. Even *if* the Jade Falcons repudiate the truce, I expect the Wolves to be the ones to take Terra. I may no longer be the Clans' leader, but I will not have my Clan surrender its leadership."

Vlad felt his chest swell pridefully, but he did not let himself become carried away with fantasies of his own rise. Such imaginings could only be predicated on the deaths of the two Wolf Khans and, hate them though he might, he did not think the Jade Falcons were sufficiently talented to kill either one.

"I tell you this, Ulric: if you fall on Butler, we will win here and go on to win on Wotan."

Ulric smiled again, but Vlad knew it was not in appreciation for his comment, but based on something else. As always Ulric had held something back and, as always, Vlad had blundered into it unknowing. "Such action will not be necessary, Vlad."

"I do not understand." Adding to Vlad's confusion were the three tones sounding throughout the JumpShip. *The signal to jump, but we're already at Butler.*

Ulric nodded. "I know. I must apologize to you—as I wish now I had apologized to Phelan. You have worked as hard planning our assault on Butler as he worked on my defense before the Grand Council. I am sorry I wasted your time."

"Wasted my time?"

The anger rising in Vlad blossomed as bright as a fusion reaction when the ship jumped. It felt as if his flesh had been flayed from him in one piece that kept stretching and stretching to contain the energy of the fury burning inside him. Just as he reached the point where he must surely burst, the *Dire Wolf* emerged back into normal space, thirty light years away from Butler.

Vlad's flesh snapped back onto his body, then the ship jumped again. In contrast to what he had felt a second before, his flesh became tight on him, like a water-soaked sheet wrapped snugly around him. Pain spread out from the scar on his face and raked lightning talons over his body while his flesh shrank another size and another. It restricted his breathing and his lungs began to burn for want of oxygen. He tried to arch his back, to force his air into his lungs, but all he succeeded in doing was unbalancing himself.

In the eternity that jumping made out of one second, Vlad started to fall.

He hit the ground soon after the *Dire Wolf* returned to Euclidean reality. The truth behind Ulric's remark slammed into his brain and left his head spinning. "We came in slowly not to give me time to do my calculations, but to hotload the Kearny-Fuchida jump coils. Expecting us to fight at Butler, the Falcons would only have defenses on worlds one jump away, not two."

"Yes, I expect the Falcons are as surprised as you are." Ulric stood above him and offered him his hand. "Come on, Vlad. Time to get to our 'Mechs. We'll be fighting in six hours."

"Where are we?"

Ulric smiled. "You have to ask? You did the assessments.

Attacking Wotan with two Clusters would have been suicidal. But with what we have now, and with those troops of Natasha's that survived Twycross, we have a chance of destroying the Falcons right here, in their own nest." He pulled Vlad to his feet. "Welcome to Wotan—the world that will decide our fate. Yours and mine, Vlad, and the fate of every other man and woman of our Clan."

42

There are two gates of Sleep, one of which is held made of
horn and by it real ghosts have easy egress; the other shining
fashioned of gleaming white ivory, but deceptive are the visions
the Underworld sends that way to the light.

—Virgil, *Aeneid*

Avalon City, New Avalon
Crucis March, Federated Commonwealth
10 December 3057

The urgent shouting awakened Francesca Jenkins, but in the
misty dimness she could not see who spoke. She felt cold lying on the floor, and she slowly realized that the chill fog
drifting over her would not hide her nakedness from the
shouting people. This strange place where she found herself
seemed to be illuminated only from below and had neither
walls nor ceiling that she could see.

More shouts drew her attention to the floor. Its cool, slick
surface leeched warmth from where her body pressed
against it. She thought it was glass, but she could not be
sure. With the mist and the cold and her nudity and the
shouts, everything was confused, unlike anything she'd
known before. Something was wrong and she began to feel
fear.

Looking down through the floor, Francesca saw what she
eventually, tentatively, concluded was an operating theater.
Blue-frocked doctors and nurses labored feverishly over a
body on a stainless steel table. "She's arresting. Get me epi-
nephrine, stat! Ready the defibrillator."

"Pressure's dropping."

"Bag her. Get the cardiac pump going, now!"

Someone moved as another person approached the vic-
tim's head and she saw herself lying there on the table. As
the medtech pressed the oxygen mask to her face, Francesca

felt the ghost of pressure over her own mouth and nose. She looked down again and stared, concentrating, and suddenly realized the person they were working on was *her*.

She gathered her legs beneath herself and knelt there, supported on hands and knees as she watched the physicians working on her. *I'm here watching, but I'm also down there. How can it be?*

Ahead and above a strong light flashed out to spotlight her. Francesca recoiled, then a silhouette appeared, limned by the strong light. "Don't be afraid, Francie. You cannot be hurt anymore."

"Mother?" Something insider her said it was impossible for her mother to be speaking to her, but the voice and shape were right. *But my mother is dead.* Then the light and the mist and the looking down at her own body all crashed in on her like a resonance striking deep within her brain. "I'm dead, too."

Her mother nodded slowly and regretfully, the way she always had when Francesca had done something wrong. "It could be your time, yes."

"Mother?"

"Francie."

Gooseflesh puckered her skin. "Is this heaven?"

"You are on the road. You will get there eventually." In the light from the floor Francesca saw her mother smile distantly. "We will be reunited, and I cannot wait for that day."

"Can't I be with you now?"

"I wish that you could, Francie, but you must first atone for your sins."

"Sins? What sins? I have only done what you would have wanted, Mother. I saved Joshua Marik." She touched the twisted flesh over her hip and beneath her breastbone. "I almost died."

She glanced down and saw the doctors working on her again. "I did die."

"Your sins are not entirely your fault, Francie. You were deceived."

Francesca's head came up. "No, I fooled them. The Davions never suspected that I was a Jirik. Your parents told me everything, Mother, everything you would have if you had lived."

Cold dread coiled in her stomach as her mother shook her head. "Dear, dear Francie, I left Castor with your father because I loved him, but also because there was nothing left for me in the Free Worlds League. My grandfather Jirik was killed during the Civil War, before I was born, because SAFE thought he was a collaborator with Anton Marik. And then SAFE got my parents when Castor was taken over by the Federated Commonwealth. The only reason they didn't kill me too was because I was out with your father that night."

"But they said . . ."

"Hush, child. They said what you wanted to hear. Why do you think I changed my name to Jenkins and not Jirik after I divorced your father?"

"To keep yourself safe from the Davions."

"No, Francie, no. I did it so you would grow up as someone from the Federated Commonwealth. I did not want to tie you to my past. We made a good life here. This is your home, but you betrayed its people. Because of that, until you atone, we cannot be together."

Emotions and thoughts and the buzzing-thump from repeated attempts at defibrillation below all raced around in Francesca's mind. She wanted to be with her mother again, but the pain in her mother's words tore at her. From that internal pain came a fury first against the people who had pretended to be her grandparents, but then became a conflagration to immolate anyone even vaguely anti-Davion.

"How can I atone, Mother?"

The woman in the mists smiled at her. "Use what you were taught and will yet learn. They fashioned you into a weapon—now you must be able to cut the hands that shaped you. Those you thought were your enemies will help you salvage your honor. Your mother's heart will leap with joy."

The mists thickened and the light behind her mother began to wane. "Be strong, Francie. Those who would destroy your benefactors must be made to pay."

Francesca tried to stand and reach out toward her mother's dimming shape, but the mists swirled and so did her equilibrium. She sagged forward and caught herself on her hands. Then her elbows buckled and she fell to the floor. Looking down she saw a doctor approach the body again with the electrode paddles.

"Clear."

She heard the sound and felt a tingle run over her body. *I will return to life, and I will atone.*

"I have a pulse, Doctor."

Francesca Jenkins smiled and let darkness enfold her.

Galen looked at Curaitis and the small man beyond him. "Congratulations, Dr. Simons. I think you did it."

Simons shrugged and adjusted his glasses. "Thank you, Secretary Cranston. It was just a variation on the technique the Assassins used to guarantee the loyalty of their members. They would use drugs to render them unconscious and transport them to a splendid palace. The subjects were told they were in Heaven and their every desire was attended to for three days. Then they were drugged and returned to the real world. Their 'mystical' experience fortified their belief in the dogma.

"With Francesca I was able to accomplish the same thing using standard icons from our cultural inventory. Combined with better psychoactive drugs and the wonderful video display from below, the evidence we provided her and the conclusions we drew for her were undeniable and inescapable."

Curaitis nodded toward the room. "The operating room sequence came from the holovid miniseries about Jenkins."

"I thought I'd seen it before," Galen said. "The actress playing her mother, that was Gina Winters, wasn't it? She played Francesca's mother in the series about her life, as I recall. How did we get her?"

Curaitis smiled, the first time Galen remembered ever seeing that expression on his face. "Ms. Winters wanted a chance to appear on the Prince's arm at some cultural event. She believes the exposure will help her career."

"And *you* agreed to let her get that close to the Prince?"

"The Prince was willing to indulge her."

Galen narrowed his eyes. "But isn't there a very good chance she'll tell people about this?"

Curaitis' grin broadened. "We had an auditor in the Department of Revenue Services point out to her that the money she spent on icefire and other illegal synthetic pharmaceuticals could not be deducted as medical expenses. The bad publicity would kill her career."

Galen nodded and looked down through the viewing port above the soundstage that they created for their show. Francesca lay on the glass floor sleeping, looking small and innocent as a child.

"Sleep well, Francesca," he murmured. "Once you wake, you may never know such peace again."

43

History will absolve me.

—FIDEL CASTRO

Final Drop Approach, Drop Ship Lobo Negro
Wotan, Jade Falcon Occupation Zone
10 December 3057

A warning klaxon brought Vlad's head up. Through the viewscreen of his *Timber Wolf*, he saw the lights go from white to red, plunging the 'Mech bay into a night as dark as the space through which the ship traveled. Papers and others debris swirled through the DropShip's hold as the crew blew the hatches and the atmospheric pressure equalized.

He glanced at his secondary monitor, then keyed his radio. "Star Colonel, drop bay doors are open at a kilometer. Anticipate touchdown in two minutes."

He heard Ulric's voice through the speakers in his helmet. "On schedule, good. Did you get that message sent?"

"Affirmative."

"And you did not listen to it?"

"No, Star Colonel." Vlad had been tempted to review the message Ulric had asked him to send out through ComStar, but he knew he would have lost a point in their little game if he had. *I did see that it had been recorded on thirteen September, before your trial. Why you sent it now, I do not know. Nor do I want to.*

"Good. You will form your Star up on me. The others have been given their orders, but we have a special task."

"Sir?"

"We will be hunting Khan Chistu. He is there, on Wotan. We will find him and kill him."

Vlad frowned. "He challenged you?"

"I was surprised as well." Ulric's voice carried with it a resignation toward the Jade Falcon Khan's foolishness. "The Falcons' inflexibility is what will destroy them."

"It would seem this is truth," Vlad said. "One other thing, Star Colonel."

"Yes?"

"You recall I did not like the choice you gave me concerning my duties if you die and I survive here on Wotan?"

"I do."

"I believe I have found a third choice that I like much better."

A wary note entered Ulric's voice. "And that is?"

"If the truce is repudiated by the new ilKhan, the survivors and I will race forward and take Terra before they have a chance to take it themselves."

The silence before Ulric's reply surprised Vlad. "I had hoped, Vladimir of the Wards, that the alternative would not occur to you. I think it will be best for all if you die here with me today."

The landing horns blared before Vlad could answer Ulric. His 'Mech swayed as the DropShip touched down less than gently and smoke from underbrush burned by the landing jets swirled into the 'Mech bay. A green light flared to life on his command console, so he paced his *Timber Wolf* forward, following in the wake of a *Black Hawk*. Though the confines of the 'Mech bay did not allow for speed, the 'Mechs quickly cleared the bay and stepped into the darkness of the Wotan night.

All around him the night was alive with activity. Drop-Ships sprouted on the rolling hills at the southern edge of Borealtown like metal mushrooms. They disgorged their cargo, then lifted off again on great silvery jets, withdrawing to rendezvous points where they would pick up survivors and evacuate the planet if things went badly.

Aerospace fighters shot through the black sky, heading north toward Borealtown. Ruby darts shot up from various points within the city, lasers seeking to knock down the Clan Wolf fighters. In return the Wolf pilots launched their own multiple missile flights. Explosions lit the night, and the darkened city began to glow with fires and the light of secondary explosions.

Vlad had helped make the assessments for the whole campaign. He knew that four Jade Falcon line units awaited the Wolves there in Borealtown. But even the addition of the troops remaining from Twycross was not enough to replace the losses Ulric's forces had taken on the long road to Wotan. Assaulting a fortified position with less than overwhelming numbers of troops was suicidal, yet Vlad had the feeling that such ironclad rules of warfare did not apply here, on this night.

With his Star deployed around Ulric in a ring, Vlad led the advance toward the town, his heart filled with confidence. He did not know if he would live or die on this world, but he felt no fear. *Was this how it was for Natasha when she chose to stay behind on Twycross?* For the first time since Vlad had learned of her death, he understood why she had done what she had done.

Vlad knew he was not immortal, but he felt part of something that would become immortal. The outcome of the fighting here on Wotan would mold the fate of the Clans for the next ten years, and perhaps would help shape what would come for the next twenty or two hundred or two thousand. What Aleksandr Kerensky had begun three centuries ago would be somehow finished here, in Borealtown, in a battle that would never be forgotten.

His skin prickled with a kind of animal prescience, a hyperawareness that had him bringing his *Timber Wolf*'s arms up the instant he sighted an odd shape in the shadow of a corrugated tin building. Even before his computer had found a match for the silhouette, Vlad was dropping the gold targeting crosshairs on it and tightening his index finger against the trigger on the left joystick.

One of the three pulse lasers in his 'Mech's left chest stitched a line of glowing holes across the shoulder of the half-hidden *Ryoken*. The Falcon pilot pulled his 'Mech back behind the warehouse. Without remorse or thought, Vlad nudged the crosshairs over, entering them on the warehouse's facade, and hit both thumb buttons. A blazing wave of heat rushed into the cockpit as the *Timber Wolf*'s twin particle projection cannons released their hellish azure beams.

The tin sheets sheathing the building had roughly half the thickness of a ferro-fibrous armor plate, but only a thousandth of its energy-dissipating ability. The two artificial lightning bolts cored through the building, igniting the boxes stored within, and stabbed deep into the *Ryoken*'s torso. Its left arms dangling from the ruins of the torso, the 'Mech reeled back from the burning warehouse, then staggered and crashed to the ground.

Any other time, Vlad would have poured more fire into the damaged 'Mech, which was still capable of rising to continue the fight. In other battles he would have claimed the right to kill the *Ryoken,* adding its death to the long list of foes he had defeated. It would have become part of his legend, but personal concerns now seemed insignificant.

He pressed on. Glancing briefly at the map of the city Ulric had downloaded into his computer, he saw it marked with the place where Chistu was supposed to be waiting for Ulric. Vlad believed they would find the Jade Falcon Khan there, but he knew intuitively that danger lurked all along the way. This concerned him, because he had no intention of leading Ulric into an ambush.

For a moment it struck him as absurd that he, a Crusader, would be the one to bring a Warden to a place where he could kill a Crusader Khan. With that thought Vlad realized how certain he was that Ulric would destroy Chistu, yet the thought caused him no alarm. He had moved into something beyond a Warden/Crusader fight. This was Wolf against Falcon and—just as Ulric had predicted—Vlad valued his identity as a Wolf more than his affinity with the Crusaders.

I am a Wolf, and so shall I ever be. I could never descend to the level of the Falcons.

Stalking through the concrete canyons of Borealtown, Vlad saw other 'Mechs. Some were Wolves, but most were Jade Falcons. He traded shots with them, his PPC beams and lasers lighting up whole blocks. In one series of exchanges, his *Timber Wolf* and a *Vulture* left molten armor trails down parallel avenues. It ended when the *Vulture* lost a leg in an intersection next to the burned-out remains of one of the *Timber Wolf*'s pulse lasers.

Vlad led the way up the small hill near the center of the town. The terrain leveled out there into a small circle that had once featured a statue set on a tall iron pillar. The buildings surrounding the park had all been constructed in the style of Terra's ancient Hellas, complete with columns and friezes. Had the pillar still been erect, or the buildings not been damaged by the Wolves' bombing runs, the place might have looked very much like the Olympian paradise envisioned by its creators.

On the far side of the circle a lone *Gladiator* in Jade Falcon colors stood in the plaza in front of what appeared to be the Ministry of Justice building. The humanoid 'Mech scanned as a normal configuration for that model omnimech. The anti-missile system and the extended-range small laser were relatively useless, but the 'Mech carried a reasonable amount of armor, so it could weather a lot of abuse. The rapid-loading autocannon in the left arm could inflict considerable damage, as could the PPC in the right arm. Not that it would matter much—nothing would stop Ulric from killing Chistu.

Coming into the circle Vlad moved off to the left and stationed himself in front of what had been, before the coming of the Clans, the Ministry of Budgets and Taxation. The others in his Star spread out to the right and Ulric stepped forward of their line.

From his vantage point Vlad saw that MechWarriors Jenni and Karl were closer together than he would have liked them in a war zone, but the park appeared to be the eye of the martial storm. There was danger here, but for Chistu and Ulric, not him and his people. *Still, they should know better.*

Ulric's voice boomed through his helmet's speakers. "Greetings, Vahn."

"And to you, Ulric. When I suggested this duel I had no idea you would bring seconds."

"You can consider them seconds if you wish. For me, they serve as witnesses."

The Jade Falcon Khan laughed. "My gun-camera video will be witness enough to your death."

"Possibly, but such things are often damaged when a 'Mech is destroyed." Ulric's humanoid *Gargoyle* opened its arms. "Do you require some sort of formal declaration of intent, or shall we begin?"

"It has already begun, Ulric."

That remark struck Vlad as hopelessly bizarre, then he saw the muzzle of the small laser tucked beneath the *Gladiator*'s chin begin to vibrate back and forth like the tines of a tuning fork. He reached over and punched a button on his command, changing his holographic display from starlight to ultraviolet. With that he saw a purplish blade of light scything back and forth, touching all the Wolf 'Mechs in the circle save himself and MechWarrior Andrew opposite him.

The small laser is configured for targeting. He's feeding telemetry to missile Stars. "Ulric, it's a trap!"

Vlad never knew if Ulric Kerensky heard him or not as salvo after salvo of long-range missiles arced up over the Ministry of Justice building and rained down upon the Wolves. The explosions came fast and thick, filling the circle with a nova-glare that banished night and burned shadows into the stone where they struck. Angry and boiling, the fire became hotter as air rushed in to feed it. A gout of flame shot into the sky like a fiery demon released from hell.

The last Vlad saw of Ulric was an image of the *Gargoyle* lunging forward, its arms reaching toward the *Gladiator*. Brilliant fire swept over the 'Mech, smothering it like a blanket. When it parted Vlad thought he saw the blackened silhouette take one more step forward, then disintegrate into ash, torn apart by the titanic force unleashed with the Jade Falcons' missile assault.

The ground rippled beneath Vlad's 'Mech, and he had to fight to keep the *Timber Wolf* upright. The 'Mech lurched to the right and Vlad felt it start to topple. Cursing, he wrenched his body around and forward, then brought the 'Mech down into a crouch. By lowering the machine's center of gravity he regained control, but in doing so had twisted around so that the *Gladiator* no longer stood in the firing arc of his weapons.

On his holographic display he saw the Jade Falcon 'Mech shift its autocannon toward where Andrew's bulky *Summoner* had stumbled to its knees. The *Gladiator* aimed carefully, then fire vomited from the slender muzzle that was its left arm. The swarm of autocannon projectiles blasted into and through the *Summoner*'s cockpit, dropping the 'Mech to the ground like a man just decapitated.

Vlad brought the *Timber Wolf* up and spun it to face Chistu's *Gladiator*. "You treacherous slime. You're so low that when you look up all you can see are *freebirth* soles!"

"Ulric killed them, not me. I did not want witnesses." The *Gladiator*'s arm swung toward the *Timber Wolf*. "I had hoped to use you, Vlad of the Wards, as a rallying point for the Wolves who remained, but Ulric has seen to it that I cannot."

"*I* will see to it that you cannot!" Vlad targeted the *Glad-*

iator and tightened up on his triggers. Heat scorched him, but it didn't matter. He was a Wolf, and he would avenge his Khan and cleanse his Clan's honor, even if it cost him his life. *By my hand you will die!*

One of the two PPCs missed, exploding a Ministry of Justice transformer behind Chistu. The other one combined with the *Timber Wolf*'s two remaining pulse lasers to carve deep furrows into the *Gladiator*'s torso armor. The *Timber Wolf*'s short-range Streak missiles peppered the *Gladiator*'s arms and legs, but destroyed only armor.

The *Gladiator*'s autocannon spat out a double-load of projectiles and hit the *Timber Wolf* dead center. The depleted-uranium slugs pulverized the ferro-fibrous armor and gnawed into the internal support structures that held the OmniMech together. Sparks flew from consoles in the cockpit, and smoke combined with the heat to choke the pilot.

Worse than the damage done by the weapon was the sheer effect of the transference of kinetic energy to the *Timber Wolf*. The impact of the shells lifted the torso up and drove it back. Vlad tried to balance the 'Mech, but only succeeded in making it stumble backward. It half-turned to steady itself against the Ministry of Budgets and Taxation building, but the earlier missile explosions had shaken the structure with the force of an earthquake. Vlad's *Timber Wolf* burst through the wall and crashed onto its back against the marble floor, scattering support pillars like tenpins.

I must get up! Chistu must die! Vlad shook his head to clear it, but in the heat and the smoke, and with all the warning sirens blaring, he could not concentrate. *I must get up! I must.*

He struggled even harder, then looked up through the cockpit canopy. Above him, for all of a second, he saw the night sky and the stars spread across it. Then a black void swallowed it. With each instant seeming to stretch into an hour, Vlad saw the walls and roof of the building sag inward, faster and faster. When they hit his 'Mech, the impact shook the machine harder than the explosions and harder than Chistu's autocannon fire.

Somewhere amid the shaking, the star-swallowing void came to Vlad of the Wards, and fight against it though he did, it gobbled him whole.

BRED FOR WAR

44

> But the Persians suffered from that most dangerous tendency in
> war: a wish to kill but not to die in the process.
>
> —HERODOTUS

Icegrief Pass, Australarctica
Morges, Lyran Alliance
13 December 3057

Sitting in the cockpit of his *Wolfhound,* Khan Phelan Ward
felt as desolate within as the vast white expanse around him.
The currents of emotion running through him were as fierce
as the frigid winds of Icegrief Pass as they drove billowing,
ground-hugging clouds of snow and ice before them. All
around him he saw ancient, long-frozen mountains twisted
into bizarre shapes by the winds, the forms echoing the man-
gled heaps of sentiment and memory inside him.

*The only difference between out there and in here is that
outside is all white while inside I am nothing but blackness.*

It had been two days since he'd received the news of
Natasha's death on Twycross. The moment he read the brief
ComStar transmission, he realized that they'd both known at
their parting that she would not survive this fight. But it
wasn't that he thought Natasha had harbored a death wish or
decided to commit some warrior's form of suicide. Somehow he sensed that the Black Widow, after more than eight
decades of life as a warrior, must have realized she could
add nothing more to her legend. She had become too good
at killing and, by any standard, had so far surpassed other
warriors that there was nothing left for her to do.

And, for the fearsome Black Widow, there could never
have been retirement. Phelan smiled in spite of the void he
felt inside. Natasha had always railed against the Clan tradi-

tion of retiring warriors at forty-five years of age and using them merely to raise up a new crop of warriors.

Alone in his cockpit, Phelan reflected on all this and felt a kind of acceptance of Natasha's death. Then came another message, the one from Angeline Mattlov at dawn, containing the news that Ulric Kerensky had been slain on Wotan. She noted that some Wolves had survived and escaped off planet, but she assured him they would not reach Morges in time to make any difference in their battle.

This information, Phelan was certain, was intended to demoralize him and his people, but Mattlov could never have guessed that her words would have exactly the opposite effect. Phelan did not doubt the news of Ulric's death or that the Wolves had lost the battle for Wotan. If it had been otherwise, Angeline would not be planning to engage the Wolves and Hounds today.

Ulric Kerensky, from the time Phelan had first met him up to the last time he had seen him, had always been in control of any situation in which he was involved. Anticipating each turn of events, he would plot out a strategy for victory. And, in Phelan's experience, his aim had always been true.

And now Ulric was dead.

Instead of shaking Phelan's confidence in Ulric, knowledge of his death only intensified his regard for the man. Phelan chose to believe, and so communicated to his people, that Ulric trusted so completely in their ability to destroy the Jade Falcons and preserve Clan Wolf that he had willingly accepted a role in a plan that he knew would probably kill him.

The other thing Mattlov's message gave Phelan was extremely good news. The Wolves may not have won Wotan, but they had been formidable enough to seriously hurt the Jade Falcons in the fighting. Otherwise, Mattlov would have mentioned the arrival of her own reinforcements along with his. Even more telling was the fact that the Wolves had managed to retreat from Wotan in such good enough order that she considered them possible reinforcements. This suggested to Phelan that at least a Cluster must have gotten away.

If she were to finish her campaign against him before Wolf survivors could reach Morges, Mattlov would have to push for a quick and decisive battle that would break the Wolves. The idea heartened Phelan because it meant the Jade Falcons would have to come at his people hard and fast. Since his force was already in prepared defensive positions, and had adequate air cover, the battling would be costly for the Falcons.

Angeline Mattlov knew this as well as he did and, as he expected, she had grounded her forces on the lowlands near the Bay of Broken Hope. It was a tactically inferior position, but the best she could do and still be within engagement distance of the Wolves. The meteorological survey facility on the bay was insufficient to house all the Falcons, but it was preferable to sleeping on a DropShip.

Phelan's people had all taken up positions in the Highlands, where they would defend key points to deny Mattlov access to the snowfields beyond the first ring of mountains on the icy continent of Australarctica. Phelan had supposed Mattlov would strike first at the Kell Hounds, so he had put them at Icegrief Pass, the most easily defended location. To get to it Mattlov would have to push a hundred kilometers across treacherous terrain, then start the climb up the sharp incline into the teeth of the Hound defenses.

"Wolf One, Hound Command here."

"Roger, Dan, what have you got?"

"A Jade Falcon lance, er, Star of light OmniMechs at the base of the pass."

"Roger. Your discretion, your optimum range."

"Roger, Wolf One. We'll let you know when the shooting starts."

Phelan keyed up a vector graphic image of the pass. The defensive lines had been set up in an elongated hexagon. The long lines at the top and bottom of the hexagon cut perpendicularly across the pass, generally on the reverse of any small dip in the pass itself, providing the 'Mechs cover from the direct fire of Clan missiles and beams. The sharply angled sides of the hexagon were smaller than the defensive lines and angled up and back away from the main line of the pass. By retreating to the right or left, 'Mechs would be offered cover by the mountains and a route that would take them to the next defensive line.

The angled sides went through natural terrain chokepoints that would slow retreating 'Mechs down, but would present even more of a problem to any Clan 'Mechs in pursuit. As enemy 'Mechs tried to come through those smaller side passes, Phelan's people could direct a withering amount of fire at those spots. More important, every defender had the coordinates of those points locked into his or her battle computer. Provided those passes were in the firing arcs of their weapons, Phelan's troops could direct their 'Mechs to aim and shoot at one of those points automatically, even if they could not see it.

The whole thrust of their defense was to hold on to each line for as long as they could, then pull back. The first and second ranks were already filled with 'Mechs. Once the front rank fell back, it would travel to the third rank and be prepared to support the second rank in the same way the second rank had supported them. Even if the Jade Falcons captured one line, crossing to the next one would be just as costly as taking the first and so on.

Angeline Mattlov might have decided that the Kell Hounds were the easiest unit to tackle, but Phelan figured that before she took the second line of defense she'd be contemplating a retreat. She thought of the Hounds as mercenaries—which they were—but she did not equate that with their being elite professional warriors. He also doubted she realized the Hounds were using OmniMechs of their own, salvaged from the battlefield at Luthien and supplemented by the 'Mechs the Red Corsair had used to attack their home base at Arc-Royal two and a half years before.

"Wolf One, we're about to go. Holovid feed on Tac Seven."

"Good luck, Dan."

Phelan punched the holovid feed into his holographic display. Five light OmniMechs pushed forward through the snow into the lower precincts of the pass. The ice on the stony walls had frozen into blue cascades. Little snow-devils swirled and chased each other down through the Clan formation. In the lead were two Omnis—a *Dasher* and a *Koshi* with the boxy *Puma* in the middle and two *Ullers* at the rear.

Phelan studied the 'Mechs pictured on the display. The *Ullers* and the *Puma* had been configured as missile-boats. The *Dasher* and *Koshi* did not show missile racks, so he assumed they'd been outfitted as spotting units. They were fast enough to be difficult to target—especially the *Dasher*—and the other 'Mechs boasted enough missile firepower to seriously hurt most Inner Sphere 'Mechs. Knowing that the weapons of Inner Sphere 'Mechs have considerably shorter effective ranges, Mattlov had figured she could use this Star to probe and harass Phelan's defense.

"Hunters, fire at will," came Dan Allard's voice through Phelan's neurohelmet.

The Kell Hounds First Regiment, known as The Wild Hunters, opened up *en masse* on the Falcons. Their fire patterns had two companies engaging *each* Jade Falcon 'Mech. Configured to use energy weapons almost exclusively, the Hound 'Mechs filled the pass with red, green, and blue darts of energy in a light show so bright Phelan had to turn his eyes away from the display. In doing so he glanced out through his *Wolfhound*'s canopy and saw, thirty kilometers way, a riot of light playing through the low clouds hovering over Icegrief Pass.

"*Freebirth*, what is that?" Phelan heard over the Wolf's tactical frequency.

"First blood for our side, and it goes to the Hounds."

As swift as the *Dasher* was, it went down quickly under fire from twelve 'Mechs firing an average of four weapons each at it. Pulse lasers burned through the armor on its legs and then on through them, taking the limbs off at the knees. The cerulean spear of a PPC beam penetrated the 'Mech's chest, melting its torso in half. The *Dasher*'s faceplate exploded as the pilot ejected, but the 'Mech had been so brutally stricken that the ejection seat burrowed straight into the snow of the pass and the 'Mech fell down heavily on top of it.

By the time Phelan shifted his attention to the fate of the other 'Mechs, all he could see was the imploding golden plasma ball from a fusion-engine reaction running unchecked and the *Koshi*'s burned black skeleton lying in sharp relief against the ice into which it had melted.

Phelan fed those images to all the 'Mechs of his Fourth Wolf Guards Assault and 279th Battle Clusters. "The Hounds did that as easily and cleanly as we would have. Next time any of you decide to use the term 'freebirth' as a curse, just remember that freeborn is what they are, each and every one. In that old battle between nature and nurture, I'd say nature's ahead five nothing."

45

There is no instance of a country having benefited from prolonged warfare.

—SUN TZU, *THE ART OF WAR*

Marik Palace, Atreus
Marik Commonwealth, Free Worlds League
15 December 3057

Thomas Marik studied the scarlet datastream scrolling through the space over his desk. "Ah, very good, the resistance on Castor has been put down."

Precentor Malcolm nodded. "It turns out that the leader of the guerrillas was Karl Jirik. According to a report from your SAFE intelligence, his family has a long history of treasonous activity against the Mariks. His grandfather died in the aftermath of the Civil War and a brother was killed when SAFE evacuated Castor a quarter-century ago. It seems he was helping expose SAFE agents to the Federated Commonwealth. Karl was only a child at the time, but he apparently considered his brother a martyr."

"It must have been in the blood." Thomas gently rubbed his face with his left hand, feeling the rough tracery of scars beneath his fingertips. "I've seen first-hand the kind of passions aroused by familial love and hatred."

"Yes, Captain-General."

Thomas smiled politely. "This, then, ends the contention for all the worlds we lost to the Federated Commonwealth in the Fourth Succession War."

"Yes, sir. There is still scattered fighting on some of the worlds—Nanking, most notably—where your mercenaries secured footholds for Sun-Tzu's troops. The rest of the Sarna March is fragmenting into independent worlds or multiple-world associations. Sarna and Styk have formed their own defensive alliances with nearby worlds and are sending ambassadors here to Atreus and on to New Avalon."

"They ignore Sun-Tzu?"

"They are aware, Captain-General, of where the true power rests."

"I see." Thomas pursed his lips for a moment, then hit a button on his desk that banished the datastream. "Well, the only reason for having power is to use it, is that not so?"

"That is what the Blessed Jerome Blake believed, as well you know, sir." Precentor Malcolm looked down at his noteputer. "Calling up program five-seven-one-two-one-four Pol/Mil will give you the breakdown of forces in the Sarna March and some likely targets for our next strikes."

"I don't think that will be necessary."

"You have already selected the targets, then. I should have guessed."

No, Malcolm, you could never have guessed. "No, to the contrary. I am going to send a message to Victor, offering him a truce."

Malcolm's jaw shot open. "You can't be serious, sir."

"No? You forget, Malcolm, that I started this war because of what my son and I suffered at the hands of Victor Davion. My anger was righteous and my actions justified. My troops have taken back the worlds the Federated Commonwealth took from us, and we did it without seriously damaging our economic base. So far, the fighting has not been costly. Of all our forces, the mercenaries have taken the most damage."

"But the whole Sarna March lies open to you."

"And to take it would leave me vulnerable to attack. You know as well as I that Victor Davion has not struck back because of a temporary dearth of JumpShips. As things stand now, he will strike at worlds owned by Sun-Tzu once he solves that problem, not at me. Moreover, if I were to push deeper into the Sarna March, I would anger Sun-Tzu. Though his nation is small, he is most vexatious in his tenacity and paranoia. Were Victor able to woo him to his side, or were he to sponsor Kai Allard-Liao in some Capellan civil war that toppled Sun-Tzu, he would regain all he has lost *and* have a dagger pointed at my nation's belly."

Malcolm hesitated, clearly searching for some argument that could sway Thomas from his chosen course. "But what *of* Sun-Tzu? Will he not be angry with you for ceasing your support of his efforts?"

"Indeed, he might. I will mollify him. I will issue orders for mercenaries to reinforce Nanking and give him his *Wolverine* factory. If he wants more, I will offer to sell him the contracts for my mercenaries. Then if he chooses to push *his* war with Victor, I will wash my hands of him."

Precentor Malcolm laid the noteputer on the desk. "I still fail to understand. You know what the Word of Blake teaches about unbelievers and how they must be persuaded to embrace what we teach. This is your chance to bring billions of people into the fold and enlighten them."

Thomas took caution from the hints of betrayal in Malcolm's pleading. "Understand this, please, Precentor Malcolm, because what I will tell you is *critical* to our realizing the vision of Jerome Blake, a vision that ComStar has betrayed and defiled."

"Blasphemers and heretics all."

"Indeed. They have secularized ComStar and have purged it of the spiritual guidance it once provided. In this, ComStar errs grievously because they look to technology alone as the means by which humanity will realize its destiny. Perhaps their confusion is understandable because they believe that if was technology alone that defeated the technological juggernaut of the Clans at Tukayyid.

"What they forget is how important was the role of the spirit of the defenders on Tukayyid in deciding that fight."

"They do not forget it, but they underestimate it, Captain-General. As the Blessed Blake said, 'The outcome of a battle depends not upon numbers, but upon the united hearts of those who fight.' "

"Yes, Malcolm, Jerome Blake was fond of quoting Kusunoki Masashige." Thomas slowly shook his head. "We must never let our fervent loyalty to the spirit divorce us from reality. Jerome Blake was a good man, a wise man, but not the *only* good man or wise man ever. His greatness came in his ability to understand the past and project its lessons into the future. The future he envisioned was a Dark Age into which humankind must fall, and out of which ComStar would raise humanity back up into the light. The situation is directly analogous to the recovery of Europe on Terra after the collapse of the Roman Empire. ComStar serves as the Christian Church did then to lead the way."

"But ComStar rejected its role, sir."

"Yes, and you overestimate the Word of Blake's role. You have forgotten, or refused to acknowledge, that while Europe was in a dark age, the Arab, African, Chinese, and Mayan cultures flourished. Indeed, a vast amount of scientific information discovered by the Greeks was almost lost in that Dark Age. The only reason it was not was because the data was preserved by the Arabs and then was later uncovered with the liberation of Spain. In other words, Malcolm, the dire collapse you see as necessary is an illusion. The important thing is to present the people with an example and a means to finding the right path. It is not a battle between the secular and the religious, technology versus spirituality, but the necessity of showing the people that the two can be integrated."

Malcolm glanced up at him. "Your Knights of the Inner Sphere are a step in this direction?"

"Yes, Malcolm, yes, they are. Those warriors combine superior technology and skills with pure spirit and a commitment to making the universe finer. By combining the drive and abilities of the Word of Blake with the technology possessed by great states like the Federated Commonwealth, we can build a great society, create an interstellar ideal, to which people will flock of their own accord."

Thomas smiled slowly. "I will offer Victor peace, provided he returns my son's body and feeds us research so we can modernize more than our weapons factories. I will even continue to produce war material for him in exchange for a promise from him to re-direct his efforts toward the Clans. I will not oppose him in any attempt to stabilize his Sarna March—less, of course, the worlds I have taken back into the League—provided he agrees not to try to take my worlds from me."

"You will require him to make a public announcement about all this, yes?"

"No, Malcolm, I will not. I will permit him to save face and even publicly refuse to relinquish ownership of the worlds we have retaken, if he so chooses. A threat from without unites those within, and one should never deprive an enemy of the opportunity to present one face to his public while pursuing different policies in private. That sort of contradiction often proves valuable later."

Malcolm smiled. "As it did with the unfortunate death of your son."

"Exactly." Thomas thought for a moment of his Joshua, the boy's laughter and intelligence and happy smiles in the time before he fell ill. "Had he lived, Joshua might have done great things. Now it is up to us to do great things in his memory."

=== 46 ===

Nothing helps a fighting force than correct information. Moreover it should be in perfect order and done well by capable personnel.

—CHE GUEVARA, MEMORANDUM

Daosha, Zurich
Zurich People's Republic, Capellan Confederation
18 December 3057

Xu Ning lowered his glasses to the tip of his nose and then smiled as Colonel Burr entered his office. With the single desk lamp as the only illumination, the room was like a dark cavern. Xu took his glasses off and laid them on top of the disks he had been reviewing, then stood and extended his hand to the mercenary leader. "Thank you for coming so promptly, Colonel."

"My pleasure to serve you, Director."

Xu Ning noted a reduction in the melancholy that had seeped into Burr's voice whenever they'd spoken over the last month. "You have heard good news, Colonel? Your pilfering problem?"

"We have, in fact, solved the problem of the theft of some of our munitions, yes. We found a warehouseman at Kaishiling stealing det-cord and plastique. The man has been shot."

Xu ning winced. "I wish you had not done that. He might have had information."

Burr's face closed up. "To be effective, justice must be swift and sure."

"This I understand, Colonel." Xu well knew Burr did not like the information extraction methods his SecCom employed when interrogating suspected terrorists, but narcotic combined with torture seemed very swift and very sure to him. "Have you catalogued your losses in explosives?"

"Five kilos, more or less. A minor amount." Burr shrugged stiffly. "But I came in response to your summons. You have something you wish to tell me?"

"Tell? No, I have something I wish to ask of you." Xu expected to see Burr frown and begin to make excuses, but the man did not revert to his usual behavior. *This does not bode well.* "A month ago you mentioned steps I should take to end the threat posed by the Dancing Joker. Though I doubt you expected me to heed your advice, I did. I have an agent inside the Dancing Joker's organization."

Burr arched an eyebrow. "You do?"

Xu could see Burr wanted to ask more, but that he was restraining himself in the interests of security. "The man was brought into the organization by relatives, so he is considered completely trustworthy. In fact, SecCom had picked him up for black market activity even before he joined the Dancing Joker. He has sold us other information for money that he uses to maintain a mistress here in Daosha. According to his information the Dancing Joker intends to strike at the Jihuaide Chumai power station two nights from now. The reason I asked you to come today was to ask whether you would participate in the operation to take him apart?"

Burr slowly began to smile, but the expression was restrained. "In two nights? Yes, we would be happy to participate. Think of it as our going-away present to you, Director."

Xu Ning's eyes narrowed. " 'Going-away present?' You are leaving us?"

Burr nodded and Xu suddenly understood the source of Burr's recently elevated spirits. "Captain-General Marik has decided that it's a waste of money to leave us here cooling our heels on Zurich. On the twenty-first we leave for Nanking to rescue what's left of Smithson's Chinese Bandits."

Xu Ning dropped back into his chair. "So, you will be leaving us defenseless?"

Burr shook his head. "No, I'll kill your problem—the Dancing Joker—and then I'll go kill the Bandits' problem. A mercenary unit thrives on action, Director, and finally the Black Cobras will get to see some."

47

Nobody blunders twice in war.

—LATIN PROVERB

Stanleyfield, Australarctica
Morges, Lyran Alliance
20 December 3057

Warm inside the cockpit despite the howling blizzard outside his *Nova,* Phelan glanced down at the map on his secondary monitor. "By the map, we're right on top of them. Weapons control positive." He punched all of his OmniMech's weapons online. "Remember, Ghost Wolves, in this cold you can run hotter than normal. Keep shooting."

In a staggered line the Fourth Wolf Assault Cluster pushed forward toward the Jade Falcon position. Far to the west, in fighting at Carson Rift, the 279th and Sixteenth Battle Clusters were slowly being driven back by a concerted assault from the Fourth Falcon Velites Cluster, 89th and Fourth Striker Clusters, and the Peregrine Eyrie Cluster. Garrison troops had also secured the Falcon base at Broken Hope. All the way around to the eastern side of the continent, the Fourth Striker Cluster and 17th Falcon Regulars were keeping the Fourth Wolf Guards Striker Cluster and the 328th Battle Cluster pinned down at Archangel Glacier.

Despite their successes, the battle at Carson Rift was eating up a significant amount of ordnance for the Falcons. Because the Wolves were in defensive positions, killing them was very difficult. The Jade Falcons' overwhelming fire power was winning them ground, but only at a high cost in ammunition. Pressing their attack meant the Falcons had to be resupplied from Broken Hope, and the Fourth Wolf Guards were out to see that didn't happen.

Moving through the blizzard, Phelan knew he'd gotten lucky. The blizzard that was hiding his unit had blown in from the east to settle over Australarctica like a blanket, freezing all units in place, including the resupply convoy that had started out from Broken Hope. Before the storm had become so dense that no satellite observation was possible, an old mineral survey satellite had passed over the pole and pinpointed the concentrations of 'Mechs on the southern continent. When a mass of metal showed up in a position where it wasn't supposed to be, Phelan knew he had a group of Falcons caught out on the open plains of Stanleyfield.

The Fourth Guards—newly christened the Ghost Wolves in honor of their white camouflage—reconfigured or traded their OmniMechs for other machines within the Wolf force. They became a lighter unit than usual, with speed as their primary concern. Their weapons were swapped out for armaments suitable to short-range battling and sloppy target acquisition situations. The fight would be tight and decidedly nasty.

And, if we're lucky, it will be short.

The problem Phelan faced was that he had no accurate way of assessing the strength of the forces arrayed against him. Though he was fairly certain they would be garrison troops, that hardly meant they were harmless. Phelan didn't want to fall into the same error Angeline Mattlov had committed by underestimating the Kell Hounds because they were mercenaries.

As Phelan switched his scanners over to magnetic resonance, the holographic display started tagging targets out on the snowy expanse. Choosing a humanoid silhouette that the targeting computer identified as a *Hellhound* he dropped the golden crosshairs on it. As he did so, his squat *Nova*'s arms came up. When a gold dot pulsed in the center of the crosshairs, he punched his thumb down on the firing button on his joystick.

A wave of heat surged into the cockpit, and a tone told him the targeting computer had locked all three pulse lasers onto the left side of the *Hellhound*'s torso. Three volleys of ruby darts sizzled through the storm and hit the Falcon 'Mech hard. In two seconds, more than a ton of ferro-fibrous armor plates were converted into vapor that immediately condensed into a thick, gray fog. As the fog drifted away from the *Hellhound*, the 'Mech staggered but managed to stay up.

The Falcon brought his 'Mech's weapons up and pointed them at the *Nova*, prompting Phelan to fire the bank of pulse lasers built into his 'Mech's left arm. The *Hellhound*'s large laser sent a green energy spear wide to Phelan's left and one of the medium lasers missed high, but the third beam slashed a line through the armor over his *Nova*'s right flank. A warning buzzer sounded in Phelan's cockpit, and the armor diagram on his auxiliary monitor reflected the damage, but nothing had gotten through the armor to cause real problems.

Another tone accompanied Phelan's return shot in which all three pulse lasers poured their fire into the wound gaping open on the 'Mech's right side. Gouts of smoke jetted from the muzzles of the two lasers mounted on that side of 'Mech's body. Glowing structural supports dropped from the cavity and sank steaming through the snow. The *Hellhound* started to lost toward the left, then fell backward as the pilot overcorrected and lost his balance. The giant machine went down, and the dead 'Mech was immediately blanketed in snow.

All around him Phelan saw the phantom 'Mechs of the Fourth Wolf Guards move into the Falcons' makeshift camp. To his right Ranna's blocky *Warhawk* stabbed two green laser lances into the right side of a *Goshawk*, boiling away every bit of armor on that side of its chest. The elegantly slender *Goshawk* returned fire, but only hit with two pulse lasers. One melted a scar on the *Warhawk*'s left breast while the other boiled armor from the big 'Mech's left leg.

A gust of wind suddenly raised a white wall between Phelan and Ranna, and when it fell Phelan found himself at point-blank range with a *Man O'War*. The eighty-ton, solidly built OmniMech was constructed as if to be the very embodiment of physical power and strength. It outmassed the *Nova* by thirty tons and was built to take a lot of damage.

Phelan cut his 'Mech hard to the right and pushed down on the throttle pedals to build speed. The *Man O'War* brought its right arm up and fired both of the particle projection cannons built into the 'Mech's forearm. Two blue bolts of synthetic lightning missed to the left, but the medium and large pulse lasers built into the 'Mech's left arm hit home perfectly.

The red energy darts nibbled away at the armor over the *Nova*'s right thigh. The green laser flechettes from the larger weapon bubbled armor off the left side of the *Nova*'s chest, reducing its effectiveness by more than sixty-five percent. *One more shot like that and I'm hurting*. Phelan didn't even want to think about ejecting from a 'Mech in the middle of this storm, much less leaving the combat.

The *Nova* stabbed both arms forward and tracked the *Man O'War* as it slowly twisted to follow the *Nova*'s movement. The crosshairs dipped low on the Falcon 'Mech's outline, a gold dot appearing when the sight settled on the 'Mech's right knee. Bracing himself for the heat, he hit both thumb triggers on his joysticks.

The tone he got in response to his shot warbled, which meant not all of the weapons had locked onto the same target. One pulse laser sent its ruby needles wide between the *Man O'War*'s legs, but the others peppered the right leg. Molten armor melted a swath through the snow behind the 'Mech. The lasers sliced through the thick myomer fibers above and below the knee, leaving them dangling like worn cord.

The *Man O'War*'s pilot managed to keep the 'Mech upright and fired again at Phelan's *Nova*. The PPCs missed again, but Phelan knew that had more to do with luck and his being inside their minimum range than any deficiency on the part of the Falcon pilot. The medium pulse laser in the 'Mech's left arm stitched a line of burning craters across the center of the *Nova*, while the other laser fire missed high and wide.

Even at this temperature, he's got to be running hot. Phelan's own indicators showed the *Nova* to be a bit above optimal heat levels, but he had to risk his computer shutting him down because of excessive heat. Again he centered his crosshairs on the *Man O'War*'s body, but couldn't correct enough to target the leg again. When he got a targeting dot, he fired all his weapons and listened in vain for a tone.

His lasers swept fire across the left side of the *Man O'War*, evaporating armor from its arm, leg, and flank. One of the lasers even scored armor on the 'Mech's extended right arm, but none of the attacks penetrated the ferro-fibrous carapace protecting the *Man O'War*'s vital mechanisms.

Even without doing internal damage, the assault did have an effect. The lasers evaporated more than two tons of armor, causing a shift in the weight of the OmniMech's torso. As the machine continued to track to its left, following Phelan's *Nova*, the pilot lost control. He tried to steady the 'Mech by leaning it back to the right, but that only put pressure on the skeletal right leg. The leg buckled, the fire-blackened femur sliding forward out of the knee joint. The 'Mech wavered for a second, then collapsed in the snow, landing on its right side.

Using the momentum and speed he'd built up, Phelan pushed his *Nova* on into the center of the supply convoy's camp. Without slowing, he targeted the heavily laden hovertrucks and picked them apart with laser fire. In some spots, when the laser darts hit the snow-covered payloads, the cargo exploded. SRMs and LRMs had their rocket motors ignite, shooting the missiles off in all directions. Autocannon ammunition cooked off, spraying hundreds of rounds into vehicles—starting yet more conflagrations in a hideous chain reaction.

A Jade Falcon *Peregrine* came jetting forward from the other side of the compound, the large pulse laser in its chest spitting green energy darts at Phelan's *Nova*. They ripped into his 'Mech's left leg, dotting the armor with half-melted pits. The medium pulse laser in the *Peregrine*'s right arm hit the same target, leaving the armor on the *Nova*'s left leg a steaming ruin.

Phelan tracked the *Peregrine* as the 'Mech came in for a landing. Just before it touched down he got a pulse in the center of his crosshairs. The tone sounded loud and clear as he hit both trigger buttons. All six of his pulse lasers burned their way through the right side of the flying 'Mech's barrel chest and devoured the internal structures on the right side of its torso. Their energy unabated, they melted armor over the 'Mech's heart from the inside out, and with it ran the central supports in the *Peregrine*'s chassis.

When the 'Mech's broad feet hit the ground, the torso telescoped down onto its legs. When the shoulders hit the hips, the upper half of the body rebounded up and ripped free of the structural bits on the left side. With the right arm spinning wildly off through space, the upper body slowly rotated up in the air, then landed head-down in the snow.

A Jade Falcon *Vixen* appeared on Phelan's left side, but before it could exploit the damage done by the *Man O' War* and the *Peregrine*, Ranna's *Warhawk* intervened. Ranna's two large pulse lasers laid the *Vixen*'s left arm and leg open. The twin PPCs mounted in the *Warhawk*'s left arm finished the last of the armor on the small 'Mech's left leg, then liquefied the ferrotitanium bones. The azure beams ate up into the left side of the 'Mech, destroying both the armor and the internal structures making up the *Vixen*'s left flank. The left arm dropped away, and the smoking 'Mech fell to the ground a second later.

"Thanks, Ranna."

"My pleasure, even though these are solahma."

The disgust in her voice struck a chord in Phelan. Solahma units were suitable for chasing bandits, nothing more. Angeline Mattlov had made a big mistake in entrusting her supplies to their protection. The Fourth Wolf Guards ripped through them faster than they would have any Inner Sphere line unit. More important, the Fourth Wolf Guards' losses could be tallied in armor plates.

Ranna's *Warhawk* prodded one overturned hovertruck with its arm, and uncovered the cargo. "Phelan, Mattlov was having them bring up energy weapons for her OmniMechs."

"Yes!" Phelan smiled broadly as the Fourth Wolf Guards line swept past him in pursuit of the fleeing Jade Falcons. "She's seen her mistake, and we stopped her from getting weapons that don't need ammunition."

"My Khan, your language has deteriorated disgracefully."

"Thank you for reminding me, Star Captain. It shall not happen again."

"You expect *me* to believe that, *quineg*?"

Phelan laughed. "If any of this stuff is recoverable, let's haul it off. If we can't, destroy it all."

"As you wish, my Khan." Phelan heard Ranna sigh over the line. "Angeline Mattlov will never make this mistake again."

"Remember, Ranna, it is up to us to make certain she never has the *chance* to make this mistake again. That is what Natasha and Ulric wanted us to do—and believe me, we will because I'd rather be haunted by a million Jade Falcons than the shades of either one of them."

48

The military value of a partisan's work is not measured by the amount of property destroyed or the number of men killed or captured, but in the number he keeps watching.

—JOHN SINGLETON MOSBY, WAR REMINISCENCES

Daosha, Zurich
Zurich People's Republic, Capellan Confederation
20 December 3057

Waiting in the cold, Cathy Hanney shivered, but her shivering was not solely because of the weather. The position she and Fabian Wilson had taken up on the hillside overlooking the northern approach to the Jihuaide Chumai power station *was* exposed to the wind, and the early winter breezes did cut like a knife. Even so, she thought she could have endured them without suffering had other conditions been more comforting.

She did not like being saddled with Fabian Wilson on his rookie mission. She'd sensed from the meeting in the restaurant that things might not work out well, and she'd tried to communicate her foreboding to Noble, but when talk turned to missions, Noble disappeared and the Dancing Joker took over. Where Noble would have been sympathetic, the Dancing Joker was resolute, reminding her that if she could successfully train Fabian, their future missions would be easier and more secure.

The only way Fabian will make a mission secure is through having his tongue ripped out. Cathy knew, from long years of dealing with people in traumatic situations, that Fabian's chatter came from nerves, but it bothered her. And it distracted her, the last thing she needed while trying to look out for Noble and the others.

Wilson, squatting at the base of a wind-twisted pine tree, shook his head. "You know, Cath, I gotta tell you, I nev

igured Noble for the secret agent type, you know? I mean,
when old Foxie brought him to me to buy a computer, I said
o myself, I said, 'This is a school teacher. Quiet, unassum-
ng, bookish. I bet he wants to write action novels so he can
ive out the adventurous life he never had.' I was wrong, but
'm man enough to admit that."

"That's big of you, Fabian." Cathy intended her tone to be
utting, but Fabian seemed not to notice the sarcasm. "We
hould be listening."

"What, like my whispers are going to drown out the ap-
roach of 'Mechs? Listen, Cath, I drove a loading 'Mech in
ny warehouse days. Walking earthquakes. Trust me, if the
Cobras are slithering our way, we'll know it."

Cathy looked at her chronometer, then keyed her radio. "Po-
aris clear." She knew there would be no reply. The insertion
eams would be running under radio silence until the action
tarted—*which should be any time about now.* Cathy would
ave given her right arm for just one word from Noble, but
he realized he'd be in full Dancing Joker mode at this point,
nd even torture couldn't have made him to speak with her.

"So, Cath, when did you first find out Noble was a Davion
gent?"

Cathy dropped to her haunches. "Look, I don't know that
or certain. That's point one. Point two: you know that opera-
onal security means I can't talk to you about him. The more
ou know, the more you put him in danger. Just like I don't
now where you and your wife and Fox are being stashed, so
ou can't know about Noble without jeopardizing him."

"Hey, hey, take it easy. I was just making conversation."

"You should be listening."

"Sorry. Look, I can understand you want to be protective
f him. I mean, you feel for him what I feel for my wife,
ght?"

*I suspect I feel for him more than you're capable of feel-
ng for your wife.* "Right." Something snapped in the woods
ff to her right. "Shhh. What was that?"

"I didn't hear nothing."

Some surprise, that. Cathy slid her hand into her parka
nd took hold of the machine pistol holstered beneath her
eft armpit. But before she could draw it, she heard Fabian
ock his pistol and then felt the heavy pressure of the muz-
le against the back of her head.

"Don't even think it. Your wool cap won't stop a bullet."

"What are you doing? Are you mad?"

"No," his voice announced from behind her, "just playing for the side that will win. Come on in, she's neutralized."

Her thumb snapped the safety down on her pistol. Before Fabian could puzzle out the significance of the muffled click from inside her parka, she'd pulled the trigger. Burning nylon and smoking goose-down jetted out toward Fabian as the three-shot-burst blew through her parka and hit him in the stomach and chest. The muzzle flame burned her armpit and recoil made the pistol rise.

Behind her, the bullets' impact picked Fabian up and started to spin him around. His finger tightened on the trigger, but his pistol had shifted away from her head enough that the shot missed. Still the muzzle blast peppered the left side of her face with burning powder and the report deafened her. Worst of all the bright flash of light blinded her. Trying to cut to her right to flee, she slammed straight into a tree.

Rebounding, Cathy tried to draw her machine pistol, but the cocking lever caught on the inside of her coat. She felt herself begin to fall, then a sharp blow to the right side of her face snapped her head around. She dropped to the ground as if her bones had evaporated. A heavy weight pounced on her chest, then she felt the sights of a gun cutting into the flesh beneath her chin.

Through the ringing in her ears she heard someone say, "Viper Team One, north secured. Go in."

Those words bored through the shock in her mind. *Fabian betrayed us. The Black Cobras are here. They'll kill everyone, including Noble. I failed to warn him. It's all my fault.*

Even as she began to sink into despair, a brilliant light illuminated the night sky and outlined the silhouette of the trooper sitting on her chest. She knew it was an explosion even before she heard the faint report.. *North, north.. The only target there is the Cobra base at Kaishiling! The Dancing Joker hit there instead of here. That's the end of Xu Ning's third power base!*

Cathy wanted to laugh aloud, but the weight of the trooper sitting on her chest made it impossible for her to draw enough of a breath to do so. She settled for a smile. *You've done it, Noble. I know you'll come for me, and when you do we'll topple this Xu Ning together.*

$$=== 49 ===$$

Loyalty is the marrow of honor.

—PAUL VON HINDENBURG, *OUT OF MY LIFE*

Tharkad City, Tharkad
District of Donegal, Lyran Alliance
20 December 3057

Katrina Steiner, wearing a white knit dress under an ice-blue woolen jacket, smiled as her secretary ushered the visitor into her private office. "I am so pleased you were able to come to Tharkad."

The short, stocky man returned her smile and bowed his graying head in her direction. "I am honored by your willingness to see me."

"I agreed to see you if the token your representative brought me was impressive enough." Katrina reached down and lifted the bronze mask from the blotter of her desk. "Being presented the death mask of the man who took Keid from me did indeed impress me, Tormano Liao."

The older man shrugged. "I have, over the years, developed assets to match those of my nephew and his mother before him. I regret that doing so may have necessitated sending agents to worlds of the Federated Commonwealth, but the migration of my people to worlds outside the Capellan Confederation over the last three decades made that a natural expansion of my interests."

"Please, Mandrinn Liao, be seated." Katrina sat behind her desk and set the serene mask of Roland Carpenter's face on the counter of her desk. "I was correct in assuming this was a *death* mask?"

Tormano nodded slowly. "Mr. Carpenter was greatly enamored of power and resisted being removed from it."

"And the counter-revolution?"

"Ah, that was a native product. It would have been uncovered early on, but I had infiltrated agents into Carpenter's government and they happened to be in charge of counter-insurgency. Once Carpenter left office, installing the Duchess was simple."

The Archon rested her elbows on the blotter and steepled her fingers. "And you have many agents in the Sarna March?"

"*Had*, Duchess. As you know, over the last eighteen months my resources have been severely reduced."

"You mean since Kai deposed you as the leader of the Free Capella Movement."

Tormano nodded stiffly. "He has taken over many of the functions I had in that role, but he has not replaced me entirely. He abandoned my intelligence network, but over the last six months he has been less than vigilant in preventing me from renewing contacts. Even so, with my limited resources, I have been able to act in only one or two places. Keid was one, Zurich another."

Katrina arched an eyebrow at him. "The Dancing Joker is your agent?"

"No, though I wish he were. My agent works under the name of Jacko Diamond. He is not as successful as the Dancing Joker, but my organization is in a position to exploit any gains he makes."

"I see." The Archon folded her hands together and rested them lightly on the desktop. "So, now you come to me to ask for help in funding your operations?"

Tormano smiled slowly, as if he were indulging a child, and that frightened Katrina for a moment. "That would be one of the outcomes I would hope for from this meeting."

"Yes? Then, perhaps it is time you informed me of the purpose of your visit here."

"Indeed, Archon, I would very much like to do so." Tormano unbuttoned his double-breasted jacket and slid forward in the tall leather chair until he sat perched on the edge of the seat. "I have been watching you with great interest ever since we met on Solaris, Duchess. Yes, I was impressed with your beauty, but even more than that, your ability to manipulate people captured my attention. It is something every politician must learn, though many never succeed. Yet it is a skill you understand instinctively. You know how to persuade people to do what you want almost without effort."

Tormano's head dipped every so slightly. "This ability would make you unassailable except for—"

"Except for what?"

"Your youth, your immaturity and, most of all, your lack of vision."

Katrina's face flushed and she started to speak, but Tormano held a hand up.

"Indulge me, Archon, for what I say is not meant to inflame you, but to show you how I would be able to help you. Because of your youth, you lack a full understanding of the traditions and rivalries that are the mainspring driving the Inner Sphere. Victor does, but this is because his military training instilled in him the history of his nation and his regiment.

"And when I speak of immaturity, I refer to a penchant for impulsiveness. When Sun-Tzu took Keid and Northwind from you, you saw that as an attack on you. Yet it was obviously meant as a test of Thomas' resolve to expand the war. Thomas refused to take the bait and you complained to him and to the Kell Hounds before I could offer you my services."

"I see." Katrina bit her words off angrily. "And my lack of vision?"

"I have heard rumors to the effect that you plan to release JumpShips to your brother *without* any concession for their return. Though it is true this gives the public appearance of benign neutrality for the Lyran Alliance, you, your brother, and I are under no illusions about the depth and permanence of the division between your realms. Were it not necessary to maintain a link to provide a legitimate claim by each of you upon the other's realm, you would have made a clean break of it. You are separate nations now, and a nation will not prosper unless it wins a prize from other nations for its actions."

Tormano smiled as he opened his arms. "The Steiners have traditionally been admired as great merchants. You should be *selling* those ships back to Victor, and slowly, as well, so he never has a number sufficient to cause you trouble with them."

"I see." Katrina's anger almost prevented her from assessing the wisdom of Tormano's words. The fact that he pointed out the flaws in her performance heightened her anger, and that made her lash out. "So, you, a noble whose holdings were reduced to one estate and a scattering of loyal minions, a noble who has never ruled a state for even as much as a minute, you would have yourself installed as my advisor? Either you are here on behalf of my brother to betray me as Justin Allard did your father, or you are even more insane that your dead sister and her daughter combined."

Tormano's face remained impassive despite the savage attack. "The chance that you would judge me so harshly was not unanticipated. Let me ask you, though, to think on the fates of the leaders of your father's time. Takashi Kurita is dead. Janos Marik is dead, and Thomas is only alive today because ComStar worked to resurrect him for a year and a half. Katrina Steiner, your namesake, is dead. Your father is dead. Your mother is dead and, yes, my father and my sister Romano are dead. However, my sister Candace has ruled over Saint Ives since before your mother was born. And I, a landless noble, have survived decades of meddling in and of the internal politics of the Capellan Confederation without being killed. Let me assure you, that is no mean accomplishment in and of itself. If the Liaos are anything, we are survivors, and your realm, trapped between the Clans and the Free Worlds League, needs to be a survivor as well."

Whether it was the calm of his tone or the obvious wisdom of his words, something drained Katrina's anger away. "If I were to accept you as my advisor, what would you want in compensation?"

Tormano smiled slowly. "My needs are few. The Sarna March is now a region of space contested by the Federated Commonwealth, the Free Worlds League, and the Capellan Confederation. Internally it is a shambles, with the various worlds forming their own alliances to keep themselves safe. A state of confusion reigns, yet you have one of the most legitimate claims to it. You will recall that when the area was taken from the Capellans by your father, he awarded it to your mother—a Steiner. And now you are obviously the heir to the Steiner tradition. What I will want from you are the resources necessary to maintain influence in the area. Together we shall keep the maelstrom stirred up, distracting the attention of everyone involved.

"But what you will give me is far less important than what I will give you, Archon. I will be loyal to you, both because I make that pledge and because no one else will have me. I am yours until you reject me. With my loyalty comes my willingness to act as your sounding board and your conscience. I will also be your confidant and carry out faithfully those missions with which ordinary people cannot be trusted. I even have enough standing to negotiate on your behalf with other sovereign rulers. From me you will get the counsel you need because I do not fear you, nor am I in love with you."

The Archon half closed her eyes. Deep down inside she knew that her ability to manipulate and influence people left her feeling contempt for all those she was able to control. The strong ones, the people she could not bend to her will—Morgan Kell, her brother Victor, and now Tormano—were the ones she wished to have near her. Morgan and Victor had made themselves her enemies. She did not know if he could ever come to fully trust Tormano, but she could respect his frankness and forthright manner.

And if she were to take on an adviser, at the very least it would have to be someone she could respect.

The Archon stood and extended her hand to Tormano Liao across the desk. "I believe, Mandrinn Liao, that my realm will see great things as a product of our alliance."

Tormano took her hand and lightly kissed it. "Most assuredly, Archon. Great things indeed."

=== 50 ===

Laws are dumb in time of war.

—CICERO, PRO MILONE

Daosha, Zurich
Zurich People's Republic, Capellan Confederation
20 December 3057

The cold drizzle falling in a light curtain between Xu Ning and the mercenary was no insulation from Colonel Burr's fury. Around them the Kaishiling base lay in ruins. Little piles of debris scattered haphazardly over the parade ground burned like votive candles to some chaotic godling. Fire-fighting teams, aided by Black Cobra 'Mechs, labored to douse the fires caused by the Dancing Joker's attack.

Xu looked over at Burr. "I understand your ire, Colonel, but it could have been much worse. Had your people not been away from the base trying to defend Jihuaide Chumai against the Dancing Joker, the attack here might have killed many of them."

Burr stopped and stared at Xu as if he believed the Director to be utterly mad. "You act as if you thought his strike here was serendipitous. Of course he didn't kill my people. The buildings he blew up here were a distraction so he could make a run against our warehouses for supplies. He would have gotten away with plenty of it, too, had we not already packed up everything to take with us tomorrow."

"And had your security forces not counterattacked to drive his people off."

Burr's nostrils flared. "Yes, but that left our DropShips unprotected during the firefight."

Xu raised an eyebrow. "Unprotected? Those ships bristle with weapons. They can never be unprotected."

"Those weapons are designed for counter-'Mech fire, not antipersonnel fire."

"Still, I heard your Captain Haverhill report to you that there was no sign of partisan sabotage aboard your ships."

Richard Burr scowled and stamped out a small fire. "Lack of evidence is not evidence of lack, Director."

"Does this mean you intend to delay your departure?"

"You would like that, wouldn't you?" Burr shook his head. "No, we'll finish loading our ships and leave by noon tomorrow."

Xu frowned. "You smile, Colonel. Is there something amusing about your departure that I missed?"

"I don't know, Director. I do imagine, though, that the Dancing Joker will be surprised and pleased to see how quickly his action apparently forced our departure. I daresay, even at his most audacious, he would not have imagined our fleeing within twelve hours of his attack."

You are but mercenaries, why would he imagine you would do anything but *run*? Xu nodded slightly. "Ah, yes, I imagine he will be very impressed with his potency for the few days he has left alive. However, when the woman your people captured is interrogated, she will give him up. I was led to believe she was his paramour."

"That could be. All I know for certain is that she was very dangerous." Burr smiled unashamedly. "She shot your quisling before he could kill her."

"Ah, the admiration in your voice reflects highly upon her." The Director clasped his hands at the small of his back as he began walking toward the gutted building that had once been Burr's headquarters. "Have your people turned her over to *mine* yet?"

Burr bit his lower lip and remained silent for a moment before answering. "There are regulations governing the treatment of prisoners, Director. As a mercenary I have agreed to honor certain conventions."

"Yes, yes, Colonel, I understand, but this woman is not a member of a legitimately constituted military organization. She and this Dancing Joker have murdered hundreds of people and even attacked you and your people. She and her ilk are enemies of the state and little more than very clever, very common criminals. Moreover, even if she proves to be a Davion agent, or in league with one, she would still be guilty of treason against my government."

"Fine, Director, I will have her executed for you."

Xu Ning laughed politely. "A good joke, Colonel, but a dangerous one. You skirt the edges of treason yourself. Give her to my people."

Burr nodded stiffly, obviously reluctant to acquiesce.

"Thank you." Xu looked down as one of a string of lights crunched beneath his heel. "Ah, Christmas lights. You are a Christian, then?"

"I think of myself as one."

"Then perhaps I should send for water that you may wash your hands of the woman's fate?"

Burr ignored the remark, letting his gaze travel around at the damage done. "I will not be sad to leave this place, though I will regret one thing."

Xu turned to face him. "And that is?"

"I'll regret not getting to watch the Dancing Joker finish what he has begun here."

"I do not think you will miss anything, Colonel." Xu Ning shook his head. "In fact, I will have you back here as my guest and over dinner, served on his grave, I will tell you exactly how I put an end to this Dancing Joker."

=== 51 ===

Military action without politics is like a tree without roots.
—ATTRIBUTED TO HO CHI MINH

Sian, Capellan Commonalty
Capellan Confederation
21 December 3057

The fact that he did not feel outraged or betrayed both surprised and pleased Sun-Tzu. Had his mother entered into an
alliance with Thomas Marik and then learned that Thomas
had offered Victor Davion an olive branch, she would have
exploded in fury and ordered the wholesale slaughter of anyone with connections to the Free Worlds League in the last
three generations. The streets would have run with blood,
and bodies would have dangled from every tree and street
lamp on Sian.

Fortunately, I am not my mother. Even after Thomas had
issued orders for the Black Cobras to go and secure Nanking, Sun-Tzu had known that the overt display of support
had presaged some sort of betrayal. He also knew, when he
complained to Thomas about the premature cessation of hostilities, that Thomas would respond with some aphorism
about patience and virtue. *Every pearl of wisdom known to
mankind might not have fallen from Jerome Blake's lips, but
you'd never guess it from the way his disciples quote him.*

Because he had anticipated what Thomas would do, Sun-
Tzu did not feel betrayed. Besides, he could see that the in-
vasion either had to end or else escalate to engulf the whole
Inner Sphere. As desperate as he was to re-gain the worlds
Hanse Davion had stolen from the Capellan Confederation,
Sun-Tzu did not want to see the outbreak of total war. No

matter that other Houses of the Inner Sphere stood between him and the Clans or that they were hearing rumors of the Clans fighting and fragmenting each other. The Clans were a threat to them all and would be on the march again soon enough. When that time came, Sun-Tzu did not want to see the Inner Sphere weakened from within.

Katrina Steiner had begun to offer to sell JumpShips back to her brother. If Victor accepted, it would not be long before he could start delivering troops to the Sarna March to reverse Sun-Tzu's gains. Thomas obviously saw the Sarna March as a buffer between Victor and the worlds the League had retaken. Though Sun-Tzu resented having his worlds seen as battlefields by other nations, he acknowledged that those planets also formed a buffer zone for him. Were the Marik-Liao invasions still hot by the time Victor got his transports back, he could choose to finish the job his father had started and nibble away at the Capellan Confederation itself. With a truce in place, Victor would launch operations to take back worlds that had been his, not conquer new worlds.

Sun-Tzu sat back in Justin Allard's chair and smiled. The one universal fact about the Davions—the fact his grandfather had ignored and the fact that had given his mother nightmares—was that the Davions believed in retribution. Take something from them and they would take it back. Kill something of theirs and they would kill something of yours. This meant Victor, ever the perfect miniature of his father, would try to recapture the worlds Sun-Tzu had taken back before he pursued new conquests.

Having concluded that, Sun-Tzu wondered briefly if he were making a gross error in anticipating Victor's actions based on what he knew of the man's dead father. In the time he and Victor had trained together on Outreach, he had believed the son would be more dangerous than the father just because of Victor's desire to escape Hanse Davion's shadow. Since Hanse's death, however, Victor had made a string of errors that had already cost him half his realm. It was as if Hanse had been his son's landmark, and with him dead, Victor no longer had any point of reference.

Being a Davion, steeped in Davion lore, he reverted to type. Victor's apparent lack of feeling about his mother's death was just the sort of emotionless display Hanse would have made. Using a double to replace Joshua Marik was also the kind of trick that would have suited Hanse Davion. Victor had stumbled about until he found himself marching in his father's footsteps, and chances were he did not even realize he was doing it.

It was exactly the thing Sun-Tzu had to avoid. He must at all costs not fall into the extremes that had plagued the ruling Liaos throughout this century. He also knew that complacency would destroy him. He could assume Victor would tend to behave like his father before him, but he had to test that assumption. He had to test all of his assumptions. For him to operate on *belief* instead of *knowledge* was to leave himself open for attack. *And there are plenty of places from which it might come. Tormano, Candace, Kai—even my sister Kali might strike against me. And I mustn't forget that Isis Marik might be used against me too. If we wed, and then I am slain, Thomas could claim the Capellan Confederation and absorb it into the Free Worlds League. That would be better than having Kali on the throne, but I could never abide the thought of my nation being ruled by someone outside the House of Liao.*

"The other thing I must do is to continue to make the others underestimate me." Sun-Tzu smiled broadly and steepled his fingers. "When Thomas tells me he has concluded a peace with Victor Davion, I shall thank him. I shall even ask him if he wants his daughter back with him on Atreus. That should start him wondering about me and my plans. Meanwhile I go about consolidating the worlds I have taken and prepare for the next opportunity to return to my realm that which is rightfully mine."

=== 52 ===

> Wild animals never kill for sport. Man is the only one to whom
> the torture and death of his fellow-creatures is amusing in itself.
> —JAMES ANTHONY FROUDE, OCEANA

Daosha, Zurich
Zurich People's Republic, Capellan Confederation
21 December 3057

Despite her right eye being almost swollen shut and the blinding light glaring down from above, Cathy Hanney recognized Xu Ning when he stepped into the cold chamber. Knowledge of his identity came not from the way her tormentors snapped to attention at his arrival, but in the suave and simple way he translated his initial shock into a casual shrug. Had she any saliva left in her mouth she would have spat at him.

"Miss Hanney," he began in oily tones, "you must realize that your resistance is quite futile. We know you are exhausted and in pain from the beating the Black Cobras gave you. These first four hours, of course, have been filled merely with questioning because we would rather not take more drastic measures with you."

Cathy remained silent as her thoughts raced. *Four hours? Try eight—I've watched the clock grind through transplant operations, when every second counted, and I know how long I've been here. How long I've held out. He's coming. Soon. I can wait.*

Xu Ning's hand felt cold as his fingertips traced the bruise on the right side of her face. "You have shown bravery and intelligence in your time with the Dancing Joker. Let me tell you what will happen from this point forward. Because you have given us nothing, we must find a way to stimulate your cooperation. We have two choices: physical torture or narcointerrogation. The latter is, of course, the more effective, but in this case time is a key factor. If we use drugs to pry information from you, we must let you recover from those drugs before employing pain to verify your answers. Using pain first, we achieve the answers we want even more swiftly than might be imagined because the oblivion of drugs can be dangled before you as a reward for giving us your answers."

She remained silent. *I will say nothing. He is coming for me. He will be here. He will rescue me and destroy all of you.*

Xu Ning folded his arms and stepped back until he was a silhouette framed by the open door. "Your resistance is predicated on the mistaken belief that the Dancing Joker is coming to rescue you. That is a false premise. You are currently in a location well removed from Daosha and you were not followed here. This area is well protected so that even were he to come here, he would die."

He is coming. I know it. He will rescue me.

"Of course, you have failed to grasp the full import of your situation. You might not have been captured except that the Dancing Joker set you up. He assigned you to work with a traitor—a traitor he suspected but about whom he told you nothing. Had he not been suspicious of Fabian Wilson, he would not have switched targets and the Black Cobras would have captured him."

He is coming.

"You were abandoned." Xu Ning gave a brief laugh. "In many ways I admire him for sacrificing you so. It guaranteed that we would not guess his change of plans. Your Dancing Joker is almost cold-blooded enough to succeed with his counterrevolution."

"He is coming."

"Ah, she speaks. Good." Xu Ning presented Cathy his profile as he looked over toward her chief torturer. "Let us not be too brutal with her. Electrical stimulation should be effective, I would think. Farewell, Miss Hanney, and should be unable to speak with you later, thank you for your assistance."

"He's coming. He will come for you."

"I'm sure he will, my dear young woman, but by then you will have told us all you know about him." Xu Ning's laugh stabbed deep into her heart. "And with that information, I will destroy him."

53

> There is only one tactical principle which is not subject to change. It is: to use the means at hand to inflict the maximum amount of wounds, death and destruction on the enemy in the minimum of time.
>
> —GEORGE S. PATTON, JR., WAR AS I KNEW IT

Bay of Broken Hope, Australarctica
Morges, Lyran Alliance
25 December 3057

Phelan looked out across the pristine snowfield and saw in the distance the snow-covered colony of DropShips that had brought the Jade Falcons to Morges. Though snow and ice capped them, the emerald-green hue of their hulls marked them as being as alien to Australarctica as the Clans were to the Inner Sphere. The presence of snow on the ships meant that they were not ready to travel and that confirmed Phelan's fears about Angeline Mattlov and the Jade Falcon host.

They're not going to run.

It was ridiculous for them to stay. Their assault on Carson Rift had hurt the Wolves, but it had been costly for the Falcons as well. It stalled when supplies failed to get to the Falcon field units. The Peregrine Eyrie Cluster had fought rear-guard action as the others pulled back to Broken Hope. At the same time the Ninety-fourth Striker Cluster and Seventeenth Falcon Regulars had retreated from Archange. During the retreat the Kell Hounds Second Regiment had poured down out of Icegrief Pass and mauled the Seventeenth Regulars.

Of the five line clusters Mattlov had brought to Morges she had enough 'Mechs to bring just three of them up to full strength. Yet even that was illusory because her supplies were running low, which meant most of her 'Mechs and a

nost all of her aerospace fighters were operating without
oads for more than half their weapons. The Peregrine
olahma unit had fallen so quickly and easily because its
:lose-in weapons—SRM launchers and heavy autocan-
10ns—were without ammunition.

While the four garrison units that had held Broken Hope
vere untouched in battle, Phelan assumed they were suffer-
ng similar ammunition shortages. He also guessed that their
BattleMechs had been used to rebuild other 'Mechs that had
aken partial damage at Carson Rift and Archangel. Though
he garrison troops were respected within their Clan, they
vere subordinate in status to the line units and the fate of
heir equipment was out of their hands.

A light started to flash on his command console commu-
1ication panel. He punched it and was surprised to see
Angeline Mattlov's face appear on his primary monitor.
Star Colonel Mattlov. To what do I owe this communica-
ion?"

The woman looked highly indignant. "I knew you held
1e Clans in contempt, Khan Phelan, but I never expected
ou to totally flout our ways. You attack without first inquir-
1g what forces I shall use to defend my position."

"I have done no such thing, Star Colonel. The condition
f your DropShips tells me that you are not going to evac-
ate even part of your force, therefore I assume you are de-
ending with all of it. Do you forget that you were the
ggressor here? A string of misfortunes does not turn you
1to the defender. I am under no obligation to tell you any-
1ing about my force, and you have done nothing to make
1e inclined to be generous to you. If you wish to leave,
owever, I could be persuaded to withhold the coming as-
ault."

The old woman recoiled as if she had been slapped. "If
ou mean to suggest we would run . . .".

"Hardly, Star Colonel. You have better than a half-dozen
lusters here. Go back to the Clans. Yours is probably the
nly Falcon Galaxy with any command integrity left. If you
ve the Clans half as much as you believe I hate them, you
ill realize your duty is to leave here."

"My duty is to destroy you."

"Then your fate is to die here." Phelan narrowed his green
ves. "Let your people know: survivors will be permitted to

live, but they will never become bondsmen to our Clan. I
they want to live as warriors they will live as mercenaries."

Phelan hit the communications button and cut off her re
ply. "Wolf One to Wings Leader."

"Wings leader here."

"Carew, two runs. Have the Hounds keep them off you."

"Roger. Wings Leader out."

Phelan took one last look at the snow-shrouded building
that had once been mankind's only meager foothold on th
ice continent. "You may want to die here, Angeline, but
have no desire to join you."

Orbiting above the battlefield, Caitlin Kell watched as th
flight of Wolf Clan fighters looped out over the ocean to th
west of Broken Hope. The aerospace fighters turned an
headed due east, intending to strafe Falcon positions in
line parallel to the Wolf and Hound BattleMech front. A
they prepared to do that, the Falcon DropShips launche
flight after flight of aerospace fighters into the sky.

"Raven flight, we're on the lead element," she heard Cap
tain d'Or announce. "Go to it."

With her wingman Spider Hearst following, Caitlin kicke
her *Stingray* toward the first Falcon flight. She knew th
Jade Falcons were aware of the mercenaries' presence, bu
they had made no attempt to drive them off. Refusing t
fight anyone except other Clansmen seemed somewhat suic
dal to her, but she was not a Jade Falcon. If their stupidit
was going to make her job easier, so much the better.

She centered her crosshairs on a Clan *Visigoth*. When sh
got a target lock she triggered the PPC in the *Stingray*'s nos
and the large lasers in either wing. The PPC's blue lanc
skewered the *Visigoth*'s slender fuselage, coring armor an
destroying a heat sink. The lasers' green scalpels carved a
mor from the right wing and engine cowling.

Caitlin broke right and saw the flashes of Hearst's weap
ons as he attacked the same *Visigoth*. More armor peele
away from the right wing, fuselage, and engine area on th
fighter. Caitlin's computer reported a spike in heat emission
from the fighter, so she assumed Hearst had gotten anoth
heat sink as well.

As the *Visigoth* bounced to the left and started to div
away from them, Caitlin hauled her stick back and to th
right, inverting her *Stingray* and diving straight after hi

The *Visigoth* might have a bigger power plant and more thrust, but the *Stingray* was far more maneuverable. While the *Visigoth*'s move would have shucked off the pursuit of most other fighters, Caitlin hung with it and targeted the wounded craft again as it began to level out.

Her PPC and one of the large lasers raked away all but a thin coating of armor from the 'Mech's fuselage, splashing another heat sink and destroying a thrust vector louver. The other laser nipped the tip off the right wing, which combined with the louver problem to start the *Visigoth* shaking in flight.

One more pass and I'll have it.

"Caitlin, break left!"

Without thinking she slammed her stick to the left, kicking the *Stingray* into a tight barrel roll. As the horizon spun and then leveled out again, she saw a storm of green laser bolts shoot past her right wing tip. A second later another Clan *Visigoth* dove through that space and Hearst flashed past on its tail.

Hitting the rudder pedals, Caitlin slewed her ship to the right and dove after Hearst. *He covered me. Now it's my turn to cover him.*

Ground-bound, Phelan could only watch as the aerospace fighters above him wheeled, dove, and turned. He knew his sister was up there and, though the *Stingray*'s swept-forward wings made for a distinctive silhouette, the aerial action moved too quickly for him to pick her out. *Good hunting, Cait. Don't let them even scratch your paint.*

As the Kell Hound fighters scattered the two dozen fighters the Jade Falcons had launched, the Wolves' air forces came sweeping in and down on Broken Hope. The Falcon DropShips lit the sky with red, green, and blue beams as they fired their energy weapons, but the Wolf fighters threaded their way through them, then poured fire down on the small settlement. Wave after wave of fighters strafed the ground, reducing Falcon 'Mechs to fire-blackened skeletons and sowing Broken Hope with uncounted explosions.

"That must be the hottest time that town's ever seen," commented someone over the radio network.

Before Phelan could snap an order for silence, he heard his father's voice. "Be quiet! What's happening to the Jade Falcons is neither funny nor wonderful. It's a tragic necessity to prevent more of our own from dying. Before you feel so inclined to gloat, you'd do well to remember our own friends and comrades we've lost here."

Phelan keyed his radio. "Thank you, Colonel. Heads up, everyone. Wolves are coming in for their second pass. Once they're through, we go in."

Spider finally sent his *Visigoth* down in flames. The Clan fighter exploded when it hit the ice over the bay and left burning pieces scattered all over the ice pack. Spider turned off to the right and stayed low to the deck while Caitlin opened her turn, pulled back on her stick, and kicked the overthrusters in. Like a rocket she shot up and rose beneath a Falcon *Sulla* lining up to make a pass on the Wolves as they began their second strafing run.

Caitlin fired as she pulled up and through the *Sulla*'s six. One of the large lasers drilled green fire into the engine cowling while the PPC and other large laser burned tons of ferro-aluminum armor from the slender fighter's left wing. None of the attacks damaged more than armor, but Caitlin's auxiliary monitor showed a fifty-eight percent reduction in the left wing's protection. *Another shot or two there and that wing comes off.*

The Clan pilot immediately stood his fighter on its left wing and began to break to the left. Anticipating his next move, Caitlin inverted her *Stingray*. When the *Sulla* went over into a barrel roll and pulled out, heading west, Caitlin started a dive, then pulled a hard turn to the right and bounced right up behind him again.

Her PPC sliced into the left wing again, reducing all but the last bit of armor to vapor. The large lasers bored into the engine and fuselage. An explosion and the appearance of a yellow vapor cloud told Caitlin she'd gotten one of the ship's heat sinks. That was useful, but she didn't expect the dogfight to continue long enough for heat to become an issue.

Then the Clan pilot dove.

Caitlin followed him down to the deck and through a turn back north again. As he leveled out, she began to smile. *Broken Hope won't offer you cover.* Then she looked off her starboard wing and saw the flights of Wolves coming in on their second strafing runs. *Oh, hell!* To make matters worse, the *Sulla* bore in at two of the Falcon DropShips, making her a target for their fire as well.

Committed to her flight path, she dropped her crosshairs onto the *Sulla* and triggered *all* of her *Stingray*'s weapons. *I'll run hot, but that's the least of my problems right now.*

The PPC sent a shaft of artificial lighting into the *Sulla*'s right wing, stripping armor off in sheets. One of the two medium lasers missed, but the other combined with the two large lasers to rake through armor on the fighter's fuselage. Two more heat sinks burst in yellow clouds. Another explosion on the left side of the craft jetted debris into the air, but Caitlin wasn't able to mark the source of that damage immediately.

She juked her *Stingray* up and a bit to the starboard. While that did take her closer to the incoming Wolf fighters, it moved her away from the DropShips. She also knew the *Sulla* had to move right to get through the gap between the DropShips. Through her course would take her wide of him, she would be able to pounce on the other side of the DropShip wall.

What the hell is he doing?

The *Sulla* shuddered when it should have drifted right. The tail fin cut around hard to the right in a move to swing the plane around and drive it to the right, but all that managed to do was to make the fighter begin bucking. The left wing came up, letting Caitlin see that the thrust-vectoring outlets on the left side of the *Sulla* had been fused shut, which explained the difficulty in maneuvering to the right. Unfortunately, as the left wing came up, it caught too much air and started to invert the fighter. At the same time the momentum imparted by the desperate tail flap adjustment pushed the fighter around so it was traveling belly-first along its line of flight.

The needle-bodied *Sulla* slammed into one of the *Overlord* Class DropShips, shearing the fighter's nose and cockpit off. That half of the plane pierced the DropShip's hull and ricocheted around inside the bridge level. The aft half of the fighter spun wildly through the air, rising briefly, then hammered into the ground and exploded. Pieces of it spread all over Broken Hope, mixing with all the other debris.

Caitlin threw her stick hard to the right and stood her *Stingray* on the tip of its right wing. Hauling back on the stick, she pulled her fighter around until she was running directly at the waves of Wolf fighters coming in. Easing the stick forward again, she stayed up on her right wing, presenting as narrow a target as possible for the Wolves, and shot out beneath their flight path. Once she cleared their line, she righted her ship and began a long turn out over the bay.

Gaining altitude she looked back at the settlement, but she could see little more than fires amid the clouds of black smoke. "Spider, where are you?"

"Angels Eleven, Cait. We're clear."

Clear, yes, thank God. She took another look at Broken Hope, then started to climb. *Down there it's hell itself.*

To describe what the Wolf BattleMechs found opposing them as resistance was to exalt the Jade Falcon response to their advance. The strafing runs had been devastating. Laser and PPC fire reached out from the defensive lines to attack the Wolves, but it was sporadic at best and always answered with overwhelming return fire. As the Wolves and Hounds closed in on the sooty settlement, Phelan gave the order for his troops to use suppressive fire. A nearly constant steam of red, green, and blue beams crackled through the crisp air, pinning 'Mechs behind defensive embankments.

As Phelan moved into the Jade Falcon position, a cold chill ran down his spine. The aerospace fighters' lasers and PPCs had vaporized armor and snow into a black fog that condensed almost immediately. It coated BattleMechs with an onyx flesh that fouled sensors and blinded pilots. Twisted black rivulets had been frozen as they ran from the legs of 'Mechs—looking like necrotic ivy rooting slain 'Mechs in place.

Every Falcon 'Mech he could see had gaping rents in its armor. Many had lost limbs and weapon systems. Some 'Mechs stood covered in black ice with their canopies open. One Falcon 'Mech had squatted down and used the flamers built into it to keep a small building burning. A knot of dejected Falcon pilots stood huddled between the 'Mech's legs for warmth and protection.

Phelan stopped his *Wolfhound* and keyed his external speakers. "Where is Colonel Mattlov?"

Most of the pilots shook their heads, but one or two pointed off deeper into Broken Hope.

Phelan pushed on, with the rest of his Cluster moving forward and around him to forestall any of the Jade Falcons attempting to win the battle by taking him down. Phelan knew, as did the attackers and all the defenders, that the battle was long since over, but he also knew that if he left himself open, the Falcons would try to kill him. They were Clansmen after all, and that was the way of the Clans.

On Tukayyid and other worlds Phelan had seen greater destruction of a 'Mech force, but no other place had seemed so desolate and cruel. As the wind rose, it drove the smoke away. Granules of black ice washed over the landscape, building dark little snowdrifts that covered the bodies of fallen 'Mechs. He realized that new snow would soon cover over all evidence of the battle, preserving it, broken and lifeless, in this sterile and barren place.

Back toward the edge of the bay he found Colonel Mattlov. Her *Daishi* trailed its right leg behind it, the limb attached only by the myomer fibers dangling from the hip. The metallic femur had been melted away by fire from the fighters on their strafing runs. The rest of the 'Mech's armor was in little better condition. Angeline's hunched 'Mech looked like a wounded animal that had been gnawed on by a herd of scavengers.

Up in the cockpit of his 'Mech, Phelan looked down at Angeline Mattlov in her 'Mech. He could see from the snow and ice how she had dragged herself two hundred meters in the direction of the DropShips. He opened a radio frequency to her. "It is over, Colonel."

"Never, *freebirth*." Mattlov's 'Mech levered itself up on its right elbow and thrust its left arm at him.

Phelan drifted his 'Mech to the left, letting the pair of PPCs and pulse lasers shoot through the space where he had been standing. Dropping his crosshairs onto the *Daishi*'s left shoulder, he fired all his weapons. His large laser melted the thick myomer muscles that had once given the stricken 'Mech's left arm movement. The trio of pulse lasers mounted in the *Wolfhound*'s chest stabbed a cloud of ruby laser needles into the joint itself, changing the ferrotitanium bones from a dull silver to a brilliant white before they evaporated. The arm dropped away, bouncing off the 'Mech's left thigh before landing in the snow.

"Next I'll take your leg, then your other arm."

"If you had any honor, you would engage me in single combat."

"We have been engaged in single combat, Angeline. You and your forces were pitted against me and mine." Phelan's *Wolfhound* opened its arms to take in the mix of Wolves and Hounds surrounding them. "You were out-matched, out-maneuvered, outwitted, and out-fought. The only thing single combat would accomplish would be your death, and I do not feel inclined to grant you such release."

"Then you are a coward." Anger heated her words. "You have betrayed everything for which the Clans stand, but who could expect more from an Inner Sphere *freebirth*? The Clans exist to create the best warriors and you weaken us. You are every bit the traitor Stefan Amaris was."

Phelan felt the muscles in his jaw clench. "I have not betrayed the Clans, Angeline, but the Crusaders have. You say the Clans exist to produce the best warriors, but is that not merely as a means to an end? In founding the Clans, Nicholas Kerensky set us on this path as the *means* by which we, the Clans, would one day be strong enough to protect the Inner Sphere. Our ancestors left the Inner Sphere to escape the power struggles that tore the Star League apart, and Nicholas charged us with the duty of defending the Inner Sphere against threats from without.

"The Crusaders are that threat, Angeline. The Crusaders have decided that the Inner Sphere has debased itself so it is no longer worthy of our protection. The Crusaders would come in and deprive the people of the Inner Sphere of their freedoms—the very things we were charged to protect and preserve."

"You are a fool, Phelan, and think me a greater fool if you think I believe you understand what it is to be a member of the Clans. We are who we are. We are warriors. We were bred for war, and three centuries of such breeding has created a people who are not only worthy of reestablishing the Star League, but capable of doing it."

"Yet I, someone born in the Inner Sphere, was able to rise to the pinnacle of the strongest Clan there was."

"Only because Ulric shielded you."

Phelan couldn't help but laugh at that. "There you are, Angeline. More evidence that damns you. Even in defeat you cannot accept the fact that I have done more, better and faster, than you or any other product of the Clan breeding program."

"You are a Wolf and a Warden. That hardly makes you of the Clans."

"It could be as you say, Angeline, but if it is true, then it is the Clans' loss." Phelan slowly shook his head. "You believe the purpose of war is to raise the level of combat to new heights. Only those who win, who excel, who distinguish themselves are allowed to breed. You would make it some martial form of Darwinism, part of humanity's evolution.

"But war is not something beneficial. There is one reason for war, and one reason only. It is why we fought here. It is why Natasha and Ulric and all the others fought against you Jade Falcons in your occupation zone. It is the reason the Inner Sphere has fought against the Clans. That reason is freedom.

"Oddly enough, that is the reason you opposed us. You saw Ulric as an obstacle that denied you Crusaders the freedom to breed and grow stronger, but what you failed to see is that the Clan way denied you that freedom. Without war you could still breed and get better, but only through war, by fighting you, could the people of the Inner Sphere defend their freedom to determine their lives. Nicholas Kerensky created the Clans to prevent someone or something from taking such freedoms away from the Inner Sphere."

"You, *freebirth,* cannot know what was in Nicholas Kerensky's mind."

"No? Why not? Nicholas Kerensky was a freebirth, *quiaff?*"

Angeline's hiss of outrage crackled through the speakers in Phelan's neurohelmet. "How dare you dishonor him with that word!"

"The truth dishonors no one, Angeline, except those who will not acknowledge it." Phelan pointed his *Wolfhound*'s right arm at a DropShip. "Round your people up and leave. Go back to your masters, go back to the Clans and let them know that I live. Let them know that I have with me the genetic material of the Wolves. Tell them we have found haven here in the Lyran Alliance. We are committed to remaining true to Nicholas Kerensky's dream of a free Inner Sphere. Be it next month, next year, or a decade from now, whenever the Clans decide to renew their Crusade, the Wolves they believe they have destroyed will oppose them. And if they wish to ponder the outcome of new battles, remind them of Morges and let them consider their actions with the utmost of care."

54

The reluctant obedience of distant provinces generally costs more than it is worth.

—THOMAS BABINGTON MACAULAY

Avalon City, New Avalon
Crucis March, Federated Commonwealth
25 December 3057

Sweat stinging his eyes, Victor awoke with a start. He looked down at his clawed hands and was surprised to see they were not bleeding. Without comprehending the true import of that fact, he tore back his bedclothes and bounded across his bed chamber to stand naked before the full-length mirror in the corner. His fingers prodding and twisting his face, he stared at his reflection as reality displaced dreams in his mind.

It's my face in the mirror, not my father's. It is mine, truly mine. He shivered, mostly from relief, but also from the chill air shrouding his sweat-soaked body. Raking wet hair back from his face and staring frantically in the mirror to see whether it was white-blond, not the ruddy hue of his father's, he took a deep breath. *That was a most evil dream.*

Victor stumbled back toward his bed and moved to the center where the sheets were dry. The fact that they were also cold did not comfort him, but he clung to the sensation of cold and used it to banish the last of the uneasiness in the dream he had left in him. He closed his eyes for a moment but knew he would not fall back to sleep, so he jammed pillows between him and the headboard and sat up.

The dream—*definitely a nightmare*—had been born of the clash between Thomas' offer of peace and what Victor thought he should do in response.

His father would have rejected the offer outright. By making the peace bid, Thomas had shown he had no belly for the fight. Worse yet, the only reason Thomas had reaped his successes was because he had used Katherine against Victor. Without the ships that Katherine was now willing to *sell* him—Hanse would have had Tormano's head on a stick for *that!*—Victor's ability to oppose the Free Worlds League had been severely curtailed.

That would not have concerned Hanse Davion. He would have stripped every transport in the Federated Commonwealth and turned it into a troop carrier. He would have delivered ample amounts of troops to blast Thomas' mercenaries into memories and reduce Sun-Tzu's troops to twitching protoplasm. Hadn't both Thomas and Sun-Tzu shown, in the nature and strength of their attacks, that they had learned how to wage war by studying the methods of Hanse Davion? Hanse would have taught them the true horrors of war and would have made them pay dearly for their little game.

That was, Victor knew, exactly what his father would have done. The Prince had even gone so far as to dig into his father's old files to see how he had organized the transport for the Fourth Succession War. Though twenty-five years had passed since the end of that conflict, the strategies were still sound and the resources were available. Replicating the massive invasion of Sarna that his father had executed would have imposed hardship on the people of the Federated Commonwealth, but such sacrifice was the only thing that would keep the realm intact.

Though Victor was prepared to do that, every time he approached that decision, something made him draw back. In the dream he had seen Thomas offering him an olive branch, but Victor had slapped the branch from Thomas' hand. Then the Captain-General's eyes had become mirrors in which Victor saw his father's image reflected as his own. When he landed a punch square on Thomas' nose, the mask Thomas had worn shattered to reveal Hanse's face. then Hanse became a crystal statue that fragmented beneath Victor's repeated pummeling, each fragment holding within it a holographic image of the statue of Hanse. And yet the legend on the pedestal bore the name "Victor."

"I am *not* my father." Victor slammed his fist into the

palm of his left hand. "I have never tried to be my father. I have never *wanted* to be my father!"

But using his methods has brought you to this point. Would you abandon his ways now? asked a small voice in the back of his mind.

Victor shuddered. *Have I really been aping what my father would have done?*

The voice did not answer, but Victor did not give it much chance to do so. His mind began racing, analyzing his actions, assessing their effectiveness, searching out their roots. *I have to know what I have done wrong and why I did it.*

The first event that brought him up short was the decision to institute a double for Joshua. He had never liked it as a solution. He had agreed to use life support devices to keep Joshua alive while the double was being inserted in his place because, until Joshua actually died, he could reverse his decision. He knew he had made the choice, ultimately, to buy himself time. Time to deal with Katherine, time to deal with Sun-Tzu, and time to break the news to Thomas.

His own natural inclination would have been to inform Thomas of his son's death, but the very existence of Project Gemini had somehow suggested to him that being forthright with Thomas was politically naive. Faced with challenges from within his family and without, he could not allow himself to show the slightest weakness.

Gemini had been his father's plan. It had been put into place to guarantee Thomas' cooperation while the Clans were storming through the Inner Sphere. With the truce won by ComStar, Gemini lost its value, but Hanse Davion died before he could shut it down.

And I let it continue because, with it, I still had a piece of my father alive.

Victor instantly knew that idea was wrong—as wrong as putting the double in Joshua's place. He was only doing what his father would have done and therein he spied his problem. *If I am not my father, why am I doing what he would have done?*

Even as he asked the question, he came up with a legion of answers. The conflicts with Katherine and his brother Peter had led him to assert control over the family, and his father was the only model for that control he knew. Moreover, the respect he had for his father and the reverence in which Hanse was held by the people of the Federated Commmon wealth had pushed him into paths where he could tap that image and emotion. Victor realized, though, that what his father could get away with as "shrewd" and "befitting the Fox" looked overreaching or petty and cruel in him.

This series of revelations led him back to Thomas' olive branch. His father would have rejected it and retaken the worlds he had lost—of this Victor had no doubt. It was true that Hanse had made peace with the Draconis Combine in the face of the Clan threat, but that was placing the greater gain over the lesser danger. The Draconis Combine had not been the aggressor in the War of 3039, and had put up a stiff defense against the Federated Commonwealth. Theodore Kurita had earned Hanse's respect, a fact that went a long way toward making a truce between their realms palatable for Hanse.

In the face of naked aggression, Hanse would have fought back—but Victor could see no benefit to fighting back against the Free Worlds League or the Capellan Confederation. The war, so far, had been relatively bloodless. And while war might be a crucible in which great individuals proved themselves—most notably the Woodstock Reservists and whoever this Dancing Joker was—it was also an insatiable maw that devoured people and material with incredible speed and facility.

It was true that the worlds taken would no longer be sending tax revenue to him, but those sums were insignificant compared to the economic benefits for the Federated Commonwealth offered by Thomas' peace bid. And even though Sarna and Styk had formed their own little independent nations, akin to the St. Ives Compact, their financial and economic ties to the Federated Commonwealth meant Victor had not lost any of his 'Mech manufacturing in the Sarna March.

Provided—he reminded himself—*the Reservists finish off the Bandits.*

Most of the various populations would be unaffected by the changes of planetary administration. Yes, they would have to learn the words to a new national anthem, but the Sarna March had been part of the Federated Commonwealth for less than a generation. The greatest hardship for most citizens would be adjusting their schedules to accommodate the changes in national holidays.

Not so for the Reservists and the Dancing Joker, people

who had actively fought against the incorporation of the Sarna March into the Capellan Confederation. If the Reservists were successful, Nanking would remain in the Commonwealth. If not, they would have to be repatriated. Repatriation would be vital for the Dancing Joker and his people and all of the minor functionaries and administrators who owed their allegiance to the Federated Commonwealth as well. They would be the target of reprisals, and Victor would never leave them open to such danger.

"Thomas will agree to repatriating my people if I suggest that the program be administrated by ComStar. That will keep it neutral."

With that problem solved, Victor knew he would make the choice his father would have found unthinkable. "These times are not your times, Father. I cannot strip my economy to move troops to fight over worthless worlds. In your day, the unification of the Inner Sphere was a noble goal worth fighting for. But we can no longer afford it. Such wars would ruin our economies and let the Clans devour us whole when they come for us. We have ten years before the ComStar truce expires—*if* that much time—and I would rather have my people preparing for war than engaged in it."

From deep inside Victor's memory the picture of his father as he lay dying came to him. Again he saw the momentary bright flash of life in his father's piercing blue eyes. Those eyes had focused on his son, then Hanse had clutched at Victor's shoulder, spoken his name, and smiled.

"You seemed to die content, Father, knowing I was there to take your place. Was that because you thought I was like you or because you trusted me to do what I must to keep your realm intact? I hope like hell it was the latter, because I am not you, nor will I ever be. In trying to act as you would have, I have almost ruined everything.

"Never again." Victor shook his head and focused on the mirror across the room. "I am Victor Ian Steiner-Davion First Prince of the Federated Commonwealth. From now on the mistakes I make will be my own, and the experience gain from correcting them will be my guide into the future."

55

He who bears the brand of Cain shall rule the earth.
—GEORGE BERNARD SHAW, *BACK TO METHUSELAH*

Daosha, Zurich
Zurich People's Republic, Capellan Confederation
27 December 3057

Xu Ning hit the Page Down button on the detached screen of his computer, but a beep told him he was at the end of the file. Glancing at the time display in the corner of the flat screen, he saw that he'd been reading until well after midnight. That struck him as ironic and even funny because in his days as an academic he would never have touched an escapist thriller like the Dancing Joker's attempt at a novel. If for no other reason, he would have avoided it because it was apparently meant to be the second in a series! Now something he would have considered beneath him had kept him up far later than he might have imagined.

It was not that the writing was great fiction, or even much more than literate. The prose was riddled with clichés, but the story was paced well. Only the central character, Charlie Moore, was given any sort of depth, however. Xu knew this was because the novel was obviously autobiographical, and Charlie Moore was Noble Thayer's alter ego.

The desire to know the mind of Charlie Moore—and therefore know the mind of Noble Thayer—had pushed him on through the book. Cathy Hanney's interrogation had provided enough information that they'd been able to raid the Dancing Joker's last habitation, but all they found were some personal items, including a small SecCom noteputer and the disks Thayer had used to write his books. Though the SecCom staff had worked hard to put together a profile of Thayer, it was nowhere near as illuminating as the novel.

Even the title, *The Hunter's Charade*, told Xu more about Noble Thayer than the file his people had compiled. The string of acts attributed to the Dancing Joker made it quite apparent that Thayer was no chemistry teacher. His leadership skills and ability to cover his tracks proved that he must have been trained as a Davion agent—just as had Charlie Moore. Like Thayer, Moore had come to Zurich to infiltrate an enemy revolutionary organization. Once the revolution took place, Moore began organizing a resistance movement to fight the government of evil Chao Shaw—a phonetic mixture of Italian and Farsi that translated to "goodbye king."

The Director had not found his characterization in the novel flattering, but the points Thayer had chosen to criticize gave him insight into the man's thought processes. Thayer had portrayed Shaw as a vain egotist whose grip on reality had been loosened by a decade spent hiding in remote guerrilla camps. He used Shaw's indulgence in a variety of strange sexual practices as an allegory for the inherent contradiction of a man who chooses to make himself superior so he can create a classless society, and in that allegory Xu Ning felt the most sting.

In the novel Thayer had fictionalized Deirdre Lear and kept her on Zurich as Dr. Dolores Larson. She served as Moore's love interest and was captured by Shaw and the evil mercenary band, the White Vipers, in the penultimate confrontation of the novel. The book ended with Moore, as the King of Death, planning an all-out assault meant to bring him face to face with Shaw to free the woman he loved from the dictator's clutches.

Xu tapped the screen to clear it, then set the LCD table on the table along with his computer. "I wonder how you would have ended it? Would you have had Shaw kill Larson as I have killed Miss Hanney? Would you have had Shaw's compound turned into a fortress to await your attack? And would your planning of the strike change if, in contrast to your novel, your paramour broke under interrogation and gave up all your secrets?"

Those questions filled Xu Ning's mind and he knew he would not get to sleep easily. He touched a button on the intercom beside his computer. "Tsin, please bring me a glass of warm milk with an ounce of Napoleon brandy in it."

"At once, Director."

As he disrobed in preparation for retiring, Xu Ning considered himself rather lucky after a moment's reflection. Thayer's novel had gone into great detail about how the bombing of the armory had been accomplished and how the raid on Kaishiling had been organized. Had Thayer turned his skills to assassinating him, Xu had little doubt the man would have succeeded. Of course, the revolution would have stood because another would have taken his place. Instead, by attacking the support structures of the revolutionary society, Thayer had come perilously close to toppling his government.

Xu Ning drew on his silk robe and knotted the purple sash at his waist. The Dancing Joker had not taken into account the capture and surrender of Cathy Hanney. The information she had given up had cut the Dancing Joker off from his base of operations and forced him to run and hide. That was an overwhelming setback and quite likely the thing that had saved Xu's revolution from destruction.

A nagging bit of doubt robbed Xu of taking any satisfaction from that conclusion. Xu Ning concentrated and instantly identified the paradox that was causing him a problem. He had decided the Dancing Joker had not anticipated Cathy Hanney's capture, yet the in the novel the protagonist had made plans to deal with the capture of his lover. In the real life, however, Cathy Hanney's capture had sent the Dancing Joker into hiding, so he could not have had a chance to write about how he would deal with such a situation. Moreover, only by knowingly sacrificing Cathy Hanney could he have engineered the raid on Kaishiling. Of course, in the novel, Dr. Larson had been captured *during* the raid, so it was possible Thayer had adjusted his plans to avoid the problem he had put into his novel.

Then again, in the novel and in real life, a traitor in service to Shaw had been the catalyst behind the Larson/Hanney abduction. The arguments went around and around, with life imitating art and vice versa. Xu frowned, then turned to his desk to dig around in a drawer for analgesic tablets. *Only if the Dancing Joker purposely turned his lover over to me does any of this make sense. Even so, that act does not make sense.*

Xu heard a gentle knock at his door. "Enter." Thinking only of the steaming glass of milk on the silver tray, Xu momentarily missed the fact that the slump-shouldered man bearing the tray was Caucasian, not Asian like his houseboy. Before he could demand to know who the interloper was, he saw the silenced pistol in the man's other hand.

"Noble Thayer, I presume?"

"Call me what you will. I am the Dancing Joker." The man straightened up to his full height and set the tray on a table near the door. The gun did not stray in the least as the man closed the door behind him. "Did she tell you my name, or have you deduced it from the book?"

Xu felt ice water trickle through his intestines. "She gave us your name and your location, though she did hold out for a long time. Having read the book and the file we have compiled on you, I know your real name is probably not Noble Thayer."

The dark-eyed man shook his head. "Think whatever you want."

"Ah, then I shall assume details in the book are correct. Shall I call you Charlie?"

"Whatever is your pleasure. Is Cathy dead?"

"Has been for two days. She was strong, but not *that* strong." Xu Ning tried to speak casually and wondered what his chances were of getting to the alarm button at the far corner of his desk. "She killed Fabian Wilson, if that is any consolation."

"Saves me having to find him."

"A pity he isn't alive. It would be interesting to see who would have won the race—you looking for him or us looking for you, the Foxes, the Bradfords, and Miss Thompson."

The Dancing Joker smiled slowly. "I'd have won."

"Of course you would." Xu Ning turned to the right, gaining a half step toward the button, and pointed to the computer. "In your line of work you've got to have a healthy ego, don't you, Charlie? I saw it in the novel—there the King of Death even destroyed the White Vipers. Pity life doesn't imitate art."

"Oh, but it does. One of the things I'd planned for a late chapter was the Security Committee introducing a virus into its computers by hastily duplicating and analyzing a disc containing the King of Death's personal journal." He gestured at the computer with his pistol. "I guess you've done that for me, haven't you?"

Xu steadied himself on the edge of his desk as a drople

of salty sweat rolled from his upper lip and into his mouth. "Very clever. I should have suspected." His right hand snaked along the edge and depressed the button built into the mahogany desk. "That will be most inconvenient."

"So will the fact that, as I intended to write in the book, I killed all your security guards, so hitting that button does absolutely nothing."

Xu Ning's knees began to quiver. "You meant for it all to come to this, didn't you? But you betrayed a woman who screamed out for you while we tortured her. She died believing you were coming for her, but you never were." He looked over at the man with the gun. "How could you throw the woman you loved to us?"

"Noble loved her, I didn't." The Dancing Joker shrugged. "By concentrating on her and what she knew, you couldn't stop me from getting my people off Zurich. They're gone, and you'll never be able to touch them. They'll end up on Bell, waiting for a rendezvous with me that will never take place. When I don't show up, they'll report my actions to Davion's Intelligence Secretriat."

"I thought you were part of the Intelligence Secretariat."

"Part of, no," The Dancing Joker laughed lightly. "Wanted by, yes."

"What?" Xu's eyes narrowed with confusion. "What are you talking about?"

"After a year on the run I came here for the same reason you survived as long as you did: the planetary constabulary was useless. Here I could hide." The Dancing Joker's smile broadened. "Having assassinated Melissa Steiner Davion and Duke Ryan Steiner meant I had to be very careful about choosing my sanctuary."

The Dancing Joker's finger tightened on the trigger and the bullet smashed through Xu's sternum, perforating his heart and snapping his spine. Pain roared through Xu, exploding out the top of his head, then he saw stars as his skull bounced against the floor. Looking down he saw his legs tangled in his chair, but he could not feel them.

The Dancing Joker came and stood over him. "Don't think of your revolution as a total loss, Director. I first came here to lay low and retire, but you reminded me how much I still love my work. Killing you is nothing personal—it's just that, well, destroying a whole planetary government will look very impressive on my resumé."

56

We have not yet lost this war, but we are overdrawn on the Bank of Miracles.

—W. J. BROWN

Kallontown
Nanking, Capellan Confederation
31 December 3057

If I'd wanted to spend New Year's Eve getting shot at, I could have gone to Solaris for the Ishiyama Open! Pay would have been better and the odds a damn sight shorter. Larry Acuff glanced at the secondary monitor in the cockpit of his *Warhammer.* It showed a diamond formation of four *Overlord* Class DropShips descending toward the planet. *Overlords*—two of which were sufficient to bring most of the Reserves to Nanking—could each carry three dozen BattleMechs. A full regiment, which is what Gubser had said was coming to relieve her, had 125 'Mechs in it, a force sufficient to wipe out the Reserves.

The altimeter put them at five kilometers and dropping fast.

A mission that had relied on miracles had gone surprisingly well until this point. Using a combination of patriotic appeals, thinly veiled threats, and promises of commercial endorsements and new marketing opportunities, the Woodstock Reserve Militia had managed to get corporations on Woodstock to equip them and ship them to Nanking. Once there they had tricked the Bandits into sending a company of light 'Mechs into an ambush, reducing the mercenary strength by a third.

They had also cordoned the mercenaries off in the Kallon Industries Factory complex, resulting in a standoff. When

Victor had promised more help would eventually arrive, the Reservists had been pleased with their situation.

Unfortunately, when help arrived, it seemed to be meant for the other side.

Four days ago, when the DropShips had detached themselves from the Free Worlds JumpShip, Larry and Phoebe had worked the approach vectors and fuel factors through the computers to see if the ships were coming in empty or full. The performance data suggested they were coming in loaded, but that still didn't tell them what the ships were carrying. A ton of scrap metal weighed just as much as a ton of 'Mech.

When the ships were two days out, they intercepted transmissions incoming to the Bandits. They unscrambled them enough to identify Colonel Richard Burr, but neither Phoebe nor Larry fully trusted the intelligence obtained through eavesdropping. ComStar had already passed the news that Xu Ning had been assassinated on Zurich and that a counter-revolution had the planet in chaos. It was hard to believe Thomas Marik or Sun-Tzu would have allowed the Black Cobras to leave Zurich in such a state of crisis.

The message they intercepted, they agreed, could have been a prerecorded holograph designed to make them believe the Black Cobras were really coming in. Of course, they couldn't discount the fact that it might also be genuine. That was the reason for ordering the Reserves into a heightened state of alert and for their deployment in defensive positions outside the Kallon Industries plant.

The altimeter counted down to thirty-five hundred meters. Larry keyed his mike. "Empress, if they're genuine, they'll blow their hatches and start dropping at a klick."

"Roger, King Crow." Larry heard dread in Phoebe's voice. "Keep thinking Alesia, right?"

"Roger, Empress. Out."

Kip Cooper, a secondary school teacher serving in Phoebe's command lance, had noted that Caesar had successfully held off Gauls in a similar position at Alesia. If some people in the unit took comfort from that fact, Larry did not. The Romans had better weapons than the Gauls and they were a regular army unit with superior discipline. No matter how proud he was of the Reservists, he was not inclined to be optimistic about their chances in the immediate future.

When the DropShips hit two kilometers in altitude and

came into plain view to the south, Larry popped his radio over to the frequency the ships had been using to communicate with the Bandits. "Colonel Gubser, this is your last chance to surrender. If your bluff fails, we won't be nearly so accommodating later."

"Watch and weep, Acuff."

The Black Cobras had long ago refitted their *Overlord* Class DropShips into what was considered the most efficient configuration for that type of ship. The central section of the egg-shaped craft had been stripped out and turned into one giant 'Mech bay. The BattleMechs occupied pods around the perimeter of the bay, each nestled between support structures of the ship's hull. Between the 'Mechs and the central elevator shaft lay all the equipment the Cobras had hurriedly loaded onto the DropShip before their hasty departure from Zurich.

Above the central bay, and accessible by the elevator shaft, were the crew quarters. In the top of the egg was the bridge. Beneath the deck of the 'Mech bay was the ship engineering section, including the fusion engines that provided the ship's thrust. All the crew members had taken their battle stations, meaning most were manning the weapons pods that dotted the ship's hull-like warts.

As the ships came into combat range, the captain ordered the central bay sealed off from the rest of the ship, then had the pressure seals blown on the 'Mech bay doors. Tarps tied down over crates flapped as the atmosphere purged itself. Air pressure within and without the DropShips equalized at .8598639 of a single atmosphere. On a simple barometer this would have given a reading of 65.36 centimeters of mercury and rising.

In fact, such a reading had been obtained on the dozen simple electronic barometers the Dancing Joker had built into detonation devices and secreted in the infantry arms ammunition and explosives crates over which his people had fought at Kaishiling. Since the insurgents had broken open and tried to drag away some crates before being driven off, the Black Cobras had erroneously assumed that the seemingly untouched crates were, in fact, inviolate.

The detonators armed themselves when they obtained a pressure reading lower than expected for air at between 800 to 1000 meters of altitude. Then, when the pressure built to

67.36 centimeters, the barometer caused an electrical pulse to feed into a pair of blasting caps secured with det-cord to a block of plastic explosive pilfered from the Black Cobras.

The fact was that the Dancing Joker had not been overly concerned with *when* the devices would detonate. They could have gone off if, say, an atmospheric low pressure system had moved through the Daosha district, arming the explosives, and then the Black Cobras had pressurized their ships for take-off. That result would have served as well for him as any other. The Joker's goal was to eliminate the Black Cobras and he was not terribly particular about how that happened.

Three-quarters of the devices functioned as intended, resulting in at least one explosion on each ship as they hit the thousand-meter mark above their drop zone. On one ship, the *Boomslang,* two of the Dancing Joker's bombs had lain undiscovered in crates full of military-grade plastique. The resulting detonation sliced through the middle of the ship, bisecting it, and scattering 'Mechs like toys spilling from a burst piñata.

Only one bomb went off on the *Sea Snake*. The force of the explosion ripped down through the deck and wiped out the primary power couplings feeding electricity to the rest of the ship. In an instant the auxiliary system kicked in, then exploded in a shower of sparks, revealing why *Overlord*s had long been notorious for problems with their electrical and hydraulic systems. With the loss of power, the engines failed, sending the ships careening toward the planet.

The port side of the *Mamba* blew out when an explosion drove two armored personnel carriers out through the hull. The *Mamba*'s engines began to sputter, but the crew managed to feed power to the attitude jets. The *Mamba* hit the ground hard, its weakened internal structures buckling and making the ship wilt over on its port side.

The explosions on the *Sidewinder* completely obliterated one of its fusion engine thrust nozzles. As the silvery ion thrust stabbed out through the starboard hull, it pitched the ship sharply to the right, slamming it into the upper half of the *Boomslang*. Both ships seems to meld together as if made of quicksilver before multiple fiery blossoms shredded them and sent them raining down over Kallontown.

Larry stared up at the sky through his *Warhammer*'s cockpit canopy. The quartet of DropShips jerked and stuttered in the sky, as if he were watching the image from a shaking camera. He was uncertain what was happening until the *Sea Snake* began to trail smoke and plunged to the ground like a silver egg. When it hit he felt the ground tremble beneath his *Warhammer*'s feet.

One moment there are four ships, the next just metal rain. On the second try Larry successfully punched up Phoebe's radio frequency. "Empress, what the hell happened?"

"Unknown malfunctions. Christ Almighty, four *Overlords gone!*"

"If the Bandits were bluffing, that ends it."

"And if they weren't?"

"Then someone either hated the Cobras, or loved us, and I'm not choosy about which it was." Larry saw a monitor light start blinking on his command console. "Message coming in from the Bandits. I'm patching you in. This is Hauptmann Acuff. Go ahead, Bandit."

Even digitization could not remove the tremors from Ada Gubser's voice as it came over the radio. "What did you do to the Cobras?"

"We don't know what happened to them, Colonel, but we do know they aren't going to be much help to you." Larry looked out at the black columns of smoke marking where one ship had crashed. "The question is, do you want to help yourselves?"

"Standard terms of surrender? We'll be repatriated with our equipment?"

Phoebe answered her. "Standard terms, provided you give us no trouble and no damage has been done to the factory."

"Okay, we surrender. Now. Gubser out."

Larry locked the Bandit frequency out of his line. "What do you think, Phoebe?"

"I think I'm glad Nanking will be part of the Federated Commonwealth come the new year." He heard relief and joy echo in her voice. "What about you?"

"I think I hope the rumors of peace are true."

"Why's that? We've won all our fights."

"That's why, Phoebe." Larry laughed aloud. "Face it. We succeeded in what was an impossible mission here. If there's more war, I don't even want to think about what Victor might dream up for us in the future. All I want is to head back to somewhere safe, like Solaris, and see what it's like to live nice and quiet and normal for a while."

=== 57 ===

Of war men will ask its outcome, not its cause.
                              —SENECA, HERCULES FURENS

Rio de Cañada, Morges
Arc-Royal Defensive Cordon, Lyran Alliance
31 December 3057

As Phelan walked across the stage to the podium, the noise in the crowded auditorium gradually diminished to a few coughs and some murmurs. His ceremonial gray leathers creaked as he walked and the wolf's-skin cape felt heavy across his shoulders, but he held his head up and kept his expression neutral. Reaching the podium, he placed one hand on either side of it and stared out at the Clansfolk gathered there.

"I am the Oathmaster! All will be bound by this conclave until they are dust and memories and then beyond that until the end of all that is."

The Wolves' solemnly chanted oath of "Seyla" echoed through his body and gave him strength.

"There has been news brought to us by Colonel Marco Hall. It concerns us all—those who fought with Ulric and with Natasha and those still streaming in from the occupation zone. It is not pleasant news, and may create a rift among us. Even if that does happen, no onus will be attached to any decision made in reaction to this news."

Phelan swallowed hard. "After Ulric Kerensky was killed on Wotan, Khan Vandervahn Chistu claimed that *our* Trial of Refusal was, in reality, a Jade Falcon Trial of Absorption."

The hall erupted with angry shouts of disbelief. Phelan had known that bit of news would shock and infuriate the

Wolves and yet he knew it was, in many ways, the least of the news he had to deliver. Chistu had made a bald grab for power because Trials of Absorption were complicated affairs that would have involved bidding by other Clans for the honor of conquering and absorbing the Wolves.

And had this been a true Trial of Absorption, my force would have been at Wotan, too, and the Falcons would never have won the battle for that world.

Phelan raised his hands, then lowered them to quiet the crowd. "Chistu laid claim to our people and our worlds and our warriors. He initiated a Ritual of Abjuration that struck from our Clan rolls the names of all the Wolves who had come away from Wotan and all the Wolves who followed me. Through the action of a Jade Falcon Khan we have been exiled from our Clan."

That information brought no uproar, but the murmuring that filled the auditorium was obviously related to a curious point. *If* the Wolves had been absorbed into the Jade Falcons, then the Abjuration would have exiled them from their Clan. Since the Absorption had been stated, but not ratified by the Clan Council, the Abjuration could be ignored. *And everyone here will ignore it.*

"Khan Chistu made his pronouncements the night of his victory over our forces on Wotan. Three days later, while clearing rubble, workers found Vlad of the Wards alive but trapped in his *Timber Wolf.* When they freed him and informed him of what had taken place, he challenged Khan Chistu to a Trial of Refusal concerning the absorption. Chistu was forced to accept the challenge and was slain in that fight."

Phelan allowed the Wolves their cheering—. Even he felt inclined to smile. Though he had hated Vlad from their first encounter—the day Vlad had captured him—he respected the man's abilities in combat. Any Wolf present on Morges ached to have done what Vlad had done in killing Chistu. Crusader though he was, Vlad had proved himself every atom a Wolf.

"Khan Crichell honored Vlad's victory but did not wholly repudiate the Absorption. Those Wolves who had been taken into the Falcons were separated from them again, but they now form the Jade Wolf Clan."

When Phelan first heard the news of what had happened on Wotan, he knew exactly why Crichell had decided to create the hybrid Clan. The Wolves who survived, by and large, were Crusaders, whose support he expected. By keeping the Wolves alive, Crichell could count on the votes of their Khans in the Grand Council. Since Ulric's Trial of Refusal against charges of genocide had failed at Wotan, a reconstituted Wolf Clan could have faced extermination. Through the blind of creating a new Clan, Crichell had found a way to reward Vlad for eliminating a rival and strengthen the Jade Falcon position in the Grand Council.

"The House of Ward of the Jade Wolves subsequently held a Trial of Bloodright. Only one person was entered into the Trial and, in honor of his killing Khan Chistu, Vlad now claims the name of Ward." Phelan slowly scanned the gathering, knowing there was not a Wolf present who would have denied Vlad his right to a Bloodname. "The Bloodright they gave him, because of the Abjuration, was *mine*."

Phelan held his hand up to forestall comment. "I stand before you stripped of my Bloodname. I first came to you as Phelan Ward Kell and was later adopted by you as Phelan Wolf. I earned the Bloodname of Ward and then was elected to the office of Khan by you. I am now just Phelan again, but no less proud.

"The Jade Falcons disowned us. The Jade Wolves have not claimed us, though they have claimed what is ours. I choose to ignore the action of the Falcons and pity the Jade Wolves. In my mind and in my *heart* I know we are still the Wolves. We will be the Wolves forever and ever and, as Wolves, we will be true to the vision of those who created the Clans."

Phelan narrowed his eyes. "It is expected the Clan Council of the Jade Wolves will elect Vladimir Ward as its first Khan. Likewise it is assumed the Grand Council will elect Khan Crichell of the Jade Falcons as the new ilKhan. Because of the severe losses they suffered in our Trial of Refusal, we know the Falcons will not attempt to resume the war against the Inner Sphere immediately. This is good, for it gives us time to prepare for them.

"The ships and garrison Clusters that traveled with us to Morges and then jumped yet deeper into the Lyran Alliance went to Arc-Royal—my family's homeworld. It is also the headquarters of the Kell Hounds. On Arc-Royal we will create our own community and continue the traditions that have brought us to this point. My father has laid claim to a massive portion of the Jade Falcon border and has pledged his Kell Hounds to defend it. I would have us pledge our strength to defend it as well, but this will be for our Khans to decide.

"I believe this is what Ulric Kerensky intended all along, and something Nicholas Kerensky would have approved."

Phelan frowned and looked away for a moment, then turned back to the silent gathering. "There may be those who believe I am in error, those who wish for reconciliation with the Jade Wolves. That is your right and I respect it. Any of you who wish to leave here and travel back to rejoin the Crusading Clans may do so, without interference or re-crimination. I ask only that you respect those of us who wish to remain true Wolves and that you will give us your best when the day comes that we must face off in combat."

Phelan swallowed hard as emotion threatened his composure. "These are my wishes and my dreams for us, but transforming my dreams into reality will fall to others. Another now claims my Bloodname. Were I truly of the Clans—born to them as you all were—I would ignore the Abjuration and Vlad's usurpation of the Bloodname I won over him. But here, now, once again in the realm of my birth I realize that I still belong to the Inner Sphere. I still admire the traditions that nurtured me. I will always be my father's son and I am proud of being a Kell.

"I am equally proud of being a Wolf, but now I must combine what is good for the Inner Sphere with what is best for the Wolves. I, who was born and raised here, will find it easier to adapt. The Wolves are welcome here—and desperately needed—but the decisions about how you will adapt to live in the Inner Sphere must come from the Wolves, not from me."

Phelan gave a slight shrug. "The matter is moot. I no longer have a Bloodname. I am not eligible to be a Khan."

From the back of the room came a voice that sliced effortlessly through the stunned silence, a voice Phelan found hauntingly familiar. "If I might, Khan Phelan, beg the indulgence of this conclave." The speaker, a tall man with a shock of white hair, slowly strode down the center aisle. He wore a simple white robe emblazoned with the golden star emblem of ComStar. His military bearing marked him a more than a ComStar functionary, and the eye-patch over his eye suggested wisdom learned through bitter lessons.

Surprised, Phelan nodded his head. "I recognize you, Anastasius Focht, and give you leave to speak." As he backed away from the podium, Phelan felt a shiver run down his spine. *What is the Precentor Martial doing here? And why didn't I know he had arrived on Morges?*

The Precentor Martial nodded to Phelan. "Thank you, Khan Phelan. I have come here to deliver a message that was entrusted to me by Ulric Kerensky." The tall man nodded toward the rear of the auditorium. "It was recorded on holodisk, and no one has viewed it until this moment."

A screen descended behind the Precentor Martial, and static played across it for a moment before the image of Ulric Kerensky appeared.

"Forgive me, my friends," Ulric began, "if this message is hasty and brief, but I record in on the eve of my trial on charges of treason by the Grand Council. I already know the outcome of the trial and the nature of the grand enterprise into which the Wolves will be launched because of it. No, I do not claim to be an oracle, but much experience leads me to this certainty about various outcomes.

"One is this: When you see this, I will have been slain by the Jade Falcons."

Phelan went cold. *Ulric knew how things would turn out, yet never shied from doing what had to be done.*

"Another is that Phelan Ward will have been successful in getting you to the Inner Sphere. He does not yet know that is what he will be forced to do. He will not like it, of course, but neither Natasha nor I could do what he will to preserve our Clan. I do not envy any of the Jade Falcons sent into the Inner Sphere to pursue you—now or in the future.

"The future is what this message concerns. It is the ilKhan's right to reward the successful conclusion of a mission. The highest reward we have to bestow—the one offered Jaime Wolf and the others who ventured into the Inner Sphere half a century ago—is the creation of a Bloodname. In this vein, I, ilKhan Ulric Kerensky, have created the Bloodname of Kell, in honor of Phelan Ward Kell. He will be the first to bear this Bloodname, a name that will be respected here and feared among those you have left behind."

Ulric's message paused and applause arose from the assembled Wolves. Phelan stared gape-jawed at the screen and then at the assembly. He had just told the Wolves that he was not really part of them, but the thrill running through him at the honor bestowed by Ulric and their affirmation of it told him he was wrong. He realized that he need not choose to be either a creature of the Inner Sphere *or* a Wolf, but that he could be both. And if he could do that, so could the others.

The ilKhan's image nodded as if in confirmation of Phelan's thoughts. "You are embarking on a grand mission that will shape the future of our Clan, the Inner Sphere, and humanity. Remember that you are Wolves. Be true to your traditions, but do not become reactionaries. Never abandon that which makes the Wolves strong, but *adopt* that which will make us stronger! The Clans were always meant to be the greatest of warriors, and we have trusted science to produce the most superior soldiers ever seen. But the events of recent years have taught us one thing. In war, as in nature, adaptation is as important as selection. We have seen in Phelan Ward the greatness of a warrior born and trained in the Inner Sphere, and this teaches us that being bred for war is not all. We have eyes to see, minds to think. We have imaginations to dream of the brilliance that might arise from a synthesis of both warrior traditions.

"Your mission now is to defend the Inner Sphere from the threat represented by the Clans. Who better than you? You must stand united to prevent war from destroying a people who have neither the means to comprehend it nor withstand it. You have Khan Phelan Kell to lead you and the courage, my Wolves, to follow."

Ulric's face froze on the screen, locked in a proud smile, but his voice continued to echo through the hall. "This, I say, is your destiny as Wolves and from it you shall not shy."

A long silence followed those last words of Ulric Kerensky, Khan of Khans, and leader of Clan Wolf, the strongest of the Clans, the one with the most revered lineage extending back not only to Nicholas Kerensky, but even farther, to General Aleksandr Kerensky, who first led his exiles from the Inner Sphere into the dangerous reaches of uncharted space. An exodus into the unknown to form something new, something that had never been seen before.

"Seyla," spoke the Wolves as one, the single word whose meaning had been lost in the mists of time, but whose import filled Phelan's heart with pride. These were his people

They accepted the ilKhan's charge for them and, in doing so, gave the people of worlds like Morges the faintest glimmer of light in the bleak darkness that had, until then, been their only future.

=== 58 ===

Avalon City, New Avalon
Crucis March, Federated Commonwealth
1 January 3058

Weary from the New Year's celebrations he'd been duty-bound to attend, Victor Davion sat alone in his office. With half the buttons on his dress jacket undone, he sat back in his big chair and put his booted feet up on the corner of his desk. One hand swirled brandy around in a snifter and the other felt as if it should have a cigar in it. He smiled, remembering the time or two he had seen his father in so relaxed a state.

But you would never have relaxed now, would you, Father? Victor's decision to accept Thomas' offer had ended the war, which gave his people something to truly celebrate. They also rejoiced in the victory of Nanking and the death of the tyrant on Zurich. Both worlds had returned to the Federated Commonwealth, giving him a slender finger of influence poking into what he had lately begun to call the Chaos March. While he was pleased to retain those worlds, part of him wondered if they would not be so tempting that Sun-Tzu would feel he just had to go after them again.

Any other time that would have been enough to cause him some concern, but other news had relegated Sun-Tzu's potential trouble-making to a minor nuisance. Early the day before he had gotten a message from Morgan Kell that proclaimed the creation of the Arc-Royal Defense Cordon, an area spanning the worlds from Kooken's Pleasure Pit

Koniz. Though that encompassed most of the Lyran border with the Clans, it left significant gaps that Katherine would have to cover or risk Clan breakthroughs above or below the Cordon.

For the Grand Duke of Arc-Royal to put such a large slice of the Lyran Alliance under his control, even for the purpose of defense, was quite an affront to the ruler of the nation. Had Victor been on the throne in Tharkad, he would either have slapped Morgan down or required an oath of personal fealty. Victor knew Katherine could manage neither the former nor obtain the latter from Morgan. What their mother's cousin had effectively done was carve a sovereign state out of the middle of the Alliance, weakening Katherine considerably without crippling the defense against the Clans.

One more thing for her to think about, which is good. Left to her own devices, or those of Tormano, she finds too many ways to make trouble for me. Victor knew he needed more time to measure the full impact of Tormano Liao's rise to the position of Katherine's advisor, but the sale of JumpShips back to the Federated Commonwealth was already a bad sign. Even so, Victor assumed Tormano would always have one eye on the Capellan Confederation.

The Prince of the Federated Suns took a swallow of brandy and relished the burn as it went down. Thinking back over the past year he realized his biggest lesson had been not to underestimate Thomas Marik. Because Thomas had been restrained by the presence of Joshua on New Avalon, both Victor and this intelligence apparatus had considered the Free Worlds League impotent and its leader a minor player in the politics of the Inner Sphere. Nothing in Thomas' background would have suggested he could engineer so skillful an operation to recover his planets.

Obviously, his fascination with technology and idealism are but the outer layers of the onion. Victor knew he could never again take Thomas for granted, and he translated that into a rule he must extend to everyone around him. *Never assume—know!*

A gentle knock at the door brought Victor's head around. "Come."

An ashen Galen Cox opened the door and stepped into the office, pulling the oaken door shut behind him. "Good, you're sitting down—and you have a strong drink in hand."

Victor pulled his feet from the desk and sat forward. "You

look as if you've seen a ghost, Jerry. What's the matter?" A thousand possible scenarios ran through his brain, but only the renewal of war with the Clans struck him as one that could have made Galen look so stricken. "You're the one who looks like he could use a drink. Get one and tell me what's happened."

"After, my lord. I want to get this straight." Galen held up two fingers. "Two things, one minor and one major. The minor one comes first because it provides a perspective on the major one."

"I'm listening."

"You remember, of course, the trio of Liao agents who were at the hospital and were killed trying to get to Joshua?"

"Yes."

"The war shifted some of our intelligence assets around and made League codes and ciphers a priority down in Crypto. It wasn't until after things slowed down that some of the backlog started to get cleared up. Part of that was processing the orders sent to the Liao agents. Once that was done we discovered that the message had been encrypted with a routine we had tagged, in the department, as 5707. That means it was the code sequence being used in July of last year."

Victor nodded. "I follow you. Go on."

"The thing of it is that we had 5707 in the computers because we had picked up the key to it when the Maskirovka first tried to get it to their sleeper agents and we prevented its being passed on to them. I'm fairly certain the Maskirovka knew we had the key because they sent a new code—one we didn't get—and through *that* transmission we identified their back-up system for code transmission. Our efforts with 5707 should have prevented the agents from being able to decode the orders when they got them.

"The problem is that the 5707 code key appears to have been re-sent in place of the 5709 code key to agents here on New Avalon. The message that the Liao agents got in September used the July code a code the Maskirovka should have known we had cracked. This means, in short, that the July code was sent here again *and* the message encrypted with it followed. On no other world was the 5707 code key repeated and, in fact, we picked up a variety of 5709 keys.

Victor frowned. "What you're telling me is that someone sent an old code and, by implication, an old message to the sleeper agents here. This would imply ComStar or Word

Blake. I guess it was the latter, given our cordial relations with ComStar at the moment. This further suggests, however, that the Word of Blake sent the message to Sun-Tzu's agents to create an incident to set off a war. An attempt on Joshua's life could have forced disclosure of the switch."

Galen nodded. "I think we have to consider the fact that Thomas knew we had put a double in his son's place. He laid the groundwork for the war and then went out and prosecuted it."

"And by using Liao agents he does not jeopardize his own people, points me at Sun-Tzu, and even provides himself an excuse for turning on Sun-Tzu later if Sun-Tzu tried to defy him. He got a number of bonuses from one simple act that he knew would not endanger his son." Victor gave a low whistle. "I'm even more impressed."

"Wait, there's more." Galen took a deep breath. "You remember, when the war started, you told me you wanted to duplicate the genetic tests Thomas was claiming proved the double was not his son?"

"Yes. And you gave me the results of the tests a week later."

Galen shook his head. "No, I gave you the result of *some* of the tests. They were the crucial ones, the father-son match. Lab techs, well, they're the sort of folks who operate in their own world. As far as they're concerned, anal retentive is not only hyphenated, it's capitalized and printed in bold italics."

"Obsessive are our lab people?"

"Even more so than you, sir."

Victor arched an eyebrow. "Is that possible?"

"Yes, but only because they have no life outside the lab and, therefore, no real understanding how important information can be. At seven PM today, while I was getting ready for your reception, the head of the genetic identification department dropped some files to me with a note saying he thought he'd sent them before, but had forgotten. They were the results of the rest of the blood tests.

"When Joshua originally came here, and throughout his time here, his family sent whole blood for use when he needed transfusions. The lab people used that blood to do the genetic testing. Not only did they test the double against the family, but they tested the *real* Joshua against his family. As expected, the real Joshua matched with his mother and father, but he didn't match against Isis."

"Of course not, she was his half-sister."

"Highness, *no* match means *no* relationship. They're not brother and sister, at least, not blood relations."

Victor's head came up. "You mean Isis' mother was impregnated by someone else, then claimed her child was Thomas'? If I recall my history correctly, she was born about a month after the bomb attack on Thomas. She was proclaimed his daughter while ComStar had him stashed away being healed up."

"That's correct, but you're missing the point. At the time of Isis' birth, Thomas was believed dead. To prove paternity, Isis had a DNA identification done that matched her with blood taken from Thomas and held in case of medical emergencies."

"I know, I know, I've had plenty of liters taken from me for storage in hospitals in case I'm injured. So you're saying, then, that because there is no match between Isis and Joshua that Joshua isn't really Thomas' child?"

Even as he asked the question, the paradox struck him. "Wait, Joshua matched his father. Isis matched her father, but the two of them *don't* match. That means her father isn't *his* father."

Galen nodded slowly. "Which means Thomas Marik isn't Thomas Marik."

Victor's mouth went dry. "Everyone thought Thomas dead for eighteen months, then ComStar brought him back and set him up on the throne of the Free Worlds League. That was during Myndo Waterly's reign as Primus of ComStar. With her Thomas—whoever he really is—on the League throne, she could have directed a war that would have made the Inner Sphere over into some sort of a Blakean theocracy."

"But now she's dead and he still rules the League."

"And as her agent I would have imagined him embracing the Word of Blake, but he seems content to fend them off."

"And he's not repudiated ComStar entirely."

"Which means this Thomas has his own agenda and all the tools necessary to advance it."

Galen nodded his head. "Precisely, Highness." He held out his hand. "Can I have that drink now?"

"Please." Victor drained his snifter and held it out toward his friend. "I'll take a refill, then wait for you to get caught up. If this is the omen that marks 3058, it'll definitely be an interesting year."

85 TONS

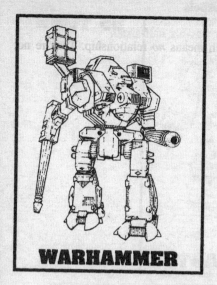

WARHAMMER

·HEAVY MECHS·

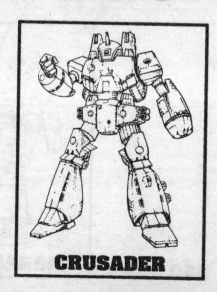

100 TONS **CRUSADER**

85 TONS

BATTLEMASTER

·ASSAULT MECHS·

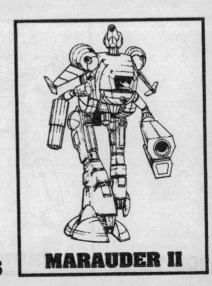

100 TONS

MARAUDER II

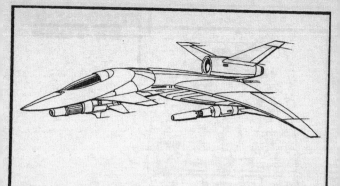

SULLA

·ASSAULT FIGHTERS·

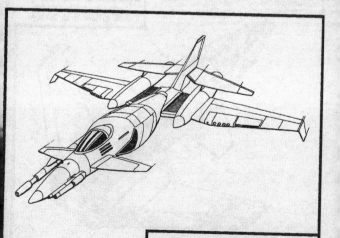

VISIGOTH

DROPSHIPS

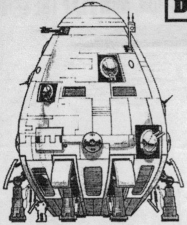

OVERLORD

AEROSPACE FIGHTER

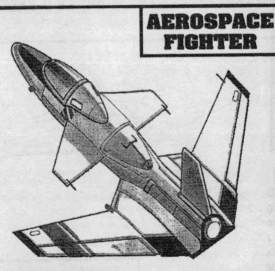

STINGRAY

YOU'VE READ THE FICTION, NOW PLAY THE GAME!

IN THE 30TH CENTURY LIFE IS CHEAP, BUT BATTLEMECHS AREN'T.

A Dark Age has befallen mankind. Where the United Star League once reigned, five successor states now battle for control. War has ravaged once-flourishing worlds and left them in ruins. Technology has ceased to advance, the machines and equipment of the past cannot be produced by present-day worlds. War is waged over water, ancient machinery, and spare parts factories. Control of these elements leads not only to victory but to the domination of known space.

The story continues in
I AM JADE FALCON
by Robert Thurston,
author of the
Legend of the Jade Phoenix
trilogy. The Wolf Clan
and the Jade Falcons clash
on Twycross, where
Natasha Kerensky and
Star Commander Joanna
meet in a duel
to the death.

On sale from Roc Books in
February 1995.